P9-EME-239

TRACERS

A Selection of Recent Titles by Adrian Magson

The Harry Tate Thrillers

RED STATION *
TRACERS *

The Riley Gavin and Frank Palmer Series

NO PEACE FOR THE WICKED
NO HELP FOR THE DYING
NO SLEEP FOR THE DEAD
NO TEARS FOR THE LOST
NO KISS FOR THE DEVIL

* Available from Severn House

TRACERS

A Harry Tate Novel

Adrian Magson

Falmouth Public Library
Falmouth, MA 02540

This first world edition published 2011
in Great Britain and the USA by
SEVERN HOUSE PUBLISHERS LTD of
9–15 High Street, Sutton, Surrey, England, SM1 1DF.
Trade paperback edition first published
in Great Britain and the USA 2011 by
SEVERN HOUSE PUBLISHERS LTD.

Magson

Copyright © 2011 by Adrian Magson.

All rights reserved.
The moral right of the author has been asserted.

British Library Cataloguing in Publication Data

Magson, Adrian.
    Tracers. – (A Harry Tate thriller)
    1. Intelligence officers – Fiction. 2. Fugitives from
    justice – Fiction. 3. Terrorism risk communication –
    Fiction. 4. Baghdad (Iraq) – Fiction. 5. Suspense fiction.
    I. Title II. Series
    823.9'2-dc22

ISBN-13: 978-0-7278-8013-0 (cased)
ISBN-13: 978-1-84751-338-0 (trade paper)

Except where actual historical events and characters are being
described for the storyline of this novel, all situations in this
publication are fictitious and any resemblance to living persons
is purely coincidental.

All Severn House titles are printed on acid-free paper.

Severn House Publishers support The Forest Stewardship Council [FSC],
the leading international forest certification organisation. All our titles that
are printed on Greenpeace-approved FSC-certified paper carry the FSC logo.

MIX
Paper from
responsible sources
FSC
www.fsc.org   FSC® C018575

Typeset by Palimpsest Book Production Ltd.,
Falkirk, Stirlingshire, Scotland.
Printed and bound in Great Britain by the
MPG Books Group, Bodmin, Cornwall.

As ever and always, to Ann

ACKNOWLEDGEMENTS

With grateful thanks as always to David Headley, for his help, enthusiasm and insights; to Kate Lyall Grant, who took the punt on Harry Tate and gave him a happy home; to everyone at Severn House who made this a proper book; and to all the readers, reviewers and friends who have voiced their enthusiastic support and made this second in the series a thoroughly enjoyable must-do.

PROLOGUE

Baghdad – Al-Jamia District – August

The dead don't need food, the man in the black leather jacket and dark glasses thought coldly. He plucked a tomato from the delivery of vegetables being wheeled towards the kitchen door of the heavily fortified villa in the west of the city. As he bit through the ripe skin, a burst of voices from the local *Dijla Radio* rose momentarily from inside the building, then faded abruptly as the heavy door slammed shut again.

It was time. Holding the tomato to his mouth to shield the lower half of his face, he ducked his head and left the compound through a reinforced door set in a high wall, stepping past a watchful armed guard. Glass shards and razor wire glinted atop the barricade, and the door groaned under the weight of steel plate. The guard studied him as he passed, blinked with uncertainty, but said nothing. Bolts rattled into place. The door closed behind him.

As he crossed the sun-baked square outside, he tossed the tomato aside and took from his pocket a mobile phone with a single, pre-programmed number on speed-dial. The device felt awkward through the bandage on his hand and he winced, recalling the moment he had cut it on some glass while clambering over the outside wall to dispose of incriminating papers in a brazier along the street the previous evening. He shouldn't have bothered, he knew that, because it would soon all be gone. But old habits die hard and he was being watched too closely in the house. Only the foolhardy tempt providence by not being sufficiently prepared.

He thought about what would happen in the next few seconds. A brush of warm air – deceptively gentle at first – would turn into a lethal pressure-wave. Then a monstrous roar, invading the atmosphere and sucking the oxygen out of every space, collapsing lungs and buildings alike. Heavy objects would smash against the walls around the square and, amid the splintering glass and crumbling structures, screams would rise, some old and faint. Others young and shrill.

But that could not be helped. *Insh'allah*. It was the will of God, may His name be praised.

Next would be heard a patter of small sounds, like hard rain. Falling on the rooftops around the square, growing in intensity and tearing through thin structures and fabrics, it would bring a thick, choking dust, boiling through the narrow streets and alleyways like an angry fog. Amid the wails and shouts of alarm there would be the first signs of response from the security forces.

They would be too late.

Behind him, the door in the compound wall groaned again and a man's voice called after him. It was the guard, recognition coming too late, duty overcoming doubts. He was asking – but respectfully – where he was going and why he did not have anyone with him.

He ignored the man and increased his pace, lips moving soundlessly in a steady, silent mantra. He was sweating profusely and his heart was pounding. But not simply because of the borrowed leather jacket. Beneath it were extra layers of clothes into which he could change at a moment's notice, skilfully discarding one appearance for another, as surely would be needed in the minutes or hours ahead if he were to get away safely. He passed two small boys, a scavenging dog and an old man sitting in the shade of a leather goods shop. They spoke but he ignored them.

In the distance, the speck of a US helicopter gunship was circling a column of heavy, black smoke. The thud of rotors rose and faded, sunlight winking off the canopy. He ignored that, too; it was a common enough sight here and too far off to be of concern.

The guard called out again, sharper this time and shrill with concern. Or was it fear? He continued walking, heavy dust muffling his footsteps. As he reached the corner of the square and the shelter of a deserted *madrassa*, he murmured a soft, final incantation.

Then he pressed the SEND button on his mobile phone.

He did not look back.

ONE

England – September

The cottage lay at the end of a muddy, rutted track, surrounded by trees and bushes. To Harry Tate, it was like something out of a child's fairytale. Only darker.

A finger of cold air slid down his neck. He looked back towards the Saab, but it was lost beyond a curve in the track. To his right lay an expanse of tall reeds, cigar-top stems rustling in the chilled breeze coming over the dunes off the north Norfolk coast. The area was slipping into shadow as the day began to fade, erasing detail and leaving a leaden dullness in the atmosphere.

He turned to face the cottage. It was a scrubby, stone-built box with a faded green door, a small porch, tiny windows and a slate roof coated with bird droppings. It might have looked quaint once, but now had a forlorn air, in need of a good coat of paint and some work on the weed-strewn flowerbeds.

Beyond the cottage, the track butted into the trees, the ruts old and overgrown. The end of the line. Appropriate, he thought, considering the reason he was here. He checked the windows for movement and the chimney for a telltale plume of grey smoke. Nothing. If there was trouble waiting, it was keeping its head down.

Checking his mobile was secure under a rubber band on the clipboard in his other hand, he flexed his shoulders beneath the UPS driver's jacket. It was a tight fit but it would have to do. Who looked at a courier's clothes, anyway? People wanted the goodies, not a catwalk parade.

He knocked and waited, wishing he had the comforting feel of something solid in his pocket. A 9mm Browning would have been good. But this was Norfolk, England, not downtown Baghdad or Kabul.

A scuff of footsteps and the door opened. A man blinked into the dying evening. He was dressed in a Paisley-print dressing gown tied with a silk cord, highlighting a low-slung paunch. Bare, skinny legs ended in a pair of burgundy leather slippers, and a scraggy goatee beard gave him the look of a middle-eastern potentate in a seaside pantomime.

'Yes?' Tired eyes flicked nervously past Harry's shoulder.

Harry smiled genially. *Gotcha.* Abuzeid Matuq was a bit plumper than the photo in his jacket pocket portrayed, and he was wearing his hair a shade longer than a man of forty-six years who wasn't a rock star should do. But it was definitely him.

Transferred to London just over a year ago to run a newly established branch of the General Bank of Libya, Matuq had soon slipped into bad company. Once he was out of sight of head office and his beloved Colonel Gaddafi, it hadn't taken him long to find a whole new direction in his life, and to disappear with a large amount of Libyan money. He was now being sought by bank officials and the Serious Fraud Office. Along with, most likely, the more vengeful elements of the Libyan secret police.

'Got a delivery.' Harry slapped the logo on his breast pocket. The light wasn't brilliant, but he thought Matuq had an unhealthy grey tinge for a man his age. Fat lot of good the money had done him, then, ending up in this drab, shadow-filled hideaway.

'A delivery? Not for me.' Matuq shifted slightly, but stayed where he was. It was a reminder for Harry that desperate people sometimes do rash things when confronted by pursuers.

And right now, Matuq was partially shielded by his front door.

Harry got ready to move. There was no telling what the Libyan might be holding in his concealed hand. As one of his old MI5 instructors would have said, even small, furry rodents have sharp teeth when cornered.

'Uh . . . Mrs Tangmere? Stokes Cottage?' Harry glanced at his mobile and shifted the clipboard until the white blob of Matuq's face appeared in the centre of the screen. Not quite sharp enough, but it would do. He keyed the button, freezing the face.

'There is nobody of that name.' Matuq's voice was soft, like his appearance, the accent pronounced. His eyes slipped instinctively to the large brown envelope Harry produced from under the clipboard. It was addressed to an imaginary Mrs

Tangmere in bold handwriting. Another good lesson learned: it was the detail that got you in, the lack of it that got you found out.

'Took me ages to find the place.' He hated this part, having to go through the play-acting just to give him an excuse to leave without alerting Matuq. But finding the target's location was just one part of the assignment, albeit a critical part; next he had to get the photo to Jennings to prove it. He gestured down the track. 'Had to leave my wheels down the end and leg it.'

He shivered briefly and smiled again to dispel any impression of threat. Visitors promising violence or incarceration rarely comment on the weather or the state of the roads. Nor do they carry clipboards. Harry was a bit under six feet, but probably looked worryingly big to a small man on the run.

'Sorry. I cannot help,' Matuq murmured regretfully, beginning to close the door.

Harry let him. He'd done what he came for. Now he just had to wait for instructions.

'No problem. Sorry to have disturbed you.' He turned and walked away as the door closed, followed by the rattle of bolts being thrown. He squeezed a glance across the tips of the reeds in the marsh bed separating Stokes Cottage from the village of Blakeney. The air here was damp and sour, a ghost of mist adding to the chilled atmosphere. He caught a faint shine off the Saab's roof as he rounded the curve in the track and hoped Matuq hadn't seen it. A UPS delivery driver with a clipboard was unremarkable; the same man in a mud-spattered car was not.

He dodged puddles, automatically checking the ground for tyre tracks. A single set but not fresh. Matuq must have a vehicle tucked away behind the cottage. If the Libyan decided to split, he'd have a job tracking him down again. Runners, once spooked, rarely allow their pursuers a second chance.

Out over the reed beds, a startled bird took off with a clatter, wings beating the air. Others followed, scattering wildly into the darkening sky. Harry wondered if his presence had set them off. He brushed subconsciously at his neck and lengthened his stride.

This place was already giving him the creeps.

TWO

I n the car, Harry checked the picture on his mobile against the hard copy in his pocket before sending it on the next stage. If Jennings was on the ball, he should have instructions within minutes. Then he could be out of here, with or without a package.

He yawned and shifted the passenger seat back and placed a foot on the dashboard, knuckling the tiredness from his eyes. There were times when he felt too old for this business; covert surveillance and tracking was for youngsters; those who were time-rich, who didn't find themselves thinking of all the better things they could be doing instead of getting stale and stodgy in the front seat of a car while the world slipped by outside. Not that forty-something was old, exactly. He probably needed some TLC and a good holiday. With Jean, preferably. He leaned forward and checked his face in the mirror. Could do with a shave; hair still good – a bit long on top maybe but no traces of grey among the light brown; teeth not bad, either.

He lowered the window a fraction, allowing the smell of salt and decay to drift in. He shifted uneasily and eyed his surroundings. There wasn't much to see here: the reeds, some woodland and dull, camouflage-coloured undergrowth. Beyond that and out of sight lay the coastline of dunes and the cold North Sea. The overall impression was unwelcoming and unnaturally quiet, as if all life had been turned off at the mains.

He eased the door open and stepped back out, treading with care in the mud. Out here was a steady rush of low-level noise produced by the breeze among the trees and rushes. Apart from that, there was nothing visual to disturb the scenery: no people, no movement, no vehicles. Just a car engine rumbling faintly from somewhere over by the village. He left the Saab and strolled the few yards back to the main road, using up time while waiting for Jennings to call back.

To his right, the road was empty, burrowing into the gloom before abruptly turning a corner as it followed the line of the coast. To the left, a hundred yards away towards the village, a white utility van stood on the grass verge, a red warning cone near the offside tail-light. The rear door was open, showing a jumble of tools inside. A long metal mains key stood against the side of the van. There was no sign of the driver.

He strolled back to the Saab and climbed in, taking a ten-day-old copy of the *Telegraph* off the back seat as he did so. He'd already tried the crossword but wasn't in the mood. He flicked through the pages for something of interest. Another bombing in Baghdad and the death of a so-called major Iraqi figurehead; a critical setback to the handover of full power, according to the leader writer, who was clearly deluded enough to believe that one man was all it needed to solve the problem. Harry felt a surge of relief that he was no longer a part of that whole sorry mess. All in the past, thank God.

He thought about Matuq, wondering if he'd have to take him back. He didn't like taking in runners, whatever their alleged background or problems. It changed the whole dynamic of the hunter–prey situation. Tracing them was one thing; it was done remotely, avoiding all physical contact until the last possible moment. Doing the knock wasn't always necessary, either, depending on the client's requirements. But sharing car space with the target afterwards and having to listen to them justifying their actions was a step too far.

The phone buzzed. Jennings.

'You may leave.' The voice was smooth and bland, smug even, and Harry pictured him behind his executive desk in west London, pinstripe suit and polished brogues on display, self-satisfaction turned up high.

'You sure about that?' The last thing he needed was to drive all the way back to London only to have to come out here again because of a change of heart.

'I'm sure. Someone else will handle it from here.' A click and Jennings was gone.

Harry switched off the phone and placed it on the central console. Jennings had few obvious social skills and seemed determined not to improve them; maybe he'd been dropped once too often as a baby. He tossed the paper over his shoulder, distracted. Something was niggling at him. Something about the call. But it wouldn't come.

He reached up to check the rear-view mirror, settling himself for the long drive back. He'd stop somewhere for a meal, if he saw a place open. Something with chips. Or salad.

In the mirror, two bursts of light flared briefly against the darkening sky.

The source was from the top of the track near the cottage. There was no sound, but Harry knew instantly what it meant.

THREE

He was out of the car without thinking. He clicked the door shut and crouched by the rear wing. No sound after the flares of light; no indication of anything wrong. Yet there was something. Had to be.

He stood up and opened the boot. Reaching inside, he located a heavy metal box with a dial, which he moved two clicks to the right. Seconds later he flipped open the lid and took out the familiar weight of a semi-automatic and inserted a loaded magazine.

This is not clever, he told himself. Crazy, in fact. But what he'd just seen in the mirror was the reflection of muzzle-flash. Gunfire. He'd be even crazier going up there empty-handed.

He sighed and closed the boot. Took a deep breath.

Like old times.

The layout of the track was familiar enough, but he took it at an easy walk, keeping to the side away from the reeds. He'd done this kind of thing too many times in too many places before and knew that hurrying wouldn't help. Whatever had happened at the cottage was done; going in on the run wouldn't change it and could easily get him killed. And with the light fading fast, the ground was too uneven to take at a faster pace.

When the cottage came in sight, he stopped.

The door was wide open and a blaze of light was spilling out across the front step and painting the track a dirty yellow.

It was a bad sign: runners don't leave doors open. The sense of being pursued is with them always and the security of enclosure is what they crave most. Open doors bring unwelcome visitors with a tendency to chat. Chatting allows secrets to slip out. And he'd heard Matuq close and bolt the door.

He waited, tuning in to the night. Above the breeze a faint rattle echoed from the reeds behind the house, like the distant applause of a concert audience. A bird took off. High overhead, a plane droned unseen across the sky.

Staying clear of the light, Harry circled round the side of the cottage, one eye on the windows. There was no sign of movement inside, no sound from the outside. A flimsy wooden carport stood away from the house. It contained a dark-coloured Renault saloon with pale streaks of dried mud down the side. He touched the bonnet. Cold as mutton. If this was Matuq's car, he hadn't used it for a while. Then he noticed the vehicle had an odd tilt to it.

The tyres had been slashed.

He stepped towards the rear of the cottage and peered round the corner. A cold breeze was slicing in across the reeds from the sea, and he hunkered down in the lee of the wall. The back door was less than three feet away; wood-panelling at the bottom, glass at the top. Adequate for holiday lets but too flimsy for serious security.

He leaned over and tried the handle. Locked.

Ducking beneath the windows, he returned to the front of the cottage. Still no sound or sign of life. He stepped up alongside the front door, weapon held two-handed in front of him. With a conscious effort not to take in an audible breath, he stepped inside.

FOUR

Abuzeid Matuq was lying on his back against the far wall of the small main room, bare legs splayed out before him. The former banker wore a shocked expression and looked somehow diminished in size, as if death had robbed him of solidity. His Paisley-print gown showed two black holes in the front, and in the depression between his stomach and his chest, a dark, liquid mass had pooled like oil on sand.

Harry stepped across the room and knelt by the body, although he knew from the Libyan's posture that he was already beyond help.

A burst of noise came from the rear of the cottage. Harry reacted instinctively, reaching out to hit the light switch and plunging the house into gloom. He waited, breathing barely audible in the room, eyes on the emptiness outside the windows. He could just make out the back door. It was still closed, so he turned to cover the front. Anyone deciding to storm the place would come in the easy way.

More noise, this time a recognizable clatter of wings. A pigeon landed in a tree nearby, closely followed by another, crashing through the foliage like a flying brick.

Harry let out a long breath. He took out a slim Maglite torch and flicked it on. Other than the front door and the entrance to the kitchen, there was one other exit – a slim one to a narrow flight of stairs. He went up, gun held in front of him. Although the heavy silence in the house told him it was deserted save for the dead banker, it paid to be sure. Getting back-shot through carelessness was no way to live a long and happy life.

He found a single bedroom, a bathroom and toilet. The minimal signs of Matuq's presence signified a brief stay: a few clothes, a washbag and a suitcase which he checked. Just clothes.

Back downstairs, he played the torch over the body. He didn't know if Matuq had been a religious man, but whatever kind of afterlife he'd been bound for, he doubted he'd have been planning on reaching it just yet. He did a brief survey of the room. It was basic and drab, even allowing for the torchlight, and in need of a paint job. It was impossible to tell if anything had been moved, never having been inside before; there were usually signs if a place had been searched, no matter how carefully it had been done. But in this light it was a non-starter.

He prowled around, careful not to touch anything, noting a scattering of newspapers and magazines, a couple of DVDs on the arm of a chair and some rumpled outdoor clothing in need of a wash. The table held the remains of a meal, a mug of warm coffee and a radio. The latter, a small multi-band receiver, lay on its side, as if Matuq had inadvertently knocked it over when turning to answer the door. A bunch of keys lay next to it, secured to a Renault badge by a heavy clip-ring.

He peered through the window by the front door. All he could see was the bulk of the bushes screening the Saab and the dense mass of trees on the far side of the track. To his left lay the dark bed of reeds, their swaying heads just visible, bobbing in the breeze. The dying light had faded the dull colours of day to a standard charcoal to match the sky. In spite of that, he knew that anyone waiting out there for him to leave would have a clear field of fire.

He checked the tiny kitchen, which held the basic equipment for a holiday let. The sink was full of soiled dishes, the pedal bin overflowing with fast-food packaging. A scattering of breadcrumbs covered the worktop. Three empty wine bottles stood clustered together on the small drainer, each with a cork balanced neatly on the top. It was an indication that Matuq had found time weighing heavy on his hands. The back door had a large key in the lock.

He glanced through the side window at the carport. Whoever had done this had hobbled the car first in case Matuq tried to run. That did away with the idea of a rural burglary gone wrong. Burglars rarely carried handguns, even now, and the car would have been easy pickings for a quick sale, no questions asked. Harry flicked his torch across the room to confirm that there were no signs of even a cursory search; no torn cushions, open cupboards or drawers; no spilled papers or scattered magazines, none of the rumpled carpets showing the place had been turned over indiscriminately. So, no hayseed crackheads looking for a quick score.

He went back to Matuq's body and knelt down, holding his torch close. In the V of the dead man's dressing gown lapels, a heavy red patch showed just above two ugly bullet wounds. But what drew his attention was the pool of blood on the clothing. Caught in the sticky liquid were what appeared to be bits of cotton stuffing, like loft insulation.

Harry recognized the material. It was wadding – the kind used in homemade sound suppressors, or silencers. A tube lined with baffles, the gap between them packed with the material, it was a short-term but effective way of reducing the muzzle sound of a gunshot. Some of the wadding inevitably came loose under the intense pressures, as had happened here.

The beauty was, the tube could be disposed of afterwards and few would give it more than a second glance, a nameless piece of junk. It was probably lying in the reeds nearby, if anyone cared to look.

He glanced up as an alien sound interrupted his thoughts. A starter motor was turning over, insistent and high-pitched. The noise continued for a few seconds, reluctant to catch, then the engine coughed and caught, running fast as the accelerator was depressed.

The utility van.

Harry jumped up, the wadding forgotten. The killer had been close by all along. He'd found an alternative approach to the cottage. And a quick way out.

FIVE

A flick of the torch outside revealed a short stretch of unkempt garden running from the back door to the edges of the reed bed. A rusted wheelbarrow stood mired in long, twisted grass in one corner amid the remains of what might have been a rockery, and a straggly tangle of rose briar curled in on itself like an octopus.

Harry pointed the torch and instantly spotted a narrow footpath leading away between the bushes bordering the track and the waving reeds. The tenants probably used it as a short cut to the village and the main road.

He studied the ground around the drooping wire fence. Fresh footprints showed in the damp soil, and there was a gash where someone had skidded. He stared into the gloom, knowing this could be a trap. Whoever had come down here had the advantage of knowing the layout of the ground, and might be waiting for him to follow.

He shook his head and eased off the safety. Standing here wouldn't accomplish anything. He started down the path.

The going was soft and the path narrow, with room for one person at a time. The smell here was heavy and sour, hemmed in by the reeds on one side and the bushes on the other. Something scurried away as Harry passed, and a splash echoed among the vegetation. He used the torch sparingly, flicking it on to gain a sense of direction, but ready to throw himself off the path.

Something glinted at ground level a few feet ahead. He estimated he could be only yards from the road, probably close to where the van had been parked. He slowed but didn't need to use the torch to see what the shiny object was; the backlight behind the keys showed it was a mobile phone. He stepped quickly to one side of the path and bent to scoop it up.

The combination of movements probably saved his life.

He heard a violent scuff of movement from close by, followed by a sharp exhalation of breath. Something hissed past his head. He felt a flash of intense pain in his shoulder and his torch tumbled away from numbed fingers. Reacting instinctively, he threw himself sideways away from the reeds and the soggy ground underneath and brought up his gun. But the attacker was already moving away, his footsteps fading along the path.

Scrambling to his feet, Harry snatched up the mobile and used its light to find his torch, then set off in pursuit, wincing with pain from his shoulder. It didn't take long to reach the road.

As he burst out from the path, he was just in time to hear a vehicle roaring away into the darkness and see a brief flash of brake lights as it disappeared from view in the direction of the village.

Harry muttered in disgust and looked at the mobile. He'd fallen for the oldest trick in the book: the killer had dropped it to distract him and nearly caved his head in. He was willing to bet that the mobile had once belonged to the late Abuzeid Matuq.

He wondered what the killer had been trying to accomplish. Doubling back along the path to lay in wait had been a risky manoeuvre. He'd already got back to his van and was clear and ready to leave. So why do it? There was only one explanation: he was improvising on the move, looking to distract attention from himself by leaving someone else lying near the body.

Harry walked back up the path until he reached the point where he had been attacked. He cast around with the torch until he saw a gleam of metal among the reeds. It was a long mains water key with a T-piece on one end and a heavy-looking prong on the other. Just right for caving in a man's head.

He left it and walked back to the Saab, a deep feeling of unease settling on him. What had started out as a simple job of chasing down a runaway banker had suddenly become a lot more complicated. Now there was a killer involved. And whoever he was, he was resourceful and quick on his feet.

A professional.

SIX

As he drove south through the village and out the other side, Harry rang Jennings with the news. He kept it brief. The lawyer was silent for a few moments, then said briskly, 'There's nothing you can do. It was probably the Libyans. There was a danger they might take direct action if they located him – especially somewhere remote like that. They probably reasoned it would look bad if someone else recovered the money for them.'

Harry felt a prickle of irritation. 'And you didn't think it worthwhile warning me?' He didn't mention that he had been armed, so therefore not exactly incapable of defending himself. Carrying a gun was no guarantee of survival, and there were some things Jennings was better off not knowing.

'Time to move on.' The lawyer ignored the question. 'Someone else will come out to deal with Matuq. Report to my office tomorrow morning. Noon. I have an urgent job for you.'

'What about Param?' The other assignment on his list. So far, he had done no research on this runner, an investment manager from a London firm who had disappeared along with sizeable sums of money siphoned off through a batch of illicit accounts.

'My office. In the morning.' The connection was cut.

Harry dropped the mobile and concentrated on driving, trying to push Matuq's murder to the back of his mind. It wasn't easy. After a stint in the army, including Kosovo and

Iraq, followed by several years in MI5 on the anti-terror and anti-narcotics teams, death was no longer a stranger to him. Even less so after a drugs operation had gone wrong and his near-fatal punishment was a posting to a security services outstation in Georgia that he wasn't meant to survive. But each death he'd seen had carried some kind of explanation or motive, some reasoning – even if not always a rational one. The shooting of Matuq, however, seemed pointless. Random.

Yet he knew it wasn't.

It had been too efficient. Like an execution.

'Christ on horseback.' It seemed only minutes later when he sat upright and stared through the windscreen at the road ahead. He'd been driving on automatic pilot, the miles being eaten away without conscious thought or awareness. He gazed around; saw familiar landmarks streaming by under the glare of overhead lights, and a steady rumble of late night trucks on a motorway. He was just crossing the M25 around north London. He rubbed his eyes, gritty through lack of sleep, and lowered the window to get a blast of air on his face. He felt guilty at this loss of concentration; how he'd driven from a rural backwater to the outskirts of London, all without being totally conscious of the road before and behind him.

Backwater.

Suddenly he knew what had been puzzling him about Jennings' earlier comment; what had finally jerked him back to reality.

The only thing he had sent Jennings from Blakeney was the photo of Matuq taken on his mobile. There had been no details other than his name. No location, no directions, no indication of where it was taken – not even a county. That would have followed later when asked for. Confirmation first, then specifics; it was how Jennings liked to work.

So how could the lawyer have known that the location was 'remote', or where to send his people to deal with the body?

SEVEN

'**T**his is a priority job.' Jennings selected one of two buff folders from his desk and slid it across the glossy surface. It was noon the following day, and if the lawyer was surprised by Harry's display of punctuality after the events of the night before, he was careful not to show it. His secretary had shown Harry in moments ago, then retreated to her small office just off the main entrance hall.

Harry picked up the folder. Inside was a single sheet of paper, a plain brown envelope and a six-by-four black and white photograph. It showed a slim, doleful-looking man with dark shadows under his eyes and closely cropped black hair dotted with flecks of grey. His cheeks were pockmarked, with what might have been a large birthmark just below his right eye. He had a neatly trimmed beard lining his chin, and his age could have been anywhere between fifty and seventy. The sad expression in the man's eyes spoke of something tragic about his past. Or, thought Harry cynically, maybe a lack of confidence in his future.

'What's this one done?' he asked, putting down the photo. 'Run off with his firm's piggy bank?'

Jennings gave him a cool look. 'That's not your problem. Somebody wants him found. It's all you need to know.'

'It may not be an issue,' Harry explained reasonably. 'But it helps to know if he's bent or not. Or has a contract on his head.' Jennings didn't appear to understand, so Harry explained, 'Crooks behave in a different way to those who've just gone AWOL for other reasons, like stress. They might turn nasty when I show up on their doorstep and ruin their day. Some might even have cosied up with a heavy to watch their backs.'

Jennings opened his mouth, then gave a half-nod. 'Fair enough. I can see that.' He appeared to give it some thought, then shifted in his chair. 'He's not . . . bent, as you so quaintly put it. His name is Samuel Silverman. Professor. You'll find what we have in the briefing document. He's gone missing from his home in Haifa. Simply left his house and disappeared without warning. Three days later, he was seen by an acquaintance arriving at Heathrow, coming off a Lufthansa flight. That was on the twenty-seventh, two weeks ago. Since then, nothing. His family is very worried and thinks he may have suffered some kind of trauma.'

'From what?' In Harry's opinion, living in Israel must be enough to traumatize anyone, all that danger and tension. Small wonder if some found it too stressful and wanted to jump the reservation.

Jennings studied his fingernails. 'His daughter was killed by a car bomb, along with a grandchild. He took it badly. He stopped going anywhere socially without explanation some time ago, and they think it may have been a precursor to walking away. That's all I can tell you.' He looked up as if daring any further questions.

'Was he travelling solo?' The majority of runners travel alone, prisoners of their circumstances, trusting no one. But occasionally they pick up company along the way. That it sometimes turns out to have been planned beforehand is usually one of the reasons for their vanishing act in the first place. If Silverman had hooked up with someone, it would leave a bigger footprint and might make tracing him a little easier.

'Yes.' Jennings made no further comment.

'Did they try the police? Immigration?'

'No. It was considered a waste of time.'

Harry frowned. There was something Jennings wasn't telling him. Whatever Silverman's reasons for running, surely it seemed unlikely the family would hire his kind of private expertise without trying the conventional agencies first.

Unless there was something in his background they didn't want made public.

He picked up the briefing paper and scanned it. It told him almost nothing. No address, no family details or names, no work history. Someone had written 'LH4736 T2 27th' in the margin. A brief note saying he'd suffered a cut to his right hand. The item might have been useful had the person they were looking for been a one-legged asthmatic with a dodgy foot, but Silverman seemed to possess no such characteristics other than a bandage. 'What was he a professor of? And how did he come by the injury?'

'He is – was – a professor of theology, I'm told. But that's irrelevant. The cut was believed to be a domestic accident. I've included it only because he might need to visit a hospital to change the bandages.'

'It's not much to go on,' said Harry. Actually, it was bugger all. He was beginning to feel depressed. 'Are you sure this is it?'

'I'm certain. Everything we have is in there. I'm reliably informed there was nothing worth considering in his home.'

'But he's a professor. The last academic's office I saw was a mess of paper. They ooze the stuff. Confiscate their pads and pencils and they start biting the furniture.'

Jennings remained unmoved. 'As I said, it's all we have.'

Harry picked up the brown envelope. He tipped it up and a single piece of lined paper slid into his hand. It was brittle to the touch and brown along one edge. He lifted it to his nose and sniffed. It smelled charred. 'Where did this come from?'

'His office. A metal waste-bin. There was no explanation, but . . . they thought it might be helpful because they couldn't explain it.'

'They?'

Jennings leaned forward, easing his neck clear of his shirt collar. 'Silverman has certain connections. I cannot go any further.'

'Connections,' Harry echoed. 'Israeli government connections?' He studied the scrap of paper, which had a faint line of writing on one side.

'That's right.'

'If he's one of theirs,' said Harry, 'I'm surprised they haven't provided more information. I'd have thought they'd be pleased to have help.' As he was speaking, he heard a small click from a door at the rear of the office, behind Jennings' shoulder. He'd assumed it led to an executive toilet, the kind of personal ego attachment a man like Jennings would value. But maybe not. The door was open a fraction, and he was sure he caught a small movement through the crack.

Jennings was looking impatient and shifted in his chair. 'There's a condition attached to this job,' he added seriously.

'Go on.'

'Silverman is not to be approached. You find him, you tell

me where he is, you get paid, you don't ask questions. End of job.' He raised his eyebrows to invite understanding. 'You don't go near him. Merely report in as soon as you locate him.'

'Because of his connections?' Harry wondered what was going on. With no information other than a photo and the barest of details, he was on the back foot before he started. And any mention of Israeli government 'connections' automatically implied banging his head against a brick wall if he tried probing into Silverman's background. 'If he's such a sensitive target,' he pointed out, 'why don't the Israelis find him? They're good enough at hunting down Nazi war criminals years after the event; they can pinpoint Hamas and Al Fatah targets whenever they feel like it. Tracking down a runaway university professor should be a doddle.'

'Are you saying you don't want this assignment?' Jennings' voice was cool with an edge of tension. 'If so, I can always find someone else.' He glanced at his watch as if indicating that doing so wouldn't take more than a few minutes and a phone call.

Harry reached for the folder and closed it with a slap. The door behind Jennings had now closed. 'I can do it. Crossing the tees, that's all.'

'Good. Get on to it right away. Keep me informed.'

'And Param?'

'He'll keep.'

'If you say so.' The lawyer had still asked no questions about Matuq's location, nor made any reference to his murder. There had been nothing in the morning news, either. It was as if none of it had ever happened. 'There's a problem about Matuq.'

'What kind of problem?'

'I was the last to see him alive. Second to last. I might have been spotted in the area. It's not a thriving metropolis and I wasn't exactly keeping a low profile. Nor,' he added grimly, 'was I expecting him to get popped.'

Jennings looked unconcerned and Harry wondered if the man had even considered the situation. The local police might have heard of a stranger seen driving up to the cottage and leaving. A water company van in the area would be common enough; they come and go all the time. Part of the street furniture almost.

But a stranger in a high performance car late at night wasn't that easy to miss – especially when a local visitor gets drilled by a professional hit.

Yet Jennings wasn't buying it. 'A sleepy place like Norfolk? I doubt you were even noticed.'

'I hope you're right. Seeing the same car twice is probably a thrill a minute in those parts; murder must be way up with UFOs and fish on bicycles.'

'It's been taken care of,' Jennings said eventually. 'There will be no comeback.' He indicated the door. 'Don't let me keep you.'

Outside on the pavement, Harry flipped open the slim folder on Professor Samuel Silverman, late of Haifa, and wondered what Jennings wasn't telling him. He also wondered who had been listening in on their conversation behind the door, and whether it had anything to do with Matuq's early death.

EIGHT

Jennings watched the former MI5 officer cross the pavement to a muddy Saab parked in a residents-only bay, and felt a prickle of disquiet. Tate was an odd character. He had come on the recommendation of someone trusted, although with the proviso that he'd been round the block a few times and had a reputation for doing things his own way. There was also a whisper about something in his background which would have made interesting reading had his contact in the security services been able to gain access. But that part of his record was sealed. All his contact had been able to tell him was that Tate had left the service in mysterious circumstances, yet without a noticeable black mark, which was intriguing in itself. Since then, he had worked in private security here and overseas, occasionally hooking up with a former MI5 IT and communications expert named Ferris. Ferris also had a sealed record and had left the security service at the same time as Tate.

Tate was a rebel, in other words, used to doing things his own way. Jennings didn't mind that. For the right jobs, rebels had their uses.

He turned as the door at the rear of the office opened, and a man entered. Dressed in a dark, ill-fitting suit, the newcomer was wiry and intense, with the compact build of a jockey. He looked oddly out of place in the confines of the office, like a caged animal, with eyes of cold grey set in a tanned and weather-beaten face. His mouth curled at one corner as if permanently snarling at the world, and his hair was cropped harshly at the sides and lank on top.

The newcomer went by the name of Dog. It had been his call sign years ago in the back runs of Belfast and Londonderry, when personal names could mean the difference between life or sudden death. Jennings was one of the few people who knew the man's real name of Gary Pellew, but he'd always thought there was something in his manner and appearance that suited the pseudonym much better.

'He sounds like trouble,' Dog murmured. 'He questions things.'

'Stay on him,' said Jennings, ignoring the comment. 'And keep me informed. I'll let you know what action to take.'

Dog turned and left without a word, and Jennings knew that his instructions would be followed to the letter. Unlike Tate, Dog didn't have the same level of skills at tracing runners. But what he did have were certain rare attributes that would never get him any kind of desk job. It was these skills which gave Jennings cause to shiver whenever he was in the man's presence, although he took great care not to show it.

He was always quietly relieved that Dog was on his side, but never more so than when the man had left the building.

Still, he couldn't quite dispel an evidently shared feeling of unease about Tate, although he wasn't about to tell Dog that he agreed with him. What particularly surprised him was the ease with which Tate had managed to track down Matuq. A week or ten days might have been the norm, given the Libyan's head start. But Tate had hardly given him time to breathe before he was on him like a rash. Maybe he had underestimated the man's capabilities.

He shook off his concerns and opened the middle desk drawer. Inside was a slip of paper bearing a name and telephone number. The number led to a contact deep inside the Ministry of Information in Libya's capital city, Tripoli.

It was time to confirm the successful completion of another assignment.

NINE

Raymond Param's house stood in leafy seclusion at the end of a short cul-de-sac in London's Highgate. With a double garage, large garden, eyelash gables and a majestic sweep of roof, it was impressive and solid in the evening sunlight, a fanfare to design, prosperity and the rewards of capitalist enterprise.

It also had a brooding aura hovering over it like a dense cloud, as if the owner's sudden change of status had infected the area, draining whatever light there may have been out of the atmosphere.

'Nice gaff,' said Rik Ferris, studying the facade. He scrubbed at his head of spiky hair which refused to be tamed. A bit, Harry decided, like his unusual taste in T-shirts, although he'd toned them down a bit lately. The current one was dark blue with a vivid splash of orange across the chest. The blue matched the Audi TT they were sitting in. Rik had agreed to meet him outside the house for a briefing on Param's background. 'I thought you said Jennings wanted him left alone.'

'So he did. But I haven't yet sorted out how to start on the latest job he gave me. A runner named Silverman – I'll tell you about it later. In the meantime, we might as well do something positive.' Harry took out the briefing paper on Param and scanned the main points. Raymond Param, investment manager for Boulding Bartram, an investment partnership in London. Aged forty-three, Anglo-Indian, his mother British, he went to the London School of Economics, did some time in the States, then joined Bouldings. Married, no children. Solid performer, reliable, steady, then one day, gone. No notes, no goodbyes, no shoes on the beach. He checked a six-by-four photo which accompanied the briefing notes. It showed a sleek individual in a conservative pinstripe, with receding black hair and an easy smile.

'Why are they hot to find him?'

'His employers found a bunch of dummy offshore accounts after he'd skipped. All empty. They think he set them up so he could dump small amounts of money over several months, then cleared them out once he was ready to go.'

'Small? Is it worth all the trouble, trying to get him back?'

'The small amounts added up to about three million.'

'Ouch. Painful. Sounds like their systems slipped up.'

'Just a bit. No warning, out of character, never done this before, highest integrity, honest as the day is long, blah-di-blah. Now rich and on the lam.' He passed Rik copies of the briefing documents. 'We need to check out anything you can find on him; clubs, friends, recent trips, financials – the usual.'

'No problem.' Rik folded the sheets and put them in the glove box. Like Harry, he was a former employee of MI5. He had an extensive knowledge of government systems and a widespread hacking community he could use to blur the lines of any illicit searches he needed to conduct. It had been his misuse of IT resources that had led to his own downfall, and his posting to the same remote station where he and Harry had first met.

'Where do we start the physical stuff?'

'Right here. The wife's staying with her sister, so we've got full run of the house to do the audit, including, with luck, his computer and financial records.' The audit was the term Harry used for trawling through a runner's background, checking every file, document, scrap of paper, phone and email records, financial detail, and even searching their clothing and cars, all in the hope of finding a clue to the runner's where-abouts. Mostly, it worked. Like it had with Matuq, turning up a colour postcard of a cottage in Blakeney, Norfolk. It hadn't been the one he'd been staying in, but enough to point Harry in the right direction. The rest had been down to Rik checking phone calls and emails made by the Libyan from his office and home. Harry looked at him. 'First, though, I'd like to check the wife actually is with the sister and hasn't snuck off to Las Vegas to join hubby Raymond on the blackjack tables.'

'Cynic,' Rik murmured drily. But he knew Harry was right; Param wouldn't be the first partner or husband to skip with some ill-gotten gains with the connivance of his better half. He yawned. 'Tomorrow first thing?'

'Why – you got a hot date?' Rik had a variety of girlfriends, none of whom seemed to last long. Most were victims of his irregular lifestyle and his obsession with technology . . . and possibly, Harry figured, his taste in garish T-shirts and his spiky hair. Their passing didn't seem to bother him much.

'I did. She blew me out. Something about visiting her sister in hospital.'

Harry laughed. 'Christ – they're not still using that old chestnut, are they?'

'At least I'm still finding out,' Rik sneered. 'When did you last go on a date?'

Harry didn't rise to the bait. He was beyond dates. Dates were for new beginnings, tentative relationships with a faint whiff of potential failure about them. He was more into a relaxed night in with a decent bottle of wine. And Jean. Fortunately, she concurred wholeheartedly with that. The willowy owner of an upmarket flower business, she had an easy grin and an earthy laugh and actually concurred very nicely. But not tonight. She was out with friends at a hen party in the Cotswolds. 'You haven't said anything about the Libyan . . . Matuq? How'd it go?' The electronic sweep Rik had conducted had provided nothing useful, save that his credit cards and bank account had not been used. With no other identifiable source of money, they had concluded that he was using a pre-drawn fund of cash on which to exist until the fuss died down.

'I found him. He's dead.' Harry described briefly what had happened.

'Jeez, that's tough. Remind me never to steal anything from Colonel Gaddafi.'

The house looked no less imposing the following morning at nine thirty. The local school run was over, always a time when nobody had time to notice anything, in Harry's experience, as he led the way through the front door and across a broad hallway to a small green box on one wall.

'You have twenty seconds to key in the number,' a tearless and artfully 'traumatized' Mrs Param had told him half an hour earlier. It was all the time they had, she had warned, sitting regally in her sister's front room, before the private security company she had insisted her husband use came to investigate.

She had given grudging permission for them to look around, but only after the intervention of her husband's former employers.

'How long do I have to put up with this?' she had demanded coldly. She was attractive in a glossy, brittle way and, if she had shed any tears at her husband's disappearance, there was little evidence in her manner or the precision of her make-up. Harry thought she needed a swift kick up the pants, but kept his thoughts to himself. Somehow, given the acerbic comments voiced by her sister about her absent brother-in-law being nothing but a gambler and wastrel, he doubted it would be long before Mrs Param returned to clear the place out for a quick and vengeful sale.

'A few hours,' Harry had told her. 'A day at most.' He hadn't mentioned that if they had to enter the fabric of the house to see if her husband had hidden files or documents inside the walls or beneath the flooring, it could take a lot longer. That sort of decision was down to Jennings and his client.

After keying in the security code, he stood and breathed in the atmosphere for a moment before walking through the house. Rik hung back, humming quietly. This was Harry's area of expertise, a time to acclimatize himself to the feel of the place and soak up the colour and tone of Raymond Param's former life.

The house was richly furnished and comfortable, with gold-embroidered chairs and sofas set with precision around a large living room overlooking a neat rear garden and patio. The carpet was pale and expensive throughout. Apart from a huge kitchen, a utility room, dining room, study and a downstairs bathroom completed the ground floor layout, like the pages of a property catalogue. It was the domain of a childless couple: no clutter, no toys, no signs of disarray from careless teenagers or rampaging tots.

But there were signs that the police had been through the house, evidenced by the minute shift of certain items, the slightly opened drawers and small depressions in the carpet where furniture had been moved and put back a fraction out of place.

There were a few photos, carefully positioned for maximum effect, like exhibits in a gallery. Other than people who were probably unnamed members of the extended Param family on both sides, they were mostly of Param and his wife, Saskia, arms artfully entwined and heads close but never quite touching. None of the shots displayed any obvious warmth between them. It was as if they had been concentrating more on the professional than the personal touch, like mannequins in a photo shoot. Raymond Param was athletic, well dressed and groomed, from the brushed hair and crisp shirts, to the display of a large Rolex and the chunky cufflinks at his wrists. His wife wore her clothes and make-up with the ease of a professional model, smiling carefully at the camera but not once at her husband.

'Nothing blindingly obvious,' said Harry. There had been little in the way of clues or suggestions from Saskia Param as to where her husband might have gone, and he'd dismissed further questioning of her as a waste of time. It was down to sifting through whatever they could find in the hopes of uncovering a lead. The one thing he was sure of was that this house had ceased to be a centre of marital bliss a long time ago.

'I'll start on the study.' Rik was looking through the doorway at a grey PC sitting on a desk.

Harry nodded. 'Go to it. I'll do the rest.' He made his way upstairs and began working methodically through the rooms, beginning with the master bedroom. He wasn't hopeful of finding anything because Mrs Param had made it clear that her husband's domain was the study, and she knew for certain that he never left anything in his suits because she always checked. This had been said without a blink of embarrassment. He looked anyway, because as he knew from experience, even the most watchful of wives missed things. And an apparently innocuous scrap of paper was all he needed to give him a trail to follow.

Twenty minutes later he closed the door to the main bedroom. The wardrobe held only clothes and the drawers contained smaller items and accessories. The en suite bathroom proved a similar blank, as did the other rooms and cupboards. If Param had left anything here, it was somewhere inside the furniture or concealed behind the walls, where nothing short of wholesale demolition would find it.

He returned to the study where Rik was staring at the PC with a concentrated look of disgust.

'What's up?'

'Nothing,' said Rik. 'It's a useless pile of crap. He cleaned it.'

'How?'

'He must have downloaded a wipe utility to sanitize the hard drive.' He tapped the keyboard in frustration. 'Kills all the data stone dead.' He gestured at a laptop on the sideboard. 'Same with that. No links to follow, either.'

'Well, although I only understood half of what you just said,' Harry murmured, 'it means he wasn't fooling. He was covering his tracks.' It also meant that it killed any chances of Param having been coerced by a third party to defraud the funds. 'We'll have to do it the hard way.' He began pulling drawers out of the large, ornate desk, and emptying them one by one, placing each item to one side after examination. There was also a sideboard, a drinks cupboard and a filing cabinet, all of which were places Param might have left something they could use. If they were lucky.

Rik scowled, cheated of the opportunity to use his specialist skills. He selected a drawer and dumped the contents on a spare piece of carpet and began sifting through.

TEN

Two hours later, they adjourned to the kitchen for coffee and a conference. So far they had come up empty.

If there was anything in the desk, they hadn't found it. Every invoice, receipt or statement cross-referenced perfectly to a household or work expense, and those that didn't, they had cross-checked with Saskia Param. It had taken several phone calls to elicit the details, along with repeated queries from her about why they needed to go through her private papers in this way.

After the first three calls, Harry had given up explaining.

'If you want to find out what happened to your husband,' he'd said bluntly during the last call, 'and get your house back, this is the only way.' It had shut her up, although he guessed only for a while. He sensed she had already lined up a divorce lawyer ready for the fray, and was impatient for them to be out so that she could move in and begin the next phase of her life.

'He's clean,' Harry said, staring into his coffee, adding in a way that made it sound an almost unhealthy trait in a grown man, 'Too bloody clean, in fact.'

'As in?' Rik had come to rely on Harry's judgement in these things. As straightforward as Harry liked to pretend to be, he had the ability to peer deep into the minds of his quarries and understand what they were thinking.

'Param's wealthy, married, no kids, great job. OK, his missus is as cold as custard, but nobody's life is perfect, right? Then he goes walkabout with a ton of money. Also not uncommon . . . for a fraudster. But this was no spur of the moment thing. Too much planning went into it.' He gestured around the spotless kitchen, a mocking reflection of what they had found everywhere else. 'It's like he sanitized the whole place before he bunked off. And that lot in there,' he nodded towards the study, now littered with piles of papers, none of which had offered a single lead, 'is uncanny. Nobody could work on a scam, then do a bunk and not leave *something* behind.'

Rik shrugged easily. 'Like you said, he planned it.' He glanced at Harry, took a tour round the kitchen, then said casually, 'Is this what you thought you'd be doing after Five, looking for runners who didn't want to be found?'

Harry had often asked himself the same question. Forced, like Rik, to leave the security service after surviving a posting to an office called Red Station in Georgia, where his name had been placed on a hit list by two renegade security services bosses, he had been in limbo. Since staying on at Thames House was a non-starter – there were too many embarrassed faces who didn't wish to be reminded of the organization's shortcomings – it had meant an end to the structure and order of his life. Even working undercover requires strict attention to habit and detail. In its place had come freedom and free choice, neither of which he had experienced much of before. Life since then had been a mix of security-related jobs and contracts, including two brief assignments in Iraq – a place he'd sworn never to go back to, but circumstances had demanded it – where Rik had learned some hard lessons in survival not normally experienced by security service IT personnel.

Yet for Harry, the link with his old employers had never been irrevocably broken. For him, there was still some unfinished business to be resolved: namely, finding his former boss, Henry Paulton. The man had conspired with a senior MI6 officer, Sir Anthony Bellingham, to have Harry and the others in the station terminated by a team called the Hit. Saved by ironic circumstance as the Russians had moved across the border into South Ossetia in a so-called protective and supportive action, Harry, Rik and an MI6 officer named Clare Jardine had abandoned the station and headed home. Recognizing that his time was up, Paulton had slipped away. Bellingham was not so lucky; he had died by Clare Jardine's hand on London's Embankment before she, too, had vanished.

Harry had no interest in Jardine. She had done what she thought was right for her. But Paulton was another matter. And that still rankled like toothache. It was something he'd never discussed with Rik, although he knew the day would come. But right now wasn't the time.

'Let's do it again. Top to bottom.' He rinsed his cup and left it on the side. It was down to sheer doggedness now, revisiting every nook and cranny, rechecking every item of furniture in the house, in case they'd missed something. If that didn't work, they were stumped.

After two more hours of effort, including a dusty trawl through the attic, Harry walked back into the study. He did a tour of the room, ticking off obvious places of interest. But it was a cosmetic exercise; there was nowhere left to look which hadn't already been searched thoroughly. And he was now certain that Param would not have hidden anything in the walls, ceiling or floor without his eagle-eyed wife being aware of it. He left the room and picked up a set of car keys with a BMW fob from a table in the hallway.

The garage was a double, brick-built affair with a concrete floor finished in a polished dark-green skim. It held one car – a blue 5 series BMW – and a few items of gardening equipment. Apart from that, it was immaculate and barren. Harry searched the car from front to boot, but found nothing. It looked as if it might have just been delivered from the showroom, with none of the usual accumulated car trash found in most vehicles.

He returned to the study and dropped the keys on the desk, then rang Mrs Param and asked her for the registration numbers of the family cars. She gave him the details with customary reluctance and he rang off before she could bitch further about the invasion of her property.

'Now there's a thing,' he said quietly, and felt the first buzz of something being not quite right. He went back to a drawer he had been working on earlier, checking and rechecking everything. Only this time he knew what he was looking for.

'What have you got?' Rik was showing signs of acute boredom, his spiked hair now limp. On Harry's instructions he had already gone through the kitchen again with a fresh pair of eyes, emptying drawers and cupboards, even poring over a pegboard of notes and postcards. So far it had produced nothing useful. Unlike Matuq, Raymond Param had shown no history of visiting isolated cottages in the depths of Norfolk or anywhere else.

'The Params own two cars – a BMW for him and a Mazda for her,' Harry explained, sitting back. 'She's got the Mazda with her and the Beemer's in the garage – and it's new-pin clean.'

Rik pulled a face. 'Why leave a car like that?'

'Because driving it would be a dead giveaway. Like a sign round his neck saying, *Here I am.*' Harry picked up a piece of paper from the drawer. 'There's a parking fine receipt here for a late-model Mini Cooper S, issued in Golden Square, London.' He shrugged. 'I saw it earlier but dismissed it. Now I'm wondering.'

He picked up the phone and dialled a number, read out the registration number of the Mini and waited. Eventually, he stirred and made a scribbled note on the parking receipt. He cut the connection and scowled at the ceiling.

'Well?' Rik looked as if he was contemplating taking a pickaxe to the furniture out of sheer spite.

'A second.' Harry went back to the drawers he had been working on and rummaged through the papers before pulling out a sheet with a triumphant smile. 'What do we know of Param's office colleagues?'

'Not much. They've all been looked at by the police and the company's own security people. Mostly long-time employees, no queries or big spending habits, no changes to daily routine.'

He frowned, realizing that Harry had found something. 'The smug old git look really doesn't suit you, by the way.'

Harry ignored the jibe and flicked at the piece of paper he was holding. It was a dusty, creased sheet he'd discovered at the bottom of a drawer, caught up among other work-related clutter of seemingly little relevance.

'This is an extract from minutes of a board meeting a couple of years back. Apologies for absence, dates of next meeting and so on. One of the notes refers to a vote of thanks to a Miss Yvonne Michaels, who served as a PA for Param and a couple of other directors. According to this, she was leaving London to go back to Cape Town, where her family lives. Sounds like they were sorry to see her go, good and faithful employee, loyal and so forth.'

'South Africans come and go all the time. There's a whole community of them here.'

Harry nodded. As Australians and Kiwis had done for years before them, now it was kids from Johannesburg and Cape Town who piled in and out of London looking for opportunity and adventure, filling in by staffing pubs up and down the country.

'The registration of the Mini Cooper S,' he explained, teasing out his thoughts along with the facts, 'booked for an over-stay in Golden Square, London W1, is in the name of a Y. Michaels.'

'Param paid the fine for her. Good bosses do that.'

'The ticket was issued on the fifth of last month.'

Rik lifted an eyebrow. 'She must have come back.'

'Or he's using her old car. Or, she never left. Either way—'

'Either way, why is the receipt in Param's desk?' Rik grinned. 'Somebody's been a naughty boy. Do we have an address?'

'Yes, we do.' Harry checked his watch. It was mid-afternoon and they hadn't eaten. Much more of this and they'd be operating on reduced batteries. He hoped the Michaels address would lead somewhere and not dump them flat. 'We'll do it another time. We've pushed our luck with this one. I need you to do some work on this new job for me.'

Rik jumped up and cracked his knuckles. 'Suits me. After all this paper, I'm getting withdrawal symptoms. What's the brief?'

'There isn't much.' He reeled off from memory what little information he'd been given by Jennings.

Rik looked doubtful. 'Christ, you weren't kidding, were you? I need more than that if I'm to get anything on the net.'

'We've got a name. We'll have to make do with that. Anyway, I thought you IT nerds liked a challenge.'

'We do. But what happens if we can't find anything? He might have disappeared completely.'

Harry smiled. He knew Rik well enough to realize that he would wear his keyboard down to the wires before admitting defeat. 'There's no such thing as disappearing completely. You in or not?'

'I'm in.'

ELEVEN

They drove to Rik's flat near Paddington to ponder on the meagre scraps representing Professor Samuel Silverman's recent life. With so little to go on, the usual audit was out. With none of the usual paperwork, they were missing their customary points of reference. A process which might normally take a couple of days, interspersed with numerous calls to check any detail that failed to match, now looked a non-starter. And with no family members or friends to speak to, usually a valuable source of information, gossip and speculation, they had no anecdotal hints to fall back on and broaden the search.

Rik opened his laptop and began feeding Silverman's name into various search engines. There were several Samuel Silvermans, some dead, some living, but none matching even remotely the kind of background to the missing professor. There were lawyers, financial experts, psychiatrists, scientists – even academics. Yet none that came close to the man they were looking for. Going on Jennings' mention that Silverman had connections with the Israeli government, he also began tentative probing of certain restricted websites, and put out feelers to contacts in the hacking community.

While Rik was Googling, Harry went out for sandwiches,

coffee and cake to spur on their thinking. After being cooped up in Param's place, the car and now here, he was glad to get out into the open, and took his time. He had a feeling there would be a lot more of being cooped up to come.

On his return, he handed Rik his brain food and prowled the room deep in thought. The furnishings were minimal and mixed, evidence of impulse buying by Rik following his recent move from home, where he'd lived with his mother. There was an L-shaped sofa, a glass-topped table with four matching chairs, a space-age steel-and-glass coffee table, a flat-screen television and music centre, but little else. The floor was wood-block and polished to a high gleam. Discreet wall lights completed the modernistic, almost clinical effect.

'God bless IKEA,' Harry commented.

'It's a place to chill, not a character statement,' retorted Rik, who had clearly been waiting for some form of comment. 'Anyway, I've had no complaints.' He smirked and fluttered his eyebrows.

Harry walked over to the window. His own place in Islington was like a second-hand shop in comparison, the furniture gathered at various times without much thought given to style or fashion, the result of a life on the move with little time spent at home. Anything matching was by chance, whereas he guessed Rik had chosen his furnishings with an instinctive leaning towards how they might look to a third party.

He peered down three floors to a twin row of shops. The area was busy, cars jostling with delivery vans to find space at the kerb, while pedestrians crossed wherever and whenever the spirit took them, instinctive survivors of a busy thoroughfare. The aftermath of an earlier fruit and vegetable market lay in the gutter like battle scars, blood-red segments of pulp and skin mixed with traces of paper bags and splinters of wooden boxes.

'How is it,' said Rik, sprawling on the sofa, waiting for the machine to do something, 'that Silverman's "people" didn't supply any financials? No bank statements, no credit card slips, no receipts, no work stuff, like letters, academic notes, agendas or jottings. There's usually too much crap, not too little. This bloke has nothing.' He balanced the disposable mug on the arm of the sofa and ripped the ends off paper tubes of sugar, stirring in the contents and glumly considering the lack

of data they had to work with. Rik's IT-trained mind preferred
to see something tangible to fasten on to, not a dribble of
detail that led nowhere. 'Makes you wonder how hard they
looked.'

Harry was only half listening. He was studying a nondescript saloon at the kerb a hundred yards up the street. It was
parked behind a battered delivery van and contained a soli-
tary figure – a man – but he couldn't see any other detail. A
tired shopper, maybe. Or a patient husband, killing time while
his wife did the weekly market run. It could be either, but
after years of undercover work, he had built up a security
man's instinctive suspicion of lone figures in parked cars.

'Unless he destroyed everything before walking away,' he
said vaguely. Some runners did that. Binned or burned everything. It was as much a psychological severing of all ties with
their past life as it was an attempt to conceal any clues pointing
to their new one.

'He couldn't destroy bank or tax records,' Rik countered.
'Not possible.'

Harry waited for a sign of movement. He'd noticed the car
earlier, when he'd gone for coffee. Something about it had
snagged at the edge of his attention without quite gelling. Yet
there was nothing he could put his finger on. Maybe it was
an aura he'd become attuned to over the years, a marker only
those with the right instincts might pick up on. Yet why should
it concern him? He didn't even live here. He put his coffee
down. Sometimes you had to follow your instincts. 'I'll be
back in a minute.'

He ran downstairs, slowing to a stroll as he hit the street.
He stopped at a fruit stall that was still packing up and bought
some grapes, then continued along the street, eyeing the
windows and pausing occasionally to peer at a display. As he
drew level with the delivery van, he turned and faced the
nearest shop window and chewed some grapes, studying a
rack of audio equipment on special offer. He bent as if taking
in the specifications. The angle gave him an ideal background
against which he could see the driver in the saloon behind the
van.

It was a man. Medium build, jowly, with dark hair and
heavy eyebrows over a pasty face. He was staring down the
street, eyes fixed on a point somewhere in front of him.

It was a look Harry had seen too many times to be mistaken: the driver was watching someone. He turned and followed the line of the man's focus, but there was too much clutter to be able to pick out any one object. Or person.

He continued his stroll, pausing to catch the car's reflection in another window, but without drawing any firm conclusion. A local cop, then. A drugs squad officer on a dealer's tail, perhaps. Or more mundane than that: a market inspector.

He crossed the street and returned to the flat by a round-about route, wondering if paranoia got worse as you got older.

'Everyone's life overlaps in some way, right?' Rik was still teasing at the lack of paperwork in Silverman's file, as if Harry hadn't left. 'There's always home stuff in their desks and work stuff at home. Until now.' He blinked, just noticing a change in the atmosphere. 'You've been out.'

'Just checking something.' Harry picked up his coffee. It had gone cold. He exchanged it for the briefing sheet Jennings had given them. He stared again at the description of Silverman, although it produced nothing he hadn't read several times already.

> Subject: Samuel Silverman (Prof. – Haifa Univ.) Age 52 – 5´8˝ – slim build – 140lbs – hair black/flecked grey – receding – usually cut short – neat beard and moustache. Skin swarthy/Mediterranean – disfigurement (pockmarking) on cheeks – dark area approx. 4˝ square (believed b'mark) below right eye. Eyes black – described as piercing – even teeth, all white – firm jaw – strong nose. Likes Med/Middle East cooking – mostly veg – non-drinker/non-smoker. No known reading/film/music preferences – no known hobbies but keen walker.

The description fitted thousands of men; like many of those walking past in the street outside. He put it down and picked up the fragment of charred paper. It appeared to have been torn from a spiral notebook, with a line of jagged holes along one edge. The writing was at an angle across the paper, as if it had been scribbled in a hurry. The letters were faded, probably by the heat, but he could clearly make out 'J.A. London', followed by a number.

He handed it to Rik, saying, '"J. A. London". A place or a person?'

Rik shrugged. 'Take your choice. And what's the six-digit number?' He fed it into a search engine in a variety of permutations, but came up blank.

'Mobile phone?'

'Maybe. Without the first half, though, we'll never track it down.' Rik could access some useful databases, but there were limits to the information he could get from them without adequate pointers to help focus his search.

'It might explain the flight to Heathrow. He decided to come over to somewhere or someone he felt close to.' Harry fingered the number LH4736 T2 written on the briefing paper. 'A Lufthansa flight number arriving at Terminal Two. It's all we've got.'

'Great.' Rik fed that into his laptop, but shook his head. 'Can't access their passenger lists. They're blocked. Do you know anyone in Immigration?'

Harry nodded. As it happened, he did. As vague as the lead was, it was their best bet. It must have seemed significant to the Israelis, otherwise why provide it? He took out his phone, checked the directory and dialled a number. When it was answered he spoke quickly, giving Silverman's details and the flight number. He ended the call and nodded. 'She'll check it out. Might take a while.'

Rik gave a sly smile. 'She? Did you say "she"? Christ, things are looking up. I thought your only contacts were hairy-arsed coppers with a drink problem.' He picked up an *A–Z* of London and flicked through the index. After a few minutes, he sighed and tossed it to one side. 'There are several places in London that fit the "J. A.": James Avenue and Jersey Avenue to name two. We need a house number, otherwise we're chasing smoke.'

Harry nodded. 'Long shot. Leave it.'

Rik opened the folder and tapped the briefing paper where it mentioned Haifa University. There were no other details, such as contact numbers, faculty, or departmental names. 'Didn't you say Silverman was a doctor of theology?'

'According to Jennings. Before he went AWOL.'

Harry chewed on that for a while. Jennings might have picked up the information at an original client briefing, but for some reason hadn't bothered including it in his notes, such as they were. Still, even if they didn't have the department, how big could the place be? The Professor must have had friends there at one time; someone might remember him and give them some background information.

'I need a phone number,' said Harry.

'I'm on it.' Rik turned to his laptop and began punching keys.

TWELVE

Harry dialled the number and waited. It rang twelve times before being answered by a gruff male voice. He asked if they had a Professor Samuel Silverman on the staff. There was a sharp reply in what he took to be Hebrew, before the phone clicked and a woman's voice came on with an American accent. He repeated the question.

'Who are you?' She sounded instantly suspicious. 'It's a holiday today. Why do you want to know?'

'I need to speak to him,' he said finally, winging it. He had no idea if the university staff were aware that Silverman had gone walkabout, and didn't want to set alarm bells ringing unnecessarily. 'He was helping my nephew with some study advice.'

The woman made a grudging noise, and he heard the sound of paper rustling. In the background someone laughed and a computer beeped. 'You say Samuel?' said the woman after a lengthy wait. 'Samuel Silverman?'

'That's right. Professor Samuel Silverman.' He waited. If she wanted the department and the subject, he was sunk.

'What's he teaching? You don't know?' The woman must have extrasensory perception. He wondered what to say. What subject or speciality would an Israeli professor, apparently much valued by his government, teach? It wouldn't be theology, in spite of what Jennings had said. Defence studies was more likely. Statistics, maybe. But they wouldn't work – not now he'd mentioned a nephew. He had to risk a bluff. 'You think my nephew tells me what he's studying?' he countered dramatically. 'He tells me nothing, like he tells his parents. I have to force things out of him. It could be theology, though – he's into all that stuff.'

Across the room, Rik shook his head in mock despair.

'Sorry,' said the woman. 'Silvermans we have plenty of, but not a Samuel. And believe me, sir, we've had the same theology staff here since Golda Meir was in small pants.'

'Oh.'

'Sorry – nobody of that name on the staff here.' In spite of her abruptness, she sounded sympathetic. 'And no visiting lecturers, either – I checked the register, in case. We have people coming and going all the time, you see. You should maybe try another campus.'

He thanked her and rang off. 'No Professor Samuel Silverman, nor ever was.'

Rik pulled a face. 'Maybe he was caught playing naughties with a student and they've blanked him from the records.'

'That would take some doing.'

'Not if he was in tight with the government. Scandals they don't need.'

'OK, so given that he's cut loose from his life in the Promised Land, what made him decide to come to Britain?' He stood up and stretched, then stared at the ceiling as if it might contain the answer. He didn't mind puzzles – relished them, in fact – but this wasn't even a small one; it was a nothing made up of vague facts.

'If he was grief-stricken,' Rik ventured, 'it might have been on impulse.'

'Or he's been here before without anyone knowing. It's always easy going back to a place the second time round.'

'Where would you go if it happened to you? If you had to disappear at a moment's notice?'

Harry pursed his lips. Good point. Not being a family man himself, the question was academic. If he were forced, really forced, he could cut and run anywhere he chose at a moment's notice. But trying to imagine himself into the lives of the people they were searching for was a habit that had often proved useful in whittling down the options.

'I'd go anywhere I could find a hole, pull the lid over me and hide,' he said eventually. 'I suppose if I was coming from somewhere like Israel, I'd want a similar climate without the people. But nowhere I wouldn't fit in and nowhere I'd be recognized.'

Rik yawned. 'Fair enough. But wouldn't you want somewhere familiar – somewhere where you knew you *could* hide?'

Harry saw what he was driving at. People on the run rarely chose a place they'd never been to in their lives before. A few did; those who could step off the edge with no backward glance and a sincere faith in their own abilities to survive in an alien location. But they were a rarity. Mostly, runners looked for a place with a similar culture or language, where the requirement to adapt was less of a struggle, or where they had local contacts to fall back on. There was no guarantee otherwise that they would find a suitable hole. It also followed that only the truly desperate, with none of the mental or financial resources required to successfully disappear, would put themselves unwittingly in the position where they stood out to the degree that people began asking questions.

Harry's phone buzzed. He listened for a few moments, then asked the caller to hold. He turned to Rik. 'There's no record of a Samuel Silverman coming through any terminals on the twenty-seventh.'

'You told her the right date?' Even as he said it, he looked apologetic. Harry wouldn't have made such a basic mistake. 'Scratch that.'

They stared at each other until they heard a whistling noise emanating from the phone. Harry put it to his ear.

'Sorry, Sandra,' he said softly. 'Surprised, that's all.' He listened, then said, 'It was a reliable source, yes.' Then he added, 'OK, will do.' He switched off the phone. 'No Silverman. If Jennings' information was correct and he came in on the twenty-seventh, he must have been using another name. And LH4736 originated in Frankfurt, not Israel.'

'He took a roundabout route.'

'Looks like it. But why?'

There was only one answer: Silverman had been laying a false trail, making it harder for anyone to follow. It made their task even worse. How to find a man they didn't know, using a name they didn't have? If the name was chosen at random, he could be holding a passport in the name of Mr Magoo for all they knew.

Harry checked the folder, but there were no other family names the professor might have used. He wouldn't be the first person in the world to have acquired a second set of papers. The reasons why a professor might do such a thing would be interesting, as would be the source of supply. But that wasn't relevant right now. It was also a pity they didn't have access to the acquaintance who had spotted him at the airport.

'We're stuffed,' Rik concluded.

'Not yet.' Harry waved his phone, not ready to give up. 'Since Nine-eleven, all CCTV recordings and digital media are sent from the cameras around the terminals to an editing service near the airport for checking, enhancing and archiving. Sandra can get us inside but we'd have to sit and check the screens ourselves. We know what Silverman looks like. If we can spot him on the screens, we've a chance of seeing where he went.'

Rik looked sceptical. 'She can do that? What about security?'

'I didn't like to ask.'

Rik groaned, his feelings clear. The prospect of spending several hours poring over flickering images was mind-numbing – even for an IT man. But it was clear that if they could spot Silverman and track him through the terminal, they might discover what direction he had taken next. It was all they had.

Harry was already redialling Sandra's number. He put the suggestion to her, then thanked her again and switched off. 'She says this evening, after hours. Tomorrow we'll bounce Param.'

'They haven't moved from Ferris's flat.' Dog was in an estate car down the street, nursing a cup of cold coffee and trying to keep Jennings happy with regular reports. Mostly the reports were identical: nothing doing.

He was accustomed to sitting for long periods waiting for things to happen. His line of work had called for him to sleep in the back of the car on many occasions. It was merely another facet of his job and took patience, stamina and a subconscious alarm system for a change in circumstances. He had learned the craft the hard way, when blending in had been a life skill not to be taken lightly. Anything less got you killed.

'They must make a move at some stage,' replied Jennings,

with a touch of impatience. 'Sooner or later they'll find something. There's no back way out they could use, is there? If they find a lead to our man, you need to be right on top of them.'

'I've got it covered, don't worry. I just saw movement at the window. They're still inside.' He didn't bother telling Jennings that the older of the two men, Tate, had come out twice earlier. He'd gone straight by without even looking, once with two coffees and the second time munching a bunch of grapes. He was probably becoming stir-crazy and needed the exercise. Dog knew the feeling well.

He cut the connection without saying goodbye.

A hundred yards behind Dog's position, in the shadow of a market trader's van on the other side of the street, another figure sat immobile in a small, dark saloon car.

The driver, named Carlisle, watched impassively as Dog's outline shifted. So far he had seen him drink and use a mobile. Other than that, the target seemed to be made of stone, barely moving a muscle.

He stifled a yawn, dispelling any thoughts of refreshments. He'd been briefed on Dog's reputation and knew it would be too dangerous to move. After a chance sighting of the man by another operative, which had resulted in Carlisle being assigned to this watch, he knew it would be the end of a promising career if he lost the target through carelessness.

Out of habit, he ran a check of his surroundings. The street was busy with shoppers and a regular flow of vehicles, and nobody was taking any notice of a single figure sitting in a car. He thought he'd been made at one point, though, when a man chomping grapes had hovered nearby. For a second he was sure the man was watching him. But after a while he'd moved on and disappeared.

He settled back with a sigh. It might have helped if they'd seen fit to tell him what the hell they thought Dog was doing here.

THIRTEEN

The centre of operations for the enigmatically named Transit Support Services was a plain, single-storey building on the fringes of Cranford. The A4 leading out of London was a steady rumble of late evening traffic a couple of hundred yards away, and a faint tang of aviation fuel mixed with car fumes sat in the air like a thin soup, a reminder of the proximity of the capital's busy airport.

An untidy car park at the front of the building added to its air of near invisibility, as did the plain front door and the heavily silvered windows throwing back a reflection of the road and surrounding scenery. Only the powerful security lights that gave the area a day-like clarity betrayed the fact that this building was not simply a backwater business selling office stationery.

Rik parked his Audi next to a battered Nissan and switched off the engine. 'We're not going to run into a bunch of armed jumpsuits, are we? I thought this would be all razor wire and cameras since Nine-eleven.'

Harry dropped the latest copy of the *Telegraph* to the floor. 'Sandra says not. To the locals, it's an archive library and processing unit. They don't advertise what they do, so they don't need heavy security.' He levered himself out of his seat with a sarcastic grin. 'Just stick with me, laddie – I'll look out for big hairy men with Hecklers and flak jackets.'

He approached the door and thumbed a button on an intercom unit. A woman's voice invited them to enter and the door clicked open. Under the lens of a camera they entered a small, musty lobby furnished with two stiff chairs against one wall, a dying pot plant and a battered steel-framed desk holding a single telephone. There was no receptionist, but a small sign asked visitors to wait to be dealt with.

A door opened to one side and a woman in a white coat appeared. She was in her thirties, slim, with her hair scraped back and held by a clip. It gave her the austere look of a headmistress.

'You must be Tate and Ferris,' she said in a soft Scottish burr. 'Sandra Platt in Immigration said you needed help with some images.' She produced two visitor passes from her coat pocket. 'My name's Karen. Keep these clipped to your jackets at all times while you're here and surrender them before you leave. Otherwise I'll have to send the security guard to shoot you dead.' She gave a dry smile that softened her features. 'Not kidding.'

'You don't need to see any ID?' Rik smiled winningly at her but she appeared not to notice.

'No need. Sandra emailed me a very accurate description of Harry. As far as I can tell you aren't making him bring you here at gunpoint.' She gestured up at the camera. 'Anyway, we have you on tape for all eternity. You want to come this way?' She turned and stopped at the door she had come through, briefly flapping the lapel of her white coat at a small black box on the wall. 'RFID scanner,' she explained, and turned the lapel over to show them a small plastic stud on the inside. 'Anyone wearing one of these gets through the door, and is tracked and logged.'

'Tracked?' asked Harry.

'Yes. We can't even go to the loo without being monitored. Welcome to the free world.'

They were in a narrow corridor running right through to the rear of the building, with doors every few feet. It was standard government issue, with a dry, overheated smell and drab paintwork, the atmosphere silent and devoid of all signs of industry. Rik and Harry exchanged raised eyebrows and followed their guide.

'There's no one else on duty at the moment,' Karen explained, 'apart from me and Andy, the security guard. He's on a fag break out back, but don't tell anyone. The work here is strictly process-led, and nobody volunteers to spend longer here than they can manage. Besides, we're pretty much on top of things – at least until we get demands for some visual evidence from Immigration, the Met or one of the security departments. Then it's all hands to the pump. I gather you're none of the above, though.' It wasn't a question.

'In a loose kind of way,' Harry supplied vaguely.

Karen stopped at another door and waved her lapel near the black box. 'Don't worry, I wasn't asking. I trust Sandra not to send me a couple of potential terrorists. She's very good like that. Anyway, what you see here wouldn't help much if you were up to no good, believe me.'

'Unless we wanted to erase something,' suggested Rik.

She looked at him with a raised eyebrow. 'Why? Is that a giant magnet in your pocket?' She turned and stepped inside, leaving Rik flushed and confused.

The room was suffused with a dull light from discreet over-head panels, and smaller than they had expected. Four desks were crammed in the centre, each one bearing a large monitor and keyboard. The walls were lined with racks, one holding a bewildering array of DVD and CD machines, with the others holding editing equipment and printers, files, folders and tapes. A twisted spaghetti of wires bridged by rubber ramps curled across the floor between the various racks, and the immediate impression was of chaos threatening to spill over into a jungle. Yet the atmosphere was oddly calm, aided by rows of flick-ering display lights and a soothing electronic hum from an air-conditioning unit in one corner.

'Cool,' said Rik, but his face suggested he wasn't that impressed. Harry had half expected him to be like a kid in a toy shop, with all manner of equipment to play with.

'It's a mess, I know,' Karen said defensively. 'But we can't dig into the fabric, so we have to live with wires everywhere until somebody stumps up a decent budget for a purpose-built unit.' She nodded at a couple of monitors and a stack of boxes piled on a side table. 'Those are a mix of discs and hard drives from Terminal Two. Some of the areas still have old tech-nology, but most have gone over to wireless.' She shrugged. 'It takes time and money, so they're using a variety of systems depending on priorities.' She pulled a face. 'Pretty soon, they won't need us any more; they'll be able to feed and retrieve whatever they need. We're setting up archives for retrieval and image management, but we're the last of the steam age. I still think of this stuff as tape, but it isn't.'

'What's the coverage of these cameras?' asked Harry. He was wondering how they were going to get the information before anyone turned up and blew the whistle.

'The entry points from airside, the various lounges and walkways, the routes down to the Arrivals door, where the meeters and greeters stand, and the concourse to the main exits. They're all different, but if you tell me what you're looking for, I'll call up what I need. You're after a passenger arriving off a flight, right?'

'Yes. What about stairways and lifts?'

'Stairways, lifts, side corridors and all links to the other terminals are covered. I've selected the recordings which run from the confirmed landing time of LH4736, to an hour after the last passengers should have come through.' She went on, 'Some passengers get taken short as soon as they land and head for the toilets. It's not unknown for some to take their time coming out. If your man came through, you'll see him sooner or later.'

Rik said, 'There's no way he could have avoided the cameras?'

'Not unless he knew the location of every unit or changed his appearance between cameras.'

'Could he have slipped out the back way?'

Karen gave him a doubtful look, but didn't automatically dismiss the idea. 'If he did,' she said carefully, 'he had inside help.'

'Is that possible?'

'In a place that size, anything's possible, I suppose. Anyway, after September the eleventh, they resited a lot of the camera positions in the terminals and ran security exercises to double-check the coverage. They also increased the optical zooms and scope for clarity and control. So far nobody has managed to bypass them.'

She went over to the nearest machine and sat down, indicating that they should drag up two chairs and join her. She tapped a few keys and hit a button. Seconds later, an image flickered on to the monitor. It showed an interior shot of a terminal building, with a jumble of people standing around, apparently waiting.

'LH4736 landed at 13.15 hours,' Karen explained. 'This is the Arrivals exit. I've prepared what we have in chronological order. It's probably the best place to start because eventually everyone funnels through this door. Unless your man did have help, which God forbid, he'd have to pass this point.' She looked to see if they understood, and they both nodded. 'OK, from here, he could go anywhere in this or the other terminals. If you spot him, just shout, then we'll switch to other cameras to follow his progress. If we don't spot him, we'll go back and check everywhere up to the Arrivals exit.'

The screen showed a trickle of arriving passengers coming into view through a gap in the wall. Some carried hand luggage, while others were struggling with trolleys or bags on wheels. It was a commonplace scene yet, from this perspective, oddly compelling. Like ants.

'Christ,' Rik breathed. 'It's like watching *Big Brother*.'

Karen chuckled. 'It's a bit more interesting than that.'

The minutes passed, the arrivals growing and receding tide-like as each planeload moved through the Arrivals chain. It would have helped if they could have identified which flight they were seeing, but there was no way the screen could pick out such details, nor if some of the figures passing through the exit had arrived on a much earlier flight and had been delayed along the way.

At the lower edge of the screen was the ever-present crowd of meeters and greeters. Some held scraps of cardboard showing the names of arriving passengers, while others betrayed the anxious foot-hopping of family and friends awaiting someone who had probably got logjammed at Immigration.

Harry or Rik occasionally asked Karen to freeze or go back over the recording, convinced they had spotted a familiar face. Each time, closer inspection showed they were mistaken. As each possible target was dismissed and the line of passengers disappeared from view, they felt the clutch of disappointment beginning to grow stronger.

A flash of movement made Harry lean forward. It was on the lowest edge of the screen and showed two men bumping into one another. One was a new arrival, the other a uniformed airport worker. A brief flurry ensued, with both figures executing the step-sideways, zigzag dance of conver-gence, before moving on with nods and muttered apologies. Harry began to look away, subconsciously dismissing it, then froze as something about the traveller made him look again.

'Wait.' He jabbed a finger at the screen. 'Back a few clicks.'

Karen did so and played it again. This time they all leaned forward, willing to exchange hours of searching for some-thing, no matter how small. When the airport worker walked off screen and the other turned briefly towards the camera, Harry snapped his fingers in triumph.

'Houston,' he hissed softly. 'We have contact.'

A hundred yards away, Dog was watching the building with stony patience. He had no idea what function Transit Support Services performed, or how many people were inside. No doubt Jennings would have a way of finding out.

After following the two former MI5 men down from Paddington, he'd run a check of the surrounding area. At one point in the journey, he thought he'd detected a presence nearby. After years in the field, he'd developed an inbuilt radar sensitive to possible threat which he'd learned never to ignore. But whatever it was had remained invisible, and he'd slowly relaxed, aware that night-time and moving traffic often combined to play tricks on the mind.

Thirty minutes into his vigil, he'd finally found the twin needs of exercise and refreshment something he could no longer ignore. But before making a move, he needed a delaying tactic in case the two men left before he returned. Blending into the shadows and keeping well back from the glare of the overhead lights, he'd made a careful circuit of the building on foot first, checking for other exits. There were a few lights on, but with the reflective sheeting covering the windows, there was no way of telling what was going on inside.

He'd located the security guard almost immediately, latching on to the smell of cigarette smoke drifting from a rear door. Satisfied that the man was busy for a few minutes, he'd slipped into the front car park and bent down briefly by the side of Ferris's car. As he walked away, he could hear the soft hiss as one of the front tyres deflated from a puncture in the sidewall.

When he'd returned later with a drink and sandwich from a nearby corner shop, the car was still there.

FOURTEEN

Harry waited nervously as Karen froze the picture and then re-ran it so they could see the man again in slow motion. 'It looks like him,' he said. 'Let it run.'

The replay showed the man walking away across the bottom of the screen, easing through the crowd. He wore heavy glasses and was holding a dark coat, slung over his right shoulder, with a dark sports bag in his other hand. For a split second his face was clearly in view.

Rik nodded in agreement. 'It's him. Check his right hand, holding the coat.' The hand clearly showed a bandage, bearing out the briefing reference to his injury.

'And the face,' Harry added. 'Right cheekbone.'

'Is that a bruise?' Karen froze the screen again and zoomed in, but the clarity was lacking. 'Sorry – the light's not good just there.'

'Birthmark. Either way, it's a match.'

He let Karen run the recording a little longer, but he knew they had found their man. All they had to do now was track him through the terminal and see where he went.

'Easy,' said Karen, suddenly galvanized by the discovery. She ran her eyes over a schematic layout of the terminal and hummed quietly to herself. 'This chart shows me the camera location and number,' she explained, bringing up a new set of recordings. 'Unless he dodges back and forth, which would be pointless, because he'd never leave the building, he has to go past one of them sooner or later. It's just a question of finding which one, then passing on to the next in line.'

'Are you sure you have time for this?' Harry glanced at his watch. They had been there nearly two hours. He didn't want to outstay their welcome, but without Karen's help, they wouldn't stand a chance of following Silverman's course through the terminal.

She smiled excitedly. 'Are you kidding? I haven't had this much fun in weeks. Usually it's humourless plods in suits doing their own searching and keeping us at arm's length. I never to get to do this stuff unless they fuck up the machine.' She glanced at them. 'Sorry.' She checked the chart and selected another recording. 'I think I know where he'd have gone next. Let me run it and see. If I tell you where the makings are, I don't suppose one of you boys would care to make some coffee, would you?' She smiled disarmingly at Rik, who stood up and stretched.

'I thought you'd never ask.'

Thirty minutes later, coffee cups discarded, they were watching the flickering images of the inside of Terminal Two. After Silverman's little dance earlier, they hadn't been able to pick him up again. It was eye-watering work, with nobody daring to blink in case they missed something. Time after time they told Karen to stop the film, but each one proved to be a mistake. There were momentary distractions, too, in the unfolding story of the stick figures bustling about before them; brief meetings, mild collisions and near misses; the body language of the stressed, portrayed by waving arms, covered mouths and bursts of frantic activity; the tumble of luggage from a careering trolley, followed by the scrabble to regain possessions and dignity in the face of the unrelenting advance of another flush of travellers bearing down like a tidal wave.

They were nearing the last batch of recordings when Karen tapped the screen. 'Is that him?'

Sure enough, Silverman's figure appeared in the background, partly obscured by a group of Japanese businessmen in dark suits. He was standing still, head down and apparently relaxed, by the entrance to a pharmacy. He seemed to be alone, the sports bag lying at his feet.

'He's waiting for a pick-up,' said Harry, recognizing the man's body language. Impatience, anticipation and wariness all bound together.

They sat frozen, waiting to see what would happen next. It was clear from Silverman's increasing shift of position that he was growing nervous, throwing regular glances around with sharp movements of his head, the light flashing off his spectacles. After following his progress through the terminal, it was almost an anti-climax to know that this part of the chase was over, that in the next few seconds or minutes they would either learn the next stage of his journey or lose him altogether.

'How about this one?' said Karen.

A younger man had appeared on the opposite side of the picture, filtering slowly through the crowd. He carried no hand luggage, and was dressed in jeans and a dark windcheater, another greeter killing time while awaiting an incoming passenger. There was nothing overt to suggest he was connected with Silverman, and he could have been on his way to the pharmacy, except that, from their commanding position over-looking the scene, he seemed to be on a collision course with the waiting professor and kept looking towards him each time he was forced off-course by the flow and press of the crowd.

'Ten quid says it's him,' breathed Rik, but there were no takers.

The man was in his late twenties or early thirties, solidly built with the springy walk of someone very fit. He was clean-shaven, with glossy, swept-back hair and a Mediterranean appearance, but they couldn't see enough of his face to get a clear picture.

At the last second, rather than entering the pharmacy, the newcomer skirted a family group huddled together around a trolley. He stopped at one side of the entrance, idly flicking through a carousel of travel items. Then he ducked his head, as if spotting something of interest nearer the ground. The movement brought him closer to Silverman but shielded his face from the camera.

Then they saw the professor's body tense. He began to turn his head, but stopped suddenly, before looking back down at his feet. The newcomer, now less than a foot away, must have said something.

'Got you,' breathed Harry. He clapped a hand on Karen's shoulder, drawing a triumphant giggle.

Suddenly, as if galvanized by decision, the younger man turned and walked away, disappearing into the crowd. Moments later, after hopping from foot to foot, Silverman followed, scurrying through the flow of people like an erratic missile bearing down on its target.

Karen turned to her chart. 'I don't need to follow this any more,' she said confidently, 'but just in case . . .' She called up another recording and hit the PLAY button.

'Where's he going?' said Harry.

The new picture showed a panoramic view of the terminal building shot from one end. The foreground was a bustling mass of people, while further back, the screen seemed flooded with a greyish aura of light. There was no sign of the young man.

Karen pointed at a figure which might have been him, but he was too far away for a clear view. Then she tapped the edge of the screen as Silverman hurried into view, pushing his way with difficulty through a knot of schoolchildren. 'He's heading for the main exits.'

She reached across and grabbed a hard drive from a box. 'This is from an auxiliary camera outside the main exit.' They waited to see if Silverman would deviate from his course. He didn't.

'Some bloody professor he is,' Harry murmured cynically, and Rik nodded in agreement. They were both thinking the same thing: whatever Jennings' briefing paper might have said, Silverman was no simple academic fleeing under the burden of emotional trauma.

This bore all the hallmarks of something far more professional.

FIFTEEN

'Still no sign of a Mini,' said Harry. It was nearly twenty hours later and he and Rik were walking along a quiet back street in Harrow.

It was after six and the light was fading, the predominantly residential area morphing into shadows and yellow lights, and the homeward rumble of through traffic. The houses on each side were part of a small redevelopment, neatly terraced and upmarket, with a variety of large potted plants flanking the doors to give an illusion of greenery. Glossy vehicles were parked on hard standings immediately in front of each house, although none looked as if they were used much.

Only one house showed a vacant space, and had done since their first drive-by earlier that day.

'She might have dumped it,' said Rik. 'If she's in with Param, they'd know it would be too hot to keep for long.'

They had left Karen and her banks of screens late the previous evening, hopeful possessors of a tenuous lead to Silverman's whereabouts after he left Heathrow's Terminal Two. A private cab had arrived minutes after they had watched a tape of the area immediately outside the main exit. It followed a brief period of doubt, during which they thought Silverman must have ducked into a waiting vehicle. But then the younger man had appeared, prowling along the pavement and gesturing animatedly with a mobile phone pressed to his ear.

'Can we get a print of that?' Harry had asked, tapping the screen. It was the first full-face view they'd had of Silverman's greeter, and would be useful when they caught up with the two men. He was convinced that the way the man had kept his face carefully averted from the cameras until now was too deliberate to be accidental.

'Of course.' Karen's fingers danced across the keyboard. The screen blinked and a printer hummed into life. She continued to run the recording and they watched the younger man gesticulating, shoulders hunched and a finger stabbing the air excitedly. In the entrance behind him, Silverman was glancing anxiously around, the bandaged hand a small white flag in the gloom. Although the two men had still not spoken openly, it was clear they were together.

It was even clearer that Silverman, if that was his real name, was under the control of someone who knew his tradecraft.

Two minutes later, a white people-carrier cab nosed in to the kerb, and the younger man leapt forward to open the rear door. Gesturing at Silverman, who scuttled across the pavement and into the car, he jumped in after him and slammed the door. A lurch of the vehicle and they were gone.

'There's a number on the roof,' said Rik.

'Got it.' Harry noted the time on the recording and moved away, slipping his mobile from his pocket.

'You can use one of these if you like,' suggested Karen, nodding at a phone on a desk across the room. She seemed disappointed at the prospect of her part in the chase being over.

'Thanks,' said Harry with a smile. 'Best not.' Using one of the landline phones would leave a trail. With no way of knowing how often a phone audit was run on the lines in this building, it was safer if there was no obvious record of them having been here. There wasn't much they could do about the camera over the front entrance, but they would just have to trust to luck and human fallibility.

He returned five minutes later. 'The dispatcher says the driver who made the pick-up is due to clock on shortly.'

In the event, they had heard nothing more. They had decided to call it a day, not even allowing the discovery of a flat tyre on Rik's car to dull their elation at finding Silverman's trail.

Now, following their initial drive-by of the address on the parking fine for Yvonne Michaels, Ray Param's former PA, earlier that morning, they had spent the day keeping the house under surveillance. So far they had seen no sign of activity. A brief movement of a front curtain might have been a breeze from an open window, but until they were sure, they were hanging back.

Cautious questions to the neighbours had produced nothing firm, save that someone new had moved in recently. With no sign of the Mini Cooper, and calls to the cab firm yielding no reply from the driver who had picked up Silverman from Heathrow, Harry was fighting a growing feeling of impatience. As leads went, it was up in the high numbers of usefulness, but it was no cause for over-optimism. Firmer leads than this had led nowhere, but it would give them something to do while they waited to speak to the cab driver from the airport.

'Come on,' he decided eventually. 'I've had enough of this.' He crossed the pavement and turned into the front yard, and knocked on the door while Rik stepped to one side and waited.

The door clicked open and Raymond Param looked out at them from a small hallway. He was dressed in casual slacks and a white shirt. Neither had seen a recent iron, a condition at odds with the photos on display at the house in Highgate. He needed a shave, the stubble adding an extra few pounds of weight, and a hank of hair hung uncontrolled over his forehead. In spite of his appearance, he seemed relaxed for a man who had allegedly deserted his wife and home in favour of a large amount of stolen money.

'Can I help?' His eyes flicked over them in turn. If there was an indication of nerves, it was in the brief glance he threw past them at the street beyond. That and the way he remained positioned well inside the doorway.

'Hello, Mr Param,' said Harry. His tone was calm, but left no doubt that he knew who the man was. It was essential in the first moments of contact to alleviate any tendency to panic on the part of the runner.

For a moment there was no reaction. Then Param seemed to sag visibly as if the air had gone out of him in a rush. He turned away. 'You'd better come in.' If he didn't know who the men were, he knew what they represented.

He led them through the house to a kitchen overlooking a small courtyard garden bordered by a high wall covered in creepers. The room was simple in design, evidently expensive, and smelled faintly of something herbal. A rustic table and four chairs dominated the room, and the worktops were clean and free of clutter, as if the equipment was rarely used. The atmosphere was quiet, with a faint ticking sound of a boiler emanating from a cupboard at the back of the room.

'Tea or coffee?' he said, flicking on a kettle. He took out three mugs without waiting for a reply, then turned and faced them. 'Who sent you – my wife?' His expression was sour, as if he had been given yet another unpleasant surprise in a long list. 'I'm surprised you found me. Mind telling me how?'

'Parking fine on the Mini,' said Harry.

Param lifted an eyebrow. 'Bugger. I forgot that.'

Harry felt almost sorry for him. 'It's always the little things. Other than that, you nearly had a free run.'

Param made no comment, but turned back to the kettle and made the tea. He handed out mugs and gestured to the table, which held a sugar bowl and a carton of milk. 'Help yourselves.'

When they were all seated, he looked at his two visitors. 'I suppose there's no point in promising you large amounts of money to go away and forget you ever saw me?'

Harry shook his head. 'Sorry. It's not the way we work.'

'Fair enough. Just thought I'd ask.' Param gave a sad smile. 'Who's the more seriously pissed off at me – my wife or the company?'

'The company, by a short head. Your wife's bearing up surprisingly well, considering. She's at her sister's.' He kept his face carefully blank, but the information drew a wry smile of something close to appreciation from Param.

'Yes, she always had strong support on the family side. Her sister thinks I'm a waster.' Param shrugged and warmed his hands on his mug. 'Like I care. So what happens now? Is this where you drag me kicking and screaming to the local nick?' There was something almost light-hearted in his tone, as if he wasn't taking their arrival too seriously.

'Is there any reason why we should?' said Rik. 'The company wants its money back. I'm not sure about your wife, though.'

Param showed a set of even white teeth. 'My wife will want the house, the cars and my testicles, in that order. The company will want the money but they'll shy away from the embarrassment of publicity. It doesn't look good to investors when a manager siphons off a load of cash.' He sighed, the levity dying. 'Unfortunately, they're both in for a nasty surprise.'

'Oh?' Harry sipped his tea, wondering what the man had in store for them. There was something – he could feel it in the air. He eased himself back in his chair, ready to make a move.

'Well, unknown to my dear wife, who doesn't really bother herself with matters of finance, the house is mortgaged to the eaves. And there's no money, company or otherwise.' He looked apologetic. 'Sorry – the offer of cash was a dud.'

'What do you mean, none?' Rik asked.

'None. Not a cent. It's all gone.'

Harry watched the man's face for signs of lying, but saw none. Param had been much too calm and resigned. For a man caught within an ace of getting away with a large amount of money, he should have been depressed at failing. But he wasn't.

Now he knew why.

SIXTEEN

'There's nothing to take back,' Param explained. 'The house is owned by the bank, and if you want to get the money, you'll have to find Yvonne first.' He clenched his mug between his fingers, the first real sign of tension he had shown. 'She knew everything I was doing . . . had done right from the beginning. I thought she was with me all the way.' He looked bitter, his mouth turning down at the edges, although it could have been embarrassment. 'More fool me. I taught her too well. She knows as much as I do about moving money around – possibly more. And she turned out to be a natural at covering her tracks and hiding what she was doing.'

'Why did you take her on in the first place?' Harry asked.

Param tapped his fingers on the table. 'I needed someone else to help set up the accounts to take the final transfer of money. That way, even if the company auditors looked at me for some reason, I'd be clean. She seemed an ideal partner. There was no risk to her; she did everything perfectly legitimately. Unfortunately, she was even smarter than that; she'd set up some accounts of her own without telling me. I trusted her. Too far, as it turned out.'

Harry almost felt a touch of sympathy. It wouldn't be the first time a man had fallen for and been duped by an accomplice far more cunning than him, and left holding the baby. 'You got taken.'

Param nodded. 'Yeah. Tell me about it.'

'Any ideas where she might have gone?' Harry had to ask the question. He doubted that it would be their problem to worry about, but if the ball got lobbed back into their court, they would need all the information they could get. And Yvonne Michaels had got a head start. 'How about South Africa?'

'You've done your homework,' Param said with a note of approval. 'To be honest, I haven't a clue. Yvonne knows a lot of people in some strange places, believe me. South African and Zimbabwean ex-pats, mostly, and a few others with interesting backgrounds. She's got three passports that I know of. She won't be as easy to find as I was. And you can forget about the Mini; she dumped that days ago.'

'We'll have to call in for instructions,' Harry told him, then added by way of explanation, 'We're not the police; we work freelance. Our brief was to find you and confirm your location. What happens next is up to the client.'

Param nodded. 'I figured the company would send somebody after me. I suppose I'm lucky it isn't a bunch of heavies with baseball bats.' He took a deep breath and gave them each

an earnest look. 'I've no right to ask this, but is there any
chance you guys could give me some leeway – say half an
hour?' He held up a hand. 'Don't worry – I'm not planning
on making a run for it or doing anything stupid. I haven't got
the money or stamina to run, and I'm too much of a coward
to kill myself.'

'So what do you want it for?' Harry asked.

'I've got a letter to write. My parents . . . they deserve an
explanation.' He gave a tired smile. 'It's not the sort of thing
they should first read about in the morning papers, is it? Their
favourite son ruining the family name.'

Harry considered it for a moment, then nodded in agreement. It wasn't as if they could arrest Param; if he wanted to
walk out of here right now, he could do so and there was
nothing they could do to stop him. He stood up and signalled
Rik to follow.

'Thirty minutes,' he reminded Param. 'Then we have to call
it in.'

They found a teashop just round the corner, with tired lace
curtains at the window and a smell of cinnamon in the air. It
would do while they gave Param his requested leeway. The
owner was an elderly, demure lady with powder-blue hair and
thick spectacles, who fussed around them as if they were
visiting royalty rather than two late customers wasting time.
Harry opted for coffee and a slice of walnut cake over a newspaper crossword, while Rik took tea and a toasted bun.

'I like to stay open late because it's better than watching
the rubbish they call television,' the owner explained, re-
arranging the tablecloth and plates until they were just right.
'It's all bad news, crude men and tarts with tits for brains
these days, isn't it?' She bustled away to get their order, leaving
the two men staring at each other in amusement.

Harry tried the taxi firm again. The driver had called in
sick but hoped to be in the following day. The dispatcher
refused to give the man's address and primly quoted the Data
Protection Act. Harry left his number and disconnected.
Tomorrow would have to do.

Next he called Jennings. In the absence of Silverman, the
lawyer might react well to some good news on another front.

'It's Tate,' said Harry. 'We've located Param.'

'*Who?*'

'Param. Raymond Param – the investor who did a bunk?'

'Christ, how?' Jennings sounded puzzled. 'I mean, how did you have time to—?'

'Skill, mostly.' Harry wondered what was eating the man. Maybe he'd lost his Lottery ticket. 'And a bit of luck. What do you want us to do about him?'

'Do? I don't want you do anything!' Jennings snapped. 'I want you to find *Silverman*. He's the priority, remember? Everything else can wait.'

'Yes, you said.' Harry resisted the urge to snap back at Jennings. He was counting on future work, and in spite of his dislike of the lawyer, he didn't want to be responsible for jeopardizing it. He explained patiently, 'While we were waiting for confirmation of a lead on Silverman, we got lucky with Param. It was too good a lead to miss. We'll leave him if you want, but I wouldn't bet on him hanging around. There's also a problem with the money.'

But Jennings ignored this. 'Wait one.' The phone went silent. Moments later he was back. He sounded furious, his words coming down the line with more than his customary snap. 'Do nothing, you hear? *Nothing*. Stay away from Param. I'll be in touch.' The phone went dead.

From somewhere in the distance, the wail of an emergency vehicle cut through the quiet. The old lady stuck her head out from the doorway to the kitchen to listen, before disappearing again.

Harry put his phone away and relayed the gist of the conversation to Rik, who had snagged the newspaper. It was open at a half-page photo showing a scene of destruction, with armed men in uniform and an armoured personnel carrier set against a background of smoking rubble and torn buildings. It was a rehash of a bombing in Baghdad ten days or so before, with renewed speculation about those responsible. A VIP had been killed, and he caught the word 'cleric' in the headline but little else before Rik folded the paper and tossed it to one side.

'So we get to go home early. Did he say anything about payment?'

'No.' Harry stood up and left some money on the table. The call to Jennings had left him with an odd feeling of unease.

There was something shadowy lurking at the edge of his brain, but he couldn't put a finger on it. An inner warning, maybe – a feeling caused by the change in Jennings' voice and the abrupt ending to the call. 'Let's go check on Param.'

They left the car where it was and walked back the way they had come. When they turned the corner of the street where Param was staying, they stopped dead.

The scene was a hive of activity. A number of police vehicles and an ambulance were gathered halfway down, their roof lights creating a ghostly display across the face of the surrounding buildings. A crowd of onlookers had formed along the pavements, and two constables were reeling out crime scene tape and forcing people back. Another officer was ordering motorists to turn around and find other routes to their destinations. It was clear that the house at the focus of all the activity was the one without a car in front.

After the tranquil scene earlier, it was a dramatic contrast. Harry swore softly. They had lost the initiative. Param had fooled them and taken the only way out.

'What's happening?' Rik stopped a man walking down the street away from the police cordon. He was in slippers, a local resident who'd come out to investigate the commotion.

'A mugging, they reckon,' the man replied succinctly. 'Bloke answered a knock and got knifed. Dropped him right on the doorstep. He hadn't been living there long.'

'How bad?'

The man shook his head and moved away. 'Depends how bad you think dead is.'

SEVENTEEN

Jennings was in a foul mood the following afternoon. He had instructed Harry to stand by until called, while he looked into the situation surrounding Param's death. Harry took this to mean he would be quizzing his contacts in the Met for details not yet made public. Whatever he'd discovered didn't seem to have pleased him; the skin around his eyes was puffy and dark, as if he hadn't slept well, and he seemed to be

reining himself in with difficulty as he glared across the bare
expanse of his desk.

From the moment they had walked in, it was clear something had angered him, and the little Harry had said about
Param or his violent death seemed to improve matters. Beyond
a brief acknowledgment of Rik's presence, Jennings had
ignored the younger man, addressing all his comments directly
at Harry.

'What the hell were you doing there?' Jennings demanded,
as if they had been laying waste to the Home Counties with
a flame thrower. 'You were supposed to be finding Silverman!'

'I told you,' Harry reminded him heavily, 'we found a lead
to Param's whereabouts and it paid off. At least we now know
it's not Param your clients should be looking for, but Yvonne
Michaels.'

Jennings' jaw flexed briefly before he seemed to backtrack
slightly. He tapped his fingers on the edge of his desk. 'Very
well. It appears to have been a mugging, according to the
police. What were the local residents saying?'

Harry wondered why that should matter. Local reaction
around a crime scene usually follows a pattern: it spreads furiously, feeding on itself like a bush fire, is invariably wrong
and heaped with lurid speculation and ill-informed gossip. He
explained what the neighbour had said, which seemed to make
Jennings relax a little.

'I see. Did you notice anything?'

'We didn't stay long enough. It's possible we were seen
going in earlier, so we'll have to wait and see. Either way,
Param claimed the girlfriend has the money and he'd been
screwed. Do you want us to find her?'

Jennings shook his head. 'Forget it. It's a non-starter.' He
leaned back and said authoritatively, 'I suppose it's possible
she killed him; she might have gone back for something after
you'd left and they had a falling out. Still, that's for the client
and the police to worry about. Your part's done.' He blinked
as if making a mental adjustment, and asked, 'What about
Silverman?'

'We tracked him coming through Heathrow,' said Rik,
shifting impatiently in his chair and making the spindly back
creak in protest. 'We're waiting to find out where he went
afterwards. He was met in the terminal by a young guy and

they took a cab from there but we don't know where to.' He fixed Jennings with a stare, then asked, 'Are you sure he's a professor?'

Jennings allowed a few heartbeats go by before responding. 'That's what he was described as, and I see no reason why anyone should have lied. Have you any reason to think otherwise?' His glanced flickered between the two of them.

Harry shot Rik a warning look and stood up. 'Not really. He didn't look much like a dusty professor, that's all.' He smiled tightly, wanting to be out of there where he could think clearly. 'When we find out where he went, we'll let you know.'

It was as they were walking back to the car that Harry realized Jennings hadn't shown any interest in how they had fastened on to Silverman and tracked him through the airport. That could only mean that he knew about their visit to Transit Support Services to access the airport tapes.

The only question was, how?

Rik closed the car door. 'You didn't mention about the blank we got on Silverman in the university,' he said. 'Or that the professor's friend knows tradecraft. Is there something you're not telling me?'

'Patience, Grasshopper,' Harry replied vaguely, his mind still on Jennings. There were only two ways the lawyer could have known about them viewing the tapes. The first and obvious one was if Karen had told someone. They had never met her before, but he knew Sandra wouldn't have suggested it if she hadn't trusted the woman – she had too much to lose. 'Two murders, both people traced by us, yet all he's fixated on is Silverman, as if he's the answer to the Holy Grail.' He pushed back the passenger seat and stretched his legs. 'This is no more about a runaway professor than my Aunt Fanny.'

Rik was nodding. 'He was more pissed that we'd gone after Param than at the fact that the poor bugger got knifed. You want me to go back in and poke something sharp up his nose? I'd enjoy that.'

'Tempting, but not yet. Best make sure we get paid first.' He was considering the second way Jennings could have known what they were up to. At the same time, he was trying hard not to connect dots which might have no relationship to each other. Paranoia was a deadly result of this game – of any game where secrets were a major part of the background, a currency, almost. He'd got used to it in MI5, managing to compartmentalize each part of the job so that he didn't indulge in pointless speculation. Others he'd known had not fared so well, ending up with careers and marriages in ruins, fearful of their own shadows. But a pattern was beginning to form around everything they were doing which he didn't like the feel of, and all his antennae were now quivering. First Matuq, then Param . . . and the growing feeling that Jennings wasn't as put out by the deaths as he should have been. And if he wasn't put out, it meant he wasn't surprised. That only led to one conclusion.

He was having them followed.

Harry's phone buzzed. It was the dispatcher from the cab firm.

'The driver's here,' said the man without preamble. 'His name is Nasir. But don't hold him up – it's mental here and I've got drivers off sick. I need him on the road.' There was a rumble of conversation at the other end and another man's voice came on.

'I help you?' he said warily. His voice was heavily accented, but with an overlay of London vowels on certain words. 'Is no problems, right?'

'No. No problems,' Harry assured him. He turned on the mobile's loudspeaker. 'We're trying to trace a man who has gone missing, Mr Nasir. You picked up two men from Heathrow's Terminal Two on the twenty-seventh, at around two thirty. It was a pre-booked collection. Do you remember that?'

There was a short silence, then, 'Two men? Yes, I remember.' In the background, someone shouted and a door slammed. 'Was a booking. I pick up two passengers.'

'Good. Where did you take them?'

'I collect from terminal as arranged, on time. But passenger was impatient. First he say go to Slough. Not a problem for me. But then later he change his mind and say Southall, then he say Hillingdon. Also not a problem. I am flexible.'

'Where in Hillingdon? It's important.'

'Sure. You know ski centre? I drop them off in car park and they get into a Suzuki four-wheel drive. Nice car. Very strong. I am thinking of buying one for my son when he graduates.'

Harry knew the place. Hillingdon Ski Centre was a short hop from the Western Avenue, the main route into the city from the M40. 'OK, that's good, Mr Nasir. Did you see the driver of the Suzuki?'

'No. I did not notice. Sorry.'

'What was the colour of the car?'

'Yellow. Like canary. You want the registration?'

Harry wondered for a second if Mr Nasir was being sarcastic. Then he realized the cab driver was serious.

'You've got it?' He grabbed a scrap of paper and a pen.

'Sure. I have a memory for all numbers like this,' Nasir explained proudly, and carefully recited the number. 'My son also – he is going to be a systems analyst.'

'What name did they use for the pick-up? I forgot to ask the dispatcher.'

'Ah, of course. Moment, please.' There was a clunk as Nasir put down the phone and spoke to someone in the background. Then he came back. 'OK. I have it. The pick-up was in the name of a Mr Barrett. The younger man, I think. But that not his real name.' Nasir gave a knowing chuckle. 'No, sir.'

'How do you know that?'

'Because Barrett is very English name, no? But the man who spoke to me . . . the young man, he is not English.'

'What language did he speak?'

'At first, always English. But after, until I drop them off, he does not speak at all.'

'What about the other man?'

'Not him either. No words. They sit like strangers, yet they are together like brothers. Even when I speak to them, to engage in small chit-chat, you know, they do not answer except with noises. But, as they walk away, I hear them speak. First the older man, I hear him ask the other where they are going and how much longer it will be as he is tired after his journey. The younger man tells him – seriously but most respectfully – that he must not speak and soon all will become clear.'

Harry experienced the sinking of disappointment. He'd been hoping for something more definite. Then something occurred to him. 'Was this in English?'

Mr Nasir sounded surprised. 'No, sir. Not speaking English now. They are speaking my language. Very normal for them, I can tell.'

'I don't follow. Your language?'

'Yes, sir. These two men come from my country, my province. From Karbala, south of Baghdad.'

'*What?*'

'Yes, sir. Men are native-born Iraqis.'

EIGHTEEN

The atmosphere in the car was tense as they headed towards Paddington, both men trying to come to grips with the revelation about Silverman's nationality, and the fact that they had either been fooled along with Jennings or had been lied to by him.

Harry was fast coming to believe it was the latter.

'You think Nasir was mistaken?' said Rik finally.

'What? No, I don't,' said Harry. 'Unless Silverman's fluent in Nasir's local dialect.' It was a possibility, yet instinct told Harry that a man like Nasir was unlikely to make such a mistake. Whatever Silverman's words had been, they had plainly convinced the taxi driver that he was listening to one of his own countrymen.

'Great. So our absent-bodied professor moves like Action Man, and instead of Hebrew, he speaks like an Iraqi.'

Harry stared out at the passing traffic. 'I think because he is one. We can forget anything Jennings told us. He's got some explaining to do.'

'Unless we screwed up.' Rik looked worried at the prospect. 'Could we have latched on to the wrong man coming through the airport?'

Harry had no such doubts. 'If we're going by the description, it was Silverman – we're not that careless. He had the bandage and the facial marking. And it's Arabic, by the way.'

'Huh?'

'The Iraqis speak Arabic. And some Kurdish.'

'So now you're a linguist?'

'I'm all manner of things.' He chewed his lip. 'It would help if we could get a line on who owns the Suzuki.'

'No problem. I can do that. But I'll have to stop – unless you want to drive?'

'No. We've got time.' Harry still hadn't thought about what to do next. He needed a few moments to make a decision.

Rik pulled to the side of the road and retrieved his laptop from the boot. He switched it on and connected via his mobile to the Internet. Harry didn't bother watching – he'd seen it all before and it still left him cold.

Minutes later Rik scribbled a note on the slip of paper with the Suzuki's registration. 'It's listed to a B. Templeton, South Acres, near Kensworth, Luton. No known recent sale.'

Harry nodded. Unless the car had been stolen or sold without paperwork, it was a start. 'Sounds like a farm.'

'Or a caravan site. My auntie had a mobile home at a place called South Acres. Down at Highcliffe, near Bournemouth. We used to go there for summer holidays . . . until it fell over the cliff in a high wind.' He glanced across and closed the laptop. 'Are we going to take a look?'

'Not we. Me. Drop me at my place and I'll get my car. I need you to be on standby back here. And just in case we get the call to find Yvonne Michaels, you can start researching her background.'

Harry took the piece of paper and studied it. It would be easy to drop the assignment here and now; to forget about Silverman and go find other work. There was plenty out there if you knew where to look. But would it really be that simple? Quite apart from the fact that he and Rik were now linked by proximity to two murders, he was intrigued by what they had so far unravelled. Could he really put aside what he knew and forget it?

They travelled in silence for a while until Harry said quietly, 'There's something seriously off about this.'

'What?' Rik glanced at him.

'All of it. Two runners die right after we find them, and an Iraqi comes into the country on a false ticket and goes into a covert huddle. What the hell has Jennings got us involved in?'

'You think they're linked?' Rik looked nervous. 'Terrorists? An Al-Qaeda cell?' He let out a long breath at the

possibility. 'Sounds a bit wild. I can't see Param as a pal of
Osama.'

'Neither can I,' Harry agreed. 'But it hardly seems normal,
does it? Nasir the taxi man's normal. His kid graduating and
getting a car, that's normal. Not this.'

Twenty minutes later, Harry was in the Saab heading north.
He gave the M1 a miss and threaded his way instead on to
quieter county roads, using the time to think. Rik was right,
this whole business was wild. But then, the activities of terrorists and criminals usually were . . . if that was indeed what
Silverman was. How he, Matuq and Param could possibly tie
in together was, on the surface, impossible. The three of them,
given what he knew of their backgrounds, were worlds apart.
Yet instinct told him there must be a common factor. All he
had to do was find it. The idea that he might be slipping into
the kind of territory he had decided to leave behind was
disturbing. If there was a terrorist dimension to this, and the
situation was going hot, it could escalate rapidly into something beyond his control.

As he eased clear of a built-up area of housing and shops,
he checked his mirror, automatically cataloguing the traffic
behind. A couple of big trucks, a van and one or two cars.
They'd been there for a while, all of them. Nothing to worry
him. And why should there be? And yet . . .

He felt uneasy. He wasn't normally given to seeing shadows,
yet something about the past few days was beginning to get
under his skin. He noted a lay-by coming up. He waited until
the last moment, then spun the wheel and braked hard, skidding into a dipped, single-track hollow shielded from the road
by a dense layer of bushes. He pulled up and waited, the
engine running, watching the mirror.

Nothing. He counted to thirty, waiting for the first signs of
a vehicle coming in after him. Most days in most situations,
he trusted his instincts. And while the best of alarms occasionally threw up a false flag, the one time you ignored them
was usually when something was wrong.

Apart from the hum of cars and the heavier beat of an occasional truck engine, every vehicle continued on by without
slowing.

He gave it five more minutes, fighting against the desire to keep moving. Moving was good; moving stopped you becoming an easy target. When you stopped you became vulnerable. After five minutes, he climbed out and went to the boot, reached in and found the metal box. He flipped the dial and opened the lid. The handgun was concealed under a layer of foam. A 9mm Browning semi-automatic variant, it carried no identification marks, the dark steel well worn and showing signs of its passage through many hands. But it was clean and oiled and, as a quick check revealed, ready for use. He made sure the safety was on before slipping it into his pocket.

He got back in the car, wondering whether he should have left Rik in London. But Rik was a computer whizz, not a field man. Harry had taken him to a private range a few times, to give him a workout. He had shown a good eye and a steady hand, and had performed well on a defensive driving course. But it didn't make him ready to be thrown into a dangerous situation and able to cope instinctively.

Unlike himself. A hangover from being a field officer in the security service was that Harry had left with the unusual proviso of being 'carded' – permitted to carry a handgun as a civilian. It meant he was on call by the authorities if the need arose. He'd fought against it at first, determined not to have any kind of umbilical cord tying him to an organization that had tried its level best to kill him. But in the end the offer had been too easy to accept and he'd given in, persuaded against his better judgement that it might be useful. After all, what was the likelihood of him being called? They had better, younger and brighter bodies on their books.

But authorized or not, there was still a risk to carrying an automatic weapon in his car. Especially if he ran into a random police check and was unable to provide proof of his authority quickly enough. It was reason enough not to drag Rik into it . . . and one of the reasons he had never told him about being carded. Even so.

He took out his mobile and considered calling him. Two sets of eyes were better than one, and he should warn him to keep an eye out for unusual movement around his flat. But what if Rik overreacted and got himself into a jam? He decided against it. No point in raising the tension unnecessarily. First he needed proof.

* * *

A mile ahead of the lay-by, Dog sat astride a trials bike in the forecourt of a petrol station and sipped from a small bottle of mineral water. And waited.

He was dressed in worn, nondescript black leathers and a scratched crash helmet, and was watching for signs of the Saab.

Whatever had caused Tate to pull off the road so abruptly didn't particularly concern him; he was certain he hadn't been made, although that might change the longer he stayed on Tate's tail. But any deviation from the norm was a change in pattern and, in Dog's experience, such changes often carried unforeseen dangers if you ignored them.

When the familiar car flashed by ten minutes later, he tossed the bottle into a bin and dialled a number on his mobile. When a voice answered, he said, 'We're off again.' Then he switched off the mobile and powered away after the Saab.

NINETEEN

Unaware of Dog's presence, Harry was soon off the main routes and cruising through quiet back roads. He drove fast, negotiating the bends with ease and flicking past slower traffic and the occasional cluster of houses. All the while he kept an eye out for signs of pursuit, but saw nobody hovering in his wake for longer than seemed normal.

A sign came up for South Acres. A crudely painted sheet of marine ply nailed to a pine tree at the side of the road, it bore an arrow pointing down a narrow, unpaved track. The track disappeared into a thick belt of conifers and seemed to lead to the only dwelling for some distance.

Harry turned round and drove back slowly past the entrance to study the layout. The track bent out of sight after fifty yards, and wherever South Acres was, it lay screened by trees at the top of a rising slope.

A hundred yards beyond the entrance was a scrubby, unkempt field dotted with tufts of couch grass. A few weather-worn poles and uprights lay scattered, with a rusting feed bin on its side, buckled and unused. The paint on the poles was peeling and dull, and if any horses had jumped them, it must have been a long time ago. Another line of trees at the end of the field prevented any view of a house or farm buildings. A newish TO LET sign on a post stood against the fence near the road, with the agent's name followed by a phone number.

Harry spotted a gap in a group of trees just beyond the field and stopped. He reversed off the road until the nose of the car was screened by folds of soft bracken and the overhanging branches of a beech tree. He checked his watch and nodded towards the sky, where the light was already beginning to fade. Another thirty minutes and it would be safe to take a walk.

He took out his mobile and dialled the number of the letting agent that he'd seen on the post in the field.

'Dempsey's. Can I help you?' The singsong tones of a young woman echoed in the car.

Harry said, 'I've just noticed your panel in a field near a place called South Acres. Is it vacant?'

'I'm sorry, sir.' The young woman sounded distracted, as if she'd been about to leave. 'But that property's on a short let. Perhaps you could call in the morning? Our Mr Dempsey can tell you—'

'I don't have much time,' Harry interrupted her before she could put the phone down. 'I'm flying out of Luton this evening and I need to get something sorted in the next day or so, otherwise my wife and daughters are going to kill me. I need to rent a place for at least twelve months, but it's got to have stabling for three horses.'

'Yes, sir, but—'

'What's your name, miss?'

'It's Donna.'

'Listen, Donna, you could save my life and I'll tell your Mr Dempsey what a big help you've been. Let me know the name of the current tenants, so I can pop in for a quick look round, would you? If it fits what I want, I'll do a bank transfer tomorrow, first thing.'

'I'm sorry, sir.' Donna sounded interested but cautious. 'I can't do that. Mr Dempsey handles the South Acres let. All I know is, it was to a gentleman who wanted a temporary base here for a few weeks.' Her voice dropped slightly. 'He insisted on paying for three months, and since the place had been empty for a while, Mr Dempsey let it go as a special. That's all I can tell you.'

Harry thanked the young woman and rang off. Pity Rik wasn't here, after all. He could have sent him round in person. She'd have probably salivated all over him and given him whatever information he asked for.

He wondered what kind of person needed an isolated farm as a temporary base. Presumably somebody who needed space around them, and where they were not troubled by neighbours. But for what?

A few vehicles swept by, fanning the surrounding foliage. If anyone noticed the car among the trees, they clearly considered it none of their business. Harry settled back to wait for daylight to fade.

When the light had dropped sufficiently, he got out of the car and closed the door. He checked the gun in his pocket but left it where it was. He didn't know anything about this place yet, and could be on a wild goose chase. Wandering around the woods at dusk with a handgun could expose him unnecessarily if he chanced on someone innocently walking their dog.

He zigzagged through the trees, following a line roughly parallel to the road. The undergrowth was rampant, with tangles of briar and nettles underfoot, and lots of deadwood slowly rotting into the soil, making progress slow. An occasional curtain of hanging branches stung his cheeks, but although he wasn't ideally dressed for tramping through the woods, he didn't need to detour too far off his intended route. Other than the background hum of vehicles along the road, the atmosphere among the trees was quiet and sombre, the air heavy with the aroma of sap, rotten wood and damp earth. He stopped every few yards to listen and check his surroundings.

Eventually he reached the edge of the tree line and saw the field containing the abandoned jump fences. Turning away from the road, he followed a rusted barbed wire fence until he reached another stretch of twisted wire. On the other side of this was a twin set of ruts, a continuation of the track from the road.

Beyond the track was another belt of trees, dark and silent save for the faint rustle of leaves. The undergrowth looked as wild and desolate as the area he had just crossed, with fallen tree trunks and branches littering the ground.

He looked right. The track ran for a few yards before curving sharply left and out of sight. It was tempting, and would allow him to move faster. But following it would leave him out in the open if anyone came along. He decided on the trees opposite, which looked like ideal cover.

Crossing the track into a denser thicket, he eventually reached a high stone wall. The top layer showed signs of crumbling, with broken fragments lying in a jumble at the base. Moss covered the stones, filling the gaps with fuzzy bundles like small, hairy bugs, and the air reeked of damp and the permanent absence of sunlight. The structure was too high to see over, but Harry spotted a point where a stone had fallen out. He stepped across and peered through the gap.

What had once been an elegant, two-storey farmhouse stood a few yards away, with the track running across between it and the wall. Beyond the house stood a collection of ancient barns and outbuildings, the latter with moss-covered walls and iron stains from large reinforcing cross-bolts in the stonework. A rusted iron fence ran along the front of the house, and inside it, the remains of a flowerbed now peppered with weeds and tufts of rampant, coarse grass.

Rust seemed to be the predominant colour among all the outbuildings, from the corrugated metal sheets of the roofs, which had sagged away, exposing their metal trusses to the elements, to an ancient tractor standing against the barn wall. Its rubber tyres were gone, perished to husks, the engine block a solid, rusted lump beneath a dull, red bonnet. The smokestack was skewed drunkenly to one side, as rotten as soft bark.

Behind the tractor Harry could just make out the front wing of a car.

A yellow Suzuki four-wheel drive.

The farmhouse was dark save for a single, naked bulb burning in one of the upstairs rooms. Harry froze at a flash of movement. A man was standing in the lit room, his back to the window. He was gesturing at someone out of sight. He wore a plain white shirt with the sleeves buttoned to the wrists. He shook his head and turned to stare out of the window, eyes on the trees right where Harry had been walking moments before. A dark patch was just visible on his face.

Silverman.

Harry stayed absolutely still. If he moved now, Silverman couldn't fail to spot him. Then he realized the man's attention was caught by something down at the front of the house. Silverman said something, and seconds later he was joined by another figure who looked down and smiled briefly before turning away and pulling Silverman after him.

It was the young man from the airport.

Harry lifted himself on his toes and peered in the direction the two men had been looking. As he did so, he heard a crunch from the other side of the wall, followed by a cough and the throaty sound of somebody spitting. He waited, not daring to move and feeling the strain up the back of his legs.

A man walked by not ten feet away. He was moving slowly along the gravel drive, head swinging to check the scenery. Even in the poor light, Harry saw he was dressed in a bomber jacket and jeans, was heavily built and swarthy, in need of a shave.

He waited for the man to turn away, then dropped slowly to a crouch, his breathing light but his heart pounding.

The man on the other side of the wall was clearly a guard. While the shotgun he carried across his chest might have been for shooting vermin or rabbits, the semi-automatic tucked prominently into the side of his belt was anything but.

TWENTY

Harry thought about his next move, waiting for the man to walk away. Treading on a branch now would be a dead giveaway, and a shotgun blast among these trees could still be lethal. Gut instinct told him he should drop this assignment and get out fast. There were departments that dealt with this kind of stuff; he'd worked in one himself and knew the score. A phone call to the right number would initiate a scramble of men and transport, and in no time at all this place would be surrounded and contained.

If he did that, however, he would never know what lay behind the events of the past couple of days. A puzzle like that could gnaw away at you, driving a person mad with speculation.

He could do both, he reasoned. Call it in to Jennings and wait around to see what happened. See what the lawyer had in the way of clout.

He made his way back to the car and dialled the number. If things went disastrously wrong, at least he would have the satisfaction of knowing he had fulfilled his part of the contract. If it all turned out to be a fuss over nothing, well, he'd have to live with it. *Former MI5 man cries wolf.* He'd had worse things said about him.

A motorbike with a loud exhaust clattered by on the road. It was loud enough to shock a number of birds out of the trees, forcing Harry to abandon the call and redial. He noted with relief that there seemed to be less traffic going by now. If he had to get away from here in a hurry, he didn't fancy waiting for someone to let him out into a long line of commuter traffic. Not with a man waving a shotgun behind him.

Jennings' number was engaged. He counted to ten and tried again. It was time for the lawyer to tell him what the hell was going on. If he turned round and said he didn't know, Harry might as well pack up and go home. First, though, he'd drop a call to the anti-terrorist squad.

At least the boys in black might get a night training exercise out of it.

The motorbike engine was still surprisingly loud, but muffled now by the trees. It took a few seconds for the alarm bell in Harry's brain to ring. Something about the proximity of the noise wasn't right. He switched off the phone for a second, listening to the sound of the engine.

Why still so close? It should be a mile away by now.

Another clatter of exhaust, this time from deep in the woods, scared up a handful of birds. They streaked by overhead, wheeling away to the south before peeling off in different directions, pigeons, mostly, identifiable by their heavy wing beats, dragging in their wake a flock of smaller birds swooping and darting haphazardly across the sky.

The engine gave a final cackle, followed by a series of flat pops. The sudden quiet afterwards was almost numbing, with only the beat of wings fading into the distance as a few more birds joined in the exodus.

Then the blast of a shotgun tore through the gloom.

It was followed by a deathly silence. Then two flat pops, this time muffled.

Harry felt his blood go cold. There was no mistaking the sound.

Someone was using a handgun.

Moments later a car engine roared and lights swept through the trees from the direction of the house. The motor revved and whined furiously, the glow flaring through the foliage as the vehicle tore along the track towards the road.

Harry switched off his mobile and grabbed a torch from the boot of the Saab, then took off through the trees, crashing through the brushwood and hanging branches. He reached the fence bordering the track and scrambled over. This time, instead of heading through the trees towards the high wall, he turned and ran along the track and through an open gateway with a security light burning high on a stone pillar to one side.

The light was enough to show a huddled shape on the ground in front of the house. *His instincts had been right – he was being followed!*

He dodged off the track and crouched behind the pillar, his heart thumping. He peered out but saw no sign of movement. A metronomic ticking was coming from somewhere nearby, and he saw a trial bike lying at the side of the track, the ribbed front wheel turning slowly. Its rear tyre had been ripped away from the wheel rim, no doubt shredded by the shotgun blast.

Harry stepped out and knelt by the body. Flicked his torch on the man's face.

It was the guard he'd seen earlier. He was dead. The shotgun lay close by, the stock shattered, and the man's lower face was a mess of blood, the torn flesh sprouting splinters of wood.

Harry moved on, ghostly fingers crawling up his back. He stepped round the side of the house, but there was no sign of the Suzuki. So who had got away – good guys or bad?

The side door of the house was open, the interior thrown into dull relief by a single light. It gave him a narrow view of a large, rustic kitchen with yellowing, bubbled wallpaper and ill-matching chairs set around a heavy table. The floor was bare, laid with heavy flagstones worn to a shine by decades of use.

Harry stepped inside, feet crunching on grit. A smell of stale food and damp hung in the air. A battered cooker and fridge were the only light dash of colour, but like the decor, they were ancient and long past their prime. The kitchen table and worktops were a mess of dirty plates, opened tins and empty food wrappers. A bolt-hole, not a home.

A half-open doorway leading to the front half of the house lay to his right. A doorway to the left showed a narrow flight of stairs disappearing up into darkness.

Neither option looked very welcoming.

Upstairs was the logical place to go; it was where he had seen Silverman. First, though, he had to check that the ground floor was clear. The torchlight pushed back the dark, revealing a narrow view of two large reception rooms and a utility room, and a hallway running across the front of the building. More damp, more musty air and heavy furniture, but no signs of life. He returned to the kitchen and moved across to the stairs.

Holding the torch against the barrel of his semi-automatic, Harry switched it on and poked it round the doorway and up the stairs. There was no sound of movement, no blast of gunfire. He steadied himself, remembering the countless times he'd gone through the training shell they called the Clearing House. Dodging from room to room and hoping for a clean run, all the trainees had to do was face a barrage of deafening flash-bangs, pop-up targets and screaming sound effects operated by the merciless technicians on the other side of the blast-proof walls.

The difference between then and now was this was for real, with real bullets.

He bent and picked up a muddy shoe lying near the door. Stepping forward, he lobbed it underarm into the gloom, where it bounced and rumbled along the floor. No reaction.

There was only one thing for it: he breathed deep and took the stairs in three strides, hurling himself to the floor as he reached the landing and curling round to see past the banister, the gun and torch thrust out before him.

'Jesus,' he muttered, and swallowed hard.

A man's body was lying crumpled at the far end, legs drawn up to his belly. One arm was thrown across his face, and an almost delicate mist of blood had been sprayed across the faded wallpaper in the background. The man had been shot twice in the chest. Harry bent and eased his arm away.

The greeter from the airport.

Recovering quickly, he checked the bedrooms, then came back to the landing and switched on the light. The single bulb revealed a trail of blood on the wooden boards and a scarlet handprint smeared down one wall of the stairwell. It was easy to see the chain of events: the killer had charged up to the house on the motorbike, taking the outside guard by surprise in spite of – or perhaps because of – the noise. What Harry had taken to be the sound of the bike engine popping had been the first shots fired, which must have damaged the shotgun without killing the guard.

The killer had then stormed the house and disposed of the second guard, during which the first man had fired his shotgun into the motorbike wheel to disable it and prevent the attacker's escape. The gunman had simply adapted to the change in circumstances and got away in the Suzuki.

The one thing he couldn't tell was whose blood was on the wall down the stairwell. Unless the killer had taken a hit on the way in. The two guards had been prepared, but hadn't reacted fast enough. The outside man got caught in the open and this one had been standing flat-footed at the top.

Harry checked each room for papers, personal effects – anything that might tell him what had happened and why. What it revealed was an old house that had been largely uninhabited, with the majority of living space confined to the kitchen and two bedrooms. The main ground floor rooms were untouched, while the utility room showed signs of some use, with washing in the tumble dryer and dirty footwear on the floor.

But there was nothing about the men who had been staying here.

The bedrooms were the same. One room contained two sleeping bags on the bare boards and spare items of clothing heaped on two hard-backed chairs. Evidently the guards' quarters. Rucksacks in one corner showed the men had not planned on a lengthy stay, and the wardrobe and a cupboard hadn't been used. The labels on the bags and the few clothes inside were all high-street chains, readily available, cheap and disposable. A couple of DVD players lay on the floor, the accompanying discs bearing cheap, pirated labels.

The other room held a single bed against one wall, with a sleeping bag in place of bedclothes. A dent in the mattress showed the bed had been used recently.

Harry flicked open the sleeping bag. A faint smear of red showed against the fabric at the top, with a heavier patch on the inside. More blood. But this was dry. He guessed it had leaked from Silverman's hand, and might account for the blood on the stairs. Down by the side of the bed he found a grubby wad of gauze with bloodstained cotton padding on one side. Silverman had changed his bandage but hadn't had time to dispose of the old one. There was no sign of the dark coat or the sports bag they'd seen him carrying at the airport.

It looked like Silverman had been given the prime spot – such as it was – while he was here. Yet he clearly hadn't made himself so comfortable that he'd been unable to pick up at a moment's notice when necessity demanded. Harry wondered what the man had been thinking of as he lay here, guarded by his two colleagues.

Or had they been his captors?

He checked the window. It looked out over the rear of the house on to a patch of garden and more trees. It was now too dark to see anything clearly, but the window showed a small gap at the bottom, as if it had been closed in a hurry. It slid up with only the faintest protest, and he noticed a shine in the sash runners. He rubbed his finger along the groove and sniffed.

Soap. Someone had been prepared, then. But not the guards. Had Silverman escaped out the back or had he gone with the gunman?

As he turned to go, he noticed some marks on the wallpaper alongside the bed. Somebody had written on the paper. But the marks were odd, almost Cyrillic. Or were they?

He lay on the bed with his head on the pillow and looked up, studying the marks against the light. The scribbling was upside down. He was looking at a mobile phone number followed by the letters 'J.A.'

He felt a buzz of excitement. The same letters and numbers he'd seen on the scrap of paper in Silverman's briefing file! Without some additional information to clarify them, he'd dismissed them as useless. Now here it was – the missing half of the number.

He made a note of the number and initials and slid off the
bed. On the way past, he checked the body on the landing.
The man's pockets produced a French passport in the name
of Henri Taoub, a thin wad of Euros and Sterling and a mobile
phone. Other than that, Mr Taoub had been travelling light.

He left the money but took the passport and mobile for
checking later. Back outside, he checked the body at the front
of the house. This also revealed money and a French passport in the name of Marcel Yamouh, but no mobile. It pointed
towards Taoub being the one in charge. He stood up, reflecting
that since neither of the two dead men had the initials J.A.,
another person was involved – someone Silverman was
intending to contact.

He hurried back through the trees to the car. If the shots
had been heard and recognized, it wouldn't be long before
the police were on their way here. He waited until he was
well away from the immediate area before ringing Rik and
gave him the passport details, the number he'd copied off the
wall and the number from the guard's mobile phone.

'Can you crunch that lot? I'd especially like a name and
address for the phone.'

'Should be easy enough. How do you know J.A. isn't the
guy on the bike?'

'He might be, but I don't think so. Silverman was hardly
there long enough before the gunman turned up. Why write
down the number? I think he was prepared for a longer wait.
As soon as he heard the shooting, he was out the back and
away.'

'And if he wasn't?'

'If he wasn't, and the killer took him, it's because somebody wants him alive. For now, at least.'

TWENTY-ONE

'Joanne Archer? Yeah, she lives upstairs – when she's here.
Who's asking?' The gaunt individual who answered the
door to the large Victorian property was dressed in scuffed
tartan slippers and a ratty brown jersey. His unshaven face

had the appearance of soggy cardboard as he stood squarely in the entrance, squinting through the morning sunlight at Rik and Harry. A faint rumble came from the North Circular barely two hundred yards away, where it sliced through Finchley past St Pancras and Islington cemetery.

Harry gave the man a stony look and a flash of his old MI5 card. 'Police,' he announced. 'We'd like a word with her.'

Rik had crunched the mobile numbers through his laptop and come up with this address for J.A. He hadn't been able to get a copy of the call records, but that would have to come later if they needed it. After the two killings and Silverman's disappearance from the farmhouse, Harry had decided not to waste any time watching the house, but to come straight in. It was risky, but so was losing the mysterious Joanne Archer to the killer before they could talk to her and find out what her connection was with Silverman.

'She's not in.'

The house was divided into separate flats and bedsits, with a line of bell-pushes and name cards to one side of the door. The plastic square for flat No. 3 was the only one without a card, the slot grimy and rimmed with dust.

'And you are?' Harry played the deadpan cop.

'McCulloch. I own this place.' The man looked unimpressed by the ID. 'Jo's a PA or something. Travels a lot . . . sometimes away for weeks at a time. The first I know if she's back is when she appears out of the blue. She doesn't communicate much.' He looked from Harry to Rik. 'You don't look like police.'

'He's undercover,' said Harry.

'Oh. I see. She's not in trouble, is she?'

'Nothing like that, sir. We need to speak to her, that's all. It's a private matter.' He gave the landlord the kind of look meant to provoke instant respect for privacy. 'Can we see her flat?'

'I don't know about that. Shouldn't I see some sort of documentation?' McCulloch scowled and straightened his bony shoulders, a lowly individual taking a stand against official invaders. Then he noticed the uncompromising expression on Harry's face. 'I mean, it's only right.'

'A warrant, you mean?' Harry nodded. 'Probably. But that would mean going to a judge and giving reasons for wanting

access. We can do that, if you insist. It would give us access
to every flat in the building, of course. And the rental records.'
He stared up at the walls and pulled a face. 'Plus health and
safety, fire regs . . .' He smiled coldly. 'They'd be checked,
too.'

McCulloch looked appalled at the idea of an official open
season on his affairs. He stepped quickly aside. 'You'd better
come in, then. Not that I've got anything to hide, of course.
Upstairs at the back . . . number three. I'll open it for you.'

They trooped upstairs, McCulloch jangling a bunch of keys
and muttering beneath his breath. He pushed past them and
bent to unlock a door at the rear of the landing. It opened
directly into a tiny lobby laid with plastic tiles and contained
a stiff-backed chair and a pair of walking boots. The soles
and sides of the boots were crusted with dried mud, and a
few pieces had fallen to the floor, like pale chocolate flakes.

'She walks a lot,' explained McCulloch unnecessarily.
'Always off somewhere, she is. Never could be doing with
that fitness stuff, myself.'

A door led from the lobby into a living area and another
opened into a small kitchenette overlooking an untidy garden.
The decor throughout was utilitarian and sombre, but Archer
had evidently made an effort to brighten up the place by the
addition of some colourful pictures in the living room, showing
what could have been desert sunsets and a line of single-storey
buildings with white walls and black holes for windows. A
large ornate vase on a coffee table was empty save for a
yellowed chalk in the bottom where the water had evaporated
in the dry atmosphere.

'You know who she works for?' asked Harry. 'Any visitors, deliveries, that sort of thing?'

'No. She never told me anything like that. Kept herself to
herself. Wish I had more tenants like her, to be honest.'
McCulloch sniffed. 'Some of them treat the place like a
knocking shop, bringing in all sorts. Not her, though. Quiet.
Goes running and walking, like I said. Likes her own company,
I suppose. Nice-looking girl. Bit butch for my tastes, but the
meat's all the same in the dark, isn't it?'

'What about the rent?' Harry resisted the temptation to give
the man a slap. 'Does she always pay on time?'

The landlord nodded. 'On the nail. When she knows she's

going away, she pays up front. Cash.' He gave a sly smile and
rubbed his fingers together, drawing them into his little
conspiracy. 'Suits me, you know what I mean? Bloody government takes enough off us already.' He clearly didn't see them
as a threat to his livelihood, official ID or not. Even so, he
glanced nervously at Rik. 'He doesn't say much, does he?'

'He doesn't have to. I keep him for other uses. The bedroom
this way?'

McCulloch blinked and scurried after him.

The bedroom lay at the rear of the building. It contained a
single bed, a cabinet with a narrow door and a small wardrobe,
the door open. A few garments hung on the rail, but none
looked recently worn, the fabric lightly coated in dust. A pair
of trainers and some slip-on sandals lay jumbled at the bottom,
like cast-offs. The air inside smelled musty.

Harry sat on the bed and bounced. It creaked but nothing
crackled under the mattress. He'd take a look anyway, as soon
as they could get rid of the landlord. 'When was she last
here?'

McCulloch pursed his lips and studied the ceiling. 'Now
you've got me. Ages ago. When was it . . .? Oh, I know –
about three months. Yep, she paid for four up front, said this
job was a long one but she didn't want to lose the flat in case
things didn't work out. Like I said, fine by me.' He appeared
to realize rather belatedly that the two men wouldn't have
shown up without good reason. 'Here, I hope she's OK. She
was a good tenant.'

'That's what we hope to find out,' said Harry. 'Nice of you
to show concern, though.' He stared at the surface of the
bedside cabinet. A palm print showed clearly in the dust along
one edge, as if someone had bent to retrieve something, using
the cabinet for support. A small hand, like a woman's. And
recently made.

He smiled at McCulloch. 'Thanks for your cooperation. We
just need to look around . . . get a feel for things. We'll shout
if we need anything.' He nodded at the door.

The landlord seemed reluctant to move until Rik stepped
up to him and gave a hard smile.

'Right. No problem.' McCulloch got the message. 'I'll be
downstairs if you need me.'

They waited for his footsteps to recede. 'Amazing,' said

Rik with a smile. 'Saying nothing really put the frighteners on him.'

'Silence is golden. Never forget that.' Harry pointed at the handprint. 'See that?'

'Yes. Looks fresh.'

'There's another one in the kitchen. She must have dropped by without McCulloch knowing. Come on, let's get to work before Prince Charming decides to check with the local nick.'

They began to toss the place, working their way through each room, checking every drawer, cushion, chair back and crevice. The carpet lifted easily enough, but there were no loose floor-boards and no signs of anything hidden within the fabric of the room. The wardrobe slid aside to reveal nothing more than dust and a yellowed, ageing newspaper covered in splashes of paint, evidence of a long-ago attempt at decorating.

Back in the small lobby, Harry checked the walking boots. They were worn at the heel and smooth on each sole, but still serviceable except for a torn eyelet. He tried to flex one of them, but it had dried solid and unyielding. As he turned them upside down a small square of brown card fell to the floor. It was for a gym membership.

Rik joined him and peered at the card. It was topped by a logo and the name PARK'S GYM, and made out to J. Archer. The expiry date was nearly twelve months old. A membership number was handwritten at the bottom. Evidently Park's Gym had not yet embraced electronic membership systems.

'So,' mused Rik. 'She's not often here . . . she travels a lot, but we don't know where; she's a fitness freak – we know this because of the used walking boots and the gym card, and because handsome downstairs says she runs a lot.' He looked around. 'Pretty basic lifestyle. No frills to it, no softness.'

'For a girl, you mean?'

'For anyone. Where did you last see that?'

'Unmarried squaddies' quarters,' said Harry automatically. 'She's army. Or was.' He went into the living room and stared at the desert sunset pictures. 'I think she did the Gulf.' He turned to a point opposite the window where a small square of wallpaper was slightly darker than the surrounding area. He peered closely at the surface, then tapped the wall where a small hole showed in the paper. 'Looks like there used to be a frame hanging here.' He looked down at his feet and bent to retrieve a small panel pin lying against the skirting. 'I should have been a cop.'

'If she paid up her rent a month ahead,' Rik concluded, 'why come by to clear out without telling anyone?'

'Frightened? Called away on another job?' Harry shrugged. 'With McCulloch as a landlord, I wouldn't hang around either. I wouldn't live here in the first place.'

Rik flicked the gym card. 'This place might know. People with a shared interest exchange gossip without realizing.'

Harry looked doubtful. 'Yeah. I always give away secrets when I'm pumping iron.'

They closed the flat and went downstairs. McCulloch was waiting for them in the hallway.

'Any joy, gents?' he asked, ingratiating. 'See everything you wanted?'

Rik ignored the question and showed McCulloch the gym card. 'How do we get to this place?'

'Park's? It's about a mile away. Clarence Road.' He gave them directions. 'She used to go there a lot. Surprising, really – it's a bit . . . you know.'

'No.'

'Hardcore. Spit and sawdust we called it when I was younger.'

Rik gave the man a sour once-over. 'Yeah. I can see you used to work out.'

McCulloch was unruffled by the taunt. 'You know what I mean. It's not the place for a girl, exactly. Not that she was into Spandex or all that designer gear.' He blinked rapidly as if realizing he'd said too much. 'I mean, not that I'd know what she was into, would I?'

'Of course you wouldn't,' Harry growled. 'What about Park's?'

McCulloch flushed and wiped a hand across his face. 'Well, you get some rough types down there . . . a few boxers, weight trainers, that sort of thing. Not for the faint-hearted, anyway. She seemed to like it, though.' He shook his head, mystified at the ways of the world. 'I suppose I should have mentioned it to the other two, but I forgot.'

Harry was turning away. He swung back and fixed

McCulloch with a stare like a mongoose eyeing a cobra. His voice came out unnaturally quiet.

'What other two?'

TWENTY-TWO

McCulloch floundered visibly, aware of his slip, mouth working like a stranded goldfish.

'Two men,' he muttered. 'Came by just over a week ago. I thought they were coppers at first, but they were too smart. Well, one was; the other hung in the background and didn't say much. The one who did the talking flashed a card, same as you. But I can't remember what was on it. Very polite, he was.'

'What did they want?'

'They said they needed to contact her . . . something about insurance, I think. I figured they were sales reps. Anyway, I told them she hadn't been around for a while and I didn't know when she would be back.' He looked between them, his forehead beaded with perspiration. 'Did I do the wrong thing?'

'Not yet,' said Harry heavily. 'What did they look like?'

'Like I said, smart, wearing suits and that. They were both tanned, like they'd been on holiday. The quiet one was a bit of a bruiser; big guy. Didn't really look like a rep, now I think about it. I didn't notice anything else.'

'They have a car?'

'No idea. They walked down the street, that's all I know.'

'What about her mail?'

'Sorry?'

'Miss Archer's post,' Rik said clearly. 'There was none in her flat. She must have had something, even if it was only junk. What did you do with it?'

McCulloch gestured towards a half-moon table against one wall. 'All the mail for tenants is left here, so they can sort through it. They take what's useful and leave the rubbish. Anything addressed to Joanne, I'd do it for her. She was OK about me doing that – not that she got much . . . maybe two a week at most.' He licked his lips. 'I suppose I should have taken it in.'

'Should have?' Rik's voice dropped to a dangerous low and McCulloch blanched, reaching out a restraining hand as if he was about to get hit.

'*Wait* – hang on. Two days ago her mail disappeared – I don't know how. It was there, with a rubber band on it, on the table like always. Maybe a sneak thief got in and took it on spec. There's plenty of them around here, nicking whatever they can get their hands on.' He shrugged. 'What can I say?'

They left McCulloch and walked back to the car, trying to figure out who or what Joanne Archer was, why she led such a Spartan lifestyle, and why she should attract official-sounding visitors in suits.

'Do you believe the bit about the sneak thief?' asked Rik.

'No. Archer's been back. I wonder why the secrecy, though, if she's all paid up?'

They followed McCulloch's directions and found Park's Gym at the end of a cul-de-sac backing on to a small commercial estate. The area was tired and rundown, a backwater overlooked by local civic development plans and left to rot. The gym was a two-storey brick structure which might once have been a garage and showroom. A single door with the word ENTRANCE invited visitors to enter.

The air inside reeked of stale bodies, dust and industrial-strength deodorant in equal measures. The clang of weights echoed from behind a wooden door on the ground floor. Upstairs, a loudspeaker hammered out a disco track. A door marked 'CHANGING – MEN' stood off to one side, with a similar sign for women pointing upstairs.

They pushed through the wooden door and found themselves in a large, brightly lit room filled with weights, exercise machinery and a fight ring. The walls were lined with mirrors reflecting half a dozen men of varying ages undergoing several kinds of self-induced torture. The atmosphere was stale and heavy, a place dedicated to pain and effort rather than leisure.

A stocky individual in a cutaway vest and sloppy training pants left one of the weight benches and walked across to greet them. He had a bald head and an unshaven chin, and had clearly spent his life working weights, the muscles on his arms and chest like tattooed slabs of meat. He measured the two men with a professional gaze and lifted his chin. 'Hi. I'm Danny Park. Can I help?' He eyed them without a flicker of welcome, balanced and solid, relaxed.

'We hope so,' said Harry. 'We're looking for Joanne Archer. I gather she's a member.'

They waited while the information was processed. A few of the men in the background had stopped training and stood watching. None of them looked particularly friendly. The sound of the music upstairs thumped through the ceiling, punctuated by the repeated clang of weights from the far end of the gym.

'Who wants to know?' Park said at last.

Harry didn't think flashing any ID would impress the man, so he nodded to Rik to show him the membership card from Archer's flat. 'She hasn't been home and her friends are worried. We've been asked to look for her.'

Park looked sceptical. 'You're not police – so what are you?'

'We look for people. People who go missing.'

'Yeah?' Park pursed his lips and seemed to find the answer acceptable. He barely looked at the membership card. 'That's well out of date. Current colour's green. She hasn't been here for a bit. You think she's in trouble?'

'That's what we'd like to find out.' Harry bent to a rack of hand weights and picked up a ten-pound dumb-bell, turning it over as easily as he would have handled a bar of chocolate. 'I really need to get back into this. I miss the burn, y'know?' He replaced the weight on the rack with a faint chink. It wasn't true – he'd never seen the point – but the lie came easily.

'You should come here, then. We're always on the lookout for more mature members.' Park flashed a line of white teeth to show he was joking.

'I might do that. So . . . Joanne.' He raised his eyebrows.

Park turned and shouted, 'Anyone seen Jo recently?' When nobody replied, he turned back and said, 'Sorry – they're not the most talkative bunch. They'll have you two down as cops.'

'Can you tell us anything about her? It might help,' Harry said.

'Sure. She's a good kid. Tough. Came here to keep fit. Not that she wasn't already fitter than most of these sad sacks.' He smiled dreamily. 'Fitter than a lot of the guys I used to train, actually.'

Harry looked at the tattoos, which included a set of faded wings. 'Paras?'

'Used to be. Ten years and counting. Wish I was still in, tell you the truth.'

He was interrupted from further reminiscing by a boy in his teens who ambled across from a punchbag in one corner. He wore scrappy tracksuit bottoms and a pair of training gloves, and his chest was narrow and pale, but taut with muscle. In spite of his youth, he already had the battered look of someone who would never reach the top of his game, and his eyes held the slow vague expression of someone who'd taken too many punches.

'I seen her.'

'What's that, Hughie?' Park's voice was surprisingly gentle, as if talking to a child.

'I seen her,' Hughie repeated. 'I seen Jo.' He smiled, then frowned, emotions overlapping, and ripped back the Velcro strap on one of his training gloves. He picked at a stray length of cotton as if he'd already forgotten what he was saying.

'Where did you see her, Hughie?' Park prompted him. 'Where'd you see Jo?'

'Battersea,' replied Hughie after some thought. 'At the weekend. I remember, it was Park Road. Park Road, see?' He smiled self-consciously, proud at making the word connection.

'Battersea.' Danny Park gave the two men a quick look. 'That's a long way from here, Hughie. What were you doing down in Battersea?'

'Seeing my dad, wasn't I? He lives down that way . . . back of Latchmere Road.' He smiled vaguely at the memory and rubbed the knuckles of the gloves together. 'I think it was her, anyway. I said hi, but she didn't say nothing.'

'What was Jo doing, Hughie?' said Rik. 'When you saw her?'

The youth glanced at Park before answering. 'Nothing. Walking. I know it was her because of her pink bag.' He shrugged like it was no big deal. 'Maybe she didn't see me. She'd have spoke, otherwise, wouldn't she?'

Park explained, 'She had a sports bag with bits of pink . . . what d'you call it – piping – round the edges. The lads had a good laugh when she first brought it in. One of 'em said it was a big girlie bag and she was turning into a right pussy.' He smiled. 'She got him in the ring after and kicked the crap out of him. Man, it was great.'

Hughie nodded shyly in agreement, then eyed the two men carefully and waved a gloved hand towards the punchbag. 'C'n I go now?'

Park nodded and clapped Hughie on the shoulder. 'Sure, off you go. Thanks, Hughie.' He waited for the young man to move out of earshot, then said quietly, 'Hughie had a thing for Jo. Thought she was a princess. She was always nice to him when others weren't. If you go on what he says, you're welcome, but don't rely on it too much. He got knocked down by a car when he was a kid. He's fine, mostly. But he has . . . lapses.'

'He found his way to Battersea,' Harry pointed out. 'We'll give it a try.'

Park nodded. 'Fair enough. If you find her, tell her she's always welcome back.' He gave a sour look at the other men in the gym, now turning back to their training. 'Tell you the truth, she was the only thing ever brightened up this dump.'

'What did she do here?' Harry asked. 'Apart from kicking the crap out of people?'

Parks shrugged. 'All sorts, really, but to a system. She boxed, lifted weights, ran . . . even wiped the floor with me when the mood took her.'

'Come again?' Rik looked cynical.

'Seriously. I don't mind admitting it. Somebody taught her how to fight. Nasty stuff, too; none of your Queensberry rules. She didn't just know all the moves, either. She was hard with it, but deceptive. Wicked fast, too. She never said, but I reckon she'd done time in the army. She had that . . . thing about her, you know? That edge you don't get with civvies.' He shrugged. 'Like I said, tough.' He frowned for a moment and shook his head.

'What?' said Rik.

'I don't know. There was something . . . She was always so *focussed*. Like she was permanently in training. I couldn't figure it out, and to be honest I didn't like to ask. It's not what people come here for.' He scratched his head. 'The last time I saw anyone that intense was in the regiment, just before something big kicked off. Then it was everyone in his own world, you know? Dealing with it.'

Harry nodded. 'You think the training was for real?'

Park shrugged. 'What do I know? But, yeah, I reckon. Like she was on standby . . . which is stupid, right? I mean, people in Civvy Street don't live like that, do they?'

'No,' said Harry thoughtfully. 'They don't.'

TWENTY-THREE

The Corpos Fitness Centre was a modern, brick-and-glass designer cube near Battersea Park, catering to a clientele that liked to exercise in air-conditioned style and comfort. Forget about pounding around the park in wind and rain, the glossy signs and subdued lighting implied; that was for extremists, oddballs and London Marathon wannabes. Enter instead the world of heart monitors, space-age exercise machinery, designer leisurewear and your own personal trainer right out of *Sex and the City*, all for a very reasonable sum payable by credit card or direct debit, no cheques accepted.

They had located three fitness or exercise centres in the area; one was strictly men-only, the emphasis being on weight training, with no other facilities and, according to the man on reception, women were 'discouraged'. The second was at the other end of the spectrum, with lots of glitz and a fancy cocktail bar . . . and membership limited only by the size of your bank balance.

That left the Corpos. After Danny Park and his back-to-basics sweat and grunt gymnasium, it was light years away from what Joanne Archer would have been used to. But if what Park had said about her being a relentless trainer was true, and Hughie was correct in his claim to have seen her in Battersea with her pink gym bag, it seemed as good a place as any to continue their search.

For Harry, it was back to basics. Finding where runners

might have gone could be a laborious process. Nine times out of ten a link was there, usually connected to a place or element of the runner's past life. With Joanne Archer, all they had to go on was a rigorously observed fitness routine. While it wasn't much, it meant she was unlikely to break that routine unless forced by circumstances beyond her control.

Four thirty in the afternoon was evidently a quiet period in the world of exercise, sweatbands and leotards. No doubt the rush would come when people began leaving work, intent on an evening workout to ease the kinks of sitting down all day.

From their vantage point in a café across the road, Harry counted eight people entering the Corpos premises and five leaving, each armed with sports bags. Most were young, good-looking and self-aware in the latest multicoloured leisure clothing, and were greeted by the receptionist, a young woman with a startling orange tan and lustrous black hair.

She, he decided, recognizing a professional gatekeeper at work, might be a problem.

'Do you think that kid Hughie was daydreaming?' Rik asked. 'Wandering around London looking for her like a love-sick donkey.'

'Maybe.' Harry wasn't sure. Kids like Hughie had different values, different ways of looking at things. To Hughie, someone who'd treated him with kindness was a person to remember. To notice. 'We'll give it a few more minutes, then you can go and kick the doors in.'

'What makes you so sure this is it?'

'I'm not.' Harry nodded at one of the signs in the window, which read: 'Extreme Fitness and Martial Arts!' 'It sounds serious enough and fits what we know about Archer's lifestyle.'

While the minutes ticked by, they used the time to go over what they knew about their quarry, to ensure they hadn't missed something.

'She's ex-army,' said Rik, ticking off his fingers. 'Current occupation thought to be a PA but not confirmed. She's young, fit and travels a lot but keeps her place in north London on as a bolt-hole. Suddenly, from an already unusual lifestyle, she drops her routine and goes AWOL. No reasons given, no explanations, she just ducks out of sight. That's not normal.'

'Neither is the fact that Silverman had her number,' Harry added. 'I'd give anything to know how, though. And now he's also on the loose.'

'You think he called and triggered her disappearance?'

'Unless she was waiting for him to show.' It wasn't much of a theory but in the absence of any other it was workable until something better came along.

Rik floated a new idea. 'We could ask Jennings if he knows about her.'

Harry thought about that. It wasn't a bad idea, but he wondered if Joanne Archer was something else the lawyer hadn't told them about. The man was too full of secrets, that was the problem. Harry hadn't yet told him about the bodies at South Acres and the events of the previous evening, because he wanted to find out who Joanne Archer was first. In any case, it was likely Jennings already knew about the shootings; if he was as plugged in to the law enforcement network as he pretended, he would have picked up reports immediately.

'We should call him,' Rik insisted, 'or go see him face to face.'

'To say what?' The idea of Rik stomping into Jennings' office playing the heavy might be mildly entertaining, but he figured the lawyer was tougher than he looked and would be no pushover.

'If we don't, he might think we've got something to hide.'

He thought it over, and decided Rik was right. He took out his mobile and dialled the number.

'I was wondering where you'd got to.' Jennings answered the phone with typical bluntness. 'I take it you have something useful to report?'

'Depends on your point of view,' said Harry, and gave him a brief rundown of what he'd discovered at the farmhouse. He kept the specifics clouded, in case anyone was listening, referring to the bodies as 'broken items' and their method of dispatch as 'severe structural damage'.

'Where were they from?' asked Jennings, catching on fast.

'They had French papers,' Harry replied, 'but darker in tone.'

Jennings made no comment, and Harry thought he heard the rasp of a pen in the background. 'So you've no idea where the main delivery has gone?'

'We're working on it.' Harry thought the lawyer sounded altogether too calm.

There was a pause, then, 'You have a lead?'

The interest sounded genuine. Maybe Jennings didn't know about Joanne Archer after all. 'Among the papers you gave us,' Harry explained, 'was a reference to "J.A. London". It wasn't much to go on and we pretty much dismissed it. When we searched the place at South Acres, we found the same initials and a number scribbled on the wall of a bedroom. It was too significant to ignore.'

'I take it you have an address for this new item?'

Harry gave him the address of Joanne Archer's flat in north London, and her surname. 'It's no longer there but we're currently trying to find out where it might have moved to. There are also a couple of other interested parties looking for it. They could be official.'

'I'm sure they are. Don't worry about that.' Jennings didn't sound at all perturbed at the idea.

'There's also,' Harry added, drawing raised eyebrows from Rik, 'something you need to know about the main package: its source of origin is not where we were told.'

'Go on.'

'The brief said Israel . . . and academic in nature.'

'So?'

'Try further east. It also arrived via Frankfurt under different papers and was picked up from Heathrow. It was obviously a prearranged collection. None of that fits the brief.'

Jennings brushed off the revelation. 'I think you're mistaken.'

'*Oh, come on!*' Harry exploded. Jennings was treating him like an amateur. What did the man think they'd been doing all this time, for Christ's sake – playing dominoes? 'We talked to somebody with the same background.' He was beyond caring about client relations now. Too much had happened. If Jennings didn't like his tone, he could go jump. Across the table, Rik was smiling encouragingly. He decided to dispense with caution. 'How does Iraq grab you?'

'Impossible.' Jennings' response was automatic. 'Your informant is mistaken.'

'*How the hell—?*'

'Mr Tate,' Jennings cut in sharply. 'I'd be grateful if you

would inform me when you find this Archer person. As to the events of yesterday, they're no longer part of your brief. Call me the moment you have a location.' He rang off without saying goodbye.

TWENTY-FOUR

'Cheeky bugger,' Harry growled, drawing a look of disapproval from an elderly lady who had just entered the café.

Rik was grinning in wry triumph. 'He doesn't want to hear what we found crawling about under the stone, does he? Probably because he already knows.'

'If he does, he knows more than we do.' In spite of all the evidence of bodies and documents, they were no further forward in their knowledge of Silverman's true background. The guards' passports were unlisted in any of the databases Rik had accessed, and the mobile number was a pay-as-you-go disposable with no address and no previous call record. Whatever real history the two dead men had possessed was now a closed book.

Harry got to his feet and nodded towards the building across the road. 'Come on, Boy Wonder. You've got work to do.'

By the time they pushed through the glass doors in the Corpos building, he had banished all thoughts of Jennings from his mind. The foyer was peppered with posters of muscular men and women engaging happily with complicated equipment, and the decor was a mixture of fancy Greek tiles, thick carpets and tinkling fountains, with soft mood-music issuing from speakers. A corridor ran off to the left, with an arrow pointing to a studio, sauna, fitness rooms and administration. Unlike Park's Gym, a subtle smell of air-freshener and soap hung in the air, along with the merest hint of perfume.

The receptionist looked up and gave them a flash of white teeth. 'Hello, gentlemen. Welcome to Corpos.'

Harry nudged Rik forward and veered off to study a notice board.

'Hello . . . Mandy.' Rik gave her his best boyish grin and

eyed the name badge on her chest. She followed his eyes and almost blushed. 'I wonder if you can help?' His tone made it perfectly clear that she could, and even if she couldn't, it would be fun finding out.

Harry wasn't sure what Rik's precise game plan was, nor did he need to hear the lurid details. Just as long as they got the information they needed: confirmation that Joanne Archer was a member and, if possible, her current address.

Mandy seemed to lose some of her anticipation as Rik spoke, her face taking on a look of concern. Moments later, she was clicking away down the corridor on high heels, her bottom twitching fetchingly under her white coat. They watched her go, heads tilted in admiration. If she'd had eyelashes painted on her rear, Harry decided, they'd both have been winked to death.

He had already checked for security cameras and found none. The moment Mandy was out of sight, he signalled for Rik to slip behind the desk to check the monitor. From a brief glance, it appeared to be a standard client registration screen with spaces for the insertion of personal details.

'You didn't promise her anything, did you?' he said, as Rik typed Archer's name into the query screen. The machine clicked and built into a frenzied hum. He hoped it was a fast program.

'Why? You jealous?' Rik flashed him a smug look.

'Not really.' Harry moved to give himself a view of both the main entrance and the corridor. 'Just that Mandy looks the sort to expect seconds.'

'I asked for the name and address of the company's lawyers,' Rik explained, tapping his fingers impatiently. 'Said I'd slipped and fallen in the shower a couple of days ago, and needed details of her people so my people can contact their people.' He smiled proudly at his inventiveness. 'Places like this are terrified of lawsuits.'

'But you're not a member.'

'They won't know that,' Rik pointed out, 'until they check. And she didn't ask. I'm hoping we don't have to hang around long enough for it to get that far.'

They had discussed tactics earlier. They needed to gain access to the club's customer records, and Rik had volunteered to handle this without disclosing the specifics. He'd made whatever he'd got in mind sound fiendishly cunning, but to Harry, this solution was like Indiana Jones flashing a silk handkerchief instead of his trademark bullwhip.

'That's it?' he muttered, unimpressed. 'You slipped in the shower? I thought you'd come up with something . . . I don't know . . .'

'What?'

'Bold. Dazzling, even.'

The computer fan stopped. In its place they heard a familiar clicking of heels along the tiled corridor. Mandy was on her way back. But they could also hear the low murmur of a male voice and the sound of heavier footsteps. She was bringing reinforcements.

Rik was staring at the screen as if willing it to do something. Harry figured they had thirty seconds at most, probably less. He started forward, ready to intercept the receptionist and whoever she was bringing with her. If they got no luck here, they'd have to think of something else.

He glanced towards Rik just as the screen flickered and revealed a new template.

'Got it. *Go!*' Rik hissed, signalling for Harry to lead the way and hitting the BACK button to return it to its original place. They made it to the street just as Mandy turned the corner.

'Archer's got a place near here,' Rik told him. 'She's obviously keeping up her fitness routine.'

Harry nodded. Old habits died hard. 'You've got all that from one quick look?' He was impressed.

'Look at screens all day and it gets to be second nature.'

Back at the car they consulted an *A–Z*. The address was a short distance away, off Battersea Park Road.

Hughie had been right after all.

The address was a small flat above a letting agency, on a busy parade of shops. Access was by a flight of open metal stairs from a service yard at the rear.

They couldn't tell if anyone was in, and the approach up the stairs was too open to risk going near. If Archer's involvement with Silverman was anything less than innocent, two men showing up on her doorstep might be enough to set her running again. And next time they might not find her so easily.

Rik found a parking space a hundred yards away from the

flat, giving them a clear view of the stairway. Harry left him on watch and walked a slow circuit of the block, picking up a feel for the area and the flow of people. The pavements were reasonably busy, but with only one way in, they stood a good chance of spotting Archer entering or leaving. If they missed her, with daylight dropping fast, any lights going on inside would make their task easier.

After two more circuits and with no evidence of Archer being at home, Harry rang Jennings and gave him the address. He did this with reluctance; their job wasn't finished yet and he hated the idea of being cut out too early. Neither did he enjoy giving a blow-by-blow commentary of their activities.

'There's no sign of Archer,' he informed the lawyer. 'You want us to go in and check she's there?'

'No,' said Jennings. 'That's not necessary. What's the location like?'

'Could be quieter.' Harry described the layout. 'It's not going to improve until the shops shut. There are pedestrians all over.'

'Leave it,' Jennings told him. 'Your part is over. Payment will be made as usual.'

It wasn't the response Harry had expected. *Your part is over?* What was that supposed to mean? 'Is there a problem?' he queried. 'We're right here, we might as well stay on it until we eyeball her.'

'It's not necessary.' Jennings sounded calm but firm. 'Others will take over from you.'

Others?

'Fine,' said Harry. 'You're paying the bill.' He switched off the phone. 'Orders are to bug out. We're done.'

Rik scowled. 'We haven't confirmed her presence yet.'

'No need. He wants us out of here. We get paid anyway.'

Rik shrugged and started the car, heading north towards Battersea Bridge. Traffic was slow, and there was little to do but concentrate on the bumper in front of them and the occasional set of traffic lights; neither man spoke, both feeling a sense of anti-climax after the long trail they had followed.

As they reached Chelsea on the northern side of the river, Harry swore at length.

'Turn round.'

'What?' Rik stared at him.

'Go back. This is a mistake. It's not finished.'

Rik smiled, sensing some action. 'Now you're talking.' He made a fast U-turn, earning a volley of horns and flashing lights from other drivers, and stepped on the gas.

'I don't like leaving it like this,' said Harry. 'I want to see what this Joanne Archer looks like. You OK with this?'

'Of course.' Rik frowned. 'We're at a disadvantage, though, aren't we, with all this shooting?'

Harry gave it some thought. He had placed a briefcase in the back of the car earlier, but without mentioning what it contained. And so far Rik hadn't asked. 'We don't know if she's armed, and there's no sign she had anything to do with killing the two men at South Acres. Of course, if I'm wrong,' he added with dark humour, 'and she shoots you, I apologize in advance.'

'Cheers. And Jennings? He's going to be really fussed when he finds out we came back.'

'We'll let him complain to our union.'

It took half an hour to fight their way back through growing traffic to Archer's flat. By the time they arrived, most of the surrounding shops were closing and pedestrian traffic had reduced dramatically. Harry paused long enough to delve in the briefcase, then followed Rik up the metal stairs. Once at the top they were in full view of a narrow window alongside the door. There was still no sign of a light.

Harry moved ahead and reached for the door. Before he could knock, however, it swung open of its own accord.

TWENTY-FIVE

The Yale lock looked new, Harry noted. Shiny with no scratches or tarnish. But the wood where the latch should have fitted into the frame had been torn away, revealing a strip of yellow wood beneath the paint.

He used his knuckles to push the door further back. It revealed more damage to the inside of the frame and a scattering of wood slivers on the floor of the hallway.

There was no sound from inside.

They stepped over the debris into a short, carpeted hallway. The atmosphere had a dead, sad feel, as if the soul of the place had fled the scene, leaving just the empty shell. No memories, no presence, no trace of past warmth . . . and no future.

Harry used his elbow to switch on the hall light. It didn't help much, merely highlighting the worn drabness of the decor. Bedsit land in the flesh, he thought dourly, temporary accommodation for the disconnected.

The first door to the left was a bathroom with bath, sink and toilet. It was empty save for a few items of washing drying on a line and a faint smell of soap and perfume. The sink was half full of soapy water with a pale scum on the surface. Harry dipped his finger in; it was faintly warm. In the bath, a pair of tights lay coiled like a snake's skin, and one of the taps was dripping into a brown stain on the enamel with a hollow, plunking sound. A crust of dried soap sat amid a dusting of talcum powder around the rim. The cabinet above the sink was empty save for a plastic razor.

The kitchen was small and smelled of a spicy takeaway and grease. Other than a layer of dust, it looked little used. Two drawers revealed some basic cutlery and plastic bin liners, and a waste-bin contained a jumble of plain polystyrene cartons and foil lids stained with dark sauce. Whoever lived here didn't seem to be much of a cook.

'*Harry.*' Rik was standing just inside a doorway along the hall, looking down at the floor.

Harry joined him and peered past his shoulder.

It was a bedroom. A young woman was lying on the carpet, one hand pressed to her stomach. She was face down, as if she'd been trying to hide among the worn, dusty pile. She wore a plain jumper and black jeans, and had short, cropped hair and simple stud earrings. A pair of spectacles and one shoe were lying nearby. The heel of the shoe was broken, the nails protruding like a rat's teeth. She was clutching a hand towel in her other hand.

Harry bent to check her pulse while Rik moved away to check the rest of the flat.

The flesh was warm and damp, but there was no flicker of life. A worm of blood lay on the back of the woman's neck, just beneath the hairline, which was damp. Closer inspection revealed an area of scorched skin just below her ear, and a dark, puckered hole. Up close, he smelled the aroma of burned flesh and gunshot residue. By the way the fingers of her hand were twisted into the clothing of her stomach, she'd probably been hit in the middle first, doubling her over, placing her in line for the killer shot from above.

Harry felt a deep sense of outrage. Whoever had done this had acted with cold deliberation.

'Not long happened.' He wasn't sure if Rik had heard, and realized he'd spoken without intending to. The killer couldn't be far away, he reflected. They might even have passed him in the street. Another near miss, like the others. It was becoming a nasty habit.

He stood back, automatically trying to read what had happened. Without a full forensic examination it was all guess-work, but he had to try. Archer looked as if she had been surprised in the bathroom and had tried to get away. But the killer had caught her, her shoe heel breaking in the process. She clearly hadn't had time to put up a fight. The end had been brutal and quick.

He walked through to the living room. Decorated in faded yellows and sparsely furnished with a brown leatherette settee, two hard-backed chairs and a table, it was more functional than homely.

Rik was emptying a travel bag sitting on top of a neatly folded blanket on the settee. He took out a jumble of casual clothing: jeans, tights, underwear, trainers and T-shirts, a couple of cheap paperbacks and some cash in a purse. No documents, however; nothing to confirm the dead woman's identity.

The rest of the flat proved just as featureless. Nothing stood out. But then, Archer had hardly been here five minutes; there was no paperwork, no receipts or bills, none of the detritus of anything resembling an established life.

It was only when Harry returned to check the top of the wardrobe in the bedroom that he turned up anything signifi-cant. He found a brown jiffy bag containing a photograph in a plain black wooden frame. It was the sort issued by official photographers. The photo showed a group of men and two women in army camouflage uniform. They were smiling self-consciously at the camera, the way comrades and friends do, caught in a moment of time and out of context.

One of them was now lying on the floor nearby, a bullet hole in the back of her head.

Harry compared faces, identifying Archer in the photo. She looked confident and easygoing, her head cocked slightly to one side as if she'd been caught momentarily off guard. Not for the first time, Harry thought grimly. But certainly the last.

Rik joined him and peered over his shoulder. 'Regimental Provosts,' he said, pointing to a badge worn by both women and two of the men. 'Tough bunch.' He looked down at the body. 'She was an army cop.'

Harry nodded. At least he now knew where the photo frame from the flat in north London had gone. She'd carried it with her. Though it was so mundane, she must have valued it. 'Park thought she'd been trained to handle herself.'

He walked through to the kitchen, where a pair of faded yellow Marigolds hung over the edge of the sink. They were small but with a bit of pulling, fitted well enough. While Rik went to keep an eye on the back stairs, Harry carried out a more thorough search of the place, starting in the bedroom. He found a few neatly folded clothes in a chest of drawers, some shoes in the wardrobe, but not much else.

It was the same with the bed and bedside cabinet; nothing helpful, merely items for everyday living. Through to the kitchen, which showed two empty wine bottles, a mug and a glass, all wet. Maybe Joanne Archer had been a drinker, in spite of the exercise regime. He checked the cupboards, drawers and air vents. There weren't many places to look and it was soon clear that whoever had killed her must have cleaned out anything that might have helped fill in her background.

'Nobody's life is this empty,' he muttered, sensing Rik coming back to see how he was progressing. 'Even after a few days you pick up some rubbish.' He checked the small waste-bin in the bedroom. 'Not even a tissue. It's unnatural. Either the killer had help to clean up, or . . .'

'Or what?'

'Or Archer had already sanitized the place as a matter of routine.'

'Makes sense. No clues, no trail. Just like her place in Finchley.' Rik frowned. 'Heck of a way to live, though. Who the hell is this woman?'

Harry shook his head. The choice was stark, either way. It

would take a professional killer to leave the area so empty of clues, and only a person living an extremely cautious life to have so little to show for her presence.

He returned to the bedroom and studied the body. He checked the fingernails and knuckles, found them clean and unblemished.

'I don't get it,' he muttered. 'If Archer was such a hotshot in the gym, and a regimental cop, why didn't she put up more of a fight? She should at least have got one good shot at the bastard who did this.'

'Unless she knew him.'

'I suppose.'

Then Rik said softly, 'Harry.'

Harry looked up. Rik was staring past him towards the bedroom door.

When he turned his head, he found himself looking down the barrel of a semi-automatic pistol.

TWENTY-SIX

'Who the hell are you two?' The pistol was held unwaveringly at shoulder height. Behind it stood a young woman wearing a bomber jacket and jeans, with the nylon straps of a rucksack over each shoulder. She looked fit and toned, with cropped, dyed-blonde hair and nice skin. Her mouth was tight with tension and her gaze said both men would be in trouble if they made a wrong move.

She glanced down at the dead woman, then up at the two men. There was no sign of emotion and the pistol didn't move.

Harry broke the tension. 'I'm Harry, he's Rik. We didn't do this.' He wasn't sure why he thought she would believe him. 'Who are you?'

The woman ignored him and moved sideways, gesturing with her free hand. 'The bed. Sit. Both of you. Hands away from your bodies.' Her voice brooked no argument.

'Hang on a sec—' Rik began to protest, but she cut him short.

'I said, *sit*.'

Harry sat down and motioned Rik to do the same. From the way in which the woman had positioned herself, she was just beyond their reach and it was obvious that if they made a move towards her, they wouldn't get more than a few inches.

'Unusual weapon,' Harry commented, nodding at the gun, although he thought the only unusual feature about it was that she had it and they didn't. It looked workmanlike; anonymous, small calibre, no markings and disposable. 'You got a licence for it?'

She barely gave him a glance and looked disturbingly at ease with the gun. Distracting her evidently wasn't on the cards.

'Why are you here?' she asked. She moved to the chest of drawers and rested her gun on it, the barrel still pointing between the two men. Harry kept very still. He knew that resting her arm was not a sign of weakness. Guns are heavy pieces of equipment designed to stand fierce pressures and handling. But the weight can play havoc with the wrists and arm muscles, whether held by a man or a woman.

'We were looking for her,' Rik explained, nodding towards the body. 'Joanne Archer,' Harry let him speak. Since the woman had the upper hand and neither of them was about to get within six feet of her without being popped, there was little point in using delaying tactics. 'We thought she might be in some sort of trouble,' Rik added. 'Looks like we were right.'

'How do you know Joanne Archer?' The question came back instinctively, but with a momentary hesitation in uttering the name.

'We don't,' said Harry, deliberately drawing her eyes towards him. He smiled, aiming to get her to relax. 'We're paid to find people. It's what we do.'

'Paid? By who?'

Neither of them replied. Instead, Harry said quietly, 'That's not her on the floor, is it?'

He was holding the photo frame and looking down at the faces, his finger on one of the women. Although the cap and brown hair was enough to fudge the picture slightly and throw them off, it was now obvious that the woman he was looking at wasn't the one lying here.

She was actually standing right in front of them.

'She was staying with me overnight.' The comment was matter-of-fact. 'Her name was Cath Barbour; we were in the same unit. She just got out.'

'What kind of trouble are you in, Miss Archer?' queried Harry.

She blinked rapidly, then surprised both men by kneeling down by the body. If she saw either of them as a threat, she no longer seemed to care.

'It would help if you put the gun away,' Harry suggested. He was careful not to move, however; this woman was too full of surprises and might have a miniature Uzi tucked inside her bra.

'I heard you talking,' she said vaguely. She touched her fingers to the dead woman's face, then sat back on her heels. 'What are you – army?' Her voice was dull, lifeless.

'Used to be,' said Harry. He left it at that. She wouldn't be impressed by their background in the security services.

'Recently?'

'No. Not recently.'

'Then you won't be able to help.' Her voice was soft, almost regretful, as if they were not what she had been hoping for. 'You won't be used to this.'

'Death, you mean?' Harry gave a shrug when she looked up at him. 'Actually, we're more accustomed to it than you might think.'

'How?'

He told her briefly about the past couple of days, how death seemed to be following them around; about Silverman and the events at South Acres, and the trail they had followed to this flat. Something told him she wasn't about to go screaming to the police about Param and Matuq, and she clearly had a connection of sorts to Silverman, which made her a person of interest.

She took it in without comment, then stood up. She studied the gun as if making a decision and clicked on the safety, switching her gaze squarely back to the two men. 'I don't see how any of this concerns me. I don't know anyone called Silverman and I've no idea how he came to have my number or –' she looked down at the body of her friend – 'why anyone would kill Cath. She was just passing through . . . she didn't have anything to steal, either. It's . . . crazy.'

Harry studied her face. There was a flat quality to her voice which made her sound robotic. Yet she seemed almost too controlled, given the circumstances. Unless she had an unusually low panic threshold. Whoever or whatever she was, unusual seemed a fair description.

'So why are you here?' he asked, changing the direction of the conversation. 'You've got a flat in north London, you train there, you have friends . . . you've got a routine. When you're not travelling, that is.' He gestured around them. 'Why this place?'

Archer didn't reply. Her attention seemed to have drifted off somewhere far away.

'We might be able to help,' Rik offered gently. But there was still no reaction.

'I'm going to reach into my pocket,' Harry told her. 'There's something I want you to look at. You OK with that?' She didn't respond. 'Joanne?'

The sound of her name seemed to bring her back. She nodded assent, watching warily as Harry reached inside his jacket and pulled out the shot of Samuel Silverman from the airport camera. He flipped it the right way up and handed it to her. 'This is the man we're following. The one who had your phone number.'

Neither of them knew quite what to expect. Logic suggested that there was little likelihood that Joanne Archer had ever set eyes on Silverman before. The fact that he had been in possession of her phone number and initials might have been one of those inexplicable convergences of detail that sometimes pops up, in the same way that siblings who have never met occasionally discover a brother or sister living in the next street, unknown and unknowing neighbours for decades.

But Archer's reaction on seeing the face in the photograph took them both by surprise. First came a look of intense shock, then her knees buckled and almost gave way, her face draining of colour. She stared at each man in turn, her lips working soundlessly.

'This can't be,' she whispered finally, shaking her head. 'He's dead. He was blown to pieces three weeks ago!'

TWENTY-SEVEN

A car started with a tinny rattle, and a woman's laughter floated up from the street, a rising trill ending on a high note. It was followed by a volley of goodbyes and the slamming of car doors. From further away came a brief squeal of car tyres and a man shouting an obscenity. A car horn, voices, a burst of music growing louder, then fading as it went by, a roller shutter slamming down. Normal street sounds.

Harry pulled his attention away from Joanne Archer and what she had just said. He cocked his head and eyed Rik, then stood up and left the room, ignoring the gun. He went through to the front window and checked the outside. Half the pavement was visible beyond the overhanging roof above the shops, the kerb lined with cars. Vehicle and shop lights splashed the faces of the few pedestrians still going about their business. He walked down the hallway and peered through the back door at the metal stairs and the yard below. All clear. Yet he felt a prickle of anxiety. Staying here made them vulnerable. Exposed.

He returned to the bedroom, where Archer and Rik were waiting in silence.

'We have to go,' he announced. 'Now.'

They both looked round at the urgency in his voice.

'Trouble?' Rik asked.

'Not sure. But staying here can't be good.' Harry looked at Joanne, who was still holding the gun. 'Did you say your friend was just passing through?'

'Yes. She rang my mobile yesterday. She needed a place to crash for a night. She was on her way up north to see her family. I couldn't exactly turn her away, so I said she could stay. I gave her directions and she arrived yesterday evening.' She gave a bitter smile. 'She brought some wine and we gave it a hammering, talking over old times. We hadn't seen each other for over a year.'

'And you were the first to leave this morning?'

'She said she wanted to be on her way by ten, but she was feeling hungover, so I went out; I had things to do which took me longer than I expected. She must have decided to wait for me to come back and . . .' Her voice trailed off as she thought about what had happened.

'She was unlucky,' said Harry. 'Wrong place, wrong time.'

Joanne flinched at the harshness in his voice. 'What do you mean?'

'Whoever killed her got the wrong person. The killer came in, saw her and did what he was hired to do. You and she were about the same height, weight and colouring. If she was in the bathroom when he kicked the door in, and holding the towel to her face, he wouldn't have noticed the difference until it was too late. He probably didn't expect to find anyone else here but you. Then he sanitized the place to delay identification of the body.'

She stared at him as the implication sank in. 'He's been watching me.' For some reason, she didn't sound surprised.

'Bet on it. And he'll probably be back when he finds out he got the wrong woman.' Harry pointed at the gun. 'Put that thing out of sight but keep it handy. We have to go.'

'What about my things?' she protested. 'And the photo – I'm not leaving it.'

He pushed it at her. 'Take this, leave the rest. You can always buy more clothes.'

He made for the back door, leaving the other two to follow. They passed a pink gym bag in the hallway.

'Leave it,' said Harry, as she bent to pick it up. 'A colour like that is a beacon. It got you noticed once already.' He softened his tone. 'Your gym buddy, Hughie, spotted you with it the other day.'

As she stepped outside, Rik hung back and asked quietly, 'What's the rush?'

'Jennings is sending another team. After Matuq and Param, do you want to be here when they arrive?'

Rik pulled a face and followed Joanne outside without another word.

They walked back to the car with Joanne sandwiched between them, each checking vehicles parked at the kerb and eyeing pedestrians nearby. The clatter of a motorbike made Harry jumpy, the familiar sound too fresh from the night before.

They climbed in and Rik headed north, while Harry kept an eye on the surrounding traffic.

He felt pretty sure they weren't being followed, but his instincts had been wrong before and he didn't want to take chances. Ever since the prickly feeling he'd had on the way to South Acres, he'd been fighting a rising sense of paranoia, and now found himself constantly checking their tail.

It took them an hour to reach Rik's flat. Harry got Rik to change direction twice and double back on their route to throw off any possible pursuers. Joanne said little, even when addressed directly, but stared listlessly out at the traffic. Whatever vitality she had possessed on first entering her flat had drained away, and Harry guessed she was settling into a state of shock.

'Shouldn't we tell the police?' she muttered at one point, as a patrol car sped by in the opposite direction. But the question lacked conviction. When nobody replied, she shrugged and huddled deeper into the corner. The gun, they noticed, never strayed from her hand.

Back at the flat, Rik made coffee and poured three brandies, while Joanne excused herself and went to the bathroom. She walked as if she was at the very limit of her resources, shoulders slumped in an attitude of defeat.

'She needs some kip,' Rik commented. 'Or a shot of something.'

Harry agreed. But the practical side of his nature told him they needed to get her to talk first. If they left it too long, they might never find out what was going on and why somebody was trying to kill her. 'I'd like to hear what she has to say first.'

Rik gestured towards the outside. 'I'll just run a check outside. You OK to talk to her?'

'Of course.'

Rik hesitated. 'The friend staying overnight bit; did you buy that? It sounded a bit convenient to me.'

'Who for? The friend's dead.'

'Yeah, but...' Rik pulled a face. 'It sounds a bit . . . I don't know – unreal. If she's so good at hiding, how come she let some ex-army buddy track her down and get so close?'

Harry had no answer to that. People made mistakes all the time, no matter how careful they were. He shrugged and Rik left to go on his scouting tour.

Harry turned to face Joanne as she entered the room, indicating the coffee and brandy. 'We'll eat when Rik gets back. He's gone to check the bushes.'

She nodded in understanding, and Harry reflected that she was a very unusual young woman. So far she appeared to be going along with what they were trying to do without argument, and the fact that she hadn't gone to pieces after finding her friend's body spoke volumes about her strength of character. Being ex-army might have been part of the answer, but he felt certain there was more to it. He had known female MI5 officers like her, and one from MI6, and they had all possessed a similar steely quality of self-control.

As if to confirm it, she took her gun from the rucksack and began to strip it down and clean it using a small tube of oil and a cloth pad. She seemed to relax slightly as she worked, as if the routine offered some solace or distraction.

Harry watched her for a few moments, then said, 'Tell me about him – the dead man.'

She put down the cloth and sipped at her brandy, grimacing as it went down. 'You haven't told me who you are, yet. How do I know I can really trust you?'

'You don't. But if we're right about what happened to your friend, I'd say we're the only people you can rely on. Besides, if we'd wanted to hurt you, don't you think we'd have done it by now?'

The look she gave him was full of scorn, but she didn't argue. Instead, she reassembled the gun with expert economy, her eyes on him all the time as she snapped each component back into place. As a display of expertise, he'd never seen better. Then she said, 'You haven't said anything about your backgrounds. But I can see you're professionals. Where's that from?'

'MI5,' he replied, adding, 'Not any longer, though. We resigned. Went private.'

She nodded. For a moment there had been a flicker of something in her face. It might have been scepticism or disapproval, but it was gone just as quickly. 'Did you do Iraq?'

'For a while. I got bored with being a target and decided to go into a quieter line of work. It pays better and people shoot less. Did do, anyway.'

She looked at him over her coffee. 'Did you go to Baghdad?'

'Flew in but didn't stay long.'

'Lucky you. You'll have seen enough bodies, then.'

He nodded. 'There and Kosovo. Different conflict, same mess.'

'Was that with the army?'

'Yes.' He sipped his brandy sparingly, aware that he had to keep a clear head. 'Now we specialize in finding people. People who've disappeared.'

'I thought the police and the Sally Army did that.'

'Not the kind we look for.'

'Oh?'

'The criminal, the confused, the desperate . . . you name it.'

Joanne's lip curled slightly. 'You're bounty hunters. Who do you work for?'

'Whoever pays us.' Harry ignored the disdain. 'Everybody works for someone; it doesn't lessen the value just because we chase runaways.' She didn't say anything so he switched tack. 'What about your background? What exactly do you do? Only, don't tell me what you told McCulloch; you don't look like any PA I ever came across.'

She thought about it for several seconds, then said, 'I work in deep-cover Close Protection.'

TWENTY-EIGHT

The words dropped into the room with the impact of a grenade, and Harry struggled to keep his expression blank. If she was telling the truth, it explained a great deal about her behaviour, lifestyle and obvious air of resilience. 'Private or army?'

'I started in the army. Northern Ireland, Germany, Iraq – even Afghanistan for a while – and all the boring places in between. I did all the courses and a few more, got good reports and they asked me to go on the Regimental Provost course. I came out of that second in my class, which pissed off a few of the blokes, but that didn't bother me. Then six months ago, in a pub in Germany, I was approached by a man and we got talking. I was single and bored and he looked like he wanted company. We talked, he told me almost nothing about himself but asked lots of questions. After a while I realized I was being interviewed.' She shook her head, 'Right there in the middle of a pub, surrounded by other squaddies. Not that they could hear what we were talking about, but it was surreal.'

'He'd followed you.'

'Yes.'

'What did he ask?'

'Background stuff to begin with – where I came from, whether I had any family, friends and so on. Like he was interested in me. Then he began asking weird stuff, like whether I enjoyed live firing, what sort of security training I'd done, if I'd ever considered joining Special Forces. It was then I decided he must be recruiting for something a bit unusual, like 14 Company or maybe undercover with the RMP. I thought it was odd doing it like that, but for all I knew then, that's how it always works.'

'What did you say?'

She shrugged. 'To be honest, I was intrigued and flattered. After years of doing shit jobs and slogging about at everyone's beck and call, I wanted something better. Why not? I had no family or responsibilities, nothing to tie me down – it sounded exciting. I said yes.'

'Who was he?' Harry asked, 'this recruiter?'

'He called himself Douglas, but I doubt it was his real name. It's not, is it, with people like that?' She stood up. 'Excuse me – I need to . . .' She disappeared into the bathroom, passing Rik standing by the door. He shook his head to indicate all was quiet outside.

'You hear any of that?' Harry asked.

'A bit. Sounds like someone was talent spotting.' He picked up his brandy and retreated to the back of the room. 'I'll listen in.'

Joanne returned and resumed her seat, ignoring Rik's presence. She looked pale but composed. Harry wondered if talking was helping her relax. 'What made you think his name was false?'

'It didn't suit him. I don't know why. Not that it mattered, because at the end of the evening, he gave me a card with a number on it and passed me up the line. This time it was on base, and I was interviewed formally by two men in suits.

One was obviously military – he had that look, you know?
Like the clothes weren't his usual kit. The following week, I
signed a batch of papers, handed in my gear to the stores and
returned to England, where I spent four weeks being put
through a meat grinder.'

'Go on.'

'It was CP work, mostly – lots of it. Hours of live firing,
defensive driving, unarmed combat, knife work . . . basically
learning more ways to overcome an attacker than I knew
existed. There were night exercises, computer and comms
classes, more close-quarter weapons training, covert surveillance and bugging techniques, anti-device training, emergency
evacuation exercises . . . it felt endless.' She almost smiled.
'They even threw in a basic medic's course. I nearly fainted
when they shot a pig for us to practise on. But it was a hell
of a buzz after all the boring stuff I'd been doing. I was the
only girl on the course, too; great for the ego. Not that I was
allowed to fraternize with the men. We weren't told each
other's names and they chucked one bloke off the course for
asking. We were just numbers, an army of robots. God knows
what the others were being trained for.'

'Did they all last the course?'

'No. There were RTUs – Returned to Unit – all the way
through. Some of the guys right near the end must have been
gutted. I never found out why they were dropped and we
weren't encouraged to ask.'

'What next?'

'They sent me on a total-immersion language course at a
place in Beaconsfield. I joined the army to get away from
classrooms, and here I was back in one for fourteen-hour days,
non-stop.'

'What language?'

'Arabic. It went on day and night. It was torture. And I had
to learn how to prepare basic Iraqi food. That wasn't too bad,
though.'

Harry was surprised at the depth and detail of her training.
Whoever had planned it hadn't left much out. It still didn't
explain why she was connected with the man named Silverman,
but the mention of Arabic was a clue. He had a feeling that
it was bringing them closer to an answer.

'Where did they send you?' he asked.

'Baghdad.' She gave a half-smile. 'If I'd known that at the start, I'd have told them to shove it. But by then it was too late; I was so far in I didn't have the guts to back out.' She poured the remainder of her brandy into the coffee and took a sip. 'The operation was code-named Pamper. Someone's sick idea of a joke, probably. They inserted me into the area among a bunch of aid workers, then split me off and took me to a house on the outskirts of the city. I was assigned a handler – a guy named Gordon Humphries. He was about fifty-five and looked like he'd spent ten years on the bottle. But he was as tough as boots and knew more about covert ops than I'll ever learn. He was there to keep an eye on me and brief me about what I had to do. He was quite sweet, but hard-nosed, you know?'

'So what did you have to do?' Harry thought he could guess but he wanted to hear what she had to say. All that training had to have been for something truly special; the government wouldn't waste time, money and talent unless it was for something of crucial importance.

'I had to pose as personal assistant to a man named Subhi Rafa'i. He was a former cleric and something of a big cheese among the locals. I wasn't told much about him, only that I had to be with him twenty-four-seven, living in his house or going wherever he went. He'd had a western secretary for years – a Swiss woman named Siggert – but she'd just retired with a medical condition. At least, that's what they told me.'

'You didn't believe them?'

'It was Rafa'i who didn't. He said that one minute she was there and fine, the next she'd gone. But it was probably for the best because she was getting on. I just slid into her place and kept my head down.'

'Is Rafa'i the man in the photo?'

'Yes. He was a nice man. I liked him. I still can't believe he's alive. Are you sure he wasn't killed?'

'We'll get to that. What was your brief?'

'As far as anyone was concerned, I was his PA. He'd had Frau Siggert working for him before, and I was her replacement. It sounds bizarre, me being a westerner and a woman, but nobody locally seemed to think it was unusual. And that's what I did day to day; I handled his correspondence, ran his office, made sure he had what he needed. Rafa'i did a lot of lecturing at seminaries and university campuses, and he also had some business interests. He needed someone who could organize it all.'

'And you could do that?'

'Yes. It was part of the Beaconsfield course. When I wasn't learning Arabic I was picking up computer and office admin skills. That was boring.'

'But it wasn't your real job.'

She took a deep breath and shook her head. 'No. Rafa'i had a team of bodyguards, all local men who'd been trained by the Coalition forces. He was important, you see. Some said vital. He had influence with lots of leaders across the country. Because he was a former cleric, he was listened to and respected by people across the different factions. That made him valued . . . and therefore dangerous.'

'What was he?'

'Shi'ite. But he never trumpeted his origins. To him, Iraqi was Iraqi. It made him unique. There are people in the Coalition who believe that even with a properly elected and fully functional government in place, there will be a constant threat from extremist groups who'll try to overthrow them. And if the day ever comes when they succeed, there has to be someone around who can wield influence on the street to stop it all going shit-faced. It would have to be someone pretty special . . . what they called a Golden Solution.' She smiled thinly. 'A bloody saint is what they meant. That's where Rafa'i came in.'

'He's that highly regarded?'

'And some. I saw the reactions from people around him. They worshipped him.'

Harry looked cynical. 'Obviously not all of them. What about the bodyguards?'

'There were ten on constant rotation. He never travelled with less than six and they all lived in the compound around his house. It was a miniature fortress.' She looked down at her mug. 'They were all big and macho, so full of themselves it was laughable. Good at their jobs, though. They'd have had a fit if they'd ever found out what I was there for.'

'Which was?'

Joanne sighed. '"If all else fails" was how Gordon Humphries put it to me. He wasn't one for flowery words. I don't think he was happy with the situation, but I doubt there was much he could do about it. He had his job, I had mine.'

'What did that mean?' muttered Rik, speaking for the first time. '"If all else fails"'?

She gave him a level gaze. 'What it said. If all else failed and the security perimeter around Rafa'i was breached, he had to have a final backstop. That was me. I was his last line of defence.'

TWENTY-NINE

'It was quite clever, really,' she said softly. 'Any killer coming after Rafa'i wouldn't have given a woman a second look. Women out there aren't a threat – especially not a pen-pushing westerner.' She looked at them. 'The average Iraqi doesn't think much of female soldiers. Not that they knew my background, of course. It gave me a slight edge.'

Harry nodded. It was clever – but for Joanne, deadly. On a very basic level, the idea of it appalled him. She had been utterly alone, isolated by her situation and gender, not knowing where the first threat might come from. No matter how close Coalition forces had been, for all the good they could have done they might as well have been on the far side of the moon. 'It was a hell of a position to put you in. What was the plan if things did fall apart?'

'My orders were to get Rafa'i out of the house by any means possible and go underground until they could send in a patrol to lift us out. I was expected to fight my way out if necessary, although nobody put it in so many words. I figured all that special training must have been for something.' She shook her head resignedly. 'They were out of their minds, of course; I realized that the moment I arrived in the area. Apart from an open square on one side, the area around the house was a rabbit warren. Tight streets, packed with houses and barely wide enough for a donkey, let alone a car. We wouldn't have made it two blocks without being clocked and stopped.'

'What went wrong?'

'Part of the arrangement was that I had to meet Humphries,

my handler, every week for a briefing. It increased the danger
to us both, but they insisted it was necessary. I'd tell him
whatever I could about the people around Rafa'i and hand
over any other information I'd gathered.'

'Wait . . . what other information? You were spying as well?'

'That was part of it, yes. I was given some electronic equipment to take in with me, so I could listen in on meetings held
in the compound. I didn't like it; I thought it was too risky.
But they insisted it was necessary to protect Rafa'i from the
elements around him.'

'Such as?'

'They said he was under constant pressure from extremist
factions who wanted to gain influence with the Coalition. They
were nothing more than cowboys looking for a fight. They
were also riddled with distrust and rivalry, and it was vital to
weed out who was who and isolate the troublemakers.'

'So Rafa'i was their way in.'

'Yes. Whenever I met Humphries, I'd hand over the discs
so he could take them back for analysis. They also gave me
a digital camera to record anyone new arriving at the
compound, and I had to give Gordon the memory cards. It
felt sneaky, but I had no option.'

'How did you communicate with him?'

'I had a sat phone, but the signal was unreliable. It was
probably because of all the Coalition radio traffic and the
jamming signals the US forces used in the area to block mobile
phones being used by insurgents. Otherwise I'd have used it
more often.'

'Why not use the same network as the US forces?'

'Humphries didn't trust it. I don't blame him – it wasn't
as safe as they claimed. The moment they began yakking at
the start of a patrol, you could almost see the insurgents
tracking their direction of travel.'

'Did you tell Rafa'i when you were going to these
meetings?'

'Yes. We had an agreement: he knew what to do if something went down and I wasn't there. He didn't like it but he
needed the Coalition's agreement and support.'

'Support?'

'They paid him.' She shrugged. 'It's the way things work
out there.'

'Did he realize he was being spied on by the Coalition?'

Joanne appeared unconcerned by the term. 'I'm not sure. He wasn't stupid; he knew what was expected of him and he must have suspected they'd go to any lengths to watch him and those around him. But he never said anything directly to me. He was very respectful to me all the time I was with him.'

'Was Humphries MI6?' Harry queried.

'No idea. He never said.'

'But your opinion?'

'I think so.'

Rik shifted, eager to hear what had happened. 'Go on.'

'One day I got a call to a meeting. It was unscheduled, but I'd been told to expect that in case of emergencies. Humphries left a message on my sat phone. He sounded stressed. I figured maybe something had gone wrong and he was getting ready to haul me out. We usually met at a private house to which I had a key. I arrived and waited, but he never showed. I gave it thirty minutes, which was way longer than I should have done, because standing orders were that if one of us failed to show, it was probably for a bloody mortal reason and the place might have been compromised. I tried calling him but the signal was crap. There was a radio in the house, so I turned it on while I was waiting. The local news station was going apeshit, screaming about betrayal and enemies of Allah. There had been a massive car bomb in the compound where Rafa'i lived. I'd heard an explosion, but hadn't been able to place it.' She looked at them and explained, 'With the jumble of narrow streets and the thickness of the walls, sound gets badly distorted. To me, it had just been another bomb.'

'We know. What happened?'

'The place was flattened. The reports said everyone was accounted for apart from three people: a bodyguard who was seen crossing the square just before it happened, another guard covering the front of the building when the bomb went off and . . . and me. I couldn't believe it. Why would anyone do that?'

'You told Rafa'i you were going to the meeting?'

'Yes. He was fine about it; he said he'd keep his head down until I returned.'

Harry thought back to the various news reports he'd read at the time, including the rehashed report in the newspaper near Param's hideout. It now seemed a long time ago and most of the coverage had slipped by without lodging in his consciousness. Like so much of what passed for daily life over there, it was one among so many bombings, each new outrage indistinguishable from the last. He figured Joanne's information was as reliable as any. 'You think the missing guards were behind it?'

'They had to be. They weren't supposed to leave the compound. It was a security tactic to avoid a suicide bomber walking in off the street and changing places with someone on the inside. But there were other ways of getting a bomb into the compound: one of the guards or house staff could have been bribed or a delivery could have included a bomb. Someone in the crowd said a delivery truck had stopped there just before the explosion, and with the two guards seen outside the compound at the time . . . it's the obvious connection.'

Harry nodded. 'Unless that's what everyone was supposed to think.'

She blinked. 'What do you mean?'

'It's an easy explanation, that's all. Blame the missing guards . . . divert attention away from someone else. It's all politics, is what I'm saying.' He continued looking at her, trying to read what was in her face and why she had reacted so defensively. The inevitable guilt, perhaps, of the protector having failed to protect? 'What did you do then?'

She took a moment to reply, then said, 'I was switching channels trying to pick up more news reports when I heard shouting from outside. I looked out and saw a four-wheel drive stuck at the top of the street. The turning was narrow and the driver had cut the corner too tight. He'd knocked over some pots outside a small shop. The owner was going mental and screaming at the driver. Lucky for me – I knew where it was headed.'

'It could have been a rescue patrol,' Harry pointed out.

She shook her head. 'No. If they were anything to do with Humphries, they'd have come in faster and no messing. These guys weren't familiar with the area. It was quiet, but it wasn't the sort of place to hang around unless you could pass as locals – and they didn't even try.'

'You saw them?'

'I caught a glimpse of one in the back when he dropped

the window for a second. He was a westerner, in civvies and a flak jacket like most of the contractors.' She shook her head. 'He could have been army, but . . . something about them being there wasn't right – I don't know what it was. Gordon Humphries always said to rely on my instincts and not trust anyone I didn't know. I know, they were westerners, so logic-ally I'd have been safe. But not every contractor out there is working for the good guys. Some are mercenaries, just out there to do a job and get paid. I decided not to find out; I bugged out the back and made my way back to the compound.'

'Risky thing to do.'

'Not really. I was dressed as a local and I'd been taught to walk like one, so I was able to filter back into the area and join in the crowd. It was mental. Rubble everywhere, body parts, paper like confetti . . . everyone was piling in, saying it was insurgents or the Americans or one faction or another. Some were saying it was the bodyguards who'd been paid to let it happen.' She shivered. 'You have to be in the crowd to experience it, but in a place like that, everyone has a theory, and it changes every five seconds. Gossip gets blown out of proportion, but if you can filter out the crackpot ravings, you sometimes get pretty close to what might be the truth. Somebody *always* knows something, from a brother or uncle or cousin with connections. It's that kind of society.'

'What did you do?'

'I still had my phone, so I ducked into cover and tried calling Humphries again. This time I got a cancelled signal, so I called a crash number he'd given me. It was for use only in absolute emergencies. He told me on the first day that calling that number meant everything was blown and that I'd get lifted out by a Special Forces combat patrol and flown to a safe place. The number was dead. That's when I got scared.'

Harry nodded, although he had a problem imagining Joanne Archer being scared of anything. 'What then?'

'I was too far from any of the Coalition bases to risk walking it. As a woman, I didn't dare try getting a lift out, and approaching one of the American patrols in the area was too dangerous – they're so jumpy about suicide bombers, they'd have shot me before I got anywhere near. But I was running out of time. I knew the people around Rafa'i would be wondering where I'd disappeared to, and that they might put two and two together and make a giant Coalition conspiracy – with me at the centre of it. Can you imagine? "Western PA goes AWOL prior to assassination."'

Rik whistled. 'It would play for weeks in the local press.'

'Right. If they'd found me, I'd have been torn to pieces. Anyway, I remembered Humphries telling me once that he was friendly with one of the Reuters correspondents – an American – so I went round to one of the hotels where they all hung out. Luckily for me he was in, so I asked if he knew where Humphries was. He was surprised I hadn't heard.'

They both waited.

'He said there'd been a random drive-by shooting. Gordon Humphries was dead.'

THIRTY

'How did you get out of the country?' It was nine at night and Rik had sent out for a takeaway curry. Hunger had hit them all, and they were sharing the food around the table, washed down with cans of lager.

'I had a stash of alternative papers for emergencies and an open flight voucher out. Gordon Humphries called it my wild card; it would trump every other ticket and get me a seat out on the pilot's lap if necessary. I joined a bunch of aid workers and walked on to the first available flight, no questions asked. It was easier than I thought. I got back here on the same papers and . . . and that's where I ran into a brick wall.'

Harry stopped chewing. 'How do you mean?'

Joanne put down her fork and rubbed her face. Her eyes were dark and her face had developed an unnatural pallor, as if the past few hours had filtered out all her natural skin tone. When she spoke, her voice showed signs of a tremor. 'I didn't know what to do. Can you believe that – after all that bloody training? I didn't even know who I could trust, and with Humphries gone, I was cut loose with no backup.' She brushed her eyes with the back of her hand. 'As if it wasn't bad enough losing my principal, I was also out of a job.'

'But they must have given you a fallback number in case

your lifeline to Humphries got compromised or you became isolated?'

'You'd think so, wouldn't you? Only they never told me anything like that. I had the emergency number in Baghdad and one back here in the UK. I figured that was the norm. I mean, I don't know any spooks, but how many numbers and fallbacks do they need? As soon as I landed here, I dialled the number, expecting to be called in for a debrief. It was dead. I tried for two days but got nothing. Crazy, isn't it? I don't think I've ever felt so alone.' She gave a bitter laugh. 'I sailed through Immigration without being stopped, then nothing. Some bloody security.' She stared towards the window. 'I think I've only just realized what I owe Gordon Humphries: he saved my life.'

'How do you figure that?' Rik queried.

'I'm convinced he got wind of something happening and got me out of there. We'd not long had a meeting, yet he called for one on the day of the explosion. I thought it was odd, but didn't argue.'

'Good thing you didn't,' said Harry.

Nobody spoke for a few minutes after that. Harry and Rik were digesting what Joanne had told them, and the young woman herself was sunk deep in her own thoughts. The two men knew the workings of officialdom fairly well, especially in the darker reaches of the security world, and what they had heard was not so wild they couldn't believe it, given their own experience of double-dealing in high places. And going by everything Joanne had told them, it was plain she had been employed under very murky circumstances. No wonder she didn't know who to trust.

'Why did you clear out of your flat in Finchley?' Rik asked.

'It didn't feel safe,' she replied. 'Nowhere did. Maybe I was being paranoid, but I didn't have a bloody clue what to do.' She gave a wry smile. 'Put a nine millimetre in my hand and drop me into a firefight, and I'll be fine. But this . . .' She shook her head. 'I began to think I was being watched, although I never saw anyone. In the end it got to be too much and I bugged out. I suppose I wasn't being too rational, was I?'

'Your instincts weren't too far off.' Harry told her about the two callers at her flat. 'They could have been from Humphries' department.'

'If they were,' she replied, 'they'd have left a contact number. It's been like I never existed.'

'They thought you'd been killed,' Rik pointed out. 'The few people who knew about you, anyway.'

'Well,' Harry murmured, 'they certainly know different now.'

Joanne looked puzzled. 'I don't see how. They've cut all links with me, so I can't contact anyone. How would they know I'm here?'

'Bureaucracy.' Rik was on familiar territory. 'You used the wild card to get out of Iraq. That would have shown up on a board somewhere, linking it to Six or the army. A number cruncher would have spotted it and backtracked it through the system. Easy.'

'There's also the body,' Harry added, 'or the lack of one. You were unaccounted for at the compound. It probably took a while but somebody must have finally cottoned on that you'd got out and were on the loose.' He took out the photo of Silverman again and slid it across the table, face up. 'Are you certain this is Rafa'i?'

She studied it closely for a while, then nodded. 'It's him. The mark on his face was caused by an explosion when he was a boy. He and a friend were playing with an old mortar flare they found in the desert. It went off and that was the result. I'm certain, yes.' She pushed the photo away as if wanting nothing more to do with it. 'He had a way of holding his head . . . sort of lopsided. It used to make people think he was listening very carefully to what they had to say.'

'Handy trick for a politician,' murmured Rik.

'OK.' Harry left the photo where it was. 'But that opens up a whole list of questions.'

'Does it?'

'Yes. One: if he's here in the UK, how did he avoid being killed in the explosion? Two: someone must have identified a body as his. Three: who planned the explosion and why?'

'Four,' Rik added darkly, 'how did he get away safely without you holding his hand?'

Joanne looked away. It was clear by the set of her mouth that she didn't want to think about it. 'I don't have any answers,' she said finally. 'Our default agreement was that he'd wait for me to return. Maybe he got spooked by something and slipped away by himself. You don't hold his kind

of position in Iraqi society without developing some instincts
for survival. We'd talked it over enough times, so he knew
what to do. As to who identified his body – that could have
been someone covering for him . . . or maybe wishful thinking
by somebody wanting to take his place.'

'You must have got to know him very well,' said Harry.

'I suppose. I was told to stay detached, but it wasn't that
simple.'

'Would he have followed your instructions on security
matters?'

She nodded. 'When we were alone, yes. I couldn't tell him
what to do with the others around, though. Apart from being
unacceptable because I was a woman, it would have blown
my cover. I had regular one-on-one review sessions with him
about what to do if there was an attack and the guards were
overcome. He thought it was all a bit unlikely, but he never
questioned it. It was for his benefit and survival, after all.'

'How was it,' said Harry carefully, 'that Rafa'i had your
mobile number? The one he wrote on the wall.'

She thought back, then said, 'He asked me for it one day.
We'd been talking about London and England, and he said if
he ever came to the UK, and I was back here, he'd give me
a call. I didn't think anything of it because it was never going
to happen. I mean, we were hardly in the same social circle,
right? Anyway, I gave it to him because I couldn't see any
reason not to. It was one of the few normal things to happen.
Everything else was . . . unreal.'

'Has he tried to call?' Harry queried.

'No. Why would he?'

'Because he clearly intended to. Why else write the number
down?'

'I can't answer that.'

'Maybe he was psyching himself up,' suggested Rik.
'Remember, he might have thought you were dead, too.'

'Or that you'd got out in the nick of time,' said Harry. When
Joanne looked sharply at him, he added, 'Think about it: your
trusted bodyguard leaves your side for an unscheduled meeting
and suddenly the world comes crashing in around your ears.
In a situation like that, what would you think?'

She didn't say anything.

'Would you recognize him among a crowd?'

'Of course. Why?'

'Because you might have to if you ever want to live a normal life.'

Her eyes grew wide at the thought, and the silence in the room lengthened. Then she said, 'How do you plan to make that happen?'

Harry stood up. 'There's only one way. You're going to help us find him.' He glanced across at Rik. 'I'll go out and check the street.'

Dog was surprised when he saw Harry Tate appear at the front of the building, and slid down in his seat. He was sure the man wouldn't see him, not from there. But he didn't want to take the chance of light flashing off his face and giving away his position.

He watched Tate stroll by on the other side and wondered what had made the former MI5 man come out here. Maybe he suspected someone was close by. He was beginning to think that Jennings had made a mistake using this man. He was already causing problems and plainly had highly developed instincts for survival. Dog was certain he'd done nothing to blow his cover, but the only sure-fire thing in his line of work was that fate had a talent for proving you wrong.

He switched his gaze to his wing mirrors and watched Tate stop and turn, his figure outlined by the garish neon of a store window further along the street. Then he began to retrace his steps, head turning to scan the shadows.

Dog gave a cold smile, recognizing the signs. *This one's a hunter. He knows what he's doing.* He slid his hand into his jacket pocket and touched the comforting shape of his knife. He drew it out and snicked open the blade, laying it alongside his leg.

Tate walked by, unaware of his presence. Dog felt the thrill of the chase skimming through his veins. He waited until Tate was thirty yards away, then opened the car door and slipped out, closing it again without a sound. The interior light stayed off; he'd removed the bulb earlier.

Dog hadn't stalked anyone this way in a long while, and enjoyed the renewed rush of excitement it brought him. It made him feel almost light-headed. The sounds and smells were heightened, the slight metallic tang of dampness was sharp in the air, and the distant rumble of late traffic carried an almost startling clarity. He breathed easily, padding along in his quarry's wake, his rubber-soled shoes leaving no sound for Tate to pick up on.

He ran his thumb along the top of the knife blade. This wasn't part of his brief, not yet. But sometimes opportunity presented itself, a once-and-only fruit for the picking that was too good to pass up. He picked up his pace, sticking close to the buildings, his breathing coming faster as he closed in on his target.

Then a car swung round the corner behind him and lit up the street with the glare of its headlights. *Shit!*

At the same moment, no doubt alerted by instinct, Tate began to turn his head.

Dog threw himself into the doorway of a charity shop, rolling into a ball. The car drove by, and Dog pulled his legs up to his chest, adopting the stance of a rough sleeper. The light washed over him, penetrating every crevice of the doorway, but if the occupants of the car had noticed him, they evidently saw nothing to be alarmed about.

Dog waited, knowing his opportunity had gone, and let out his breath in a long, bitter flow of disappointment. So close.

There would be another time, he told himself. Very soon.

THIRTY-ONE

After a fitful night's sleep, with Harry on the sofa and Rik giving Joanne his bed in favour of a sleeping bag in one corner, the two men shared coffee in the kitchen and discussed their next moves.

'We may have a problem,' Rik announced quietly. They could hear the shower hissing from the bathroom and both men were keen to do nothing to alarm Joanne.

'Only one?' Harry muttered. 'I call that a good start.'

Rik gestured towards the front window. 'I looked out there during the night, about three. We had a watcher. Bloke in a car down the street. He moved, otherwise I wouldn't have seen him. When I checked half an hour later, he'd gone.'

Harry took a bite of toast. 'Could be we've popped up on somebody's radar.' He explained about the man he'd seen before, sitting in a car tucked behind a market van. 'I thought he was a local cop or a public health inspector. Now I'm not so sure.'

'You think somebody's on us?' Rik looked surprised.

'I'm only guessing. It could be a coincidence. But the man I saw was definitely watching somebody.'

'Joanne?'

'Or Silverman . . . Rafa'i – whatever his name is. Bound to be. After what she told us, nothing would surprise me.'

'What do we do?'

'Talk to Jennings. He got us on to this situation. He'll have to get us out.'

'And Joanne?'

'What about me?' The shower had stopped but the fan was still running in the background. Joanne was standing in the doorway, her hair still damp. It was clear she had been listening, although they didn't know for how long.

She looked tired but determined, and was fully dressed and ready to go, with her rucksack in one hand. The side of her jacket bulged out with the weight of her handgun.

Rik told her about the watcher during the night. 'It's possible someone made a connection with us going to your place. If it's the person who killed your friend, they'll have worked out by now that they made a mistake and got the wrong person.'

Joanne frowned. 'But they might not know I'm here. I should leave.'

Harry scowled at her. 'Forget it. We don't know who it is yet. He could be totally unconnected. If he pops up again, we can go out and ask him. We're just discussing possibilities.'

'Such as?'

'Like what to do with you in the meantime.' He explained about Jennings, and how the lawyer's office would be the logical place to start. 'Problem is, we don't know who got him to hire us in the first place. It obviously wasn't the Israelis, but that still leaves a big field of possibilities. Finding Silverman was just one of three jobs; we just handled the tracing bit. Like Silverman, the other two seemed fairly ordinary, but they both ended up dead.' He paused. 'There's still no reason to suggest the other two were connected with Silverman, but they could have been a useful smokescreen.'

Joanne frowned. 'What for?'

'To cover something they didn't want anyone to see. The first two jobs could have been slush; real enough, but testing the water. Silverman was the one they were really after.'

Rik glanced at him. 'You reckon?'

'I was thinking about it last night.' Harry looked at Joanne. 'Normally, when we locate a runner we call it in and wait for instructions. We don't get involved further. Our job is to confirm the find first. Then we verify the location and bug out, leaving it for someone like the cops to handle. But these jobs were different. With the first one, a man named Matuq, I called it in and was told to stand by for instructions. I saw muzzle-flashes coming from the house, and when I went back he was dead. With the second, Param, he asked for some time so he could write to his parents and explain what he'd done. We called it in and when we went to check he hadn't bunked off, he was dead, too.'

'And when Harry tracked down Silverman,' Rik added softly, 'or Rafa'i, I should say, somebody nipped in quick and did the same thing. Only they missed the main man. Or took him with them.'

'And then there was you.' Harry looked at Joanne.

'But I'm not a . . . what do you call them – a runner.'

'But you're connected to someone who was.'

Joanne returned his stare. 'Have you told this Jennings person that you'd found me?'

'We had no reason not to. You were a useful lead. Sorry.'

'What did he say?'

'We told him your address, he told us to leave it, job done. We went back instead. The rest you know.'

She frowned, eyeing them both. 'Why did you do that?'

'Pardon?'

'Go back? Why did you go back to the flat?'

The two men exchanged glances, before Harry said, 'Instinct. It didn't feel right, leaving it after all the chasing around. We wanted to see it through.' He gave a cheesy smile. 'We're conscientious like that.'

Her scepticism showed in the tilt of her head. 'Right. You departed from procedure because you felt like it.'

'We don't follow any "procedure". We work our own way. It's called having a free will.'

She nodded, accepting the logic. 'Whatever. I owe you both. Thank you.'

'So what does all this tell us?' Harry asked of nobody in particular.

'Someone's been watching us all along.' Rik's reply was unequivocal.

Harry agreed. He'd felt something on the way to South Acres; something strong enough to make him stop. And he'd been right. The biker at South Acres must have already been on his way in even as he was about to call Jennings. Yet the killer couldn't possibly have known about the place unless he was watching Harry.

'Makes you wonder who gave him the order to go in,' Rik mused. 'And what would have happened if you'd still been there.'

Nobody answered. There was no need.

'Come on,' said Harry. 'Time to go out and face the lions and tigers and bears.' He went to the hallway and checked his gun, aware of Rik's surprised look, then led them out of the flat and down the stairs.

The lobby was deserted. They left through the rear on to a small car park where Rik had acquired parking rights. He unlocked the Audi and they climbed aboard.

'Should I stay down?' said Joanne, settling into the back. Her manner was calm and focussed, as if having some kind of plan and following orders had restored her equilibrium.

Harry shook his head. 'No point. If they've tracked us here, they'll know you're with us. It might push them into revealing themselves.'

Rik drove hard through the traffic, staying on the move and repeatedly changing direction. It was uncomfortable knowing they might be intercepted at any moment, but Harry was counting on the volume of traffic in broad daylight being cover enough to get where they were going. Even so, he checked the mirrors constantly, watching for signs of unusual interest or a repeat sighting of the same car on their tail.

'Biker,' he muttered at one point. A dark green Kawasaki was edging up on the outside, the rider enveloped in

anonymous black. Since the killer had used a bike at South
Acres, it wasn't unreasonable to expect the same means might
be used here in heavy traffic. It was fast, manoeuvrable and
difficult to identify, and would be virtually impossible to follow
in the aftermath of a shooting.

A metallic click sounded from the rear seat and he glanced
back at Joanne. She had eased her handgun from her pocket
and slid it under her thigh. He said nothing. For her, the
response was as instinctive as breathing; it was what she'd
been trained for.

The bike pitched up hard on their tail, held position for a
moment, then blew past in a growl of exhaust, slipping through
a gap which barely seemed to exist and streaking ahead before
swinging down a side street. By the time they drew level, it
was out of sight, leaving a trace of blue smoke hanging in its
wake.

Thirty minutes later, Rik drew in to the kerb a hundred
yards along from Jennings' office. There were a few pedestrians about and plenty of vehicle traffic as drivers used the
quieter back streets to avoid the usual jams along the
Marylebone Road.

Rik climbed out and wandered along the street to check
the front door, then strolled back and got behind the wheel.
'Nobody in yet,' he reported.

'So what's the plan?' Joanne asked.

Harry unfolded a newspaper. 'We wait and watch,' he said.
'If he's not already here, he'll be along shortly. Then we'll
have a chat.'

Time passed, during which Harry concentrated on a crossword and Rik handed Joanne a folder of papers to hold on
her knee. If anyone took an interest, they were three people
waiting for an appointment. In an area flush with consultants,
doctors and all manner of advisers behind silver and brass
nameplates, it was a common enough sight and would go
unnoticed.

'When this is all over,' Rik ventured after a lengthy silence,
'we could have a drink.' He turned his head to look at
Joanne.

She returned the look steadily, while Harry concentrated
on his crossword. As chat-up lines went, he decided, it was
less than slick.

'I'll bear it in mind,' Joanne replied neutrally. 'Thanks.'

Harry frowned and tapped the newspaper with his pen. 'Twenty down,' he read carefully. '"Calm conversationalist". What's that? Ah – I know: *Smooth talker.*'

Rik scowled and said nothing, ignoring the sudden shaking of Harry's shoulders.

'Heads up.' Harry put the paper to one side.

It was fifteen minutes into their watch and a taxi was pulling in to the kerb outside Jennings' office. Two men got out. They crossed the pavement, the one leading the way tall and broad-shouldered, with heavy brows over a craggy face. He was dressed in a smart suit and dark coat and was lighting a cigarette. He pressed the buzzer on the entry-phone to the side of Jennings' front door. There appeared to be no answer, so he banged on the door, disposing of the cigarette with an irritable flick of his wrist.

The second man was younger, stocky and wore a plain suit with no coat. He hung back slightly, surveying the street with a casual, almost uninterested glance before turning to scan the front of the building.

Harry recognized the second man's function. He was a minder, checking out the scenery. 'Jennings has got an official visitor.'

'Did he see us?' Joanne's view of the men had been obscured by a lamp post.

'I don't think so. We'll soon find out.'

There was a gasp from the back seat. The two men looked round. Joanne had moved to get a better view of the men, and was now staring through the windscreen, her body rigid and all colour draining from her cheeks.

'What's up?' said Harry.

'That man,' she said softly, her voice trembling slightly. 'The one in the dark coat. I've seen him before.'

They both turned back to study the man. 'Where?'

'In Baghdad.'

THIRTY-TWO

Harry leaned forward. The man was now in profile. He looked bullish and determined. His colleague had his eyes on an approaching car cruising for a parking space. 'Are you sure?'

Joanne pulled her rucksack across the seat and took out the framed photograph she had been so keen to hang on to. Turning it over on her knee, she took out a small knife and slid the blade through the backing sheet. Ripping away a section of the dark paper, she revealed a small square of black plastic taped to the inside. It had one corner cut off and a golden oblong in the centre.

'It's a memory card from a camera.' Harry looked at Joanne for confirmation, remembering what she had told them about taking photos in Baghdad. 'Is this from where I think it's from?'

'Yes. Can you get me to a chemist? One with a digital photo printer? Then I'll show you.'

'What about those two?' Rik queried, gesturing towards Jennings' office. 'And Jennings?'

Harry thought about it. 'They can keep. I think Jennings has skipped, anyway. Let's check this out first.'

Ten minutes later, the three of them were in a pharmacy just off Great Portland Street, huddled round the monitor of a customer-operated digital photo-lab. Joanne slid the memory card into a slot, then tapped the screen when the pop-up menu appeared. She waited until rows of photo thumbprints appeared, then selected one by touching the screen.

'Who are they?' Rik queried. He bent to peer at the row of pictures. Most of the shots appeared to have been taken in an area flooded with bright light, the backgrounds all suggesting sandstone and bare rendering. The picture quality of one or two looked poor, but others were crystal clear.

'Just people,' Joanne replied shortly. She selected the number of copies and then hit PRINT and waited before retrieving the card from the slot. 'I could get arrested for doing this.'

She looked at them in turn with a wry smile. 'But then, you two would know that, wouldn't you?'

They said nothing. This was all moving at a fast pace, but while Joanne was helping them, they weren't about to suggest that what she had done might have contravened the Official Secrets Act.

The copies of the photo inched with agonizing slowness out of the machine, and Joanne slipped them in her pocket while Harry paid the assistant. They left the shop and returned to the car.

'This is him,' said Joanne, passing one of the photos between the front seats.

The snap showed two men sitting at a street café table. One was stocky, running to fat and in his fifties, with unremarkable features. The other was a strict contrast: large and bullish, with powerful arms and big hands, and a strong, angular face. They were both dressed in tan-coloured trousers and pale shirts, and on the table in front of them were small coffee cups and glasses of water. The tables around them were deserted. Two more men were in the background, both wearing casual clothes, flak jackets and dark glasses. They were staring off to each side away from the café scene. Both carried submachine guns and wore side arms.

'Iraq?' Rik guessed.

'Yes. It was in the suburbs, about halfway between the safe house and the compound. There was a market nearby and I was supposed to arrive fifteen minutes later, but I got there early. I'd decided to go to the market and act normal, like I was supposed to. To be honest, I needed the distraction.'

'So they weren't expecting you,' said Harry.

'No. As usual, I was dressed as a local, so they wouldn't have recognized me. I was surprised to see them. There had been a bunch of killings in the area and the streets were flooded with US troops. I think that's why they were able to sit there like that. Everyone else was indoors except for a few locals and me. When I spotted them, I couldn't resist it – I took a quick shot. It looked so bizarre.'

Rik stared at her. 'You walked around with a camera on you?' He didn't have to say how dangerous that had been. If she had been stopped in a random search by Coalition forces or Iraqi police, her cover would have been blown in an instant.

'I hid it under my clothes,' she explained. 'They wouldn't have dared touch me.' She shrugged. 'It was a risk worth taking.'

'Why did you take the shot?'

'I don't know. Instinct, I think. I'd got used to keeping records of everybody I saw, both in and outside the compound. This was just part of it. Humphries always told me to be aware of everybody and everything around me. To remember faces and names – especially of the people I met, whichever side they were on. He came across as a bit of a cynic but I think he'd learned by experience never to miss a trick. I did it without thinking.'

Harry pointed at the plumper of the two men in the photo. 'This is Humphries?'

'Yes. I don't know the other man's name. After I got the shot, I went straight to the safe house and waited. Humphries arrived alone dressed in local clothes. If he saw me near the café, he never said. But I remember he didn't seem happy.'

'He didn't say why?'

'No. He seemed distracted, like he was just going through the motions. But it was a stressful time and I figured he had a lot on his plate. He was probably running other ops in tandem with mine. Anyway, we did the briefing and he left. He didn't ask for the memory card and I didn't offer it. It was the last time I saw him.'

Harry pointed at the other man in the photo. 'What about him?'

'I never saw him again either – until now. Three days later, Humphries called me to another briefing. He said to go to the safe house and wait. It was the day the compound was bombed.'

Harry nodded. 'And the day he was killed.'

'Yes.'

'He must have known something was up.' Harry spoke with quiet conviction. 'Why else call another meeting so quickly after the last one?'

Joanne shrugged sadly. 'We'll never know now, will we?'

'It would help,' said Harry slowly, as if teasing his thoughts into words, 'if we knew something about Humphries: family . . . places he knew . . . where he lived. Did he ever say anything about his background?'

Joanne shook her head. 'I don't remember. But how would that help us? He's dead.'

'Because he's your only point of reference to this mess. It won't do any good going back to the training camp – they'll deny any knowledge and call the cops. Trying to find your way back up the chain of command would end the same way. We'd get blocked all along the line and you'd finish up being investigated for the death of your friend Cath. If we can find out who Humphries worked for, we might be able to get to someone who can help you and sort out what's going on with Rafa'i.'

Joanne shrugged. 'He never talked about himself, except . . .' She paused.

'What?'

'He once told me that he had a twin sister, Sheila. She's a teacher in a primary school in Essex. It was at one of our meetings, after we'd finished a briefing. I got the impression they were close and shared a house.' She closed her eyes. 'He even mentioned the village . . . God, where was it?'

They waited but nothing came. Finally, Harry said, 'Don't push it. It'll come.'

'OK. But she won't know anything. People like Humphries aren't supposed to talk about their work, are they?'

'You'd be surprised what spooks talk about,' said Rik. He sounded almost irritated. 'Half the secrets published in the press come about through family members spilling the beans.' He sat back with a heavy sigh.

Harry turned to look at him. Irritation wasn't Rik's usual demeanour. 'Something bothering you?'

'Matuq,' Rik replied. 'And Param. I can't get it out of my mind.'

'What about them?'

'I keep thinking about what you said before, about there being a connection. They *couldn't* have known Rafa'i. It doesn't fit.'

'They didn't have to. It's not the victims who are the connection; it's Jennings.' When they both looked puzzled, he explained by asking, 'What was stolen at any of the locations?'

'Nothing,' Rik said.

'Exactly. There's another similarity: they were killed on or near the doorstep and the killer didn't hang around afterwards. Same with South Acres: in and out, two men down, no messing. Then gone.'

'Except,' Rik pointed out, 'we don't know what happened to Rafa'i.'

'Yeah.' Harry frowned. 'I don't get that. But I still think it's the same pattern and the same man. He specializes in fast entries and exits and doesn't hang about. He's not there to steal anything – that's not his job.'

'So what is it, then?' Joanne looked at the two men in turn, although something in her face told them she already knew the answer.

'He's a specialist,' Harry replied. 'He kills people.'

THIRTY-THREE

Rik stopped the Audi at the end of the track leading to Stokes Cottage and climbed out. Everything seemed quiet; no scene of crime vans, no figures in forensic suits, no support units, no press corps. As still as the grave.

'We need to split up,' Harry had suggested earlier. He was still puzzled at the total absence of news about Matuq's murder. Rik had checked online, but not even the local papers had any coverage. It was the same with Param's death, although there was a brief mention of an assault in the area, but with no details. Yet this was at a time when knife crimes were headline news, with every attack splashed across the front pages providing further embarrassment to a Home Office already under considerable pressure to halt the rise in street crime.

Harry had rung Dempsey's, the letting agent responsible for handling South Acres. When he came off the phone, he was even more confused.

'South Acres is being renovated and is no longer on the market. The previous tenants checked out two days ago.'

Rik's mouth curled. 'I'll say – and no forwarding address.'

'The keys were dropped off and everything's above board.'

'No way. What about the bodies?'

Harry looked sombre. 'I'm guessing there weren't any. They're probably buried in the woods somewhere. I smell men in suits.'

'What do you mean?' Joanne looked at him.

'A professional is involved and the murders have been suppressed or downplayed – even Param's, although I'd guess it was too public to cover up locally.'

'We should check South Acres,' Rik suggested. 'Somebody's telling porkies.'

'It's too late for that. The workmen are already in; any evidence will have been destroyed by now. It might be worth checking Blakeney and Battersea, though.' Privately he didn't hold out much hope of finding anything. If Matuq's murder in Blakeney had been concealed, and Param's hadn't been allowed to hit the headlines, there was every likelihood that the Battersea flat was already empty.

'But who could suppress that kind of thing?' Joanne asked. 'Who has that sort of influence?'

Rik said, 'The kind of people we used to work for.'

Harry nodded. 'OK. Joanne and I will see if we can track down Humphries' sister. If we find her, she might be able to tell us something useful. It's possible he let slip something about who he worked for.'

Rik nodded. 'I'll do Blakeney. The locals won't have seen me before. Then I'll check Joanne's place in Battersea.'

Joanne looked from one man to the other. 'Why are you two doing this?' she asked quietly. 'You're not getting paid for it. You don't owe me anything.'

'Because,' Rik replied, 'if we're right, whoever took Rafa'i also killed your friend. When they realize they screwed up, they'll come looking for you.'

For a second Joanne looked bewildered. Harry added, 'What Boy Wonder forgot to mention is that they'll probably come after us, too. So we're not so much noble as a bit short on options.' He smiled to soften the words. 'Never mind, if they come too close, we'll let you use your gun.'

'Thanks,' she said faintly. 'I'll remember that.'

Now, after a fast drive from London, Rik was in Blakeney. He'd used the journey to ease the tension of the past couple of days out of his system, concentrating on driving the car as hard as conditions would allow. It was his means of relaxation, but one he could only truly accomplish without Harry in the car. Not that Harry was bothered by speed; he simply saw little point in using the full power of the car's highly tuned engine when you didn't need to.

He surveyed the ground as he walked up the lane towards the cottage, and was dismayed to see several sets of tyre tracks in the mud. Harry had mentioned only one, and clearly described the track ending among the trees, with no other houses. He had a feeling he was too late.

He rounded the bend at the top of the track and stopped. The cottage looked just as Harry had described: isolated, a little sad, even neglected. Except that the faded green door in the photo on Harry's mobile was now painted a glossy, duck-egg blue.

He checked the trees and bushes on his left, and the reeds to his right. His nerves were jangling at this latest development. Who the hell would allow someone to decorate the front door of a murder scene?

He stepped forward and pressed the doorbell, heard it echo inside. The place sounded empty. He stepped over to the front window and peered in, and felt his nerves crank up even further.

The room, far from being the drab place Harry had mentioned, was now bright with freshly minted walls and a new carpet. None of the sad decor, no half-finished meal, no oddments of thrown-together furniture.

And no Matuq lying against the rear wall.

Somebody had been busy. And definitely not the police. He checked the side of the cottage. The lean-to was still there, but there was no sign of a Renault with slashed tyres.

He was about to take a look at the back garden when a voice spoke behind him.

'Can I help you?'

He turned to see a youngish woman standing by the corner of the cottage. She wore green Wellingtons and a fleece, and had large, brown eyes. She was pretty, with glossy black hair and perfect teeth, and looked very country.

'Uh . . . yes – sorry.' He smiled and felt wrong-footed. *Where the hell had she appeared from?* 'I was miles away. I was wondering if this place was to let.' What he really wanted was to ask if she'd heard about a brutal murder committed here in the last few days, but decided that might be too direct.

The woman shook her head and smiled patiently, as if accustomed to dealing with lunatics wandering around the countryside looking for places to rent. 'It's not available.'

'That's a pity. It's in a nice location. Are you the owner?'

'No.' The woman waved a vague hand towards the village. 'I live along the road and sometimes take in the key. I was out walking my dog and noticed you here.' She frowned slightly. 'This isn't really the best place to be looking at.' She stood to one side, a clear indication that he should leave.

'Why?' Rik stood his ground. 'You make it sound like somebody just died.'

The woman's eyes flickered. It was a momentary thing and most people would have overlooked it. But Rik had spent long enough watching faces to spot it.

'There's been nothing like that,' she replied eventually. 'What a strange idea, Mr—?'

Rik ignored the opening and studied her. For a woman on her own she seemed very self-possessed, in spite of standing in an isolated spot with a stranger asking strange questions and making comments about death. Maybe they were bred tough around here.

He noticed she was carrying a mobile phone but no dog lead.

So where was the dog?

'I've got a lively imagination,' he replied, and stepped past her. It was time to go, and fast, before she summoned help. 'Thanks for your time.' As he walked back down the lane, he felt her eyes on him all the way. When he turned to look back, she had disappeared.

He drove into the village and stopped at a small supermarket. The woman on the till smiled, but shook her head when he asked about the cottage.

'Stokes Cottage? No, dear, there's been nobody there for a while. The last tenant skipped without paying the rent, they say.' She rolled her eyes at the dishonesty of some people. 'The owners must have decided to sell it. They've had workmen in, doing it up. It'll go for a good price, I shouldn't wonder.'

'Does the owner live here?'

'No, dear. London, I think. They're all from London, aren't they, these days? Why – you looking for a place to buy, are you?'

*   *   *

In Islington, north London, Harry was standing by the Saab, parked behind his flat, and beginning to wonder how stupid he'd been.

He had left Joanne sitting in the passenger seat less than three minutes ago, after returning from a wasted morning outside Jennings' office. They had been waiting for the lawyer to show up, but by the time noon had come and gone, it seemed pointless wasting any more time. Discreet enquiries at adjacent businesses had been met with politely blank looks, and the two men they had spotted earlier had not returned, nor had the office opened. Checking out where Humphries' sister lived might at least offer the feeling of progress of a sort, if only Joanne could recall the name of the village. He had tried not to pressure her to remember it, because these memory fragments usually returned in their own time.

He shouldn't have left her alone down here while he went upstairs. She evidently didn't trust anyone fully, and who could blame her after what she had been through? The temptation to cut and run once she was on her own must have been too great.

He went to the front of the building and checked the street in both directions. It was a waste of time; if Joanne had decided to run, she would have done just that. And with her skills, there was no guessing how far away she was by now.

He was about to go back for the car to make a tour of the area, when he saw a brief flicker of movement. It came from inside a vehicle halfway down on the other side of the street. He continued turning away, careful not to betray the fact that he had seen something. When he looked at the spot again, there was no sign of anyone.

He knew he hadn't been mistaken. There was a person in the car. *But was it significant?*

Then he spotted Joanne.

She was walking along the pavement towards him, fifty yards beyond the car where he'd seen the movement and on the same side of the street. There was something odd in her stance, but he couldn't figure out what it was. The rucksack, maybe, which never left her side? Her attention seemed to be focussed on a spot on or near the same vehicle where he had seen the movement.

In the same instant, he realized what was unusual about her stance: *she was holding her gun down by her leg.*

He felt the back of his neck go cold. It was a classic approach to a suspect vehicle, remaining carefully in the driver's blind spot while keeping him in sight and holding your weapon ready. The next move would be to tap on the window right behind his ear and—

Harry turned and ran back to his car at the rear of the building. It was pointless shouting a warning; Joanne had obviously spotted the watcher on her way out and had reacted in the way she'd been trained. If the person in the car, innocent or not, showed the slightest sign of resistance in the next couple of minutes, it would probably be the last thing they ever did.

He tore out of the car park, hoping nobody chose that moment to drive by. By the time he was out in the street, Joanne was already within ten paces of the suspect vehicle and bending forward slightly, beginning to bring her weapon up. He hit the accelerator, hoping he could make it in time.

The gap narrowed fast. As he began to draw level with the stationary car, he stamped hard on the brakes. The tyres squealed in protest as they tried to grip the tarmac, causing Joanne to glance up. At the same moment, a shadow moved inside the vehicle. But the watcher wasn't in the driver's seat where he should have been – he was in the back and facing the pavement, waiting for Joanne to draw close.

He'd spotted her.

'*Gun!*' Harry roared as he saw the outline of a weapon in the man's hands.

But Joanne had seen it, too. With no change of expression, she skipped sideways and ran out into the road. Caught out by the speed of her reaction, the man inside the car couldn't spin round on his seat fast enough.

Joanne's move had brought her level with the offside rear wing of the man's car. In a single movement she swivelled her body, brought the gun up two-handed and fired twice through the side window. The noise of the two shots rolled into one and was almost lost against the residue of the engine noise of Harry's car and the squealing of his tyres, followed by the tinkling of glass falling to the road.

Then Joanne ran round to the front of the Saab and dived into the passenger seat, slamming the door behind her.

'*Go!*' she yelled, and threw her rucksack in the back.

THIRTY-FOUR

'They've split up.' Dog reported succinctly. He was carefully picking broken window fragments out of his hair and trying to ignore a painful ringing in his right ear. Luckily, he could hear well enough with his left to make the call. While he waited for a response, he clambered into the front seat and started the engine. It caught with a cough and settled into a smooth hum.

Further along the street somebody was shouting. He ignored them. He felt humiliated but relieved to be alive. *Christ, nearly being bested by a woman!* He pounded the steering wheel. She was good, though, and should have been; she'd been trained by the best. It was the shout from Tate that had unnerved him. Then that move she'd pulled before opening fire was a beauty. The only thing he couldn't figure out was why she'd aimed to miss. At that distance, she should have splattered his brains all over the interior of the car. Given the same circumstances, he'd have aimed to kill.

'All three?' The drawl on the end of the line was heavy with criticism because Dog had managed to lose both Tate and Ferris. And now Archer. After the screw-up at South Acres, he could have done without it.

'I could hardly follow them all,' he replied tersely. 'I decided to stick with Tate and the girl.' He hesitated then added, 'She blew my window out in the middle of the street with a semi-automatic. You never said she was a fucking lunatic.' It was rare for Dog to swear, especially in the presence of an employer, but he felt it more than suited the occasion.

'I didn't think I had to. You know her background. Where are they now?'

'Gone. Do you want me to come in?'

'No. Stay in the open. The office is closed until further notice.'

'Closed?' Dog didn't like the sound of that. So far this assignment had not been going spectacularly well, and he had a bad feeling about this latest development. In his experience, poor planning was as much to blame as bad execution. Perhaps Jennings had overreached himself. Maybe it was time he considered getting out while he still could. Except that it went against the grain to have a failure on his record. He couldn't have that, not after all this time. 'What do you mean?'

'Don't worry about it. A minor operational glitch, that's all. I'll call you with a new location when I'm sure it's safe. In the meantime, I suggest you keep looking. This matter has now gone critical.'

The phone clicked and Dog threw his mobile down on the passenger seat. *Critical.* So critical he was out in the open and would have to stay on the move to avoid being compromised. Still, it wouldn't be the first time; some things you just got used to in this business.

As he turned a corner into a quiet square, thinking about where he could find a safe base, he smelled burning plastic. It grew steadily stronger until, seconds later, the engine coughed and juddered, then died.

It was only then that he noticed the two bullet holes in the dashboard.

THIRTY-FIVE

Joanne turned and watched the road behind them, but there was no sign of the other car. 'That should slow him down a bit.' She ejected the magazine from the semi-automatic and checked the action, then reloaded and slipped it back in her jacket. 'By the way, I remember the name of the village where Humphries lived. It's Green's Morton.'

Harry hardly dared look at her, too busy wrestling with the wheel and trying to negotiate a series of narrow back streets to shake off any chance of pursuit. It was as if nothing had happened; as if she hadn't just fired two shots into a man in a north London street, blowing out a car window in the process and probably scaring half the residents into calling the anti-terrorist squad.

'Are you nuts?' he shouted. 'You might have murdered an undercover cop!'

But her response surprised him. 'Do me a favour. If I'd wanted him dead, he'd be dead. I didn't even aim at him. The worst I did was probably make him piss himself.' She grinned like a happy kid on a Sunday outing. 'Serves him right – he shouldn't be following us.'

It stopped Harry's protests in their tracks. He realized she must have been aiming forward of the rear seats. She'd gone for shock tactics rather than something more fatal to put the man off watching them. 'You could have told me,' he said after they covered a mile or so. 'When I first came back out I thought you'd . . .'

Joanne laughed. 'What – legged it? Jesus, why would I? You guys are the only protection I've got.' She looked at him seriously. 'I trained hard for my job, but it doesn't make me a psychopath. I know when to draw the line.' She paused and looked out of the window. 'If you hadn't warned me and I'd stepped up to the other window . . .' She shrugged fatalistically. 'Thanks.'

'You did well to spot him.' Harry felt guilty for assuming the worst and jumping on her with both boots. She had exercised enormous restraint in a dangerous situation, which was more than most people would have done.

'I was lucky. One of his rear side windows got slightly fogged up. It was the kind of thing they taught us on the course.' Another mile went by before she said, 'He was no cop, though. A cop wouldn't have seen me coming.'

Harry agreed. He wondered if the man was connected with Jennings. He jerked his head to the back of the car. 'There's a map behind the seat. You find the village and I'll get us there.'

Joanne dug out the map and located the village, but still seemed doubtful. 'How do we locate a woman whose surname we don't know? She might have been married and divorced.'

'She's a teacher named Sheila,' he reminded her. 'How many primary schools can a village have? As to the rest, finding people is what I do best. Care for a bet on it?'

She curled her lip and turned back to studying the map. Her expression seemed lighter than he'd seen it so far, and he wondered if it was the result of an adrenaline rush. Danger and excitement did that to some people. 'Head east,' she added. 'I'll let you know when to turn off.'

A little while later, she said quietly, 'I'm very grateful, you know. You really didn't have to do this.'

'Actually, I think we did,' he replied easily, then concentrated on getting round a gaggle of slow cars hogging the centre of the road.

She said nothing for a few minutes, but threw him a glance now and then. 'Are you married?'

'No. Was once.'

'I'm sorry.'

'Don't be. We ended up going different ways. You?'

The question seemed to catch her off guard. She hesitated before replying. 'No. A near miss, once. He was an officer. It got smothered at birth.'

'Tough.' Harry sympathized, aware of how the intermingling of ranks was still frowned upon in the armed forces.

'Well, at least you didn't look surprised.'

'How do you mean?'

'Some men think any girl who joins up is a budding dyke.'

'Is that what your colleagues on the course thought?'

'No. Well, maybe a couple – the ones who couldn't believe a woman had any place doing that kind of work. But they never said so.' She went quiet for a while, then said, 'You two are a good team. Rik thinks a lot of you.'

Harry gave a non-committal grunt. 'He should. I taught him all he knows.'

They laughed together, and Joanne instinctively reached out to touch his arm, before drawing her hand back and studying the map.

THIRTY-SIX

He'd got company.

Rik was over an hour out of Blakeney, along a stretch of dual carriageway near Newmarket, when he realized he was being followed. One minute his rear-view mirror showed a deserted road, the next a plain blue Volvo had ghosted

up out of nowhere and was sitting two hundred yards behind
him, matching his speed.

He increased his pace. The other car picked up and stayed
with him. When he slowed down, the Volvo did the same.
He waited for a straight, clear stretch and eased up to ninety,
slipping by two slower vehicles with ease. After an initial
hesitation, the Volvo kept pace and slotted in behind him
again.

After two more miles of convoy driving, the other driver
accelerated and rushed by with a surge of power. There were
two men inside, and the passenger gave Rik a long look on
the way past. Then they were gone.

It wasn't exactly subtle and stirred the hairs on Rik's neck.
He thought about the woman outside Stokes Cottage. Also
not too subtle, and no more a dog walker than he was. He
doubted if she was local, either. He was willing to lay good
odds she'd called out the troops as soon as he left. It must
have taken them until now to locate his position.

So who the hell were they?

He checked the map. Another few miles and he'd be on the
M11 heading south. The fact that the men in the car hadn't
stopped him didn't mean they weren't planning something.
Once on the motorway, he'd be an easy mark with no simple
way off and no place to hide. All they had to do was sit on
a bridge and wait for him to go by, then tuck in behind him
or radio ahead to another car and throw a boxing manoeuvre
around him.

He saw a sign coming up. A moment's hesitation, then he
swung the wheel and took the turning at the last second,
squeezing between a milk truck and a caravan, the sudden-
ness of the move drawing a long blare of protest from the
truck's horn.

He slowed and checked the map. He was now heading west
towards Royston. It might take longer to get to London, but
if the men in the Volvo didn't know where he was, they couldn't
stop him.

He settled in his seat and concentrated on watching for speed
cameras and weaving past slower traffic, skilfully changing
down to power through bends slick with spilled mud off the
fields. He grinned to himself and flicked on the radio, enjoying
the tiny burst of rebellion and the feel of the road skimming

by. If they were really serious, they'd find him in the end . . .
but in the process he'd give them a run for their money.

After several miles he pulled into a gateway and allowed
some trailing vehicles to pass him. Local traffic, none of it
fast. He took the opportunity to call Harry and let him know
that the cottage was clean.

'It's as if Matuq was never there. And I collected a couple
of new friends on the way.' He explained about the woman
and the Volvo.

'Sounds official,' said Harry.

'Yeah – it looked it, too.' They had both spent enough
time around these kind of cat-and-mouse situations to recognize when they were on the receiving end, although Rik
hadn't got Harry's level of active experience. 'What do we
do about it?'

'We stay loose,' Harry replied pragmatically. 'Until they
show their hand and we know who they are, there's not much
we can do about it.' He hesitated. 'We had our own share of
excitement down here, too: Joanne shot a car.'

'Nice of her. Was anyone in it?'

'One man. Could be the same watcher who was on our case
all along. Where are you now?'

'Heading for Battersea. Do you still want me to check it
out?'

'Yes. If that's clean, too, there's a pattern. But take it easy
and don't get caught.' Harry cut the connection.

Rik got out of the car and cocked his ear, listening. He was
surrounded by fields and the air was deathly quiet save for a
couple of skylarks. No droning engines. If his followers had
a helicopter at their disposal, it was operating at distance.

He got back in and took off again.

The flat in Battersea looked deserted on his first drive-by.
After the second look, and with no signs of anything suspicious, Rik slipped his car into a space by a newsagent along
the main street and sat for a while watching the flow of people
and traffic.

When he was satisfied everything looked right, he got out
and strolled along the pavement, checking out the other cars
along the kerb. He had an eye out for the signs Harry had
told him about: the misted windows, the driver sitting too still,

the collection of takeaway wrappers or water bottles in the foot-well. There were no watchers that he could see, but that meant nothing; anyone worth his salt would look like an ordinary shopper, not an armed response unit member with a Heckler & Koch across his chest.

He turned the corner and glanced up at the open stairway to Joanne's flat. The door looked shut tight. If the lock had been mended, someone must have been inside. So why was there no crime scene tape anywhere?

His chest was hammering. This was the most difficult part: preparing to go through a door and knowing that somebody might be waiting for you on the other side. He almost felt his nerve go, but steeled himself. He had to see if a clean-up job had been carried out, like in Blakeney. If he freaked out now, he'd never forgive himself. And nor would Harry. He might say it was OK, but that would be it for them.

He stepped on to the metal stairway. Walked up two at a time, trying not to rattle the structure and signal his approach. A bit like hacking into someone's computer system, he thought vaguely. He still couldn't tell if the door was fixed. He reached out and put his fingers against it.

It swung open.

'*Hello?*'

If only he'd got a weapon. He was pretty sure Harry had got one tucked away somewhere. He'd meant to ask him about it, but Harry had always vetoed the idea of them outside of the range or a known 'hot' zone. If he'd got one, why hadn't he said something?

His call echoed back. The place was empty. He glanced over his shoulder to check the street. A few empty cars at the kerb, two elderly ladies struggling to get a shopping trolley up on to the path. No single pedestrians lurking with little apparent purpose, no unusual flashes of light to indicate binoculars, no sudden movement of bodies getting ready to rush up the stairs and pound him into a pulp.

He took a deep breath and stepped inside.

THIRTY-SEVEN

'I'm sorry – I don't see how I can help you.' Sheila Humphries was every inch the teacher, her hands clasped across her front as if waiting for some unruly child to pay attention. 'I think you may have confused me with somebody else.'

They had arrived barely ten minutes ago after an agonizingly slow drive in stop–start traffic, to discover that the village lay at the end of a narrow road a few miles from the coast near Mersea Island, south of Colchester. It boasted a single primary school – St Matilda's – located on the eastern fringes close to a new housing development. A modern red brick and glass structure, it had a large, open playground between the building and the road, and nowhere for Harry and Joanne to park and survey the place without attracting the immediate attention of vigilant staff or parents. In addition, a caretaker tidying up some play equipment to one side was watching them.

Harry had opted for the direct approach. They didn't have time to waste hoping Joanne might spot a middle-aged woman resembling Gordon Humphries. And there was no way of telling for certain whether they had been followed or not.

'Come on,' he'd said, climbing out of the car. 'When in doubt, ask a janitor.'

'Don't you mean a policeman?'

Harry smiled. 'You've been overseas too long. Policemen are almost extinct in this country . . . except when you don't want them.' He looked pointedly at her rucksack. 'If he tells us to bugger off, try not to shoot him.'

'Sheila?' The man eyed them both with caution and squinted against the sun when they approached him. 'She's inside. You're not inspectors giving her a hard time, are you? Only she's not been so good since her brother died.' He shook his head and nudged a marker cone into place alongside some coloured plastic equipment boxes. 'Bloody shame.'

'It's her brother we're here about,' said Joanne. 'Gordon was a nice man.'

'You knew him, did you?'

'I worked closely with him.'

'Oh.' He looked her up and down. 'You don't look like you work in oil exploration. Sorry, I'm not supposed to say that, am I? It's all equality now. I suppose there'll be paperwork and stuff to sort out, won't there? Ruled by the bloody stuff, we are. I'll tell her you're here.' He marched away and disappeared through a side door, returning moments later. 'In through the door,' he told them, 'and she'll see you in the common room third on the left. She's got a free period.'

They entered the building to find a middle-aged woman with greying hair and a melancholy look waiting for them in a plain, tiled corridor lined with pupils' work. Seabirds seemed to be the main subject.

Harry glanced at Joanne, who nodded to confirm that the woman looked like Gordon Humphries, and advanced to shake her hand. The woman gestured to an open door and followed them through. They found themselves in a staff room decorated with pinboards covered in graphs, schedules and notices, and furnished with soft chairs and coffee tables. The overall effect was of clutter and cheerful disarray.

'I know this is painful,' Joanne started, 'but we're here to talk about your brother, Gordon. We need your help.'

Sheila Humphries lifted her chin, the pain evident in her face. 'What about him? Are you from the company?'

'The government, you mean?' Joanne said gently. 'Not exactly.'

'Government? I don't follow.'

'Gordon worked for the government.'

'I'm sorry, but that's not right. My brother worked for an oil company.' She looked carefully at them both, the teacher demanding an explanation. Yet in spite of the guarded response, there was a hesitancy about her and her hands never ceased twisting and moving. 'I'm sorry, I don't see how I can help you. I should call someone.' She looked as if she was about to turn towards a phone on the wall.

Harry took out his wallet and showed her his MI5 card. If she still chose to call for help, it was likely to be an official number and would be another count against him. There was nothing else for it but to bluff their way through.

She looked at the card and appeared to relax. 'Oh. I see.'

Joanne opened her rucksack and took out the photo of Humphries and his companion at the street café. She held it out and said, 'This is Gordon, isn't it?'

Sheila Humphries reacted as if she'd been stung. She took the photo and stared at it, then gave a deep sigh and sat down on a chair as if her legs had given way. She ran her fingertips gently across the glossy surface, then murmured softly, 'Oh, dear God. You poor boy.'

They took a chair each and waited, giving her time to adjust to the shock of seeing her brother's face again. A buzz of high-pitched laughter echoed down the corridor outside and a clock ticked in the room, drawing away the seconds until she looked up.

'How can I help you?' she said.

'You know where that photo was taken, don't you?' said Joanne. She glanced at Harry for guidance, but he said nothing, not daring to intrude on the moment.

Sheila took a deep breath and nodded. 'Somewhere in Baghdad. I said he should never have gone there. But it was his work. It was what he did.' Her voice was breathless, almost muffled, as if forcing each word through a heavy gauze. 'How did you come by it?'

'I was the one who took it.'

'You?' Sheila looked stunned. 'But that means . . .'

'Gordon was my boss.' She paused, then continued in a matter-of-fact manner, 'We used to meet for briefings. I was due to meet him the morning he died. He didn't come.'

'Briefings?' Sheila Humphries suddenly leaned forward, a look of understanding dawning on her face. She stared at Joanne with intense concentration. 'He said they'd put someone out there . . . a young girl. He was appalled at the idea. Said it was horribly dangerous and he couldn't protect her. It was *you*?'

Joanne said nothing.

'He told you about it?' Harry was surprised.

'Only the once,' she replied, eyes still on Joanne. 'He was nearing voluntary retirement age. We were going to take a long holiday together. Then they asked him to stay on for

a really important job. Vital, they said. It was going to be his
last assignment.'

'I didn't know that,' said Joanne.

'Gordon loved his work. He really did. But not this time.
It was as if the spark had gone out of it for him. They'd
assigned him to another section or something, and there was
a lot of training involved. He mentioned Iraq and said they
were placing someone in an impossible situation and it was
his responsibility as handler to see that nothing happened to
them. He thought it was madness but couldn't get them to
call it off.' She shook her head. 'He wasn't supposed to talk
about his work, but I wasn't stupid – I knew what he did right
from the start. We were always close, you see.'

'The other man in the photo,' said Harry. 'Do you know
him?'

Sheila nodded without looking at the photo. 'His name's
Andrew Marshall. He was one of Gordon's superiors – a major,
I think, although he's a civilian now. They'd worked together
before in . . . well, in other places.'

'Is he one of the good guys?' Joanne asked

Shelia shrugged. 'I don't know. I always thought so. With
what they have to do, it's difficult to tell sometimes.' She
looked guiltily at Joanne. 'Sorry.'

'But Gordon trusted him?'

'Oh, yes. He trusted Andrew. Not,' she added softly, 'that
it did him any good in the end, did it?' She took out a handkerchief and dabbed at her nose. 'A step too far.'

'Pardon?'

'He always said that things went badly when you took just
one step too far. Like taking that last run down a ski slope.'
She gave a stiff smile. 'He loved skiing. Nearly broke his leg
a couple of times, taking a final run.'

'What did they tell you about it?' Harry asked.

'The accident? Actually, Andrew came to see me. He said
he didn't want anyone else to do it, not after all he and Gordon
had been through together. I thought that was very kind of
him. He told me Gordon's car went off the road somewhere
in Kuwait. But I knew that couldn't be true – he was nowhere
near Kuwait at the time. They're very good at concealing
things from families . . . they have to be, I suppose, otherwise
we'd never sleep nights. There was even a report in the paper

and a picture of the car.' She took a deep breath, a catch in her throat. 'Gordon never normally told me exactly where he was going or staying, but he did this time.'

'Why was that?' Harry waited. This could be the opening they needed.

'He had trouble sleeping, which was very unusual for him. And the last time he was home on leave, he told me what he'd been doing and where he was going next. It was the first time he'd ever done that. That's how I knew about you.' She looked at Joanne with an odd look of compassion. 'He thought you were a very special young lady. There weren't many people he said that about. He was really very unhappy about it. He wanted to protect you . . . but deep down, I think he knew that was impossible. I still don't know why you do it – any of you. But I suppose somebody has to, otherwise where would we be?'

A bell sounded along the corridor. Sheila shook herself and glanced at her watch. 'I'm sorry – I have to go. You wanted something, didn't you? Something connected with Gordon.'

Harry considered his words carefully. There was no point making her aware of what they were involved in; it would serve no useful purpose. She had been fed an official story covering the death of her brother, but had recognized it for what it was, even though she knew there must be something deeper involved than a mere road traffic accident. The truth was probably best left buried. But at least they now had a name. He opted for a direct question.

'Do you know where we can find Andrew Marshall?' he asked.

THIRTY-EIGHT

The air in Joanne Archer's Battersea flat was filled with the tang of cleaning fluid. Trapped in the stillness of the hallway, it hung in the atmosphere like a thick veil. It was enough to tell Rik he was too late; the cleansing had already taken place.

He ran his hand down the doorjamb. A new latch had been

fitted, with a fillet of wood inserted and planed smooth to replace the damaged section. It hadn't yet been painted, and whoever had been the last out must have forgotten to click the door behind them. He pushed it shut and slipped the button to lock it.

First he checked the bathroom. It was empty, scoured clean; no coiled tights, no razor, no traces of soap or powder. The kitchen was pristine, as were the other rooms, stripped of all trace of the previous occupants. No bags, no empty wine bottles, no takeaway food containers, not even a layer of dust.

And no body.

There was a patch of bedroom carpet where the dead woman had been lying. Looking at the way the edges were curled up against the wall, Rik guessed the floor underneath had also been scrubbed. Not exactly a thorough job – replacing the carpet would have been more professional – but enough to cover up what had happened to the untrained eye.

He rang Harry. 'Battersea's cleaner than a vicar's conscience,' he told him.

'Can't say I'm surprised,' said Harry. 'Best get out of there.'

'Will do.' Rik was already moving towards the door. 'Any joy your end?'

'We got a lead from Humphries' sister, but it could be a waste of time. We'll meet at your place.'

'You betcha.' Rik switched off his mobile. Heard the clatter of footsteps on the metal stairway.

Too late.

He stepped up to the door and peered out through the side window. Two men were climbing the stairs. They were both heavyset and purposeful, dressed in casual clothes.

One he recognized as the passenger in the Volvo.

He stepped back, wishing he'd got a weapon. But that was as pointless as hoping to meet Jennifer Lopez on a beach at sunset. Anyway, against two he'd be at a disadvantage. And these men looked like they meant business.

He retraced his steps to the living room and looked out of the front window overlooking the shops. Immediately below was an overhang, a section of flat roof covered with heavy felt and a scattering of gravel. It was roughly four feet wide, easy enough to walk on. The question was, would it be strong enough to support his weight?

There was only one way to find out.

The window was single-glazed and opened outwards to the side. He flipped it open and clambered out. It was a bit public, but a much better option than going down the other way and trying to get past the two men. Dropping to the flat roof, he ignored a few surprised looks from pedestrians on the opposite pavement and walked along the roof to the end of the row of shops, careful not to tread too heavily. When he reached the end, he found a convenient rubbish skip placed within easy reach, and swung down to the ground and walked away without looking back.

His car was parked on the main road, but he ignored it. Instead, he turned and walked along the access road behind the block. Each shop had its own rear door, with a stairway to the flats above every thirty yards. In between lay a clutter of vehicles, skips, pallets and other rubbish, and he used this cover to approach Joanne Archer's stairway.

He found a couple of large wheeled bins at the rear of a takeaway, and stopped, nose twitching at the sickly sweet smell of spicy food and grease.

A door slammed overhead and footsteps pounded down the stairs, causing the structure to vibrate. The two men appeared, looking grim, and Rik smiled at their discomfort. It was tinged, though, by an awareness that they had clearly worked out what he was doing and were close behind him.

Too close. Next time he might not be so lucky.

The men walked across the road and disappeared round the corner. Moments later, a familiar blue Volvo appeared and edged out on to the main road, then surged away with a brief squeak of tyres, heading north towards the city.

Harry hit the wheel with his hand and skidded into a lay-by, a cloud of dust drifting past as they came to a stop. They were only a few miles away from Green's Morton after leaving a tearful Sheila Humphries, and Harry had just ended the call with Rik about Joanne's flat.

'Damn – how stupid am I?'

'What's up?' Joanne reached instinctively for her gun, twisting in her seat to glance through the rear window.

'No, not that.' Harry climbed out and walked around the car, deep in thought. When he leaned against the front wing,

Joanne got out and joined him. 'What Sheila said about them being good at concealing things. It set me thinking: concealing is the same as covering up.'

'I know.'

'Rik was right,' he explained, frowning in concentration. 'Your friend's murder was a mistake.'

'They thought she was me. Don't remind me.'

'What if Param's killing was a mistake by assumption? The killer didn't get identities confused, he made a definite, planned move based on what he *assumed* we were doing.'

Joanne shrugged. 'You've lost me.'

'When we went to see Jennings after Matuq's death,' he explained, 'he handed us another job – to look for Silverman . . . Rafa'i as we now know him. He said it was urgent. We started on it right away, then had to wait for information about who had picked him up at the airport. While we were doing that we picked up with the Param job. We'd got a strong lead, so we used it to fill the time. We traced him to his girlfriend's place in Harrow. But when we confirmed he was there, we didn't ring in immediately.'

'You said he wanted to write to his parents.'

'Sure. It seemed reasonable, so being suckers for a sob story, we agreed. By the time we went back, he was dead. A local said it was an attempted mugging, but there's been no mention of his name in the news since. Not a word.'

'You think it's been suppressed?'

'Leaned on at the very least. And now the evidence of Matuq's death has gone as well.'

'Couldn't this man Jennings have got it cleared away?'

'He could – but I didn't tell him where I'd located Matuq . . . just that I'd got him and was waiting for instructions. There's only one way he could have known he was in Blakeney.'

'He had you followed.'

'Yes. But in London, the tail couldn't have known we were chasing down Param, because we hadn't told Jennings we'd switched assignments. He would have assumed we were closing in on Rafa'i, and as soon as we were out of the way, he went in for the kill.'

Joanne frowned. 'Did they look alike?'

'Only the colouring. To western eyes, both men looked

Asian or middle-eastern. In the dark, the killer wouldn't have noticed the difference. He was too intent on completing the job. But he was careless.'

'There's only one flaw in your argument,' Joanne said after a moment's thought. 'If the killer was the same man all along, and he thought it was Rafa'i he'd killed in north London, even if he realized his mistake and followed you out to the farm, why take Rafa'i? Why didn't he slot him there and then?'

'He couldn't.'

'Why not?'

'Because Rafa'i wasn't there.' Harry spoke with absolute conviction. It was the only explanation, and had been staring him in the face all along. Only he'd jumped to the wrong conclusion. There hadn't been time for the killer to go upstairs, find Rafa'i and force him back down and into the car. It would have taken too long. If Rafa'i was the important figure they now knew him to be, with his background of conflict, he would have put up a struggle . . . and the killer would have cut his losses and finished him off there and then. 'Rafa'i probably heard the killer approaching the farm and dropped out the back window. There were outbuildings and trees to duck into, and it was getting dark. The killer realized he was stuffed, so he left, using the Suzuki because one of the guards had disabled his bike.'

As they climbed back in the car, Joanne's phone rang, muffled inside her rucksack. She dug it out and peered at the caller display. It was an unlisted number. She looked at Harry in confusion. 'I have no idea who this is. I only switched it on a short while ago.'

'Answer it,' Harry suggested. If it wasn't a telesales call or a wrong number, he had a good idea who the caller might be.

She asked who was speaking and her face went pale. '*It's Rafa'i*,' she mouthed, then replied in a brief rattle of Arabic. Moments later, she began again, then stopped. The call had been cut short. 'I think he was scared we might be monitored. I asked him where he was, but he wouldn't say. He wants to meet me.'

'Where and when?'

'He told me some time ago that there was one particular place he wanted to visit if he came to London. He'd seen it

on television and liked the open space. Without naming it just
now, he said we should meet there tomorrow morning at ten.'

Harry made a guess at the biggest open space he could
think of. 'Hyde Park?'

'No. St James's Park and Horse Guards Parade. Near the
lake.'

Harry considered it. Was it genuine or was it an elaborate
set-up to draw Joanne into a trap? The area was open, from
what he recalled, and dotted with trees. It was also well publi-
cized on tourist sites worldwide. If Rafa'i was as well read
as Joanne had implied, he'd be aware of it. He might even
have watched the Trooping of the Colour on television. There
were several approaches to the area and it was easily overlooked, which could be both a benefit and a danger, depending
on whose side you were on. 'You're sure it was him?'

'Yes. I recognized his voice.'

'How did he sound?'

'Stressed.'

'I'm not surprised. If it was me, I'd be going mental.'

'What do we do?'

Harry started the car. 'You want to help him, don't you?'

'Of course.'

'Then that's what we'll do.'

THIRTY-NINE

Rik spotted Rafa'i first. The Iraqi was moving around
the northern perimeter of the lake, apparently deep in
thought. But his nervousness was obvious in the jerky
movements of his head. He was hovering in the wake of a
group of Japanese girls giggling and taking snapshots of the
ducks on the water, the birds parading brazenly for titbits from
passers-by.

'By the lake, north side. He's early and using cover,' said
Rik. He was following the Iraqi's progress through a pair of
binoculars, his mobile on hands-free in his top pocket. Rafa'i
wore a white shirt and dark slacks, and had it not been for
the bandage over his right hand and the dark patch beneath

one eye, could have been any other casual visitor enjoying the cool air of a weekday morning in central London.

'OK. Keep him in sight.' Harry's voice came through flat and low. He was standing on Horse Guards Parade, to the east of the park where he could watch the northerly approaches. The time was just coming up to 09.45. 'Has Joanne seen him yet?'

Joanne was sitting alone on the grass at the very end of the lake, in a triangular area between the water, some large flowerbeds and the Guards' Memorial. Her back was to Horse Guards Parade. She had a camera and occasionally pretended to take a photo, turning her body when a view seemed to appeal to her. Then she held the camera to her eye and focussed on a spot by the lake for several seconds.

It was the signal to Rik, who was closest, that she had seen and recognized the former cleric.

'OK, she's got him.'

Rafa'i slowed deliberately, allowing the Japanese girls to pull away from him. He stood by the fencing around the lake and stared into the water. Then he disappeared from sight for a while as he moved behind a section of bushes close to a lakeside cafeteria. When he appeared again, another group of tourists had moved along the path towards him and were stopping for a photo call. Laughing and pushing, they formed a ragged line and grinned at their guide, who was taking snaps with their cameras.

When they dispersed and moved away, Rafa'i had gone.

'*Damn* – where is he?' Rik muttered. 'Something must have spooked him.' He scanned the grass and pathway around the area, sweeping beyond Joanne's position and focussing on the people in the background for signs of a figure hurrying away from the park. But his view was blocked by the tourists as they swung after their guide and approached his position between the parade ground and Birdcage Walk.

'I'm unsighted,' Harry told him. 'The memorial's in the way.'

'It's OK, I've got him.' Rik gave a sigh of relief. 'He's approaching Joanne's position now.'

They were both tense, checking the area for signs of watchers, knowing this was the time of maximum threat. If the killer knew Rafa'i was here, he could make an approach from almost any direction. If he was determined enough, he might even make his play now, rather than waiting for a more convenient opportunity.

Rafa'i approached to within a few feet of Joanne. He looked nervous, but must have spoken, because Joanne looked up and smiled, then gestured to the grass alongside her.

But Rafa'i shook his head and pointed towards the Mall. He wanted to move away from the lake, and into the illusory safety of the trees. For once, Joanne seemed unsure. She hesitated, almost glancing at Rik, which would have been a mistake, then shook her head. Rafa'i responded with an emphatic jerk of his hand.

He was too scared of the open. He wanted to find cover.

From his position on the open parade ground, Harry was watching the people nearby, scanning faces and checking body language.

He had discounted a car attack as impractical; it was too easy to get snarled up in this area, with no guaranteed way out. Similarly, another motorbike, although ideal as an attack vehicle with its speed and manoeuvrability, would stand out too much in this environment.

That left someone on foot. Although still early for the bulk of tourists, there was an alarming number of them moving through the area, any one of which could be a potential threat.

He concentrated on single walkers, dismissing the elderly or infirm, anyone who didn't fit the bill of an agile and capable assassin. Pinstripe suits abounded, briefcases in hand, and smart office workers hurried across the open expanse of the parade ground. Nobody stopping, nobody loitering suspiciously. It was all very normal.

He swung back to Joanne. She seemed to be in urgent discussion with Rafa'i, leaning forward as if to emphasize a point. The Iraqi was shaking his head, casting glances around him as if looking for someone. Joanne must have broached the matter of Harry and Rik, as they had planned. He evidently wasn't impressed.

Then Joanne gave another prearranged signal. She waved her hand in a lazy motion around her head as if brushing away flies. It was the signal to move in, but slowly. If they could talk to him, they might manage to convince him of their desire to help. If not, he would keep on running until the killer caught him.

Harry began walking across the parade ground towards them, skirting a group of American ladies. He saw Rik break cover to his left and move across the grassy area around the lake. In the background was the gingerbread-like building that was Duck Island Cottage. They each had over two hundred metres to cover before they reached Joanne and Rafa'i.

The gap had narrowed to fifty metres when a flock of pigeons burst noisily into the air by the lake. It was on the perimeter path where Rafa'i had first appeared. Simultaneously, a group of tourists separated in a flurry of squeals and laughter, driven apart by the sudden noisy take-off of the birds. It left a gap showing the perimeter path and the stretch of park beyond.

A lone figure was walking towards them.

He was of medium height, slim and lithe, dressed in dark jeans and a black anorak, and had one hand tucked into a side pocket. Something about the man's appearance set alarm bells ringing in Harry's head. Then he realized what it was: unlike everyone else in the immediate vicinity, the man had shown no reaction to the flurry of birds moving off. He was focussed solely on a point in front of him, face pinched in concentration.

He was looking directly at Joanne and Rafa'i.

'*We've got company!*' Harry said urgently, and saw Rik lift his hand in acknowledgement.

They both started running.

Joanne, her attention drawn by the birds, had spotted him, too, because in the same instant, she rose to her feet. Reaching out and grabbing Rafa'i's hand, she began dragging him away towards the south side of the park and Birdcage Walk. He resisted slightly, but she spoke to him and pointed with her camera at the man in the anorak. Whatever she said was clearly enough to persuade Rafa'i to go with her.

The man in the anorak broke into a fast jog, scattering tourists and more birds. He disappeared behind the bushes for a few moments, then came back into view, covering the ground with surprising speed. It was obvious that he was fit and agile and would soon run down the Iraqi, who was having trouble moving quickly, his movements stiff and awkward.

Harry veered to intercept the newcomer. He shouted a

warning, causing a few nearby tourists to spin round. Someone
laughed, as if unsure whether this wasn't some unusual tourist
event for their benefit. A burst of Japanese echoed after the
attacker as he elbowed aside a short, squat lady festooned
with cameras.

At that moment, the man spotted Harry. He increased his
pace, jumping over a couple sitting on the grass, one hand
still in his pocket.

Harry knew he wasn't going to make it in time. He wasn't
a fast enough runner and the angle was all against him. The
attacker's line of approach meant he was drawing ahead and
was now within striking distance of Rafa'i, who was still struggling to keep up with Joanne in spite of her hold on his arm.

Then Rik appeared. He was on a collision course with the
attacker. Before the man realized he was vulnerable, Rik had
hurdled the metal fencing around the grass and struck him
with his shoulder, driving the attacker off his feet and sending
him spinning away across the ground with a savage *whoosh*
of expelled breath.

'Keep going!' Rik yelled to Joanne. He was wincing and
holding his shoulder, but was able to stay on his feet. He
turned to face the attacker, who had rolled away and was
getting to his feet, struggling for breath. When he took his
hand out of his pocket, he was holding a foldaway knife.

He flicked it open, the blade glinting in the sun.

FORTY

Harry drove on, his breathing becoming harsh. His
knees were hurting and he had a pain building in his
chest, and he wondered why he hadn't kept up a better
level of fitness. He swore loudly in frustration.

It was enough to make the knife man turn his head. When
he saw how close Harry was, he stopped and thrust out the
knife, gesturing at them with a short stabbing motion, his face
empty of emotion. Then, before either of them could get any
closer, he turned and raced away and was soon lost among
the walkers around the south side of the lake.

'Rik . . . you all right?' Harry skidded to a halt alongside him. He saw a flash of colour in the background as a police patrol car turned into Horse Guards Road. 'Heads up – police.' If the police stopped them, they could be tied up for hours answering pointless questions.

Rik bent and rubbed his side. 'I'm fine. Just winded.'

'Same here. If they stop us, it was a mugging that went wrong, OK? The victims ran off, too. We can't let them take Rafa'i or Joanne in for questioning.'

'Fair enough.' Rik took a whooping breath of air and winced. 'Shit . . . I think I did a rib in. That bastard was as hard as nails. It was like running into a tree. I wonder why he backed off.'

Harry shrugged. 'Maybe he didn't like the odds. We were lucky he didn't have anything more lethal than a blade.'

The police car drifted to a stop alongside them, the passenger window dropping.

'Everything all right, sir?' The officer in the passenger seat studied them coolly. His driver was using his radio, but didn't appear unduly concerned. In the background, a woman officer was watching from a wooden police box behind one of the government buildings.

Harry wondered how much she had seen. 'No problem,' he replied. 'A bloke ran towards a couple and my friend thought he was after a handbag. It was a mistake.' He gestured towards Rik, who was still looking winded. 'He got a stitch trying to play Superman.'

'If you say so, sir.' The policeman considered it for a moment, then said something to his driver. The car surged away, leaving them alone.

'Close,' said Rik, and took a series of deep breaths.

'Yeah. Come on.' Harry turned towards Birdcage Walk. 'Let's catch up with our runaway Iraqi.'

They followed the direction in which Joanne had hustled Rafa'i, and found her standing alone on the edge of Parliament Square. She looked annoyed and confused, but far from frightened.

'He bloody pulled away from me,' she explained angrily, gesturing towards the square, 'and jumped in a cab.' She rolled her eyes towards two policemen walking along the pavement fifty yards away. 'If they hadn't shown up, I'd have dragged his arse back out and sat on him until you got here.'

'Don't worry about it,' Harry said, glancing back towards the park. He was worried that the man with the knife would show up again. Given his past performance in dealing with his targets, he was unlikely to give up merely because they had inconveniently got in the way. 'Come on, let's find somewhere to talk.'

He led them across the square and down the steps by the Embankment to Westminster Pier. A number of Thames excursion cruisers were loading passengers nearby, but where they were standing, in the shadow of a statue of Boadicea, they were as good as alone.

He stopped and turned to Joanne. 'Did you call anyone and tell them where you were meeting Rafa'i?'

'Call who? I don't know anyone.' She looked angry at the suggestion, her jaw clenched tight under the skin.

He ignored her anger and pointed to her rucksack. 'Empty that out.'

'Why? What the hell are you saying?' She snatched the bag away as if daring him to take it from her. She was standing squarely, balanced and ready, and it was easy to see why she had stood out to the recruiter for the operation in Iraq.

'He's saying you might have a bug,' Rik suggested calmly, leaning on the wall with his back to the river. 'Either that or Rafa'i told somebody where he was meeting you. My bet's on a bug.'

With obvious reluctance, Joanne opened her rucksack and allowed Harry to go through it. He checked the side pockets and the few items of clothing inside, then examined the straps and fabric, feeling for anything unusual in the structure of the bag.

There was nothing. He handed it back.

'Finished?' Joanne muttered with a withering scorn. 'Jesus – no wonder you're single. You're paranoid, you know that?'

Harry ignored the comment. He nodded at her camera, which she was still clutching. 'Where did you get that?'

Joanne frowned. 'I bought it a few days ago. I had to leave the issue one behind. Why?'

'What about your mobile?'

She dug into her pocket and held it out. It looked scratched and well used. 'This? It was part of my original kit, along with the sat phone. I was supposed to surrender everything personal before I left for Iraq, but I held on to it.'

'What about the phone? Where's that?'

'In a sewage ditch. I dumped it the day I flew out. They searched us at the airport – I couldn't exactly pretend I was an aid worker with that kind of kit on me, could I?'

Harry took the phone from her and stripped off the back. He took out the battery and studied the SIM card, then turned and tossed everything over the wall into the swirling brown water below.

'Hey – what did you do that for?' Joanne turned on him. 'Are you nuts?'

Rik placed a gentle hand on her shoulder. 'They must have placed a tracker in the phone,' he explained. 'It's the only way that guy could have turned up just like that. He wasn't following Rafa'i. He was following you.'

She batted his hand away. 'How the hell do you know that? Anyway, if they'd bugged the phone, they'd have known days ago that I was still alive and come looking for me before.'

'They probably did,' he replied. 'Only they hadn't any leads until you switched it on and made a call. Right up until then, they must have thought you'd got caught in the blast and were no longer active.' He moved away a couple of paces to prevent anyone getting too close and overhearing their conversation.

'He's right,' Harry said. 'They'd hardly have sent someone to Baghdad to check it out after the explosion. But once they realized you'd made it out, there was every reason to start tracking you through the signal.' He gestured around them. 'They already had your number and it's easier here with all the transmitters. The moment you made a call, they had you pinpointed.'

Joanne looked unconvinced. 'Then how come Humphries didn't say anything?'

'Why should he? The whole point of operational security is that they don't tell people what they don't need to. It gets in the way.'

'That's ridiculous. He'd have told me.'

'There is another explanation,' Harry spoke reasonably, trying to take the heat out of the situation. 'The phone might have been bugged as a rescue option. If anything went wrong and you got isolated in hostile territory, they could send in a team to find you. That would have been the good guys.'

Joanne chewed her lip but said nothing, still too angry with him. But at least she was listening.

'Then along come the bad guys,' he continued. 'The ones trying to kill Rafa'i. They worked out that you were both alive and running, and decided to use the phone for different reasons. Where you and your phone went, so did the man in the anorak. Trace you, catch a lead on Rafa'i at the same time and finish the job all nice and neat.'

The silence ticked away, interrupted by the rattle and clang of a gangplank being wheeled away from one of the pleasure cruisers. A man shouted and the water around the stern began to boil as the boat moved away.

Joanne took a deep breath. 'That would be saying somebody never meant for me to come out again. Or if I got out, they could silence me. I don't believe it. They wouldn't do that – *Christ, they don't kill their own people!*'

Harry didn't deny it and didn't look at Rik. *How do you tell someone that you know different, that you were once marked down for death by people on your own side?*

'They might not have planned it that way. They might have hoped you'd get out in time and it could all be explained away. Maybe they got Humphries to call the meeting to get you out of harm's way. When the bad guys realized you'd made it out and had dropped off the radar, you became a loose cannon – a liability. Because one day you'd work out what had happened and you'd want to talk about it. And with what you knew about the operation, you were dangerous.'

'What about the good guys? They wouldn't just consign me to the dustbin, would they?' Joanne's face flushed red at the idea that she had been so casually dismissed as expendable by the people who had selected, recruited and trained her.

'Think about it,' Harry pointed out. 'You didn't surface after the explosion, neither were you at the safe house, which is where they'd have expected you to turn up. The logical assumption after a while would have been that you'd been killed. Without a thorough forensics check of the compound, they wouldn't have been able to prove otherwise. Frankly, I can't see anyone risking a forensics team for a non-attributable operation over there, anyway.' His tone was sympathetic but matter-of-fact. 'You said it yourself; you had no family, nothing to tie you down. There was nobody to tell . . . and nobody to press for an inquest. Sorry to be brutal, but it's why they chose you in the first place. You were expendable.'

Her expression said she knew he was right, but her words said different. 'I don't believe it.'

'Don't let it get to you,' said Rik, moving closer. 'If you were abandoned, it was through a balls-up, not callousness.'

Joanne hugged herself, absorbing the information and looking at them in turn. Bit by bit she appeared to relax. 'Bastards,' she muttered softly, although it wasn't clear to whom she was referring. 'How do we contact Rafa'i now? My mobile number was all he had. He doesn't know anybody else.'

'We wait,' said Harry. 'To be precise, you wait – back in the park.'

'You think he'll come back?' Rik asked. 'He might've been spooked for good.'

'I doubt it.' Harry looked at Joanne. 'He doesn't know anyone else, and you saved him from Anorak Man, so he'll trust you. Did you notice he wasn't carrying anything?'

The realization of what Harry was saying gave Joanne's voice an edge of excitement. 'He's staying nearby. I never gave it a thought.'

'At least somewhere close enough to leave his stuff.' Harry gestured back towards the park. 'Come on. Let's see if he's still around. In the meantime, you can help us understand why somebody's so intent on killing him.'

'What about the man with the knife? He might be hanging around as well.' Joanne looked unsure, but they knew it was not about her own safety. She didn't want to expose Rafa'i to another attack.

'This time we stick together,' Rik murmured. 'If he tries again, he'll come unstuck. Pity we didn't get a good look at him, though. I was too busy running to focus clearly. All I saw was a blur.'

Joanne held up the camera. 'No problem. I took a shot of him as he ran towards us. It should be clear enough to give us a face to watch out for.'

FORTY-ONE

'**W**hy does this face look familiar?' Rik was studying the six-by-four print that Joanne had produced from her digital card at a nearby camera shop. The photo was slightly out of focus, but showed the man in the anorak striding along the path, leaning forward as he broke into his attack run. His face was thin and edged with concentration, and he appeared to be staring right into the camera lens. Frozen in time around him was a scattering of people and birds, a vivid framework of motion that served, if anything, to emphasize his total focus on where he was going. The overriding impression was of a jungle cat stalking its prey, ignoring every other distraction around him as he concentrated on his target.

'You know him?' Joanne looked surprised.

'I'm not sure. Maybe the type, not the bloke.' They knew what he meant. He had the chilling aura of a hunter – purposeful and resolute, and not the kind to be put off easily. The fact that he had backed away when faced by Harry and Rik meant nothing. He had clearly judged the odds and found them unfavourable. He would simply try again when circumstances were better. The danger was, next time they might not see him coming.

Harry leaned forward. Rik was right: there was something familiar about the man, but he couldn't place him, either.

'Was he the man in the car?' he asked Joanne. He hadn't been close enough to see the man she'd shot at, merely the bulk of his outline.

'I don't know.' She fingered the photo. 'I only caught a glimpse. It was all so quick.' She looked past Harry and scanned the area behind him, sifting groups and watching for anyone who didn't fit. The two men were doing the same.

They were sitting facing inwards on the edge of the grass, not far from where Joanne had met Rafa'i. There were already far more pedestrians about than there had been an hour ago, which was making their task that much more difficult. But

without knowing Rafa'i's whereabouts, or even whether he
would come back to find Joanne or not, they could do nothing
else but sit and wait. And hope.

'He'll come,' said Harry. 'If not now, then another time.'
He was counting on the former cleric's desperate need for
help in a foreign land to bring him back to the one person he
knew he could trust. That would be Joanne. Placed in the
same predicament, Harry would have done the same.

'It's crazy,' said Joanne thoughtfully, 'but I've seen him
somewhere, too.' She prodded the photo lying on the grass
between them. 'But not here – I'd remember it.'

'In Battersea?' Harry probed her gently. 'He might have
been hanging around outside.'

She shook her head without looking at him. She still hadn't
forgiven him his treatment down by the Embankment. 'No.
Not there.'

Rik said, 'Have you still got the photo you took in Baghdad?'

'A copy, yes.' Joanne dug in her rucksack. They had left
the other one with Sheila Humphries. It would have been
almost callous to take it from her; the most recent picture she
had of her brother. She handed it over.

'I knew it!' Rik muttered with a grim smile. He held up
the photo so that they could both see it, and pointed to the
two security men in the background. One of them was lean,
the face distinct and familiar. It was the man from the park.

'He's official,' said Harry. 'That makes things worse.' A
freelance they could have coped with; someone who was
merely working for the money might give up if the opposition got too tough. But a man on the payroll of a government
department would have no such freedom . . . and would have
the resources and backup to follow the job through. He'd
therefore be all but impossible to dissuade.

'Unless he jumped ship afterwards,' said Rik. 'Or he's a
subbie.'

'What?' Joanne was still staring at the photo.

'A sub-contractor,' Harry explained. 'Most of the security
staff out there are working for PSCs. A few are ex-Special
Forces on short-term contracts to the MOD. They'll have
already been through all the security training, and if any of
them go down, it doesn't impact the official payroll.' He
shrugged. 'The government being creative with public money.'

'So he's a merc?'

'Yes. But they're sensitive souls – they don't like that word very much.' He studied the photo and the faces, and wondered how close the man with the thin face was to Major Andrew Marshall, the one sitting opposite Gordon Humphries.

They sat and waited, concentrating on watching the park. If Rafa'i was coming back, he was taking his time.

'Would he go to the nearest Iraqi community?' Harry asked. He knew that London hosted a mixed Sunni, Kurdish and Shi'a population, and Rafa'i might look for an area where he could blend in. Safety in numbers.

'No.' Joanne shook her head emphatically. 'There's a risk he'd be recognized. There are people here from the same area, although not necessarily from the same tribal group. But he's too well known; if anyone saw him, word would spread fast.' She gestured to the open park around them. 'Out here is different. People don't look too closely at other faces, especially if they're in western clothes. To them he's just another man.'

'Bummer,' said Rik, and went back to people watching.

Eventually Joanne stirred and checked her watch. 'He won't be back today,' she announced. 'It's gone noon.'

'Time for prayers?' Rik asked.

'He has a strict prayer regime, but it's nothing to do with that. One of the things I was told to impress on him was that if something went wrong and we got split up, we had to have an arrangement for meeting up again. They said to try again one hour after the agreed time, then at twenty-four-hour repeats.'

They checked their watches. It was well past the first hour already.

'And always the same place?' Harry asked.

'Yes. That way, we wouldn't have to rely on finding somewhere new to either of us, and twenty-four hours would allow any dust to settle. I never thought we'd have to use it, though.'

It made sense. This wasn't Rafa'i's home turf, so he wouldn't be familiar with the terrain. After what had happened earlier, he'd be doubly cautious, yet desperate enough to rely on using the same place again. As long as he could conquer his fear of being spotted again. 'So he'll be here again at ten tomorrow.'

'I hope so.'

'Good enough for me,' Rik murmured. 'Sitting round here is giving me the jitters.' He glanced at Harry. 'Let's hope matey with the knife doesn't come to the same conclusion. It could get crowded.'

'There's no reason why he should. He'll probably carry on looking. We'll have to watch our backs, though, maybe stay away from home for a while.'

He glanced at Joanne, aware that he'd spoiled the trust that had been growing between them. It had been heavy-handed, but a necessity. He hoped it wasn't going to get in the way of what they had to talk about next.

'I don't know enough about the situation over there,' he said, referring to Iraq. 'So what I can't figure out is why someone wants Rafa'i dead. It can't just be sectarian; that wouldn't involve westerners, and the locals have got enough of their own trigger-men to kill him a hundred times over. Knocking off one former cleric doesn't change anything.'

Joanne said nothing, returning his look with a blank face.

'It might,' suggested Rik, to break the awkward silence, 'if there was a danger Rafa'i could destabilize the order of things. Their parliament's ticking over reasonably well. OK, not great, and maybe short of a minister every now and then when the insurgents get lucky. But no worse than you'd expect with the country in the state it is. Then along comes this other bloke: well respected, popular . . . even got a whiff of the cloth about him. It makes him special – Messianic, even.' He looked at Joanne. 'What was it you said – a big cheese among the locals? Somebody like that in the background, suddenly the politicos who're in it for the power and money might get nervous, feel threatened.'

Still Joanne said nothing, so Harry joined in. 'He's right,' he said quietly, watching her face for a reaction. 'The politicians are used to one group or another vying for power. If they can't work with them, they buy them off and everything goes quiet again until the next one comes along. I can't see that they'd bother killing somebody like Rafa'i unless there was something bigger at stake.'

'What are you suggesting?' Joanne said finally. She seemed relaxed but there was tension in the whiteness of her knuckles.

'He was specifically targeted, wasn't he?' said Harry. 'That's why you were sent out there. There was a real and credible threat and he needed protection. Otherwise, what was the point?'

'They could have given him a shield of Coalition troops,' Rik pointed out, 'if he was that important.'

'He was important all right.' Harry lifted his eyebrows, waiting for Joanne to comment. When she didn't, he continued, 'If he's the one I remember reading about, wasn't he the man who believed in the oil and mineral resources being controlled by the state? That must have been seen by some as a real threat.' He paused. 'Only it wasn't the locals who were bothered, was it? They didn't have so much to lose.'

'Oh, man.' Rik spoke softly as he saw where Harry was going.

'Who would stand to lose most if Iraq suddenly turned round and locked everyone else out of their oil production programme? If someone new came along and turned the tables on western interests? It wouldn't be the current politicians – they don't have the power or the popular support.' He tore up a handful of grass and tossed it into the air, watching the fragments fall to the ground. 'But somebody with a wide national following would be a genuine threat. Reason enough to get rid of him and blame the insurgents.'

'What are you saying?' Joanne's voice was low.

'You know what I'm saying. The only ones with the means to do it would come from within the Coalition. Oil is money and money talks. That's why you saw a bunch of mercs coming to the safe house. That's why Humphries didn't make it out of Baghdad alive. This whole business is all about oil and money, and getting rid of anyone who poses a threat to the flow of both. They've probably been scratching at this particular sore since the first Gulf War.'

'You mean our *government's* behind this?'

'More likely a group or groups *inside* government. This current lot might be devious and untrustworthy, but I don't see them having the nerve to put something like this together. They'd rather go in afterwards and talk their heads off about what to do next, or blame someone else.'

Rik gave a customary scowl. 'But that would undermine the Coalition if it ever came out. Would they risk it?'

'Yes.' Joanne responded before Harry could answer. She looked into the distance, then turned back to them. 'I never took much interest in all that political rubbish. I'm a squaddie and I go where they point me. But Rafa'i said something a couple of weeks before the explosion.' She paused, her face fixed in concentration.

'What?' said Rik.

'We were alone. The security squad were patrolling outside the house and he was in a bit of a mood. Thoughtful, I mean, not bad-tempered. There had been another suicide bombing an hour or so before, a few streets away. I'd made a comment about it being a bit close for comfort. To be honest, I was considering bugging out and finding somewhere safer, or maybe getting a fighting patrol to come in and cause a diversion so we could slip away.'

'You could arrange that?' Harry looked surprised.

'Gordon Humphries could. When I mentioned it to Rafa'i, he laughed it off, saying it wasn't the insurgents he was worried about. I asked him what he meant, and he said if anyone caused his death it would be elements within the Coalition. The so-called friendly forces.' She shrugged and gave a wry smile. 'I thought he meant the Americans might drop a bomb on the house by mistake. I told him that wouldn't happen.'

'What did he say?' asked Harry.

'He said they'd already tried it once and missed. It was only a matter of time before they tried again.'

'He was right, then,' said Harry sombrely. 'Wasn't he?'

FORTY-TWO

A child complained loudly a few yards away from where they were sitting, and a party of schoolgirls in uniform giggled at two young male joggers. The sounds seemed magnified as Harry and Rik took in what Joanne had said, the normal activities contrasting sharply with their not so normal discussion.

'But surely,' Harry mused, 'that would point right at the West. The Coalition would lose all support from the local politicians; it'd be like showboating their absolute control, saying they were able to do away with anyone they didn't like the look of.'

'They've got that already,' said Rik. 'You saying the Coalition aren't still pulling all the strings out there?'

'Only while they can use locals to do their dirty work. Going in as blatant as that, though, is different.' He looked at Joanne. 'Unless . . .'

Her look was challenging. 'Unless what?'

'Unless they had a rock-solid reason for taking him out – one that would get them support from all quarters, no questions asked.'

Her face showed scepticism. 'What reason could accomplish that? It's too risky. The whole of the Middle East would be up in arms at the idea of the West killing Rafa'i – along with half the outside world. It's bad enough they blame us for Saddam's execution. I told you, Rafa'i is too important to the Coalition to lose.'

'They need him more than he needs them?' He looked doubtful. 'I wonder.'

Her look was withering. 'And of course, you've got a reason for saying that.'

'I don't, actually. I just haven't got there yet. But I will.'

Rik got to his feet, brushing grass fragments off the seat of his pants. 'Well, let me know when you work it out,' he murmured, and glanced at his watch. 'All that running made me hungry. Anybody for lunch?'

Barely ten minutes' drive from where they were sitting, a young, fresh-faced man named Allen Bentley was slumped in a Ford saloon, wishing he was in bed – preferably not alone. After a number of energetic assignations with his latest girl-friend, a second-year medical student from Madrid with an eager taste for all that London had to offer, he was dismayed at having copped a last-minute tour of surveillance duty which threatened to disrupt further activities.

He rubbed his eyes and checked his wing mirror as a trio of girls – Australians, he guessed, all golden tans and long legs – emerged from a small backpackers' hostel and wandered laughing along the street. The building was just behind Victoria Station, convenient for casual travellers needing a place to doss for a night or two.

Allen felt his anger dwindle at the thought. The place was probably stocked with female talent, all thousands of miles away from controlling parents and desperate for some action. His orders were to stay well away and not go inside, which was a pity. He might need a replacement if the *Madrileña* blew him out for not being there when she needed him, courtesy of his sodding duty officer.

He made a note in his duty log and slid it back beneath the seat. His target had just jogged along the street and entered the hostel. The only thing Bentley had been told about the man was that he was highly dangerous and all contact was to be avoided. He was to go nowhere near him and under no circumstances to blow his cover. Merely watch and report. And stay alert.

Bentley yawned and stretched both arms behind him. If he'd known this job was going to be so dull or that he was going to be kept in the dark like a bloody mushroom, he'd have joined the police force. Eight months of what he'd been assured would be fast-track training and what had he seen so far? Endless assessments and paperwork, with several specialized courses and an occasional stint of surveillance followed by more paperwork and meetings. Now this pointless bloody caper. Carlisle, his predecessor on this job, must have had some internal pull to have been able to dump this in his lap. Just wait until he caught up with him.

He watched a taxi pull in to the kerb across the street, double-parking close to a delivery van. The rear offside door of the cab opened and a tall, rangy blonde stepped out. She wore calf-length boots and a short skirt, and as she slid her feet to the ground, she showed a long expanse of smooth thigh. She caught Bentley looking and smiled.

Bloody hell, he thought, sitting up. Maybe pulling this stint wasn't so bad after all . . .

As Bentley was fantasizing about his chances with the tall blonde, the man named Dog took the stairs down to the basement washroom. He was breathing easily, even though he had jogged nearly all the way after the encounter with the two men in St James's Park. His face was flushed, and not from the exertions; he was feeling an unaccustomed burn of anger at the way things had turned out.

He kicked the washroom door back, causing a tall, cadaverous Somali cleaner to scuttle out without looking back.

It was Jennings' fault, Dog decided. Him and the idiots pulling his strings. Just a few more paces, that's all he'd needed. If it hadn't been for the two former spooks Jennings had hired, he'd have been home and dry, another contract in the bag.

He splashed cold water over his face, a trigger to calm his nerves. If he'd used a handgun back in the park, the outcome would have been very different. But waving a firearm in central London was a ticket to assisted suicide, and he'd been confident of achieving the same ends with a blade. He wouldn't make that mistake again.

He gulped some water and spat it out. He shouldn't have scared the cleaner; it wasn't his fault, and kicking off like that only attracted attention. It was time to reassess his options and adapt. It was what he'd been trained to do, and you never ignored the training; you changed your plans to move with the circumstances. The first thing to do was get some transport. Something easy to move and conceal. Something nobody would look twice at. Another motorbike would do; they were easy to pick up and practically invisible.

He scrubbed his face with a paper towel and tossed it on the floor, then walked back upstairs to the lobby. Instead of going up to his room on the third floor, he went outside. The stuff in the room was minimal and disposable; he'd got spare kit stashed in another room he'd rented at a hostel near Euston. It spread the risk and gave him options in case things blew up on him and he had to leave this place – a habit he'd learned the hard way. Best he didn't hang around here too long in case the cleaner had called the cops.

As Dog turned out of the hostel and headed along the street towards the station, he noticed a figure in a car parked on a yellow line fifty yards away. Nothing unusual in that; just another motorist among many in a busy street.

Yet a deep-seated instinct made him stop, his heart picking up a beat.

The vehicle was facing away from him, dusty and unremarkable, a couple of years old. The driver was staring at a blonde girl legging it along the opposite pavement. He was young and looked as if he was waiting for someone.

But Dog didn't think so. He took three steps and slid into

a doorway that put him in the man's blind spot, and waited. Two minutes later, after the driver made a brief, one-sided phone call, he knew he'd been right: the driver wasn't waiting – he was a watcher.

Dog stepped out of the doorway and walked towards the car. He slipped his hand into his pocket. He hugged the shadows, head down but watching the car's wing mirror, where he could see the pale oval of the driver's face. The man was still eyeing the blonde. Silly sod. The lack of professionalism made Dog angry. Not that he gave a stuff about the man himself, but the sheer disregard for the rules of the game was an insult.

He gripped the knife against his leg.

He'd been told to expect this, that sooner or later he'd pop up on someone's radar. He'd been doing this job a long time, and that made him noticeable. But that wasn't what annoyed him. Was this what they really thought of him – sending some junior, pasty-faced prick fresh out of the training centre to watch his every move?

Well, for that, he'd have to teach them a lesson.

He snicked open the blade. Stopped by the driver's window and tapped lightly on the glass. Glanced each way to check the immediate area. There was nobody close by, which gave him a small window of opportunity. He'd had worse.

The driver lowered the window instinctively and looked up just as Dog stepped in close and took his hand out of his pocket. The knife had a narrow blade, a souvenir of his last tour in Kosovo, and clearly had one purpose: it was a killing tool.

The driver's eyes fastened on it instantly, his face draining of colour as he realized his mistake. Hardly more than mid-twenties, thought Dog. Probably a university intake on his first observation. He smiled, pleased that his instincts were still sound.

'Should have kept your eyes off the girls, kid,' Dog said softly. 'That's sloppy tradecraft.'

He inserted the point of the knife into the man's ear, and with a sharp pump of his arm, rammed it all the way home.

He smiled.

The day hadn't been a complete waste.

FORTY-THREE

Rik led the way to a sandwich bar just off Victoria Street. On the way, the wail of emergency vehicles echoed over the rooftops from the direction of Victoria Station. Hopefully it was nothing to do with them, but they stayed close to the buildings, anyway. There was no sense in taking chances, even though they had no reason to think they were yet on anyone's 'watch' list.

It reminded Harry to try Jennings' number again. They hadn't heard from the lawyer, and instinct told him they weren't likely to. But he was their only point of contact to this business.

There was no answer.

Rik scooped up a selection of rolls, cakes, coffee and fruit juice all round, while Harry kept an eye on the street, less interested in eating than trying to figure out what to do next. Joanne stood silently nearby, wrapped in her own thoughts.

When they were sitting around a table and eating, Rik leaned forward and said around a mouthful of French stick, 'OK, so what's the plan? We need to get this thing moving, right? I can't stand this waiting around.'

Harry said, 'I've been thinking about that.' He peeled off a chunk of bread and chewed on it thoughtfully. Planning was something he was good at, but it only worked if you got it right and didn't trip over your own feet. Trouble was, they were all stumbling in the dark here, and there were no clear rules to follow.

'We can't make contact with Rafa'i until ten tomorrow,' he reminded them. 'Not unless we get lucky and bump into him in the street – and that's not going to happen.' He tore off another piece of bread, his appetite returning. Even Joanne was chewing dutifully, following the soldier's maxim of eating when you had the chance, because you never know when the next meal will come. 'In fact, there's more of a risk that we'll get marked by the killer before then.'

'You think he'll hang around?' Joanne paused in her eating.

'Wouldn't you? He didn't finish the job. Yes, he's still around.'

'OK. So what do we do until tomorrow?'

'We could go looking for him.' He smiled to show he was joking. 'But that wouldn't be a good idea. We need to find Humphries' contact, Marshall. He's the key to this. His sister said he was either Five or Six. Logic says Six, since Humphries was, too. But we need to make sure.'

Rik looked up. 'What if he's one of the bad guys?'

'It's a risk we have to take. Do you have an alternative?'

Rik threw a look at Joanne with a pained expression. 'He does this. Whenever we're at a sticky point and need a plan, he comes up with something and asks if I've got anything better.'

'What about you?' Joanne replied, turning to Harry. 'You were both with Five. Surely you've got contacts who might know him?'

'It doesn't work like that. Any friends we had have moved on. Those that haven't won't help.' It wasn't strictly true, and for two reasons: he'd already thought of calling Bill Maloney, his operational partner on several jobs. If anyone could get him a hearing, it would be Bill. But it might be at the expense of his job and Harry couldn't do that to him. Compromising his former colleague was not an option – not unless they were right up against the wire.

The second reason highlighted a dilemma. He did have a route into the security world – a legitimate one. But it was one he didn't want to use unless he was forced to. Any information from carded personnel would be treated as high priority until checked out. It would open up a major response over which he would have no little or no control, because the moment he made contact, the system would light up like a Christmas tree.

He pushed that idea aside. It needed to be much more focussed, to reach a man with real decision-making powers. 'So,' he said, 'Vauxhall Cross or Thames House?' The head-quarters of MI6 and MI5 were both situated on the Embankment a few hundred yards from where they were sitting. But going anywhere near either of them would be like sticking their heads into the lion's mouth. The question was, which lion and which mouth?

Joanne reacted with surprise. 'Are you nuts? They'd slap us in a cell the moment we stepped through the door.'

'I'm not saying we actually go there. But if we can get a message to Marshall, one he can't ignore, he might respond.'

'It'd have to be a good one.' Rik balled up a napkin and dumped it in his empty mug. 'Something that lit a bomb under his arse, otherwise, we'll be waiting for ever. That's if he even gets it.'

'Oh, he'll get it all right.' Harry spread out his own napkin and reached for a pen. 'What do these guys live by?' he asked. 'What governs their every action?'

They both looked blank. He wrote in block letters on the soft tissue, then spun it round so they could see what he'd written.

The words read: OPERATION PAMPER, followed by a row of numbers.

'Dude,' Rik drawled, feigning hero-worship. 'You're like, so *out* there, man.'

Harry smiled in appreciation. 'I have my moments, sunshine. I have my moments.'

Joanne stared at them in wonder. 'Would you two tell me what's going on or is this strictly a boys-only moment?'

'He's giving Marshall your operation code name,' Rik told her, 'and a mobile where he can call us. Marshall won't be able to resist it.' Then he added without apparent irony, 'These spooky-dooky types love all that stuff, like codes and numbers. If Marshall's still around, it'll draw him out.'

'But they'll trace us through the phone number,' she pointed out.

'I bet they won't.' Rik stared at Harry. 'It's nicked, isn't it?'

Harry shrugged modestly. 'It's a spare I picked up. And we won't be on long enough for him to get a fix. You two ready?'

He led them outside and along the street until they reached a small post office. Inside, he went to a rack of envelopes and selected two large, white A4-size envelopes and a plain white notepad. He paid for them and went to the writing counter near the window, and scrawled in large block letters the operational code name PAMPER followed by the stolen mobile phone number. He did this on two separate pieces of paper, then inserted one in each envelope and wrote on the outside. One was addressed to Major Andrew Marshall at Thames

House, the headquarters of MI5, the other to Marshall at Vauxhall Cross, which housed MI6.

'We don't know for sure where he works or who for,' Harry admitted, sealing the envelopes, 'but it's a fair guess it's one of them. This gives us two bites at the cherry. Now we need a delivery method.'

'How about him?' Rik nodded towards a motorcycle courier outside. He was dressed in an orange tabard and grungy leather trousers, and lounging on his machine, chewing an apple. A stream of chatter was pouring from a radio clipped to his jacket.

'He'll do,' said Harry.

Rik took some money from his wallet and reached for the envelopes. But Joanne intercepted him.

'Let me.' She took the money and envelopes and walked out the door. Moments later she was in conversation with the courier, who stopped chewing his apple and sat up. Seconds later, he was stuffing the two envelopes in his pouch.

'She's good,' Rik said approvingly. 'Better than me.'

'Prettier, too. He'd have told you to get stuffed.'

They left the sandwich bar the moment the courier was out of sight and walked to Victoria Station, where they found a corner table at a café close to one of the exits. Then they settled down to wait. The crush of travellers was an added barrier against being spotted, or being overheard by anyone if Marshall should ring. Leaving the sandwich bar had been a simple precaution; if the courier were detained and asked where he had picked up the envelopes, it wouldn't take long for an active unit to be out trawling the streets.

'What if he doesn't call?' Joanne asked. 'He might be away.'

'He'll call,' said Harry. 'Somehow, it'll get through to him.'

'You sound very sure of yourself.' Her tone was less hostile now, as if she was warming to him after their earlier fall-out.

'Actually, I'm not,' he admitted frankly. 'But when you've nothing else to go for, you have to follow your instincts.'

'Is that how you work when you're finding people – by instincts?'

'Sometimes. Planning works, too.'

'What he means,' Rik interjected, setting his chair back on its rear legs, 'is that he does the planning and I have the instinctive flashes of brilliance. It's the flashes that work best.'

He reached out and scooped up a discarded newspaper from the next table and flicked through it.

Seconds later, he sat forward with a thump. 'Christ, look at this.' He dropped the newspaper flat on the table so that Harry could see the headline.

Libyan Bank Official 'Executed', Claims Brother

In a plot worthy of a thriller writer, Libyan bank official, Abuzeid Matuq, 42, who disappeared from his London office recently, allegedly taking with him somewhere between £100,000 and £800,000 of his employers' money, has been found dead on a beach near Dunwich, in Suffolk. His brother, Muhammed, speaking from Paris, where he claims he is in hiding, says Matuq was set up by high-ranking enemies within the Libyan government and that he was innocent of any theft. This is their way, he claims, of dealing with people they disapprove of, and his brother Abuzeid has paid the price for running foul of somebody jealous of his success. Muhammed Matuq does not go so far as to implicate the country's ruler, Colonel Muammar Gaddafi, who is currently working hard to gain rapprochement with the West following 9/11, but points the finger at 'elements within his inner circle of ministers'. So far, police are not commenting on whether the death is suspicious, but have confirmed that none of the missing money has yet been recovered.

'One of the men you were looking for?' asked Joanne.

'Not just looking – we found him,' said Rik. 'Or Harry did. Trouble is, so did someone else.'

'But why dump him in the open? It would have been easier to bury him.'

'Someone must have decided it was better to have him surface.' Harry shook his head, exchanging a look with Rik.

Joanne caught the silent exchange. 'What?'

'It felt like a pro job at the time, but there was no proof, no motive.' Harry nodded at the newspaper. 'But if we're right and it was the same man who tried to kill Rafa'i, then we were used to trace Matuq so the killer could slip in and finish him off.'

'If this killer works for the British government, why would they want to kill a Libyan banker?'

'I'm not sure they do. The government wouldn't sanction killing someone on behalf of the Libyans . . . but someone with a vested interest might.'

'Jennings,' Rik muttered sourly.

Joanne looked at Harry. 'Hang on. If the killer has been the same one all along, and he was in Iraq with Humphries and Marshall, he might know what I look like. How could he have mistaken Cath for me?'

Harry had only one answer for that. 'He's a loose cannon; he's killing without thought. Maybe he's been at it too long.' He stopped as the phone on the table began to ring. He checked the caller display. It was a withheld number.

'Yes?'

'My name's Marshall,' said a man's voice. 'I believe we have something to discuss.'

FORTY-FOUR

'Give me a description,' Harry replied. He signalled to the other two to be ready to move. They had discussed tactics earlier, and were comfortable with what they had to do. Rik had warned them that if the call came from Marshall, he would already have his technical bods running down the signal. They wouldn't have much time.

'I don't follow. A description of what?' Marshall, if it was indeed he, spoke slowly, without any sign of tension. It meant he was stretching out the call for as long as he could to allow his people to do their work and get a fix on their location.

'Of yourself. A thumbnail sketch.'

There was a momentary silence. Then Marshall said, 'As you wish. I'm slim, clean-shaven, of medium height with fair hair. That enough for you, Mr—?'

'Not nearly close enough,' said Harry. 'Try again.' He cut the connection and waited.

Seconds later, the phone rang again. It was Marshall

sounding mildly contrite. 'I apologize. That was stupid of me. You know what I look like, don't you?'

'Correct.' Harry hoped the implied humility lasted long enough for him to convince the man that the three of them shouldn't be shot on sight. 'You recognized the code I sent you.' It wasn't a question.

'It rang a bell. How did you find out about it, Mr—?'

Harry ignored the baited hook. 'I have my sources. I also know about the subject of the operation.'

'What about him?'

Him. Not her. Not it. It was a small slip, but significant. 'I know where he is.'

'Really.' There was another slight delay and Harry decided he'd been on long enough. Then Marshall spoke again. 'Are you a journalist?'

'If I were, you'd have read about this over your cornflakes.'

A dry chuckle echoed down the line. 'Good point. Very well, where do we go from here? Are you suggesting a meeting?'

'Give me a number I can call tomorrow. A mobile, not a landline.'

'Actually, I'd rather we had a face-to—'

'You've got ten seconds, then I'm gone.'

Marshall read out a number.

Harry disconnected and walked across the concourse after Rik and Joanne.

They split up and left separately, each merging into the crowd. Harry had already checked for security cameras and told the others where they were. There were probably others they were unaware of, but they wouldn't be able to avoid them all. They regrouped along Victoria Street and walked north towards Green Park and Buckingham Palace, sheltering among clutches of tourists and office workers.

'What did he say?' asked Rik.

'Not much. He's trying to figure out whether his day just got bad or even worse.'

'Did you mention Jennings?'

'No. I didn't want to be on too long. I'll ask him later.'

Rik raised his eyebrows. 'Later?'

'I told him I'd call tomorrow. He gave me a mobile number.' He recited it from memory and Joanne and Rik each made a note. It was a simple precaution; if anything happened to him, they'd have a means to contact Marshall. Whether it made any difference to their situation was debatable, but at least they wouldn't be left in the dark. He glanced at his watch. They all needed a change of clothes and toiletries in case they had to stay on the move. 'We need to pick up some stuff. Joanne, can you buy some skivvies from a shop?'

'Sure. Won't your places be risky, though? If Marshall's working with Jennings, he'll have men on the way there now.'

'If he's working with Jennings, we're stuffed anyway,' Rik muttered.

'We need some transport,' said Harry. 'Rik?'

'Sure. I know where I can get a loaner. Mine's in an underground garage with CCTV. I'll need to move it.'

'OK. We'll stop by on the way.'

He left Rik to make his own way and took off with Joanne for his flat in Islington. They walked by the building twice before he was satisfied there were no watchers, then Harry went up and packed an overnight bag, leaving Joanne downstairs to watch the street. Three minutes later, he left the flat and went down to the Saab.

He drove to Rik's place, stopping on the way for Joanne to buy some essentials, then circled the block until Rik stepped out from an alleyway and climbed in the back. He was packed and ready.

'Down to the end of this road and make a right,' said Rik. 'There's a blue two-litre Renault parked next to a yellow skip. You can leave this in its place.'

'A skip?' Harry stared at him. 'You know you'll be paying for a new set of wheels when we come back, don't you?'

Rik grinned. 'No worries. I put out the word with a couple of the local lads. It'll be safe enough.'

Harry drove off as directed and pulled up alongside a battered yellow skip piled with rubbish and builders' debris. Behind it stood a dark-blue Renault Laguna. It had a high mileage but looked clean and ready to go. Rik jumped out and moved it, and waited while Harry manoeuvred his car into the vacant space and placed his and Joanne's things in the boot.

'Where's the Audi?' Harry asked.

'In a lock-up. After those two bods tagged me from Blakeney, I figured it would be best to play safe. Where to?'

Harry took out the spare mobile. 'I need to make a call. Head south, will you? We need to stay on the move.'

'Who are you ringing?'

'Marshall.'

Joanne was closing the rear door. She leaned forward. 'Marshall? You said you'd call him tomorrow.'

'I lied.' He waited until Rik was driving before touching redial. 'I don't want to give him time to set us up.'

'You said tomorrow.' Marshall's tone echoed with a hint of accusation, as if Harry had broken a minor rule of etiquette.

'Call me impulsive. We need to meet. Go to the Marble Arch underground and wait downstairs near the Oxford Street south entrance. I'll pick you up.'

'When?'

'Now.'

'Not possible. It will take me a good thirty minutes—'

'Make it ten.' Harry cut the connection and looked at Rik. 'Go for it. I'll explain on the way.'

'Heavens,' Rik lisped breathlessly, 'I *love* it when you talk tough.'

The underground tunnels beneath Marble Arch smelled of damp, decay and urine, a combination guaranteed to ensure that nobody dawdled on their way through. Most looked neither right nor left, sparing little thought for the bundles huddled beneath cardboard boxes in the darker reaches of the network, or the gaunt individuals lurking by the entrances. Apart from the concourse around the ticket office and the barriers, the walkways were ill lit, the overhead lamps casting a feverish glow and colouring everyone and everything the same drab tones.

Major Andrew Marshall paused for a moment at the top of the steps to the Oxford Street entrance, breathing in the fresh air of the Marble Arch intersection. The word fresh was relative, but it would be mildly better than what lay below. Before descending the steps he scanned the immediate area, noting people, vehicles and movement. It was just after two o'clock and the lunchtime rush had slowed to a trickle. Elsewhere was the usual bustle of activity. A bundle of passengers scurried off a coach at a nearby stop; a taxi screeched to a halt just behind the railings separating pedestrians from the rush of traffic; a man in a brilliant white *djellaba* weaved his way between the cars, casually avoiding death by inches and seemingly oblivious to his chances of meeting his Maker sooner than he'd expected.

Over against the central reservation barrier on the north-bound side stood a car with its bonnet up. A young woman was staring in dismay at a cloud of steam swirling from the engine, ignored by every other driver. London, thought Marshall, in all its glory. He took a final breath and walked down the steps. He moved lightly for a big man, skilfully avoiding contact with others and glaring as a thin youth halfway down looked up at him, about to tap him for change. Seeing the expression on the major's face, the youth snapped his mouth shut and shrank back against the wall as the large man with the military bearing strode by.

At the bottom of the steps, Marshall checked his surroundings, scanning faces. He didn't expect to recognize anyone, but he had a keen eye for detail – especially nervous detail. Satisfied he wasn't about to be mugged, he stood with his back to the wall by a rack of brochures and watched the human tide flow by.

After a moment, a man in a shabby coat and an old trilby hat appeared from one of the tunnels and shuffled up beside him. He was of medium height but broad in the shoulder. Solid. Marshall couldn't see the man's face but he could smell the feral aroma coming off him at six paces. He was contemplating telling him to shove off when the newcomer turned and moved past him, the smell suddenly stronger.

'This way, Major. Don't dawdle, now.' Then the man was off, walking quickly into the network of tunnels leading to the far side of Park Lane.

Marshall followed, carefully not looking for his own men, who had orders to wait nearby. He recognized the man's voice from the phone call and was impressed by the ease with which the stranger had made contact. But the casual display of professionalism gave him a sinking feeling in his gut, and he realized he'd already been outmanoeuvred.

He increased his pace, intending to be right behind the man when they stopped. There was a limited number of exits from

the tunnels, giving the man few options to play with. And
unless he was going to morph into a tunnel rat and slip down
a drainage gully, he wouldn't be going very far.

They entered a straight stretch of tunnel, empty save for a
tall, gangly youth with a guitar and a voice like a badly tuned
violin. A rumble of traffic came from overhead. They were
directly beneath the rush of vehicles circling Marble Arch.
Metal signs on the walls pointed to numbered exits, and the
air here was even heavier and more fetid than it had been
earlier, with an extra earthy layer to the range of smells.

Marshall felt oddly disorientated. It was an unpleasant
feeling.

They reached a gap in the wall on Marshall's left. This had
no exit number and was blocked by a sliding metal grill pitted
with rust. Behind it a flight of steps rose into daylight, the
treads covered with leaf mould and litter, long unused. As
Marshall drew level with the grill and set his gaze on the
tunnel ahead, the man suddenly turned back and kicked the grill
aside. Grabbing Marshall by the arm, he bundled him through
and pushed him up the steps before he could resist, surprising
him with the strength of his grip.

'Where are we going?' Marshall spoke as calmly as he could
manage, but he'd lost his bearings and felt an instinctive desire
to push back. He wasn't accustomed to relinquishing control
in this way.

'You'll see, Major. Keep moving.'

They continued upwards, the traffic buzz growing to a roar,
and emerged into the open. Marshall was surprised to see they
were on the central reservation area of grass and bushes
between the traffic flow of Park Lane. Not fifteen feet away
was the car – a dark Renault – that he'd spotted earlier with
its bonnet raised. The young woman who had been standing
by the front was now by the driver's door looking perfectly
calm.

When she saw them appear, she turned and slammed the
bonnet.

'You'll have to hop over the barrier, Major,' the man
instructed him. 'And get in the back, would you? We're going
for a short ride.' As he spoke, he shrugged off the coat and
trilby and tossed them on the ground, revealing him to be
stocky and in his forties, with a genial face and brown hair.

He had an easy smile and seemed relaxed, as if this kind of activity happened every day. Marshall wasn't fooled; he didn't doubt for a second that he was ready to move fast if the need arose. 'Sorry about the God-awful whiff from that coat – but you have to use whatever's to hand, right?'

Marshall stepped over the barrier as instructed and got into the car alongside a young man with spiky hair and cool blue eyes. He also looked relaxed but alert, hands resting on his knees. Marshall recognized the type; he employed one or two himself.

The young woman slid behind the wheel and started the engine. She was dressed in jeans and a windcheater and looked strong and capable. She was attractive in spite of wearing little or no make-up, and Marshall slotted her into the same category as the two men: not to be underestimated.

The older man dropped into the front passenger seat and signalled the woman to move off before turning to look at Marshall. 'Apologies for the subterfuge,' he said, 'but we wanted some of what my dear old mum called quality time, and I figured you might have brought the odd little helper in tow.'

'One or two,' Marshall agreed. He forced himself to relax, knowing that these three people had total control and there was nothing he could do about it. Worse, he didn't need to look around to know that none of his men was anywhere near. The pick-up had been neat, unfussy and unexpected, and he made a mental note to have a word with the Directorate of Training about reviewing the use of street tactics in London.

FORTY-FIVE

'We have a problem,' Harry explained to Marshall, as the car surged into the traffic flow. He wanted to get straight down to business in case Marshall had a tracking device on him. If he did, they'd soon have someone on their tail . . . and there was no time to do a body search or go through his clothing to find it. 'Oh, by the way,

my name's Harry, the one next to you is Rik and this lady is
... well, I think you probably know who she is.'
   Marshall studied Joanne's profile but shook his head.
'Actually, I don't. Perhaps you could introduce me.'
   'Really?' Harry was surprised. He checked the major's face
for signs that he was lying. But unless he was a world-class
actor, he appeared to be telling the truth. It wasn't the response
he'd been expecting. 'OK, fair enough. But before we do that,
we want to know about a man called Jennings.'
   Marshall shifted in his seat. 'What about him?'
   'You know him, then?'
   'It would seem I must. I take it you're already aware of
that fact. My question is, how?'
   'We saw you outside his office.'
   'Ah. Careless of me.' Marshall's voice was heavy with irony.
'I really should stay off the streets. So?'
   'Is he official?'
   'No. Why do you ask?'
   'Has he ever been?'
   Marshall waggled his head from side to side before replying.
'I suppose, technically, once. But he and the establishment
parted company some time ago. He preferred the opportu-
nities presented by the private sector. I believe the terms and
conditions for his special kind of expertise are a great deal
more rewarding, financially speaking. The public purse is not
unlimited, unfortunately.'
   'How sad. What expertise?'
   'He arranges things. A kind of events organizer, I think
someone once called him. How do *you* know him?'
   'We've worked for him a couple of times. Strictly freelance.'
   'Really? I hope you counted your fingers afterwards. What
sort of work?'
   'Finding people. It's what we do.'
   Marshall looked puzzled. 'Just that – you find people? Is
there a living to be made from it?' He raised his eyebrows in
innocence as Rik snapped his head round. 'Seriously – I'm
interested.' He smiled, seemingly as calm as if he were at his
favourite club, enjoying a chat with fellow members over a
glass of best malt.
   'We do OK.' Harry flicked a glance over Marshall's shoulder
through the rear window. Joanne was taking them along the

Bayswater Road as they'd planned. 'There are a lot of missing people out there.'

'So I'm told. I take it the ones you trace are not your run-of-the-mill change-of-life absconders, though.'

'Dead right. Killers, rapists, defecting bingo callers, we get 'em all.'

'How droll.' Marshall flicked something off his trousers and adjusted the crease. 'I suppose I should ask how you come to know about Operation Pamper? Or was it something you picked up during the course of your work?'

Harry gave him a cool smile. He guessed Marshall's air of calm was a deliberate device to needle them, to make one of them come out with something they hadn't intended to. He decided to save him the trouble. There was only so much beating about the bush that he could stand, and none of them was getting any younger.

'We know you trawled for, recruited and trained an operative for a special, deep-cover assignment in Baghdad,' he said. 'The operation was given the code name Pamper and the person you dropped out there had instructions to protect a high-ranking Iraqi. The operative was trained by Special Forces and told to report back on everything they saw and heard, including voice and image capture. How am I doing so far?'

Marshall said nothing. He returned Harry's look with a bored shrug. But the tension in his face was suddenly evident. Harry decided he needed to make that tension boil over.

'This high-ranking Iraqi was classified by the Coalition as something of a golden solution,' he continued, 'because of his influence across the political spectrum, which made him highly unusual – and valuable. He was there in case the new government fell apart like an old wooden shed – as pretty much everyone with a brain expects it will do one day. His name was Subhi Rafa'i. Still with me?'

Marshall gave him a wintry smile which gave nothing away. 'I have absolutely no idea what you're talking about. Is that all? May I go now?'

'Not by a mile.' Harry was unfazed by Marshall's denial. 'Because of his importance, Rafa'i had a team of local body-guards and a secure location in a fortified base. They couldn't surround him with a shield of Coalition troops because that would have compromised his position. With someone so highly regarded, it was taken for granted that he'd also have a ton of enemies, even among his own crowd. So the Coalition decided to go one better; they put in an extra layer of protection – a backstop – in case his own team failed. And that was fine until just recently, when the compound he lived in was bombed, probably by insiders. The place was destroyed and Rafa'i and everyone inside was reported killed. Including,' Harry added heavily, 'your deep-cover operative.'

Marshall shrugged. 'Bombings happen there all the time. Are we going for a drive in the country?' He gestured out at the passing scenery of west London.

Harry checked outside. A few more minutes and they'd be on the Western Avenue, where the traffic was more open.

'Unfortunately,' he continued, 'your operative wasn't the only home-team casualty that day. You also lost the handler assigned to the operation. He was killed in what was reported as a random drive-by shooting, although that now looks unlikely.' He paused for effect, then said softly, 'His name was Gordon Humphries and he was a senior officer with MI6. We still in the ballpark, Major?'

For the first time, at the mention of Humphries' name, Harry was rewarded with what seemed to be some genuine reaction. Marshall dipped his head for a moment, jaw tensed.

Finally, he murmured, 'How do you know all this?'

'Because we were hired to do what we do: to look for someone. In this case, a man called Silverman, an Israeli professor who'd arrived in Britain after a mental breakdown. But that was just a cover story. Silverman turned out to be an Iraqi. And guess what – it was none other than the recently vaporized Subhi Rafa'i. Unfortunately, we weren't the only people who knew he hadn't died. Ever since we latched on to him, somebody else has been following us around trying to finish the job.'

Marshall gave him a flat stare. 'You seem to have a lot of information. That doesn't mean it's accurate. Why should I be interested in this?'

'If you're not interested, why are you here?' Harry shook his head in disgust. 'Get your head out of your backside, Major. Your Operation Pamper has fallen apart at the seams and you don't even know it. What do I tell you next to convince you we aren't making up the whole story? You want a description of Humphries' sister, Sheila?' He waited but there was no response. 'Details of the safe house where Humphries used to meet his agents? Or how about some really gritty stuff – like the name of the operative you dumped out in Baghdad and left to die? The one you never bothered going after to find out if she was alive or dead? Oh, the name's Joanne Archer, by the way. It'll be on your files.'

Marshall flinched visibly at the name, but said nothing.

'Stop here.' Harry recognized the moment for what it was and tapped Joanne on the arm. They had gone far enough. They were drawing level with a side street. Joanne signalled and spun the wheel, pulling in to the kerb. The street was deserted save for two lines of cars. No people, nobody to interrupt them. She turned off the engine.

Marshall looked momentarily alarmed. 'Why have you stopped?' His voice was steady, but there was no hiding the tension around his eyes. Or the way he turned to look down at Rik's hands, still resting on his lap.

'Don't worry, Major,' said Harry calmly. 'We're not going to burn you. We just wanted you to meet your special operative, that's all.'

Marshall frowned, relief giving way to the beginning of anger. 'How?'

At a nod from Harry, Joanne turned in her seat. 'Hello, Major,' she said evenly. 'Or should I call you Boss?'

A few miles away, Dog was sitting astride his latest acquisition, a dull-green Kawasaki. It had new plates, courtesy of another bike left unattended in a street in Southwark, and would do him for the time being. As well as the false plates, he had added a courier's pannier and covered the tank with a leather jacket that held maps, disguising the original lines and appearance from a chance sighting by its former owner.

He'd finally heard from Jennings and now had fresh instructions. There had been a change of priorities, the lawyer had informed him. Dog had taken the information without comment; orders were orders and he would follow them through without question. Jennings had revealed with some reluctance where he was staying, and Dog had tucked the information away for later use. He didn't mind secrecy, but it was beginning to irk him that he was being left out of the loop as if he were of little importance.

He was tucked in a side street across from the river, within sight of a familiar cream and green ziggurat dominating Vauxhall Bridge. He felt safe enough here, slightly out of the public eye, although he needed to keep a watch for roving police cars, most of which would be armed response units. This area of the riverside was notoriously sensitive and covered by CCTV cameras that had nothing to do with the Congestion Charge or trapping speeding motorists. This was the MI6 head-quarters, and was probably numbered among the three or four most secure establishments in London; getting too close would be a grave error of judgement.

He eased his shoulders inside his leather jacket and breathed easily, biding his time. If anyone asked what he was doing here, he was merely waiting for his next assignment. If the same person got really awkward and pushed it, they would suffer momentarily, but he'd be away and gone before they even hit the ground.

He patted his side pocket, checking the familiar shape inside, then concentrated on watching the cars and faces moving along the street in front of him.

FORTY-SIX

'How do I know you are who you claim?' Even to himself, Marshall sounded pompous, and wished instantly he could have taken the words back. If this was a scam, it was a very elaborate one. His only excuse for such a response was that he was still trying to get over the shock of what he'd just heard.

The woman seemed unconcerned by his scepticism. 'Fair comment, Major,' she replied, and reached into a pocket. She passed over a photograph, slightly crumpled, but still clear.

It showed a street scene, and two men sitting at a café table. Marshall felt a prickly sensation crawl up his neck as he recognized himself, his companion and the location. He studied the

photo and tried not to let his emotions show. The other man
had been a friend as well as a colleague. It had been a bad
time all round, and if there were any way he could have done
things differently, he would have. But it was too late for that.

He handed the photo back, but Joanne Archer shook her
head. 'Keep it. I've got spares.'

Marshall fought to keep his voice level. He felt sick; the
kind of sickness that makes a man wonder how he'd ever got
into this vile business. 'How did you . . . get this?'

'I took it on an Olympus digital camera.' Her voice was in
briefing mode, flat and unemotional. 'I was less than thirty
feet away – I could have drilled you both if I'd been working
for the opposition. Where you were sitting was called Café
Osman and it's located in the western suburbs of Baghdad,
in the Jihad district between the centre and Baghdad
International Airport. The quickest way out there from the
city centre is on Highway 10 and down Ishmail Street – unless
you're lucky and get to drop in by chopper. It's a mainly Sunni
area but there are Shi'a as well. Most of the time they get on,
but earlier that day the Mehdi Army had made a strike in
retaliation for some Shi'ite killings a few days before. The
US marines were there in force to back up the Iraqi police,
which is how you and Gordon Humphries got to enjoy coffee
and a chat. Actually, you were only there for a few minutes
because Humphries and I had a meeting not long after in a
safe house nearby.'

'I know, but—' Marshall tried to stem the flow of words,
to say something that, however useless, would show he wasn't
uncaring. But the young woman was not to be denied her
debriefing. Especially, it seemed, this part of it.

'A couple of days later, Humphries was dead.' She waited
while this sank in. When she saw Marshall wasn't going to
speak again, she continued. 'He was dead and I was adrift.
I'm only guessing, Major, but I believe that before he died,
he got wind of something big happening and got me out of
the compound by calling a briefing at the safe house.'

Marshall blinked, his throat dry. 'Go on.'

'Unfortunately, he never made it to the meet, so I bailed
out, then found the compound had taken a hit. Suddenly, I
had no principal, no handler and I was alone in hostile territory. Is that enough for you?' Her eyes sparked with anger. 'I

can describe the training camp here in the UK and give you facials on each of the instructors if you like. The adjutant in particular was a sneaky bastard. He used to report anyone who made so much as a single complaint.' She sat back and waited, the briefing over.

Marshall shook his head. 'I don't know what to say.' He felt drained. It all rang too true to be a hoax, and this young woman had the distinct sound of the genuine article. Worse – she *was* the genuine article. There was also something in her eyes, no matter how neutral her tone, which gave a hint of powerful emotions kept in check. It was a sign Marshall had seen before in those with experience of intense combat or dangerous undercover work. If she was who she claimed – and he had no reason to doubt her – she was a very special person indeed. The thought did nothing to ease his feelings of guilt for the ways things had gone.

'I can only apologize,' he said finally, 'for everything that has happened to you, Miss Archer. You may accept that or dismiss it as you wish – I can't say I blame you if you take the latter course. I wasn't aware you'd survived the bombing. All our information led us to believe that you had died along with everyone else. And when you didn't report in . . .' He shrugged and rubbed his face with a large hand. 'I visited your flat once. Pointless, of course, but it seemed the right thing to do. Your landlord said you were away. It's no excuse, I know, but we were forced to believe the worst. Gordon Humphries' death didn't help in that regard, I'm afraid. What do you want from me?'

'Protection.' This came from Harry, in the front seat. 'And rehabilitation for Miss Archer. She's been left high and dry by your lot for too long.'

'Of course, that goes without saying. But protection from what?'

'From whom, actually,' the younger man, Rik, put in. 'We've got a psychopath on our tail. We think he's one of yours.'

'I doubt that.' Marshall's instinct was for outright denial. God knows, he wasn't privy to every backwater operation being conducted by his colleagues, nor the people they employed. Yet something about these three was turning all that he knew upside down. Why not this as well?

Harry pointed at the photo Marshall was holding, his finger

on one of the two armed security men in the background.
'This man has already killed at least three people – possibly
four – and had a go at Joanne. We believe he's got orders to
take out Rafa'i. He missed this time, but we think he'll be
back for another try.' He looked hard at Marshall. 'Like I said
– he's one of yours. Well trained.'

'I need more details,' said Marshall. He was playing for
time but it was all he could do. He listened while the two
men gave him a concise briefing of everything that had
happened so far. It stretched from Norfolk to the capital and
nothing they said sounded too far-fetched – which worried him
even more. He made notes on a small pad, then studied the
photo again, although he really didn't need to. When he'd first
seen the face of the security guard, he had experienced an
instant jolt of recognition. It wasn't good news.

'I remember this man,' he told them at last. There was
nothing to be gained by denying it. 'But only because he was
attached to my security detail.'

'Go on,' Harry prompted him.

'He stood out. The other men treated him with obvious
caution, and a fair bit of respect. It tends to make one take
notice. So I checked his record. His name's Gary Pellew. He's
former Special Forces and goes by the name of Dog. He did
valuable work for us over many years in appalling circumstances. It did things to him.' Marshall dropped the photo and
shook his head. 'Unfortunately, nobody noticed until it was
too late.'

'You mean he's a head case,' said Rik.

'Damaged, certainly,' Marshall agreed levelly. 'Not that he
would ever acknowledge such a description. He's fiercely
proud of the fact that he's never failed to carry out an order.
If anything, it's something of a character flaw.'

'You mean he's a robot.'

'I mean he won't stop until he's accomplished whatever
job he's on.'

'Cheers, Major,' said Rik dryly. 'Just what we wanted to
hear: a government-trained psychopath with a work ethic. Can't
you get him stopped?'

'I doubt it. He no longer works for us. Not long after this
picture was taken, he dropped out of sight. His colleagues
said he'd been behaving irrationally – he allegedly tried to

kill one of the other guards. He'd also taken to slipping out and doing some freelance night-sniping of insurgents.' He gave a thin smile. 'They may have been troublesome, but that definitely wasn't part of his brief.'

'He wasn't all bad, then?' Joanne's voice was laden with sarcasm.

'Sadly, he had a problem differentiating between insurgents and civilians. It's believed he shot dead at least five innocent locals over a period of several nights. Before they could stop him, he'd gone.' He looked at them each in turn. 'It's believed he may have been headhunted by Jennings as long as a year ago. Now we know why.' He let a few moments go by, then added. 'Where is Rafa'i?'

'Safe,' said Harry. 'For the time being.'

'Let's hope he stays that way. He's an important man. It would be useful if nothing happened to him while he's on British soil. I take it there's no chance of bringing him in for a chat?' He looked at Joanne Archer; she was clearly the one who knew the Iraqi best.

'You're right,' she replied shortly. 'No chance.'

'I see. And what do you plan doing with him?'

'Get him out of harm's way,' she replied. 'Back to Iraq if that's what he wants.'

Marshall's tried to keep a blank face. 'Ah.'

'Is that a problem?' Harry queried.

Marshall had already said too much. It was time to back off and get the machinery working on clearing up this whole sorry mess, starting with the psychopathic Dog. He could leave these three to take care of Rafa'i – for the time being, at least.

'No. No problem. I wish you luck – it won't be easy.' He extracted a card from the back of the notebook and scribbled a number on it. 'That's a direct number if you need to reach me. My deputy is Richard Ballatyne. I'll brief him as soon as I can and we'll be in touch on your mobile later today.' He looked at Joanne. 'I really am sorry, Miss Archer. I wish there was more I could do to rectify things.'

Rik leaned across him and opened his door. It was Marshall's cue to leave.

FORTY-SEVEN

Marshall watched the car move away and made a note of the number, although it was probably a waste of time; if the three people he'd just been speaking to were as good as he thought, they'd either get rid of it within the hour or the number would prove untraceable. But it was an instinctive part of him too ingrained to ignore. He also decided to alert Ballatyne of the situation immediately rather than wait. His deputy could at least get the team working on tracing Dog. And trawling through the Asian community networks for signs of Rafa'i.

He took out his mobile and speed-dialled a number. Twenty minutes later, a dark Rover with two men inside slid in to the kerb. Marshall climbed in, told the driver to head for Vauxhall Cross.

The man said nothing, but both looked wary. Marshall didn't bother taking out his frustrations on them; what was done was done, and he'd been responsible for putting himself in the situation where he could be lifted, anyway.

When they were in sight of the building, Marshall tapped his driver on the shoulder and waited as the car pulled in to the kerb. He liked to walk the last stretch to get the kinks out of his joints and prepare himself. Today was no different, in spite of recent events. As he strolled along the pavement, relishing the brief exposure to the cool air off the river, he wondered about the three people he had just left. Joanne Archer was who she claimed to be; he had no doubt about that. Her anger was too raw, the detail too specific to be faked. But he needed to discover the identities of the two men with her. It wasn't critical, as he was sure they would emerge soon enough. But he liked to know who he was dealing with.

Of one thing he was already certain: they were professionals. They had about them the unmistakable air of government-trained personnel; they were too calm and controlled to be amateurs, and to have picked him up so easily in a crowded thoroughfare without exhibiting some major tension really took some doing.

That thought suddenly prompted a faint jump of memory. It was from a while back, and he couldn't be certain, but while he'd been looking at the older man, Harry, he'd felt a stirring of something familiar. He didn't know the man, he was certain of that. But he knew *of* him. All he had to do was remember where from. He took out his mobile and dialled another number. It might be a wild goose chase, but it was worth a try. Know your enemy and you held the advantage. It was a maxim he didn't always agree with, but this time he was willing to give it the benefit of the doubt.

Instructions issued, he pocketed the mobile and thought about the girl, Archer. He felt a measure of sadness for her. And guilt. That there was a need for people like her was irrefutable; that it had to be young women such as she was, in his opinion, less so. Unfortunately, his concerns at the time had been overruled, to the extent that he had been prevented from ever meeting her, or even seeing her file and photo. But would he have stopped her going if he'd met her? What would he have done, he wondered, if it had been his own daughter recruited and trained for such a task, then abandoned to her fate?

A familiar figure in a pinstripe suit passed him by, nodding briefly in recognition. Something to do with Planning or Analysis, Marshall thought vaguely. They all looked the same after a while, the intelligence community's faceless army.

Ahead of him, a motorcycle courier pulled in to the kerb and took out a map. A couple of American tourists took photos of the river and a delivery van bumped by, its unsecured roller shutter clattering. After the story he'd just heard, such everyday noises and colour seemed trivial.

Absorbed by his thoughts, Marshall was only vaguely aware of the soft swish of leathers and heavy footsteps crossing the pavement. The motorcycle engine was still rumbling, and the smell of its exhaust tickled his nostrils. It took a moment for him to realize that the courier was now behind him and coming up fast—

Marshall began to turn. But he was too late. He rocked to a blow low down on his left-hand side, followed by a sharp, cold pain going right through his body. As he opened his mouth to protest, he felt a weakness spreading to his limbs, beginning in his hips and going all the way down to his feet. He staggered and reached round to his back, but that only made the pain worse. He felt dizzy, and a rush of congestion building in his throat. He coughed, saw an impenetrable darkness closing in, blotting out all sights and sounds, and wondered how he could have been so careless after all this time.

Marshall began to feel very cold. He didn't feel his knees hit the pavement, didn't hear the cry of alarm from the woman tourist. All he could think of was the things he hadn't yet accomplished.

FORTY-EIGHT

'I hate this waiting.' Rik scuffed his feet on the grass and tossed away the dregs of a coffee. They had left Harry's Saab just off the Bayswater Road and were sitting near the Round Pond in Kensington Gardens. The Renault had served its purpose and was now in an underground car park in Mayfair, gathering fines. There were a few people about, mostly walkers and tourists, but they had good all-round scope to see anyone approaching.

'It's only been an hour,' Harry murmured calmly, staring up at the sky. He had his head back in an attitude of total relaxation, as if they were out for a picnic rather than waiting to see whether Marshall rang back or turned up in person with a squad of armed men.

'I know. But it's not like we're up for a job interview, is it? If we're hung out to dry for all these killings, Marshall's our only chance of getting to the bottom of it, and of Jo getting her life back.' He slam-dunked his cardboard mug into a litter bin. 'And then there's old Ruby Rafa'i. Think what HM Government'll do if he gets slotted on our turf.'

'Subhi,' Joanne corrected him. 'His name's Subhi.' Her voice was flat, on the verge of confrontational, and it was clear that she, too, was reaching the limits of her patience.

Harry said nothing. The waiting was always the worst. It

would get to each of them in different ways. That and the uncertainty of what lay ahead.

Rik said, 'Why don't we turn the tables and ring him? For all we know, he's spent the last hour having us traced and spotted.'

Harry reached into his pocket and tossed Rik his mobile. 'You think he'll tell you, go ahead.'

As Rik dialled the number, Joanne stood up, thrusting her hands in her pockets. She did a nervous jog on the spot and flexed her neck and shoulders, her rucksack on the ground at her feet.

Rik switched the phone to loudspeaker and waited. After ten rings, it was answered by a man with a gravel voice. '*Yes?*' No identity, no indication of who he worked for.

'Is Major Marshall there?'

'*Marshall isn't available. Who shall I say is calling?*'

'He said he'd be in touch . . . him or someone called Ballatyne.' Rik rolled his eyes as a voice rose in the background and the line became muffled. Then the speaker came back. 'I'm sorry, you'll have to call back later.' The connection was cut.

'Bloody hell.' Rik stared at the phone in disgust. 'Is that what we pay our taxes for – to call back later?' He tossed the phone back to Harry, who reached out and plucked it from the air without moving from his position.

After five more minutes, Harry stood up and looked around. Rik was right to be impatient. This was all taking too long. Marshall should have got back to them by now. Every minute they stayed out in the open, they were at risk. 'Let's move,' he said. 'Back to the car.' He looked at the other two. 'If anything happens, we split up and meet in two hours at the Kensington Hilton.' It was the first place he could think of, but well placed if they were forced to split up and regroup, and busy enough inside to keep a low profile.

They were halfway back to the car when Harry's patience finally folded. If Marshall was serious about helping Joanne get her life back and pinning down Jennings, he should have been in touch by now. He dialled the number on the card.

'Yes?' A man's voice answered after a few rings.

'It's Harry,' he said. 'Is Marshall there?'

'Wait one.' The voice disappeared abruptly and Harry guessed the man had pressed the mute button. He waited, counting off the seconds, and was about to switch off the phone when the man came back on. He sounded sombre. 'Get to a secure location and wait. You'll be contacted shortly.'

'Wait. What's the—?' But the phone was dead. He slipped it in his pocket and looked at the other two. 'Something's up. They want us to find somewhere secure and wait for a call.'

'No way.' Joanne looked edgy. 'We've waited long enough. Why should we trust any of them?' She stopped, forcing the two men to do the same, and clutched her rucksack close to her chest. 'You're putting too much faith in Marshall. Don't forget he's in the same department as the people who left me to rot. Why should I trust him just because you do?'

Harry studied her carefully. He was puzzled by her change of mood. She had reacted with less anger or emotion when faced with Marshall than he'd expected. In most people it would have conjured up at least some degree of heat. But not her – until now. Delayed reaction, maybe.

'He's all we've got,' he pointed out. 'If you have any better ideas, let's hear them.'

She didn't reply, but turned and walked quickly away along the path.

Rik watched her go. 'You know who she reminds me of?'

Harry nodded. 'Clare.' He'd been having the same thoughts. Young, prickly and aggressive, Clare Jardine had exhibited the same kind of impatience and lack of trust.

He hoped Joanne didn't show her annoyance in the same cold, ruthless manner.

FORTY-NINE

Harry's mobile rang fifteen minutes later. They were seated at a corner table of a deserted lounge in a four-star international hotel along the Bayswater Road. The Saab was out the back, tucked discreetly behind a laurel

bush. A porter had departed to get them some coffee. Harry
glanced at the screen, but the number was withheld.

'Major?' he replied.

'I'm afraid not. Who is this?' The voice was hard-edged,
the accent neutral.

Harry hesitated. If it wasn't Marshall, there was only one
person it could be: his deputy, Richard Ballatyne. 'My name's
Harry,' he replied, and glanced at his watch. Anything over a
minute was pushing their luck; if Marshall was leading them
on, he could have an active unit abseiling down around their
ears before they knew what had hit them.

But the caller had anticipated that. 'Relax, Mr Tate,' he said
brusquely. 'Nobody's playing tricks here.'

Damn. They had his name. Harry was stunned. 'We know
about Ferris, too,' the man told him. 'Marshall recognized
your face from that business in Red Station, Georgia, and we
ran a search of known associates. Harry – if I may call you
that? – I've got some bad news.'

'Go on.' Christ, he thought, what was worse than knowing
you were no longer invisible and that the massed forces of
the State could pick you up whenever they felt like it?

'Andrew Marshall is dead.'

The words took a long moment to assimilate. Dead? But
how? They'd only been speaking a short while ago. The waiter
chose that moment to arrive, and Harry signalled at Rik to
get rid of the man. Even just one side of this sort of conversation was hard to disguise. Rik caught on quickly, taking the
tray before the waiter could begin to unload it and hustling
him out of earshot with a hefty tip.

'How did it happen?' Harry finally managed to ask.

'He was knifed in the back about a hundred yards from
this office. He died instantly.' The words came with the unemotional tones of a newsreader, but behind it Harry detected a
restrained sense of anger.

'I'm sorry,' he said, knowing how lame it sounded. 'When
did this happen?'

'Within the last hour. The people who found him thought
he'd had a heart attack and got him to a hospital. He'd been
dropped off by his driver to walk the last couple of hundred
yards to the office, something he liked to do. We're running
CCTV footage of the street right now. I don't hold out much

hope of seeing anything to help us, though. Someone said they saw a biker on the same stretch of pavement, but it's not much to go on. Whoever did this was a pro.'

'*Dog*.' Harry uttered the word dully, thinking of the crackle of exhaust at South Acres.

To his surprise, Ballatyne agreed. 'We think so. We're circulating pictures of him to all agencies. We believe he also killed another of our men earlier today, near Victoria Station. A knife in the ear. Our man had tracked him to a hostel. He got too close.'

'You actually had him located?' Harry felt a surge of anger at the idea that they had traced the man and had let him get away. To do this.

Ballatyne didn't try defending the decision and Harry guessed he was already feeling as bad as a man could do over missed opportunities. 'We messed up. At the time we didn't know for sure what Dog's involvement was, only that he'd dropped out of a contract assignment in Iraq while under investigation. He was on a watch list and appeared on the radar a couple of days ago. We've now got him on a Code Seven.'

'What the hell is that?' He was no longer familiar with all the security warning levels or their meanings. The world was changing too fast.

'Locate and neutralize.'

'You mean kill.' He guessed from the man's reticence that it was a Special Order, which needed neither Cabinet nor MOD approval to carry out.

'It means what it says.'

'What do we do now?' Harry asked. 'Did Marshall speak to you?'

'Yes. Where are you?'

'It doesn't matter where we are. You just need to get Dog off our backs. We'll do the rest.'

'It's Dog we need to talk about.' Then a woman's voice intruded at the other end and Ballatyne broke off. When he came back, he apologized. 'Sorry – there's a lot happening here. I'll call again in ten.' Then he was gone.

'What's going on?' Rik looked wary.

Harry gave them the news about Marshall. They both looked stunned. 'He didn't say anything else . . . just that things were happening. He'll call back.' He wondered if Ballatyne was playing them along in order to find out where they were. But he decided it was unlikely; he was pretty sure they hadn't been connected long enough for a firm trace to have been made. 'Let's give it time.'

Joanne had been looking increasingly nervous during the telephone conversation. She stood up and rubbed her stomach. 'I need something from the car.' She dropped her rucksack on the chair and pulled a face. 'Girl stuff.'

Harry nodded and handed her the car keys, and he and Rik drank coffee and waited for Ballatyne to call back. The phone rang just as Joanne returned. Harry left it muted while Rik prowled the foyer.

'Sorry,' Ballatyne said. 'Where were we?'

'You mentioned Dog.'

'Right. From what we've turned up in the last couple of hours, it looks like Dog may have been around on the same course that Miss Archer took before she went to Iraq. He was listed as still serving at the time, although he'd been out of the army for some months.'

'Somebody fudged the paperwork?'

'Either that or he was on a retained contract we knew nothing about. There are several departments running operations requiring specialist training sessions. But that's the least of your problems. We believe he has help, but we don't know what they look like. Two men, that's all we know. There's another matter we need to talk about, but that needs to be face to face.'

In the background, Joanne excused herself and walked towards the rear of the hotel, where the signs pointed to the washrooms.

Harry considered what Ballatyne had told him. If Ballatyne didn't know what these other two men looked like, there was no chance that he, Rik or Joanne could even begin to know.

'Can you give me a hint?' Then his mind whirled off in another direction as he realized something: if Dog had been on the same course as Joanne, how was it she hadn't recognized him from the photo she'd taken in Baghdad?

'Miss Archer,' Ballatyne continued with uncanny timing. 'Is she still with you?'

'What about her?' Harry had a sinking feeling in his chest. This wasn't going to be good news.

'We've checked all the security logs in Baghdad over the period Gordon Humphries was killed. There's no record of Humphries having logged an outgoing call to her, asking for a meeting on the day he died. The day of the bombing.'

'So he forgot. It happens.' Even as he spoke, Harry knew he was barking at the moon. Humphries would have been under enormous stress in Baghdad, and missing the odd piece of paperwork would not have been unreasonable. But everything his sister had told them about her brother indicated that Humphries had been far too professional to make that kind of slip.

'He might have,' Ballatyne agreed reasonably. 'But there was one *incoming* call for him logged that morning.'

'Do you know who from?'

'Not yet. There was an insurgent attack on the base perimeter at the time, and the comms corporal responsible for the log had to drop everything. We're waiting to confirm details.'

Harry stared across the lounge in the direction Joanne had disappeared, his mind in a whirl. Had Joanne called her handler?

He glanced at the chair where she had been sitting.

Her rucksack was gone.

FIFTY

Harry cut the connection and stood up. While Rik went out to scan the street, he found the washrooms and checked the cubicles. Other than a startled woman in a business suit repairing some damage to her make-up in the mirror, there was no sign of Joanne or her rucksack.

He asked the receptionist if there were any other washrooms close by, but she shook her head. He thanked her and met Rik coming in from the street.

'A black cab was just off up the road,' Rik reported. 'I couldn't see who was inside. What do we do now?'

'You heard what Ballatyne said about Dog and the others. Either Joanne's part of this or she simply doesn't trust anyone enough – us included – to hang around. Maybe she's closer to the edge than she seemed.' And maybe, he thought, the meeting with Marshall had been a step too far.

Rik looked sceptical. 'I thought she seemed pretty together most of the time. Then she just takes off. Weird.'

'She's been under a lot of strain.' He led the way towards the rear entrance. 'Come on.'

'Where to?'

'Ballatyne's agreed to meet us on neutral ground.'

Rik pursed his lips. 'Do you trust him?'

'As much as I trust anyone.' He gave Rik a straight look, aware that his friend would follow his lead. 'We've got to bite the bullet sooner or later. Now he knows who we are, he'll have our photos and service records from Thames House in circulation. We either go in voluntarily or we wait to get picked up. I don't fancy facing a bunch of nervous firearms officers with itchy fingers, do you?'

Richard Ballatyne was waiting for them at the rear of an Italian restaurant just off Wigmore Street. An elderly man in a waiter's jacket admitted them, then spun the 'Closed' sign to face out, before disappearing behind a curtain at the back. There were no other staff, no indications that the place was open for business.

Ballatyne was of medium height, with dark hair and heavy glasses. He had the slightly owlish air of an academic, but his hands resting on the white tablecloth looked strong and capable.

He nodded a greeting and stood up, gesturing to the chairs opposite. 'Can I get you coffee?' A pot and cups were on the next table.

Harry shook his head. He glanced around at the decor of plastic vines, ceramic tiles and numerous Chianti bottles in raffia jackets. A chiller cabinet loaded with bottles of white wine, San Pellegrino and soft drinks hummed in the background, and the buzz of traffic, building by now towards the early evening rush, was muted.

'Bit garish for MI6, isn't it? I take it you are Six?'

'Yes.' Ballatyne gave a bleak smile. It was sufficient to change his face from serious to almost friendly. Harry guessed he was still reeling from Marshall's death and remembered to go easy on him. Unless he pushed them too hard.

Rik walked over to the table and poured himself a coffee, then sat slightly to one side. The move wasn't lost on Ballatyne.

'No Miss Archer?' he said.

'She's indisposed,' said Harry. He had no intention just yet of telling Ballatyne that Joanne had disappeared. It could keep.

'I see. Well, in that case, it makes what I have to say rather easier.' He tapped softly on the table and seemed to be measuring his words. 'GCHQ here and at their other installations have been intercepting a series of phone calls made to international numbers over the past few months. They were on a watch and listen list, and connected with a variety of current and past investigations which I can't go into.'

'Terrorism, you mean?' Rik suggested.

Ballatyne nodded. 'One caller in the past few days was identified several times. It probably wouldn't have been noted, except that the calls originated from London and from a number they hadn't seen before. The caller was a man. Tracking back the listed subscriber proved useless; the phone was stolen or cloned. Then a name was mentioned. It was just the one time, but it rang a number of bells.' He paused for effect, then added, 'The caller was Subhi Rafa'i.'

Neither Harry nor Rik responded, both trying to work out the significance of this development. They waited for Ballatyne to go on.

'For a survivor of an assassination attempt, Rafa'i's been making a lot of international calls. Geneva, Frankfurt, Paris . . . and quite a few to Baghdad. Each of the numbers he called corresponds to a banking or finance house with strong links to the Middle East, or to individuals who control funds with Middle East connections. It was the latter who turned out to be the most interesting.'

'Are these known terrorist connections?' asked Harry.

'Yes.' Ballatyne scratched at the tablecloth. 'We think he's been gathering funds. Dirty money.'

'To do what?' Harry was certain MI6 would have already worked that one out, but whether Ballatyne would share that knowledge was another matter. He wasn't disappointed.

'We're not sure.' The answer was smooth and practised, a deflection. 'We're still analysing the calls to work out the

significance of all the people he was talking to and what role
they might be playing. It takes time to get their profiles together
. . . they're not all in one place.'

Harry knew what he meant. 'You have to ask the Americans
for the data.'

'And the French . . . the Germans . . . the Israelis.'

'But you think he's been fund-gathering.'

'Without a doubt. And where there's money like that, there
are firewalls. It takes time to get through them.' He looked at
Rik as he said it, a small but important signal that he knew
their backgrounds. 'The money we can deal with. If it leaves
a trace, we can backtrack and find the source and, hopefully,
the destination. Cut it off at both ends. The support is something else, though. I believe you know of Rafa'i's standing
with the Coalition?'

'Yeah, we know,' said Harry.

Ballatyne grunted. 'I think we can dispense with that notion
altogether. There's been a change in the wind. But he's still
a name to treat with caution in that part of the world.'

'But he's dead,' Rik interjected. 'At least, CNN thinks so.'

'Quite correct, Mr Ferris. To the outside world, Subhi Rafa'i
died in the bombing of the compound in the Al-Jamia district
of Baghdad.' He squeezed a fold of tablecloth between his
thumb and forefinger. 'What we don't know is how many
people know the real truth.'

'No chatter on the net?' Harry was referring to the intelligence network plugged into the Arab world. Any talk about
Rafa'i's survival would have become known very quickly and
spread like wildfire. News like that would inevitably leak
somewhere through friendly sources or careless talk.

'Nothing. Lamentations about his death, sad loss to Iraq,
conspiracy theories about Coalition involvement – all of that.
But that's all.' He glanced at the two men in turn with a
glimmer of understanding. 'You don't know where he is,' he
said softly. 'Do you?'

'What makes you think that?' said Rik, defensive.

Ballatyne shrugged. 'Call it a lucky guess. Somehow, I think
if you'd spent any time with him, you'd have developed an
opinion about him. He's very persuasive – even charismatic.
I doubt you've even met him.'

'So what's HMG's position?' said Harry.

'My masters are currently discussing that issue against the wider background in Iraq. There are complications.'

'Such as?'

'Exactly what he might be up to is the main one. Why he's here in the UK and how long he plans staying is another. And what happens if his presence here ever gets out.'

'I'll give you another,' Rik muttered. 'What if he gets bumped off here? That won't go down well back home, will it?'

Ballatyne looked pained. It was clearly not the first time he had considered that scenario. 'That would be . . . unfortunate.'

'Nightmarish, more like.' Rik gave him a sour look. 'Don't patronize us, Ballatyne. We can work out what the damages are just as quick as you. If he gets sliced and diced in central London, there'll be an international riot. The extremists would use it to the hilt, whether they liked him or not.'

'How about Jennings?' said Harry, in the silence that followed. 'He's the key to what happens next. If anyone can call Dog and his team off, it'll be him.'

'We checked his home address. It's been cleaned out. And I mean cleaned. He evidently knew how things might pan out. It was only a rental place, anyway; he seems to have been moving around a good deal in the past couple of years.'

'Surprise, surprise.'

'But we know he's out there. We intercepted some of his communications, which is how we discovered the presence of the other two men. He's clearly controlling all three.'

'But who,' asked Rik, 'is controlling Jennings?'

'That's what we'd like to know.'

'Really?' Harry gave him a sideways look, and the intelligence officer tilted his head to one side.

'We have some names. We're checking them out.'

'The men with Dog,' said Rik. 'Do you know who they are?'

'No. We haven't got a line on them yet. We're working through a list of names.'

'What list?'

Before Ballatyne could answer, the answer clicked in Harry's brain. 'You mean the names on the course, don't you? The course Joanne Archer was on. Just how many killers were you training at the same time?'

Ballatyne flinched. 'That's a bit melodramatic.'

'So sue me. How many?'

Ballatyne hesitated, then said resignedly, 'All the members on the course were serving personnel, with the exception of three men.'

'Don't tell me – Dog and these other two. What were they training for?'

'That's classified. I can't go into it.'

'Well, they weren't army chefs, were they?'

'It's not as simple as that. As you know, there are times when we have to use whatever tools we can get.'

'Subbies,' said Rik. 'Private military contractors.'

'Correct.'

'So what does that make Joanne?'

'She was different. Special. My guess is, we'll find these two men failed the course and Dog approached them afterwards. They'd have been sufficiently demoralized or sour to turn without too much persuasion.'

'But highly trained, even though they failed,' Harry countered. 'How long before you work your way through them?'

'There are four men unaccounted for. Two are believed to be out of the country with their units. If we can locate them, we'll know for sure who the remaining two are and have pictures circulated immediately.'

'Fat lot of good that'll do us,' Rik muttered. 'They could be all over us before we know it.'

'Why was Dog there?' Harry asked. 'According to Marshall, he'd already been through everything Special Forces could throw at him.'

Ballatyne shrugged. 'Frankly, I don't know. That's a question for Jennings. He might have been on a refresher, but I think he was there to shadow Miss Archer. She was always the one going to Baghdad because a woman was the only option to place alongside Rafa'i. The others would have been training for different assignments.'

'But why would Dog have been watching her?'

Ballatyne lifted an upturned palm. 'We think this whole operation was planned as soon as news leaked out about Archer's recruitment as a close protection operative for Rafa'i. The people behind this didn't just cobble something together on a whim; they were thinking long-term. Whatever it is they're doing, it's been carefully thought through.'

'We?' Harry raised an eyebrow. 'You said "we".'

'There are more than just the British involved. I can't say more than that.'

'So how did the news leak out?'

He glanced at his watch. 'I'm sorry – I have to get back for a briefing.' He stood up and walked towards the door, then turned before leaving. 'If it's any consolation, I know you two were given a raw deal after that business in Georgia. I read the files and I've spoken to some of the people around at the time. I can understand your scepticism, but please bear with me for a while longer. We do need your help on this one.' His eyes drilled into Harry's, then he turned and left.

'Well, cheers,' Rik breathed as the door closed behind the intelligence officer. 'That makes me feel better.'

'Ancient history,' said Harry, standing up. 'Come on. We've got to locate Jennings.'

'How do we do that?'

'How about a spot of burglary?'

FIFTY-ONE

Jennings' office was locked and silent. The street lights gave no indication of what lay inside, and the passing lights from cars and vans threw too many confusing shadows to allow more than a glimpse of vague furniture shapes through the windows.

'Are we going in?' said Rik, face pressed to the glass. 'Ballatyne's mob will have been through here already, won't they?'

'I know. But did they find anything?'

'Good point.' Rik turned away from the door and surveyed the street. He walked along to a builder's skip thirty yards away and rooted around in its depths. He came back with a short strip of metal pipe and stamped on one end until it was flattened into the rough approximation of a burglar's jemmy.

When he was satisfied, he said, 'You give me the nod, I'll get us in.'

Harry shook his head ruefully. Rik was full of surprises. He let it go. It was either this or a brick, or spend too long trying to get through a rear window. Neither prospect appealed to him, and he was not that expert at picking locks. He waited instead for something heavy to come along. Eventually, a delivery truck rattled down the street, its diesel engine echoing loudly off the buildings. As soon as it was level with their position, he gave Rik the nod.

Rik grunted and heaved and the front door flew open, the crack of the ruptured frame lost in the blast of the truck's engine.

Harry led the way inside the familiar office suite and switched on the lights. The rooms had been cleared, leaving the basic furniture. The military prints were still in place, and he guessed that the suite had been rented as seen. They set about checking each of the rooms by turn, knowing that even if Ballatyne's people had swept the place, they might still have missed something.

The secretary's office was bare, save for a small vase of wilting flowers in brown, scummy water. The desk drawers were empty and smelled unused. She had probably been a temp hired by the day. A tiny washroom at the rear held a soap dispenser, a kettle and some tea and coffee makings. No coats, no umbrellas, nothing that might contain a connection to Jennings' whereabouts.

They went through Jennings' desk, taking out the drawers and checking each one. Rik ducked underneath and felt round in the space where the drawers had been, checking the runners with his fingers.

When he backed out, he was clutching two bits of paper. One was a faded bus ticket, years old, which he discarded. The other was a National Car Parks ticket with an adhesive back. It was four days old. He showed it to Harry. It was printed with a time, date, location code, the fee paid and a number for enquiries.

'I can check this later online,' he said, 'or try it now on the phone.'

Harry shrugged. 'Go for it.'

Rik picked up the phone on the desk, listened for a dialling tone and dialled the number on the ticket.

'Hi,' he said cheerfully, when it was answered. 'Look, my idiot brother went on a bender the other day and used my car. Trouble is, he left it in one of your car parks and can't remember which one.'

'I'm sorry to hear that, sir,' said the woman on the other end. 'I'm not sure how we can help, though.'

'Easy,' he said confidently. 'I've got the ticket and there's a location code on it. He must have kept the ticket instead of leaving it in the car.' He gave her the code and added, 'When I get my car back, I'm going to charge him for the excess.'

The woman tapped keys and came back a few seconds later with the answer. He thanked her and looked at Harry. 'Ruislip.'

It was a slim lead, but the only one they'd got. Harry picked up the phone and dialled Ballatyne's number. The intelligence officer wasn't there, but one of his colleagues offered to help.

'I need Jennings' car registration and model,' he told the man. 'And home address if you've got it.'

'I'll have to check this out with Mr Ballatyne, sir,' the man said. 'I'll get back to you directly. Are you on a landline?'

Harry gave him the number and put down the phone. He had a feeling it wouldn't take long. He was right. Ballatyne called back within three minutes.

'What do you have?' he asked.

'Not much. A parking ticket from Ruislip. It means he's got a vehicle. If we can trace that, we might find out where he is.'

'Ruislip?' Ballatyne sounded intrigued. 'He rented a flat in Twickenham, but we've already checked that out and he's gone. It's being renovated, so there's nothing to see. The landlord doesn't have a forwarding address.'

'Ruislip could be a bolt-hole he kept in reserve, then.'

'Maybe. But if he's got a car, we don't know what it is. Nothing showed up on any of our trawls. He might have leased it through a blind company account somewhere.'

It was like the cottage in Norfolk, the Battersea flat and the place at South Acres: dead ends and blind alleys. Having the locations of the killings and anywhere he'd lived stripped bare and redecorated was a neat way of hiding all traces. He wondered aloud if that might provide a trail for Ballatyne's investigators. Somebody must have paid for the work.

'Probably a cash job, but worth checking,' Ballatyne agreed. 'I'll get on to it.'

Harry rang off and said to Rik, 'Looks like we'll have to do it the hard way.' He led the way out of the office.

There were few vehicles left in the public car park at Ruislip by the time they arrived. Since they didn't know the make, model or colour of the car, they were, literally, operating in the dark.

A portacabin to one side of the entrance showed a light still glowing from inside, and Rik tapped on the door. It was opened by a large man in a yellow fluorescent jacket and dark uniform trousers. He was carrying a bag and looked as if he was about to shut up shop.

'Hello, gents. Lost your keys?'

Rik handed him the ticket from Jennings' office. 'We're looking for the car that forgot to display that,' he said. 'It might still be here.'

The man dropped his bag on a table behind him and studied the ticket. 'This doesn't tell me much. Hang on, though.' He stepped back to check a ledger on the desk and leafed through until he found a note. 'This is a guess, but there's a car down the far end that's been there a few days. They don't usually stay that long unless by arrangement, and we've been meaning to get it moved. My colleague made a note because there was no ticket displayed. He'll get towed if he doesn't turn up soon. Are you the police?'

Harry flashed his ID. 'We're looking for a government official who failed to show up for work. We're concerned about him and we'd like to take a look at the car.'

The man looked doubtful, but shrugged. 'OK. Follow me. There's no body in it, though, I can tell you that. We'd smell it, otherwise.' He grinned at this attempt at dark humour and led the way across the car park to a dark-green Subaru parked against a fence. There was no tax disc in evidence.

Rik tried the doors. As was expected, they were locked. The boot wasn't, and Harry asked the attendant if he could borrow a torch. He could have used his own, but he wanted the attendant out of the way for a few minutes.

'What for?' The man shifted from foot to foot. 'I can't let you go rummaging around in there – it's still private property. You should shut the boot.'

Harry handed him his mobile and said, 'Ring the last number dialled. Our boss's name is Ballatyne. He'll vouch for us and he'll ring your supervisor if you ask him to. This is a matter of national security. We're not here to nick the car.'

The man looked down at the phone, hesitated, then handed it back. 'No need.' He delved in his jacket pocket and came up with a large rubber torch, which he switched on. 'I've only got my dog to go home to, and she sleeps most of the time. I could do with a bit of excitement.'

While he held the torch, they checked the boot. It held a faded blanket, a pair of walking boots and some old newspapers, but nothing of interest. Harry stepped round to the front of the Subaru and looked at the attendant. 'If this is against your principles, you should look away now.'

The man smiled, a gold tooth gleaming. 'Wait one second.' He walked across to his portacabin and returned with a length of wire, which had been fashioned with a hook on one end. 'This usually works handsome,' he told them. 'You'd be surprised how many owners leave their keys at the office. Don't know how they do business, some of them.'

Seconds later, he stepped back from the car and clicked the door open with a flourish.

They searched the inside in detail, unearthing just a single piece of paper – a garage receipt from the car's customer service folder, where it had been wedged behind the User Manual. The work had been for a damaged exhaust, and the customer address was in Harefield, Middlesex. The customer's name was Parsons.

The date was a month old.

'This has been sanitized and dumped,' Rik said quietly, while the attendant was out of earshot on the other side of the car. 'You ever had a car this clean?'

Harry shook his head. It was clear the vehicle wasn't going anywhere. Whoever had owned it before had finished with it, and he was willing to bet that if it really was registered to someone named Parsons, it would turn out to be a cover name.

'Harefield's not far from here,' the attendant offered helpfully, and insisted on giving them directions. 'Shouldn't take you long this time of night. I hope he's OK, your bloke.'

Harry slipped him a note and thanked him for his help, and told him they would arrange collection of the car.

'No problem.' The man was happy, his evening made by the small interlude of intrigue. 'I'll secure it and leave a note for my mate. If you want to . . . you know, look into another vehicle any time, and need someone to hold the torch, drop by.'

FIFTY-TWO

The address on the garage bill led to an anonymous terraced cottage on the edge of a small development. Open fields spread out into the darkness in front, and a few houses showed lights to the rear. The properties either side were dark and silent, and in the glow from the street lights the area looked neat and well maintained.

Harry parked a few doors along and walked up the front path. He pressed a button to one side and heard a bell ringing inside. There was no answer. He tried the handle but it was locked. Leaving Rik to keep watch, he went to check the rear.

The back gardens were small and laid mostly to patios or decking, with gravelled beds sprouting ceramic flower pots and exotic grasses. Harry pushed through the gate and negotiated the gloom to the back door. When he touched the handle, the door swung open.

He stepped back, eyeing the windows. He couldn't hear anything, as there was just enough ambient night noise to block any sounds from inside. He turned and walked back to the front and led Rik to the car.

'Back door's open,' he said quietly, and opened the rear of the Renault. He leaned inside, then swore softly.

'Problem?' Rik joined him and immediately spotted the metal box with the combination lock. 'What's that?'

'What does it look like?' Harry muttered, and tried again to open it. But the mechanism was jammed solid. He ran his fingers round the combination dial and felt a sliver of metal wedged firmly into one side. This was no accident.

Rik looked at him. 'It's a hot box!' He sounded shocked. 'I was meaning to ask you about that—'

'Ask me some other time. We'll open it later.' He looked back towards the house. There was still no sign of life. In spite of his reservations about carrying weapons, having the backup of a gun right now would be an enormous psychological advantage. 'Come on.'

Leaving Rik to cover the front door again, he made his way to the back and stepped inside. The only sound was the ticking of a heater. The air smelled musty and dead. He brushed his hand across the wall by the door and flicked on the light. He was in a small kitchen, tidy except for a plate and wine glass standing in the sink. The base of the glass was crusted with dried red wine.

He walked through the cottage and opened the front door. 'Anything?' Rik was scowling, but looked fully alert.

'Doesn't feel like it,' Harry whispered. He gestured towards the stairs. 'I'll do up there.'

He went up the carpeted stairs before Rick could ask more questions. He reached the landing and stepped into a bathroom. Empty. He crossed the hallway and found a small bedroom containing a single bed, a cheap pine desk with a PC on the top, and a chest of drawers.

He stepped into the last room and switched on the light.

Jennings was lying across the bed, dressed in a shirt and pants. His legs were white stalks, hairless and devoid of colour or muscle tone. He looked as if he might have been dressing to go out. A pair of shiny black brogues stood by the bedside cabinet, and a tie lay across the pillow. A suit was hanging on the front of a single wardrobe.

Harry called down. 'Up here.'

Rik joined him and moved across to the bed. A small hole was visible in Jennings' throat, just below the chin, and a heavy trickle of congealed blood had wormed its way down one side of his neck. Another had run from the corner of his mouth and puddled on the coverlet. Harry checked the skin around the wound. There were no signs of scorch marks.

'He was shot from the door,' he concluded. 'Small calibre. Doesn't look as if he had time to react.'

They checked the house from top to bottom, but other than the PC, there was nothing to help them in their search. The PC would have to go to Ballatyne for his experts to go over and analyse in depth.

'You want me to take a look?' Rik offered.

It was tempting, if only to get a jump ahead of Ballatyne.

But Harry shook his head. 'Jennings will have used codes or
password protection. We don't have time.'

They gave the house another once-over, each taking the
rooms previously done by the other. This second search
revealed a small paper carrier bag by the side of the pine desk
in the spare bedroom. It was empty, but when Harry peered
inside, he saw a tiny triangle of paper under the edge of the
cardboard stiffener at the bottom. He pulled it out. It was a
single, new fifty-Euro note.

He studied the bag. It had crease lines down the sides, as
if it had once contained something heavy and roughly oblong
. . . like packs of banknotes. Was this what Jennings had been
killed for – a pay-off that had turned nasty?

Harry dialled Ballatyne's number and reported their find-
ings. The duty officer coolly noted the details, including the
number off the fifty-Euro note, and said he would pass it on.
'We'll notify the police, but we'll have our people check the
place first.' He added that it might be unwise for them to be
found in the vicinity.

'This bloke doesn't waste time thinking on moral dilemmas,
does he?' said Rik. 'It was just like the others: in, do the job
and out again.'

'Similar. But there are two differences. He got here before
us and he took something away with him.' The same signature was here just as surely as if he'd spray-painted his name
across the walls.

Dog.

The hostel near Victoria was in darkness by the time Dog
returned. A digital clock in a shop window read 02.30. He'd
been unable to sleep, his mind full of what he had to do
tomorrow. He hadn't intended being out this late, but time
had slipped by unnoticed, his thoughts piling in on each
other as he considered his future after he'd taken care of
Rafa'i.

He pushed at the front door, half expecting to have to
hammer on the glass to rouse someone, but it swung open
without resistance. The cubicle where the night-porter-cum-
security-guard watched a tiny television was deserted. Grateful
for small mercies, he moved past the desk and walked quietly
up the stairs, feeling the pull of stiffness settling in his leg

muscles. He was tempted to do some warm-down stretches but it would have to wait. He needed sleep more.

He entered his room and stripped off, then took a shower. He made it part of his routine whenever he was able to, cleaning himself with almost ritual care, ready for whatever lay ahead. He enjoyed the soothing effect standing under the warm jet, letting it cascade over him until the water began to cool. He turned off the shower and shook himself free of excess droplets.

Drying himself quickly, he took out his gun and knife. He cleaned the blade with a pad of tissue, paying particular attention to some dried flecks of red around the handle which he'd missed after the job in Harrow. He felt a bristle of annoyance; that one had been a mistake, for which he blamed Jennings. If the lawyer had kept him fully informed, he'd have been ready for Tate and Ferris to alter their plans.

Still, he'd taken care of it and nobody was the wiser. He'd actually taken an unusual pleasure in seeing the man – Param, Jennings had said he was called – staggering back from the door, the life ebbing from his body, an expression of dismay on his dumb face.

He put the knife in his jacket and stripped the gun, laying out the parts on the bed with something close to reverence. It was a routine and one he could have followed in the pitch dark. When they were cleaned and reassembled, he placed the gun on the floor by the bed, within easy reach. He didn't entirely trust some of the other residents not to come calling if they thought they could snaffle something in the wee small hours.

Next he cleaned his shoes and laid out his clothes, consigning his dirty skivvies to a plastic bag for disposal in the morning. He could easily buy new ones. Then he lay on the bed, relishing the cool air on his naked skin and staring at the ceiling. He started going over what he'd accomplished so far – and what lay ahead.

He was slipping into mission mode, as he had done so often before, checking and rechecking his options, going back over earlier preparations and discounting one by one the various errors that might have been made. For a while, he was back in a meadow outside Armagh or in a hovel of a B&B in the back streets of Belfast, listening to the traffic, wondering if the vehicle slowing nearby had come for him.

It was oddly calming being here in London, listening to the sounds of the street, of late cabs cruising for fares, of night cleaners going about their work. He felt himself beginning to drift and smiled, enjoying the sensation of gradually letting go.

After Rafa'i, Dog knew there was nothing to keep him here. This was the end of the road for him, and probably the end of his work. He'd had a bad feeling about Jennings right from the start, though; he should have listened to his instincts. The man was a cheapskate, interested solely in his own future. After tomorrow morning, though, when he'd complete his final job, he'd be done for good.

The truth was, he was relieved it was over. There was only so long a man could go on doing this kind of work, and he'd been at it longer than most, lasted far longer than his contemporaries. The odds of continuing unscathed were not in his favour. It was time to move on. To disappear. Dog was good at disappearing for long periods.

This time it would have to be for good.

As his eyes began to close under the pull of sleep and his breathing began to settle to a steady rhythm, he wondered vaguely about the absence of the night porter. The man had always been as quick as a rat down a drainpipe before to intercept arrivals. He should have been there, street crime being what it was in the area. You couldn't trust anyone these days—

He heard a faint rasp of noise close by.

Somebody else was in the room.

Dog kept his eyes closed and his breathing unchanged. He lowered his hand slowly to the floor, reaching for the gun. Whoever was in here was going to regret it: they had invaded his space. Probably some bloody crack head looking for an easy score. He'd have a sharp word with the night porter in the morning.

He located movement over by the door; recognized the shift of fabric, the brush of a shoe on the scrappy carpet. He smiled. Careless. The intruder had betrayed his location as surely as if he'd struck a match.

Dog swung his feet to the floor and stood up in one fluid motion, bringing the gun to bear on the door. In the glow of a neon display from the hostel sign just outside his window, he saw the room as clearly as day. In the same moment, he saw a patch of darkness – but it wasn't where he'd expected.

The intruder was standing against the wall by the wardrobe, tucked into the corner.

A truck rattled by outside, its engine roaring. In the same instant, a light flared, the white flash painful to the eyes. Dog heard a sharp crack, almost drowned by the noise of the truck, and something punched him with unbelievable force in the chest. He staggered back, shocked and breathless.

He fought to regain his balance, dragging his weapon round to bear on the other person and trying to pull the trigger. *Why was it so difficult? It was never this hard. All you had to do was pull—* But his finger wouldn't work. He tried again, focussing all his strength on that simple task, something he'd done so often it was as natural as breathing.

Then, in the sweeping lights of traffic flushing across the front of the hostel, he saw the face of his opponent. He experienced a bitter sense of fury. And pain.

It started in his chest, blossoming out and invading his whole body. It was like nothing he'd experienced before – and Dog was no stranger to pain. His body told him he needed to lie down, but his mind rebelled, unwilling to let go. Then he could no longer control the physical functions as the motor system governing his body began to shut down. He moved backwards, and the edge of the bed hit the back of his legs and tipped him off-balance.

His gun dropped and bounced away in the gloom, no longer of any use to him.

FIFTY-THREE

Rafa'i was early again. This time he approached the park from the Mall, skittering along the pavement as if his feet were on fire. It was just gone nine thirty. He looked uneasy, huddled in the same long, dark coat Harry and Rik had seen him with on the airport cameras.

After a fitful few hours' sleep in a backstreet hotel near Marylebone following their discovery of Jennings' body, they had breakfasted in a coffee shop and discussed tactics. If Rafa'i failed to show, they were back to square one, in which case they might as well contact Ballatyne and wait to see what happened next. On the positive side, if the cleric did show, everything that followed would depend on his reaction to their presence. Without Joanne, they might have a problem talking him round. It would depend on how highly he rated his chances of surviving alone without help.

Before driving here, Harry had gone to the boot of his car and forced open the hot box. He'd taken out two semi-automatics and handed one to Rik.

'This is strictly last-resort use,' he said sombrely. 'If you take this out, it's because you intend to use it. You intend to kill. Right?'

'Right.' Rik had nodded, any argument about the box and its contents forgotten. He'd checked the gun and put it away under his jacket, apparently calm. But Harry could tell he was nervous. Nerves were OK, though; nerves would get him through this and make sure he reacted with caution rather than haste.

Then they had set off for the park.

They were in luck. Joanne was standing by the railings around the lake.

Rik was unimpressed. 'I don't get it.'

'Take it easy,' said Harry calmly, and walked across to her. He was careful not to spook her, and made a show of being relaxed, unthreatening. She watched them approach, her face tight, but no longer with the haunted look they'd seen before. She had one strap of her rucksack slung over her shoulder, but was clutching the bulk of it to her front. One hand was visible, Harry noted, resting on the railing. The other was tucked inside the rucksack.

He stopped alongside her and turned to watch the area by the Mall. Rik moved away without acknowledging her, heading towards the path to watch their flanks.

'What happened to you?' Harry asked quietly.

'I needed space,' she replied. 'It all got too much, especially seeing Marshall and talking about what happened.'

'No problem. You OK now?'

'I don't know.' She turned away, chin dropping. 'We'll see, won't we?'

Harry saw Rafa'i emerge from under the trees. He stood looking shakily around him, his nervousness obvious and out of place, like a crack head in a tea room. Rik was thirty feet away, being tapped for money by an old woman in a scruffy coat, but still alert. He looked up and nodded, signalling that he'd seen the Iraqi, too. His gaze dwelt for a long while on Joanne, and he shook his head.

Harry ignored him. He was waiting to see what Rafa'i would do. If they approached him, he might run for good. Better to let him come to them once he felt safe. He rechecked the area. If Dog was going to make his move, he would do it any time now. Then he'd make his getaway. This was the window of maximum danger.

'It seems,' Harry said casually, 'that there are some question marks against your Mr Rafa'i.'

'You've just discovered that?' Her reply was acid, resentful, the words as sharp as carpet tacks.

He glanced at her, surprised by the venom in her voice. She was shaking her head as if Rafa'i being questionable was a given. It was in odd contrast to the way she had talked about him before, when she had expressed almost a closeness in their working relationship.

'Come again?'

'I used to think he was the whole shilling,' she explained flatly. 'But there were things he said . . . people he met that made me wonder. He said a couple of times that he wanted Iraq free of the outside world. I took that to be the Coalition, especially the Americans.'

'Well, nobody could argue with that. We're hardly welcome guests, are we?'

'He meant everyone: advisors, aid workers, army, engineers, contractors, the lot. All out. Even people like me. Especially people like me.'

'Well, there's no pleasing some people.'

The attempt at humour didn't carry. Joanne said angrily, 'It was like he wanted to build a wall around the country and turn it in on itself. And after everything we'd done to help. Oh, I know the arguments . . . that we shouldn't have been there, anyway. But still.' She stopped, breathing heavily.

Harry said, 'Why are you so angry?'

It was as if she hadn't heard him. 'Then he spun the whole

thing and said he was just describing an old Iraqi dream. But
it wasn't his dream, he said. It was the people's dream. And
the people had a right to have what was theirs. He only wanted
a peaceful country again.'

Harry wondered where this was going. Where the change
in tune was coming from. She seemed to be rambling, as if
seeing Rafa'i once more had revived an old discussion, ripped
open old sores. But which ones?

'Everybody wants peace out there,' he said coolly, trying
to figure her out. 'But if Dog gets his way, Rafa'i won't live
to see it.'

She made a noise but said nothing.

'Still, at least,' Harry continued, 'we know what he looks
like . . . unlike his two mates.'

Her eyes flickered. 'What?'

'He's got help. Two men. Word is, they're on their way
here. Unfortunately, we don't know what they look like.' He
was about to add that she, on the other hand, might do, having
been on the same training course, but decided against it. It
wasn't the time or the place.

'You don't know much of anything, do you?'

'Sorry?' It was a coldly dismissive comment, uttered in a
dull, flat tone. But she shook her head and chose not to elaborate, so he let it go.

All the same, he felt a stir of unease.

FIFTY-FOUR

'What's his problem?' Joanne was staring hard at
Rik, her expression hostile. She had been
watching him intently for a few minutes now, as
if suddenly troubled by his lack of warmth towards her.

'Rik? He trusts people . . . takes them at face value. It's
something I'm trying to cure him of.' When Harry looked
across at him, Rik turned away. Rafa'i was beyond him, waiting
in the background.

'He's too close to Rafa'i,' she said. 'He should move away.'

'He's fine where he is.' Harry couldn't see the problem,

and put her attitude down to last-minute nerves. For some reason, she and Rik were rubbing each other up the wrong way.

But she wouldn't let it go. 'Rafa'i won't come if he sees him standing there. He needs to move to one side.'

Harry sighed and signalled to Rik to move aside a few feet, which he did with reluctance, the old woman tagging along. 'That do you?'

'Yes. You have to wait here.' She walked away without waiting for a reply, clutching her rucksack to her chest.

Harry wanted to go after her and demand to know what was on her mind, but he didn't. Rafa'i still hadn't moved from his position by the trees. In fact, he'd retreated a few feet and was now in dappled shadow, casting around him like a startled deer ready to bolt. Something about the situation must have spooked him.

Rik prised himself away from the old woman and joined Harry, watching as Joanne moved into an empty space where Rafa'i would be able to see her.

'What did she have to say?' he muttered darkly.

'Not much.' Harry's phone rang. 'Keep an eye on her.' He took it out and thumbed the button.

'Harry?' It was Ballatyne. 'Is Archer with you?'

'She's close by. Why?'

'Where are you?'

He hadn't told Ballatyne where they would be this morning. The intelligence man's instinct would have been to swamp the area with men in boots and jumpsuits. Rafa'i would have spotted them immediately and disappeared.

'We're waiting for Rafa'i,' he replied enigmatically. 'Problems?' He checked there was nobody nearby and switched his phone to loudspeaker so Rik could hear.

'You could say that.' Ballatyne's voice sounded tinny in the morning air. 'We've had a call from the Met. We asked them to alert us if anything out of the ordinary happened. A former Special Forces man, Gary Pellew, has been found shot dead in a hostel near Victoria.'

Dog.

'They say he's been dead several hours – sometime between eleven last night and five this morning. Difficult to tell without forensic results, but we won't get those for a while. It was a single shot to the chest, that's all we know. His room was clean apart from a change of clothes, a knife and a semi-automatic with a full load and a spare mag.'

Fighting kit. Harry glanced across at Rafa'i, still hovering beneath the trees, then at Joanne, who was checking the immediate area, her head swivelling constantly like a lioness on the prowl. Most of the time, he noted, she was watching him and Rik.

The threat had been three-fold. With Dog down, that left two to be accounted for. *So who the hell had shot him?*

'Do they know what calibre weapon?' Harry asked.

'No. Small, I'm told. Why?'

'Jennings was shot with a small calibre.'

Rik muttered and flicked open his jacket. Harry could just see the butt of his semi-automatic.

'Noted,' said Ballatyne. Then in a bleaker tone, 'We've also had more info from the Ops room in Baghdad. The comms corporal who was on the log the day Humphries was killed has come back.'

'Go on.'

'When we asked for the original check, we were only concerned with outgoing calls, to check on any arrangement Humphries had made. They were all normal business, all checked and cleared. But the corporal confirmed that the call Humphries received that day was on a secured line. That means it was an agency or military source. Humphries left the office immediately. Forty minutes later, he was dead.'

'Somebody drew him out.' Harry glanced at Rik, who was shaking his head in silent disgust. He didn't want to ask the next question, but he had to. 'Do we know who?'

'It was a woman. She used the code name Pamper.'

Harry sighed, feeling the blood rushing in his head. He didn't need Ballatyne to finish driving in the final nail.

'The call originated from the sat phone issued to Joanne Archer.'

FIFTY-FIVE

Harry looked up to find Joanne watching him. Her eyes were empty of expression, her face set. He thought she looked tired, resigned. But there was something else, too.

She knew.

He tried telling himself that the comms corporal had misread the log; that Joanne's sat phone might have been stolen and used by someone else. But he recalled asking her what she'd done with it, down by the pier at Westminster Bridge. Her answer had been unequivocal.

'*I dumped it the day I flew out.*'

So it was true.

Beyond Joanne, Rafa'i was stepping out tentatively from the trees, a bundle of nerves, his head snapping back and forth.

'Why?' Harry felt a surge of anger. 'It doesn't make sense.'

'It does,' Ballatyne replied, 'if we tie it in with some other information just in. We've been checking Jennings' calls over the past few weeks. He wasn't as secure as he thought. There were more than thirty calls between him and Archer since Rafa'i's compound was destroyed. All the calls were to or from Archer's personal mobile, and the vast majority were made within the last *three* days. They must have realized the bomb had missed and Jennings was directing Archer's movements, waiting for Rafa'i to surface.'

In other words, waiting for Harry and Rik to run him to ground.

'So what was Dog's function?'

'Probably a backup, originally, in case Archer failed or needed help. Then, when it looked like she'd got out of Baghdad safely, she became a liability. Dog was there to clean up afterwards. No witnesses, no fuss. Only he got to like the killing too much. In the end, it was he who became the liability and had to go.'

Harry watched Joanne moving towards Rafa'i. As she did

so, a flicker of activity dragged his attention towards Horse
Guards Parade. He saw two men in military uniform striding
briskly across the open square. A number of tourists were
grinning and taking snaps as they passed, and even at this
early hour, it seemed, there was no opportunity to be missed
of getting a good photo.

'There's a clincher.' Ballatyne spoke with what might have
been an air of resignation, as if he'd been keeping something
in reserve.

'Christ, what?'

'Archer had exclusive use of the Pamper code name, along
with a numeric suffix. She was the only person who could
have got through to Humphries using that code and got an
instant response. Anyone else would have got the runaround.
Nobody else but the comms staff in Baghdad knew the suffix.'

The two soldiers had been forced to stop by the wedge of
tourists wanting to take their photos. Both men carried small
shoulder bags, and one elderly Japanese man seemed to be
asking the two men to put them aside while they took their
happy snaps. But the soldiers were shaking their heads
resolutely, their focus fixed on a point beyond the snappers.

'There's something else we've just discovered. When
Humphries set out for that last meeting, he hit a panic button.
It sent a search and rescue squad on the way to the safe house,
with orders to secure the location and wait. The personnel
were posted to other assignments down near Basra the
following day, so their reports have been late coming in. The
team leader says they arrived in the street at the safe house
after the alarm was sounded, but it was deserted. They'd got
held up on the way by an IED alert, so they were late. If
Archer had been there, she must have decided it was too
dangerous to hang around and bugged out.'

'Couldn't that be true?' Even as he said, it Harry recalled
Joanne's description of the four-wheel drive entering the street
and an altercation with a shopkeeper. It had been enough for
her to decide to leave. He also recalled suggesting that it might
have been a rescue patrol, but she'd denied it, saying they
were in civilian dress. Mercs. He put it to Ballatyne. 'Would
they have been army?'

'No. We use contractors for that kind of operation. The few
military personnel still there are stretched enough as it is

without being used to pick up stray specialists.' He paused. 'I'm sorry, Harry. I know you find this hard. But somewhere along the way, Joanne Archer was got at and turned. Whether that was before going to Iraq or after, only she can tell us. It's a safe bet, though, that she was primed to kill Rafa'i if the bomb didn't do it.'

'So why kill Humphries?'

'I think he was on to her and hit the panic button to have her taken out. He must have said something to alert her and she got rid of the only person who could stop her.'

Rik leaned in and said, 'So why go to the safe house? Why didn't she just go to a control post and identify herself?'

'Possibly,' Ballatyne answered, 'because she knew Humphries would have left word about where he was going and who he was meeting. If she'd deviated from that and missed out the safe house altogether, it would have looked suspicious.' He paused again. 'There's also the timing. We had someone check the route. She'd have had just enough time to leave the compound and intercept Humphries before making her way to the safe house. If, as she told you, she was still there when the patrol arrived, it was because she was also late getting there. Now we know why.'

Harry felt sick. She'd been lying all along: about her role in Iraq; her closeness to Humphries and Rafa'i; who had called that final briefing meeting; her feelings of betrayal and abandonment – everything. She had even sabotaged the hot box in his car as a precautionary tactic by jamming the combination mechanism with a nail file. He'd found the plastic handle lying in the boot where she'd snapped it off. He even knew when she'd done it: at the hotel in Bayswater, she had slipped out to the car, hinting at 'girl's stuff'. She'd been gone easily long enough to fix the lock and he hadn't given it a thought. Idiot.

'When was the last exchange on her mobile?'

'Early yesterday morning. After that, the signal ceased.'

It would, thought Harry. Phones tend not to work too well when you throw them in the Thames. He wondered if the shot that had killed Joanne's friend Cath Barbour in the Battersea flat would match the weapon she was carrying. Somehow he knew the answer to that, too. Barbour had turned up at the wrong moment and instantly became a liability. It also explained why Joanne had cleaned her gun at Rik's place: training and habit make you clean your weapon at the earliest opportunity after a discharge.

Another piece of the puzzle dropped into place: the killing of Dog. Joanne was missing last night, her movements unaccounted for. It would be a major stretch proving it, but if they were connected, and Dog had lost the plot, Joanne wouldn't have dared risk him getting caught and made to talk. And now, with the meeting in the park set up, his part of the job really was over. It must have been a nasty surprise for the professional killer to have realized he was surplus to requirements.

'You trained her well,' Harry said bitterly. 'She's self-sufficient and ruthless, and now she's cleaning up behind her. The only thing I don't understand is why she didn't finish Rafa'i off in the park yesterday, when Dog attacked.'

'Because you and Ferris were too close. She would have been counting on you to give her a clear pass when she'd finished the job. Who better? Dog would have been the ideal fall guy.'

Harry noticed that the two soldiers had finally pushed their way through the knot of tourists and had now split up. One was heading towards the Mall, where Rafa'i was standing, the other had veered away towards the lake.

They were now carrying their shoulder bags in their hands and their demeanour looked far too purposeful for a stroll.

The truth suddenly hit him. This is what she'd been waiting for. They were *her* helpers, not Dog's!

Rik had noticed, too. '*Contact!*' he snapped, and set off towards Rafa'i, reaching under his jacket.

'What's up?' Ballatyne had heard the shout.

'Rafa'i's here,' said Harry, 'and we've got two bandits coming in fast.'

'*Christ,*' Ballatyne replied. 'Where's Archer? *For Christ's sake don't let her anywhere near him.* I'm sending a team – what's your location?'

Harry told him and switched off the phone, cutting short the intelligence man's orders not to do anything until his men arrived. 'Too late,' Harry breathed, and began to run towards Joanne. 'Too bloody late.'

FIFTY-SIX

Rik sprinted across the grass, skidding on a damp patch. He switched his focus between Rafa'i and the soldier who was approaching his position. The soldier looked sharp and fit, and there was an extra intensity about him that clearly indicated his intentions. Rik was also aware of Joanne Archer approaching Rafa'i, although she seemed to be completely ignoring the other two men.

The soldier broke into a run, clawing into his shoulder bag and casting it to one side. His hand came out holding a large knife with a serrated edge.

Rik stopped and felt his gut shrink. He was too far away to intercept the man; as quick as he was, there was no way he could cover the distance in time. He hesitated, aware of the people and surroundings, and wondered what Harry would do. Then he dropped to one knee, dragging the gun from under his jacket. A part of his brain knew that this was lunacy, that Harry would probably throw a fit. The danger of carrying a handgun in this area was beyond imagining. But there was no other option. If he didn't do this, Rafa'i was dead meat and the fall-out would be disastrous.

Cupping the butt of the semi-automatic in his hand, he centred on the chest of the soldier with the knife.

'*Stand still or I fire!*'

Cries of alarm came as people scattered among the trees, a few quick-witted individuals dragging others out of the way or pushing them down out of harm's way. A woman screamed and in the distance, a siren began whooping, the sound muffled by the buildings.

The soldier ignored Rik's shout and continued to bear down on Rafa'i.

Rik checked his line of fire, remembering the lessons on the range and the live firing course, Harry shadowing his every move with calm advice. Back then it had been fun, a flood of adrenalin hitting him as he learned new skills. Now he felt sick. The area was clear of onlookers and there was nobody behind the soldier. A few windows, maybe, but mostly trees and, beyond them, the thick, grey walls of government buildings.

He had a clear shot.

'*Wait!*' It was Joanne's voice, dragging his eyes away from his target. She was facing him from thirty feet away, the barrel of her handgun pointing right at him.

He ignored her, no longer surprised, and turned back to the soldier. He imagined himself facing the familiar target cut-outs, computing the strength and direction of the breeze and other prevailing conditions that might affect his aim. He could even hear the range-master's steady, monotonous voice in his head: *Focus on the target and ignore all other distractions. Focus. Breathe. Squeeze.*

Jesus. Rik tried not to dwell on the image of Joanne's gun or the way his hands were trembling. *Some distraction, this. If he lived through it, he was going to get shit-faced.*

If the soldier had heard Rik's first warning shout, he gave no indication. He probably wasn't expecting any opposition and was here to perform a quick, silent job, then make his escape through the park.

Rik repeated his warning shout. He'd still got a clear line of fire and the man was now within a dozen paces of Rafa'i. He had three seconds at most to make a decision. The soldier or Joanne? When it was clear the soldier had no intention of stopping, Rik took a deep breath and squeezed the trigger twice in quick succession.

The bangs were frighteningly loud. A volley of pigeons and other birds burst into the air, and several people screamed. With the unique view of the marksman, Rik saw the target – the soldier's tunic – jump with the impact of both shots.

The man looked shocked and lurched to one side. His legs went out from under him and he flipped on to his face and lay still.

Harry swore loudly as Rik opened fire, and saw the soldier fall. But he was less concerned by Rik's action than Joanne's. She had dropped into a crouch, casting off her rucksack and aiming her weapon at Rik. Her face was cold and pale, her expression focussed. Rik was a target to be dealt with. No more, no less.

Harry pulled out his own gun and shouted, although he wasn't sure what he said: the words were lost in the noise of her gun as she opened fire. Once, twice, three times, she pulled the trigger in quick succession, the shots blending into a roll that echoed back and forth across the park.

Then Rik was no longer upright, but was flung across the grass on his back, where he lay still.

'*No!*' Harry roared. The sirens were growing in volume and proximity. Any second now he could be lined up in a marksman's sights and they wouldn't know in the confusion who was who. Anyone carrying a weapon would be seen as a threat and therefore a legitimate target.

He dismissed the thought, caught in the moment. *He didn't want to do this. He didn't want to be responsible for what was unfolding. Surely she wouldn't force him—*

Then matters were taken out of his hands. He heard a rush of movement and was hit broadside. It was the other soldier, running interference. They both grunted with the impact and rolled in a tangle across the grass, dead leaves showering around them.

Harry scrambled to recover. A flash of light curved inwards and he saw the shape of a blade scything in towards him. Behind it was the snarling expression of the other man, his mouth flecked with spit.

Harry scrabbled away, instinctively crossing his wrists in front of him in an effort to block the knife thrusts. Cuts to the hands were bad, but preferable to a stab to the body. If that happened, it was all over.

He desperately tried to thumb off the safety catch, but his fingers were suddenly slick with his own sweat and moisture, and the gun slipped from his grasp and span away.

The soldier came in again, kicking desperately against the ground to gain momentum. He was so close Harry could see specks of dirt and grass on his uniform and that one button was missing. He rolled away, feeling something grind hard into his back. He grunted with pain, thinking his attacker had managed to cut him after all. Then he realized what it was.

His gun.

The soldier saw it, too, and made another lunge, the knife raised high.

Harry was quicker. Scooping up the gun, he thumbed off the safety and fired all in one movement.

The man flopped to the ground and gave a long sigh.

Harry struggled to his feet, eyes on the dead man's face. A stranger. Never seen him before. He felt nauseous and winded. Then he looked up and saw Joanne, and realized that what had happened had taken just milliseconds.

It had felt like minutes.

He saw her glance to where Rafa'i was standing, half hidden by a tree, his mouth open in shock. She turned to face Harry and shook her head, the gun lining up on his chest. Whatever she was thinking was hidden behind a mask, unrecognizable from the face he had come to know. She backed away towards Rafa'i, and Harry realized she was putting herself within certain killing range. As she moved, the people around the Iraqi seemed to sense that he was the focus of her attention and scattered, leaving him isolated.

She stopped, the gun still pointing at Harry. Her legs bent fractionally and her finger curled around the trigger. The body language of the shooter. He wasn't going to have time to bring up his own weapon, and he felt annoyed at not being more prepared for this outcome.

Then a piercing whistle cut through the air, carrying across the park and the open parade ground. It was shrill enough to stop everyone and make heads turn; close enough to drag Joanne's attention momentarily away from Harry.

Rik was sitting up, elbows resting on his knees, gun cradled in his hands. There was blood on his shirt and a red smear across one cheek. He was gritting his teeth, no doubt fighting against the shock of his wounds.

'Don't do it, Jo,' he croaked, imploring her. 'Please. You can't win—'

But Joanne wasn't listening. She hesitated, then screamed in fury and spun round, firing twice. It was probably her over-reaction that saved Rik's life. The first round ripped a chunk of bark off a tree just behind his head; the second gouged into the ground by his foot, kicking up fragments of grass and dirt.

Harry wanted to close his eyes, but couldn't. She was now sideways on to him. He knew Rik's ability with a handgun, knew what was about to unfold. And there was nothing he could do to stop it.

With a feeling of infinite sadness, and before Joanne could fire again, he brought up his gun and squeezed the trigger.

Rik did the same, their shots merging into one.

FIFTY-SEVEN

The sirens were all around them now, cars converging from all points. Men in uniform were running towards them with weapons raised, moving crab-like as they identified potential threats and prepared to retaliate. Some were shouting, telling them to drop their guns and to get down on the ground. Others were urging shocked onlookers to safety. The official machinery of armed response was in full swing.

Harry saw Rik drop his weapon and lie back on the ground, then roll with difficulty on to his belly with his arms wide as a policeman stood over him with plastic cuffs. He did the same, knowing there was no choice. From the corner of his eye, he saw Rafa'i sink to the grass. The man looked shocked by the turn of events, and he wondered how long that would last. The former cleric no doubt had a fallback plan in mind.

Through a veil of grass stalks in front of him, Joanne's face was turned towards him, eyes open but unseeing. The snarl was gone now, leaving her calm, void of expression. Then an armed officer in a dark jumpsuit moved across his line of vision and placed one booted foot on her arm before stooping to remove the gun from her hand.

Ballatyne arrived minutes later with a brace of helpers. He singled out Rik and Harry, ordered them to be released from their cuffs, and told two of his men to get Rafa'i out of sight. He looked around at the scene, taking in Joanne Archer's body and the two dead soldiers, which were being covered with dark sheets, and shook his head.

'What the hell happened here?' he demanded. 'Don't you two get enough greens? This is a blood bath.' He lifted a corner of the cloth away from one of the soldiers and bent to peer at his face. 'Yeah – that's one of them. Clever move, coming in uniform. Who would have thought, eh?'

He turned as a constable approached holding Joanne

Archer's rucksack. Inside was a plastic bag full of money, Euros of every denomination.

'Someone had a good pay day,' Ballatyne murmured. 'I think we can guess where that came from, and the banknote number you found at Jennings' place should confirm it. She probably got Dog's pay-off as well. Jennings didn't take any chances; cash payments to hide the trail, then everyone disappears into the sunset. Unfortunately for him, he chose the wrong people.' He told the constable to bag and tag the rucksack, then stared at Rik, who was being examined by a paramedic. The gunshot wound had been to his shoulder, but other than some blood loss and looking sickly, he seemed to be coping. 'You were bloody lucky, Ferris,' he said mildly. 'That girl could shoot the eye out of a gnat, according to her record. Still, I suppose we all have our off days.' He turned to Harry. 'I need to speak to you – alone.' His expression was unfriendly and Harry reflected that Marshall had left behind a tough and capable replacement.

'Just a second,' he said, and walked over to Joanne's body. He lifted the cloth and studied the wounds, then dropped it back in place.

He followed Ballatyne across the grass to the lakeside path. Two armed policemen walked a few paces behind and stood by, silently watchful. A crowd of people from the lakeside cafeteria had gathered near the entrance and Ballatyne delegated one of the officers to push them back fifty yards.

'Bloody people think it's a tourist show. Ferris'll be arrested, you know that, don't you?' He was watching Rik being led to an ambulance with a paramedic supporting him and two armed officers close behind.

'Don't talk wet,' said Harry bluntly. 'If you arrest him, you'll have to arrest me, too.'

'It doesn't work like that and you know it.' Ballatyne watched a duck swimming past a few feet away. 'You're one of the privileged few, authorized to carry. He's not.' He peered sideways at Harry. 'Your record makes interesting reading.'

'Rik was helping me. He saved my life – ask any of that lot.' He gestured towards the crowd of onlookers who were being marshalled into a line by officers, ready to be interviewed.

'We intend to, don't worry. Not that it'll help. You know

how unreliable witnesses are: they'll all remember something different and nobody will recall the good guy doing a heroic deed. To them, anyone with a gun is a villain – even the cops. Ferris will do time and there's nothing I can do to help.' He paused for effect. 'Face it, Harry, he shouldn't have been armed. What the hell were you thinking?'

Harry felt like pushing him into the lake, but controlled his anger. For someone spouting the law, Ballatyne didn't seem all that serious, in spite of his expression. It was as if he were leading up to something.

'If Rik hadn't been armed,' he said quietly, 'I'd be dead. So would Rafa'i and possibly a fair number of innocent tourists. You'd have an international incident on your hands and half the Islamic world shouting about how one of their leaders had been kidnapped out of Baghdad and assassinated in a royal park just a spit away from Buckingham Palace and Downing Street. Oh, and the assassin? A member of the British Army, hired by members of the Coalition and helped by two other members of the British Army. That'd make great press.'

'Former members,' Ballatyne corrected him. 'Those two bozos handed in their papers a while back. And records will show that Joanne Archer died heroically in Baghdad trying to protect an Iraqi VIP. Anything else?'

'So how do you explain a dead female assassin in the centre of London?'

'Who cares? If we have to, we lie. Haven't you heard of spin? It's been all the rage since ninety-seven.'

Harry felt hollow. Ballatyne seemed to have all the answers. But he wasn't about to roll over just yet. 'Before you do that,' he said, 'you might want to think how it will run in tomorrow's media.'

Ballatyne blinked and studied Harry's face. 'You'd never do that.'

'Is that what my record says? A lot's happened since then. The story's already written. Somebody would print it – if not here, then elsewhere or on YouTube. Throw in what went on when Paulton and Bellingham tried to kill us both in Georgia and there'll be a feeding frenzy.'

'Like I said, you'd never do it.' Ballatyne's jaw was firm, but there was a flicker of doubt in his eyes.

'You've known my status long enough. Yet you still chose to use me – and Rik – because it suited you to have Rafa'i's killers taken out without official involvement. Try screwing me on this and it'll come back and bite you on the arse.'

Ballatyne sighed and looked away across the lake at a clutch of Canada geese making their way towards them. 'I should come here more often, you know. It's a nice place. Peaceful. I like ducks. They've got no agenda.' He paused. 'All right. But I want a quid pro quo. A big one. I want you to take Rafa'i back to Iraq.'

FIFTY-EIGHT

Harry stared at him. So this was what he'd been building to all along. Ballatyne didn't give a stuff about Rik breaking the rules; all he wanted was leverage. The man was nuts. 'Rik goes free. No prosecution.'

'Yes. We want Rafa'i off our hands, the sooner the better. What he gets up to once he's back in that bugger's muddle called Baghdad, we don't care. He's too dirty for us.'

Harry grunted cynically. 'So much for the Coalition's golden solution.'

'Well, let's say he turned out to be low-grade gilt. Apart from the fund-gathering, we've had confirmation from two sources in Iraq that Rafa'i knew about the intended bombing of his compound in advance. I won't go into all the nasty details, but it looks like he got wind of an attempt on his life and decided to use it to his own advantage. We'll never know for sure, but it's my guess he took Archer's disappearance to a meeting as a signal that something was about to happen. He might not have known what her part was in all this, but probably figured she was being withdrawn so they could take him out without harming her. He may have counted on playing them at their own game and using Archer to vouch for him once he was over here.'

'So what has this all been about?'

'Propaganda. Power. Pecking order. The man's no fool; he's

learned to read people. He's a politician. He knew it was only a question of time before someone in his own community took a pop at him. But what if he turned it on its head? His survival and reappearance, followed by a triumphant entry to Baghdad, would be like the Second Coming. And with the funds and support he's been gathering, it would create havoc. He'd be in a position of incredible power – for a while, anyway.'

'What do you mean?'

'It wouldn't last. They'd use him for his contacts and influence, then get rid. It's the nature of things over there. A lot of people don't want him to get even that far.'

'Like?'

'Oil people. Money people. Some members of the new Iraqi government.'

'What's the Coalition view?'

'I really couldn't comment on that.'

Harry tilted his head in disbelief. 'You know who they are, don't you? The people behind this.'

Ballatyne appeared to consider his words carefully before answering. 'Some of them. We know who organized the assassination attempt and this follow-up farce. One of them is an official in the new Iraqi administration. He was over here recently, and met with others who have connections to the oil industry here and in the States. We're moving on some of them right now. We'll leave the rest for later.'

'They must be insane.'

'Scared, more like. Scared that if Rafa'i gets to power, he'll lock the gates to the oil wells and throw away the keys. It would plunge his country back into the Dark Ages and send the price of oil through the roof. And there are plenty of people who don't want that to happen.' He shrugged. 'But there are other problems attached to Rafa'i's continued safety. Which is where you come in.'

'Go on.'

'You were correct, in your own bullish way: if Subhi Rafa'i were to die here, God only knows what would happen. We think the bomb plots so far have been bad? The repercussions of him dying on British soil would close this country down for years. There's hardly anyone in the Middle East who wouldn't believe it was all some Coalition plot.'

'So you want him back in Baghdad.' Harry frowned. 'Isn't that what *he* wants?'

Ballatyne gave the ghost of a smile. 'Not quite. We'll be dropping him back in Baghdad, but there won't be any triumphant entry. We're letting it be known that he allowed his own people to die in the compound to save his own skin. We've got proof and we can leak it in such a manner that nobody will know where it came from. There's also the matter of how some of the money he's been gathering has "stuck" in a private bank account in the Caymans. He'll be discredited for good . . . especially among the money men.' He studied his hands as if looking for dirt. 'I wouldn't rate his chances of survival too highly after that.'

Harry shook his head, wondering at the minds that had been thinking about this situation all along. 'So what's this big favour?'

'Well, as you know,' the intelligence man continued smoothly, 'we're pretty short of good people at the moment, what with all the trouble spots we're trying to police around the world. We need all the experienced hands we can get.'

Harry waited, wondering what was coming.

'How do you fancy a trip to Baghdad? All expenses paid, of course. Not like this one – which I remind you, you got into by yourself. Incidentally, I should ask to see your card, just for the record.' He waited, eyebrows raised, until Harry took out his wallet and extracted a credit card. It was made out in the name of a minor finance house and looked no different to any normal card.

'Fair enough.' Ballatyne waved it away without examining it. 'No need to go any further. Bloody things are probably easy to falsify now, anyway.'

'So what next?' Harry put the card away.

'You'll have help on the ground, filtering our troublesome cleric back into his home district. You should be back out within two days, three at most. Then we'll drop you somewhere quiet to recuperate. Long enough to get the press concentrating on something else.'

'Rik's not in any state to travel.'

'It didn't look that serious. Small calibre . . . minimal damage.' Ballatyne chewed his lip. 'OK. We can hold Rafa'i for a couple of days while the shoulder gets patched up. But that's the limit. This is urgent.'

Harry remembered Rik's reaction on seeing the hot box in the Saab and realizing that Harry was carrying a weapon. That issue still hadn't been explained. He gave Ballatyne a level look. 'What if I refuse?'

The intelligence man snorted. 'You could try. You're still on the reserve list, remember? Why do you think we allowed you to run with this once we found out who you were? You were highly regarded, you know, before you went private.'

'Really?' said Harry evenly. 'Pity nobody thought so at the time.'

'Yeah, well – our loss. Still, we can't grumble, can we? It turned out OK.' He began to move away, then turned back. 'I'll give you some extra motivation.'

'You can try.'

Ballatyne was holding a five-by-four colour photo. He handed it over. It showed an anonymous street with cars, pedestrians and smart office buildings. The sun was shining and people were dressed in lightweight summer clothes. They looked relaxed, unhurried. One man was frozen centre-frame, about to step into the open door of a taxi only yards from the camera. He was wearing a smart linen suit and carrying a briefcase, a businessman on his way to a meeting. Although slightly grainy, the photo was clear enough for instant recognition.

It was Harry's former boss, now on the run from the security services.

Henry Paulton.

He felt the earth tilt and looked at Ballatyne. 'Is this a joke?'

'No. One of our spotters recognized him while on another job. She couldn't do anything without blowing her cover so she took a shot on her camera phone. Not too bad, considering.' He took the photo back and put it away. 'Do this job for me and I'll let you have a copy. I'll even tell you where it was taken.' He grinned nastily. 'I imagine you and Paulton must have lots to talk about.'

FIFTY-NINE

'What was all the chat about?' Rik rejoined Harry. He looked unsteady on his feet and had an unhealthy pallor, but was managing to stay upright. 'Why did they take the cuffs off?' He winced and moved his shoulder gingerly.

'We're off the hook,' Harry said, and nodded at Rik's wound. 'Does it hurt?'

'Only when I get my arm twisted. What do you mean, off the hook? We shot people in public. How do we get off a thing like that?'

'A favour for a favour.' Or rather, two favours, Harry reflected. He explained Ballatyne's demand. 'Two days' work followed by a paid holiday, then we can go back to doing what we do, no questions asked.'

'There's got to be a catch.'

Harry shrugged and moved away towards the lakeside cafeteria. There was always a catch. He needed a stiff drink, although he wasn't sure if they served anything stronger than tea or coffee. His eye brushed across the covered hump of Joanne's body on the grass. No, he needed to get further away than this. He leaned against a strip of fencing.

Rik said, 'You were going at it with Ballatyne. What was that all about?'

'Horse trading,' Harry replied. 'He took some convincing, that's all.' He didn't mention his threat to go public with the story, since the chances of pulling it off were infinitesimally small, anyway. And Rik would be all for spewing it on to the Internet without a second thought for the consequences.

Rik wasn't happy. 'No. That's not what it looked like. You and he were talking like . . . like equals.' He stopped. 'Jesus . . . *I bloody knew it!* You're – what do they call it . . .?' He snapped his fingers. 'I know – *carded*. That's what got us out from under this, isn't it? Otherwise we'd be on our way to Paddington high-security nick!'

Harry didn't say anything.

'Why didn't you tell me? That's why you had the hot box in your car, isn't it? I thought you'd tooled up in case stuff got critical. But you're still on Five's payroll!'

'It's not like that.'

'So what is it, then? Tell me.'

'They asked,' said Harry simply. 'When I handed in my papers, they asked me to stay attached. I said OK.'

He kicked some dirt with the toe of his shoe. Trying to explain that he was, as Ballatyne had said, one of the privileged few, would merely rub salt into the wound. Rik wouldn't understand. The truth was, they had offered the situation to him and he'd taken it. Not right away – he'd made them sweat a bit first. Childish, maybe, but it felt right at the time. A sort of acknowledgement that they'd screwed up over the way they'd treated him. But eventually, he'd said yes. They couldn't afford to lose good people, they'd said, the situation being what it was. Ballatyne had echoed the same words.

'And you agreed – after all they did to us?'

'I thought it might be useful, a way of keeping in touch. But it's not without strings; they get to call on me whenever they feel like it.'

'You've done this before?'

'No. This was the first.' Not that I knew it, he wanted to add. Not until it was too late, by which time we were both in it up to our necks.

'Did you know all about this Rafa'i stuff?'

'Of course I bloody didn't. No more than you did. According to Ballatyne, once they discovered who I was, they let us run with it.'

Rik laughed bitterly. 'So why not say? Didn't you trust me?'

Harry turned and walked towards the Mall, then stopped and came back. He couldn't let it go like this. There was too much riding on it. Friendship, for one. And Rik, for all his casual attitude, was bullish enough to gnaw at it like a dog on a bone. It would eat away at the bond they had formed since Red Station. And Harry couldn't let that happen. 'I never thought they'd call on me,' he said, 'and they didn't. Christ, it's not as if there's a national shortage of manpower.'

Rik lost the angry look. 'How many others are carded?'

'I don't know. Not many. Special Forces, mostly . . . a few

specialists. I figured that as time passed, my name would slide down the list and eventually fall off the end.' He shrugged. 'As it happened, they didn't need to call because I was already in the middle of it.' He gestured towards the covered shapes on the ground. 'I haven't said thank you – for back there. I owe you. I'm sorry you had to do that.' He couldn't think of anything to say that wouldn't sound mawkish, so he started walking.

'*Wait!*' Rik hurried after him. 'Hang on. I'm stupid for getting out of shape about it, but hear me out, all right? In Five, you were operational, I was in support – I get that. There's a big difference. I shouldn't be surprised they'd want to retain you. The others in Red Station – Mace, Clare, Fitzgerald – they talked about you, did you know that?'

Harry said nothing. He was sure they had, out of curiosity if nothing else. But he was trying to forget about them . . . trying *not* to forget about Paulton. Wouldn't be able to, even if he'd wanted. Not now he knew the man was out there. And reachable.

'First off,' continued Rik, 'you clearly didn't give a monkey's for the party line. Second, Clare admired you because you made everything look so easy. You knew exactly what you were doing and you had *instincts*. We all wanted to be able to think like that.'

'Good for you,' Harry countered. 'So?'

'So why wasn't I carded?'

Harry stared at him. He'd expected Rik to be annoyed because of the secrecy, of not confiding in him about the card. But not this. 'Are you kidding me?'

'I'm just asking.'

'You just found out why not! You get the authority to carry a gun – big deal. You want a normal life? Forget it. You want to be on edge every time there's a terrorist incident, waiting for the phone to ring? To be dragged out of the cupboard whenever someone like Ballatyne feels like it because they've run out of options? You want to get pushed into the firing line when they don't have anyone else handy? *Ferris is young, unattached and expendable – nobody will miss him if he screws up.* Believe me, you really don't want that. Stick with computers – it's what you're good at.'

'You came out OK.'

'She didn't.' Harry nodded across the grass at Joanne's body, his throat tight. 'Neither did you, in case you hadn't noticed.' He let that sink in, knowing the shock of the shooting still hadn't registered fully on the younger man. That would come in the hours and days ahead, when the sudden overload of adrenalin had worked its way out of his system. For now, he was coping, ready to believe a bullet wound was an easy trade-off for what they had gone through. But Harry had seen what Rik hadn't: the gunshot wounds on Joanne's body. There were two wounds to her left side, where Harry's shots had hit home, and one to her right shoulder. Rik's shot, going high. Shock from a wound and the adrenalin rush would do that: make the body wobble just enough to throw off the best of aims. But seeing the target react and fall would still make it look like you'd got a centre hit.

Rik was thinking he'd got off easy, that he'd taken Joanne down in exchange for a relatively minor wound. The fact was, he really had got off easy: he hadn't killed Joanne at all – Harry had. It was something he would need to know before very long. Before he dismissed it as something you did, then moved on.

Ballistics would confirm it.

Harry took out his wallet and extracted the card he'd shown Ballatyne. 'This is what they give us. Allows us to do what we do.' He dug his thumbnail along one edge and tore off the outer layer, exposing another layer underneath. It bore his photograph and a short paragraph addressed to all law enforcement and military agencies, ending with a signature and a telephone number. His stay-out-of-jail card. He thrust it into Rik's hand. 'Here – you want one, take it.'

Rik said nothing, confused by Harry's response.

'It didn't do me any good.' Harry felt the beginnings of something like relief, now it was out in the open. 'And in the end it cost too much,' he finished quietly.

Rik nodded and winced as the movement translated down his shoulder. '*Shit*, that hurts. Look, I'm sorry about . . . Joanne. I know how you felt.'

'You don't know anything,' Harry growled.

'OK. But hear me out. Didn't you get a real buzz out of the last few days?'

'*What?*'

'Come on, I know you did. All the rummaging around and secret squirrel stuff . . . you love it. It's what you were trained for. That's why you said yes to the card in the first place, isn't it?'

Harry stopped and glared at his friend, trying to find the words. But they wouldn't come.

Rik was right: he *had* felt a buzz. The investigation, the tracking, the questions – all that. But it had nothing to do with the card, the state's authority allowing him to carry a lethal weapon and use it *in extremis*. Nor would it ever. Right now, though, he was tired and angry and wanted to get away from this place and sit down with a very strong drink. Maybe if he asked him nicely, Ballatyne would pass the Rafa'i ball to someone else. But even as he thought it, he knew that wouldn't happen.

He found himself thinking about the days ahead. The headache-inducing drone of the C-130 flight to Baghdad, the hours of boredom followed by the sudden belly-lurching drop to the hot tarmac; the sights and smells, the alien atmosphere, the operational briefings, the smell of military gear, the waiting. The outcome of flying into a hornets' nest with the reluctant Rafa'i in tow.

The possibility that things might not go as planned.

Yet somehow, perversely, he was looking forward to it and to coming out the other side. To being able to deal with some unfinished business.

That was what it was all about. His problem was, he didn't trust Ballatyne to keep his word about the photo. Not that it mattered.

'How long would it take to track down details from a foreign car registration?' he asked.

'I don't know.' Rik frowned, distracted by the abstract. 'It would depend on the country. Some databases are high-tech and easy to access, others are so primitive they're virtually impossible. A lot of them still use data-card entry methods—'

'How long?' If he let him, Rik could go on all day like this.

'Can you narrow it down to a country?'

'Not yet.'

'I'd need to work on it, maybe feed it out to the community. Someone should be able to recognize the format and get back to me. After that, it'd just be a matter of searching. What's that got to do with anything?'

'Just a thought.' Harry was remembering the photo Ballatyne had shown him, of Paulton crossing a pavement. It could have been any town, any country. But not a backwoods place – it looked too smart for that. Somewhere modern, with banks and offices and lines of communication. The kind of place a former high-level spook on the run would be attracted to, to visit occasionally to collect funds and bend his ear to the ground for gossip about potential danger. Most of the cars at the kerb were nose to tail and looked sleek and shiny, exuding an air of anonymous prosperity. Except the vehicle nearest the camera: a Mercedes with its registration plate just visible.

It wasn't much, but he'd memorized the number.

Just in case they got back safely and Ballatyne decided not to keep his word.

'Come on,' he said. 'I'll tell you about it over a drink. Then we've got work to do.'